BOOK TWO IN THE DESCENDANTS SERIES

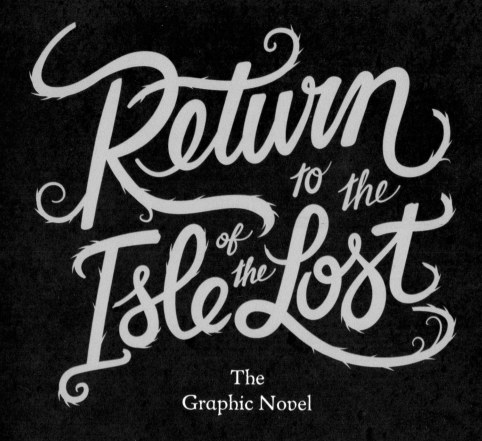

Return to the Isle of the Lost

The
Graphic Novel

#1 *New York Times* best-selling author
Melissa de la Cruz
Based on *Descendants*
written by Josann McGibbon & Sara Parriott

Adapted by
ROBERT VENDITTI

Art by
KRZYSZTOF CHALIK

Lettering by
CHRIS DICKEY

First Edition, July 2019
10 9 8 7 6 5 4 3 2 1
FAC-038091-19165
Printed in the United States of America

ISBN (hardcover) 978-1-368-04098-3
ISBN (paperback) 978-1-368-04187-4
Reinforced binding
Visit DisneyBooks.com
and DisneyDescendants.com

SUSTAINABLE FORESTRY INITIATIVE Certified Sourcing
www.sfiprogram.org
SFI-00993
Logo Applies to Text Stock Only

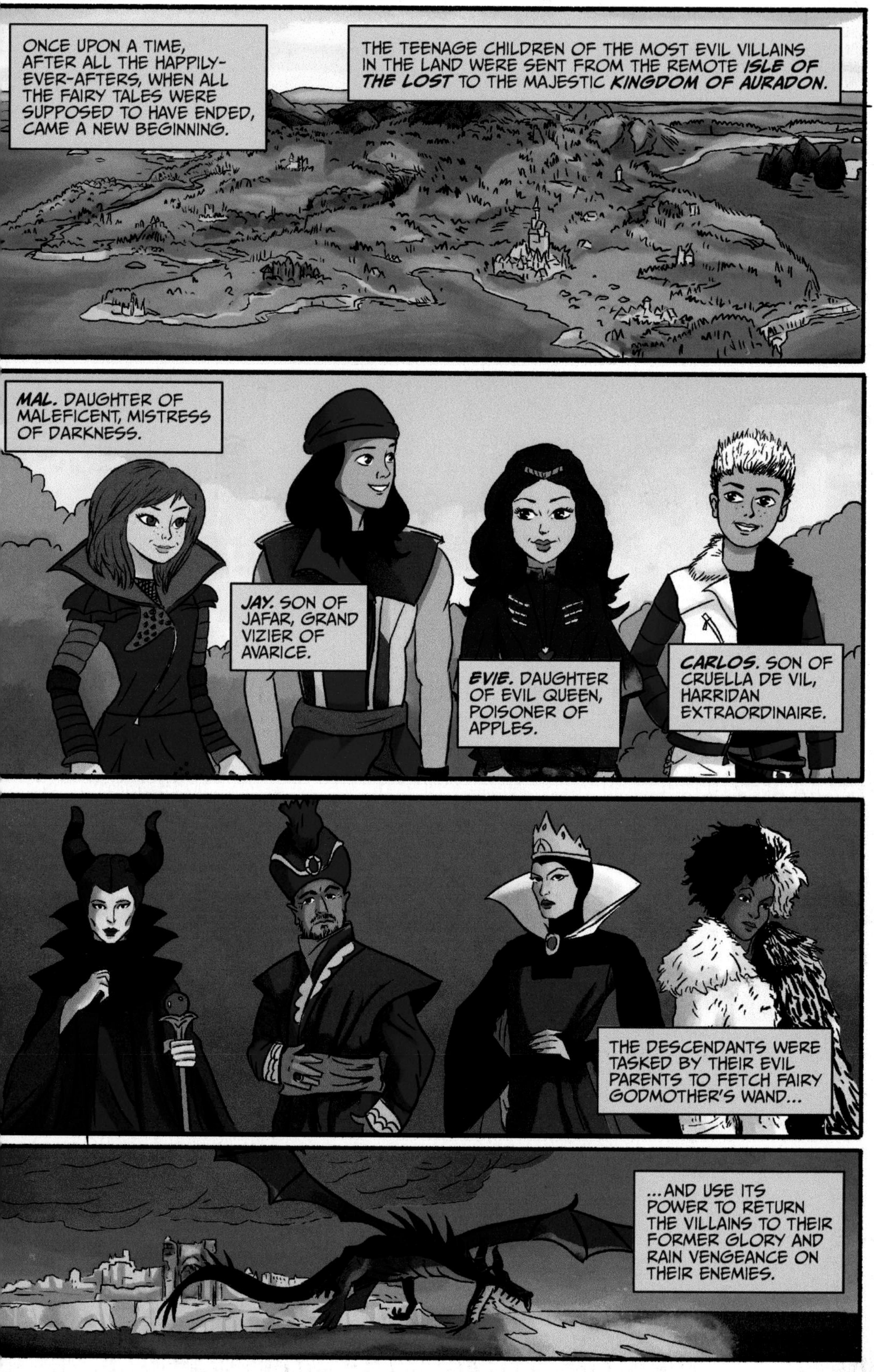
ONCE UPON A TIME, AFTER ALL THE HAPPILY-EVER-AFTERS, WHEN ALL THE FAIRY TALES WERE SUPPOSED TO HAVE ENDED, CAME A NEW BEGINNING.
THE TEENAGE CHILDREN OF THE MOST EVIL VILLAINS IN THE LAND WERE SENT FROM THE REMOTE ***ISLE OF THE LOST*** TO THE MAJESTIC ***KINGDOM OF AURADON***.
MAL. DAUGHTER OF MALEFICENT, MISTRESS OF DARKNESS.
JAY. SON OF JAFAR, GRAND VIZIER OF AVARICE.
EVIE. DAUGHTER OF EVIL QUEEN, POISONER OF APPLES.
CARLOS. SON OF CRUELLA DE VIL, HARRIDAN EXTRAORDINAIRE.
THE DESCENDANTS WERE TASKED BY THEIR EVIL PARENTS TO FETCH FAIRY GODMOTHER'S WAND...
...AND USE ITS POWER TO RETURN THE VILLAINS TO THEIR FORMER GLORY AND RAIN VENGEANCE ON THEIR ENEMIES.

BUT MAL, JAY, EVIE, AND CARLOS STOOD TOGETHER...

...AND IT WAS MAL WHO WON THE BATTLE AND WIELDED THE WAND.

IN THE END, HER POWER FOR *GOOD* WAS GREATER THAN HER MOTHER'S TALENT FOR *EVIL*.

MALEFICENT WAS TURNED INTO A TINY LIZARD, REDUCED TO THE SIZE OF HER HEART.

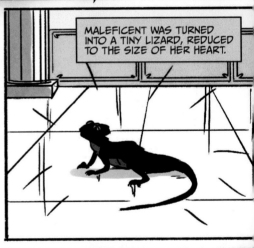

SHE WAS LOCKED AWAY, HER PRISON PLACED UNDER CONSTANT GUARD.

THE DESCENDANTS RETURNED TO THEIR STUDIES AT AURADON PREP.

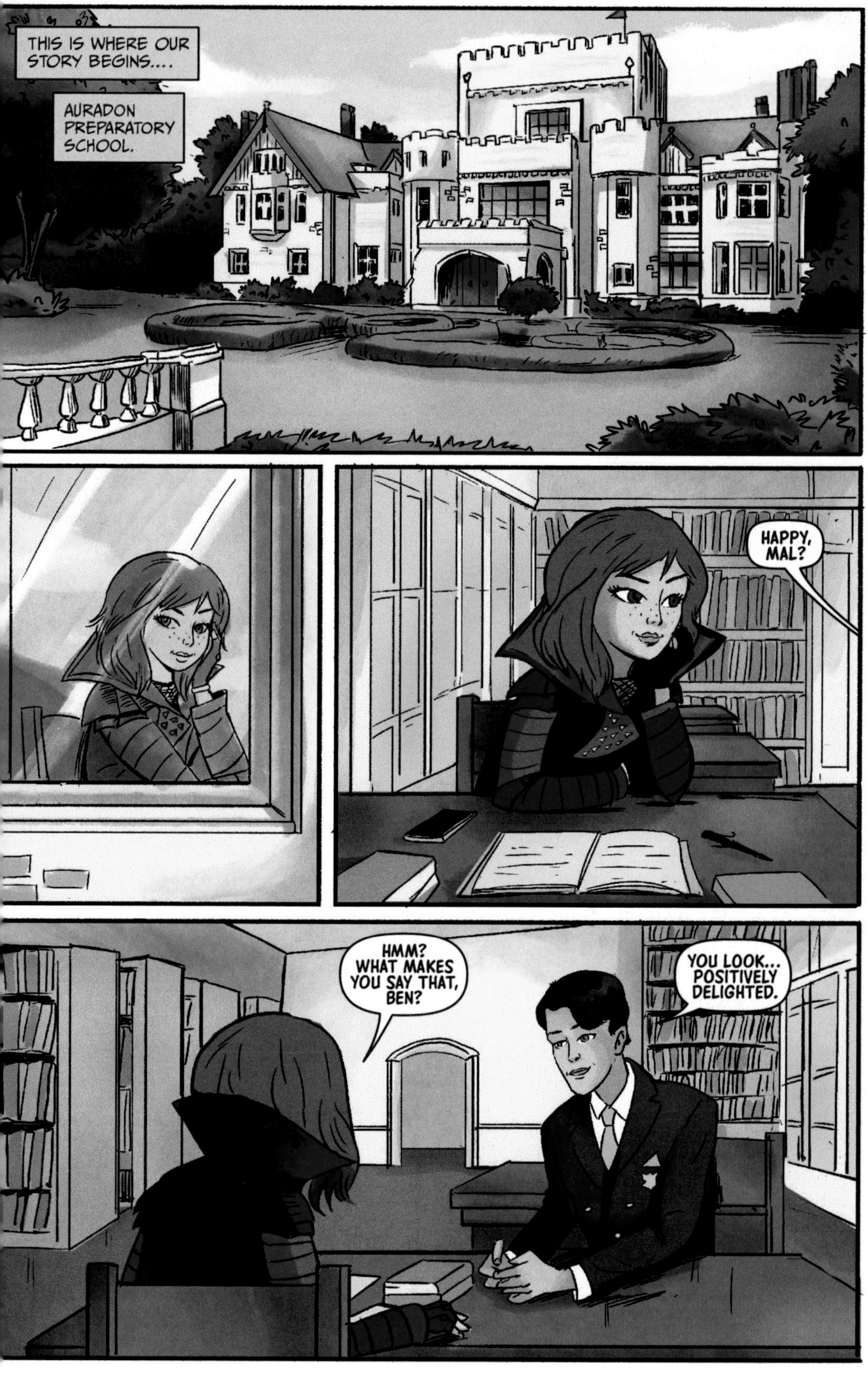
THIS IS WHERE OUR STORY BEGINS....
AURADON PREPARATORY SCHOOL.
HAPPY, MAL?
HMM? WHAT MAKES YOU SAY THAT, BEN?
YOU LOOK... POSITIVELY DELIGHTED.

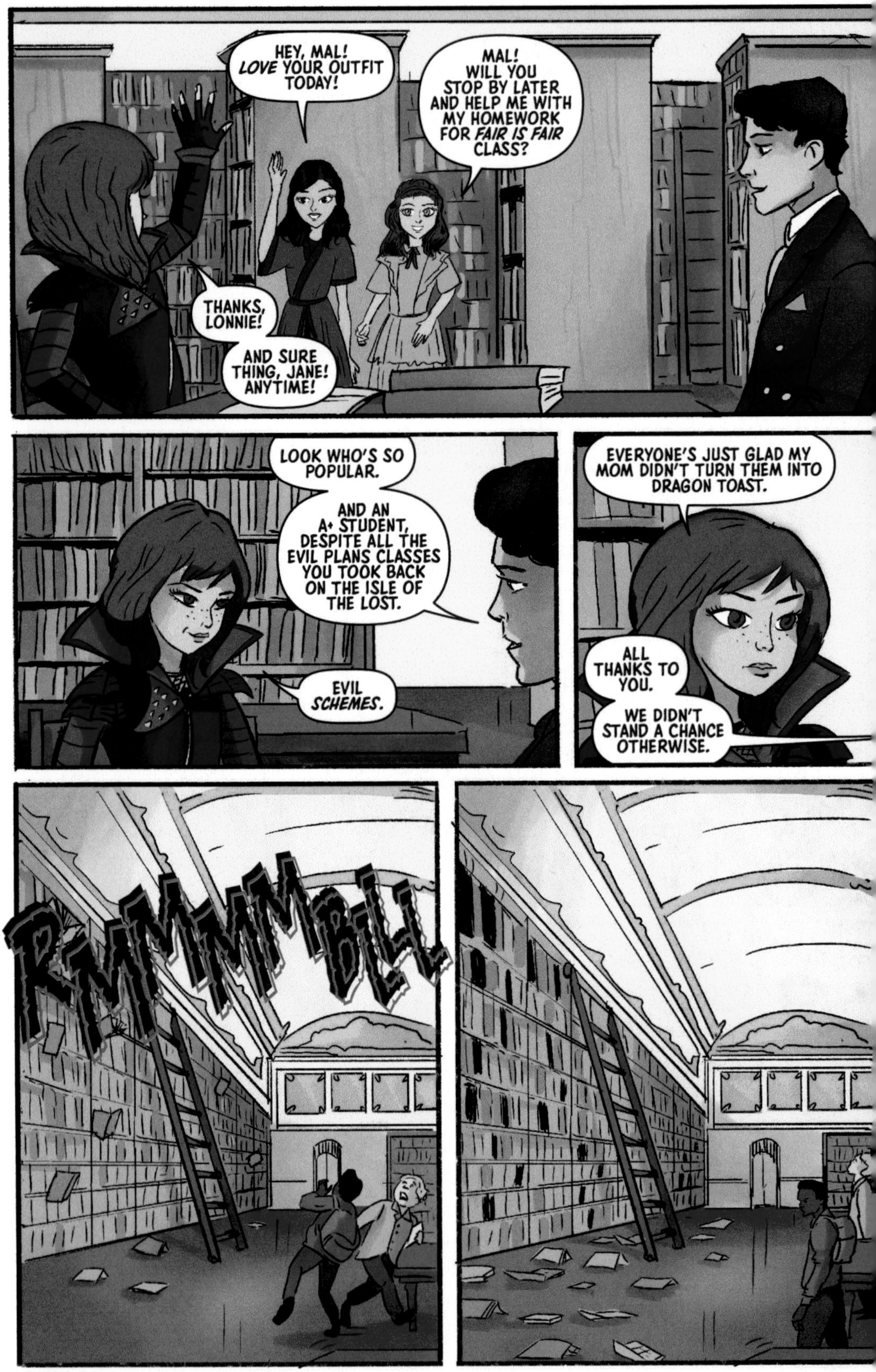
HEY, MAL! *LOVE* YOUR OUTFIT TODAY!
MAL! WILL YOU STOP BY LATER AND HELP ME WITH MY HOMEWORK FOR *FAIR IS FAIR* CLASS?
THANKS, LONNIE!
AND SURE THING, JANE! ANYTIME!
LOOK WHO'S SO POPULAR.
AND AN A+ STUDENT, DESPITE ALL THE EVIL PLANS CLASSES YOU TOOK BACK ON THE ISLE OF THE LOST.
EVIL *SCHEMES*.
EVERYONE'S JUST GLAD MY MOM DIDN'T TURN THEM INTO DRAGON TOAST.
ALL THANKS TO YOU.
WE DIDN'T STAND A CHANCE OTHERWISE.
RMMMMBLL

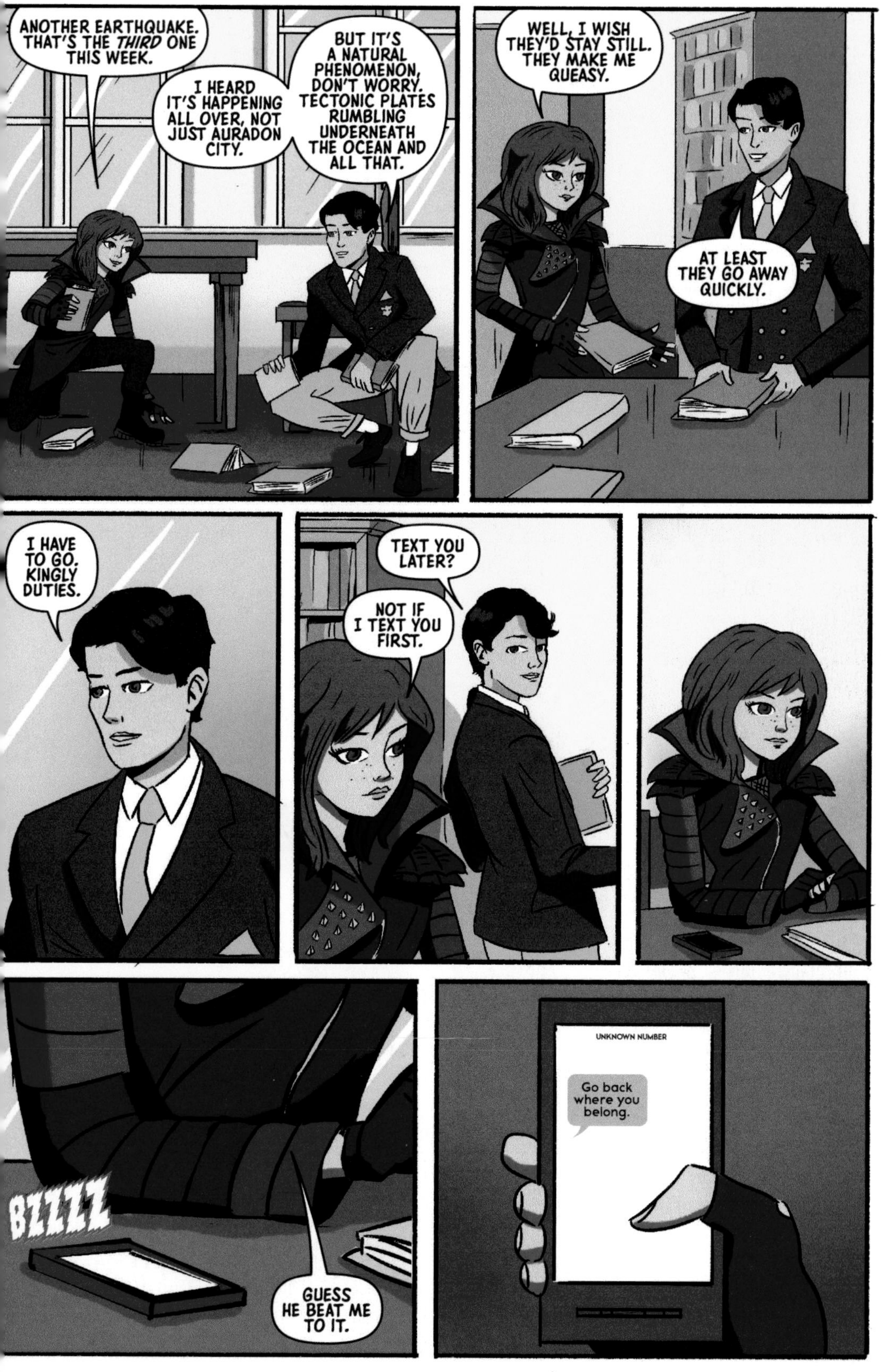
ANOTHER EARTHQUAKE. THAT'S THE *THIRD* ONE THIS WEEK.
I HEARD IT'S HAPPENING ALL OVER, NOT JUST AURADON CITY.
BUT IT'S A NATURAL PHENOMENON, DON'T WORRY. TECTONIC PLATES RUMBLING UNDERNEATH THE OCEAN AND ALL THAT.
WELL, I WISH THEY'D STAY STILL. THEY MAKE ME QUEASY.
AT LEAST THEY GO AWAY QUICKLY.
I HAVE TO GO. KINGLY DUTIES.
TEXT YOU LATER?
NOT IF I TEXT YOU FIRST.
BZZZZ
GUESS HE BEAT ME TO IT.
UNKNOWN NUMBER
Go back where you belong.

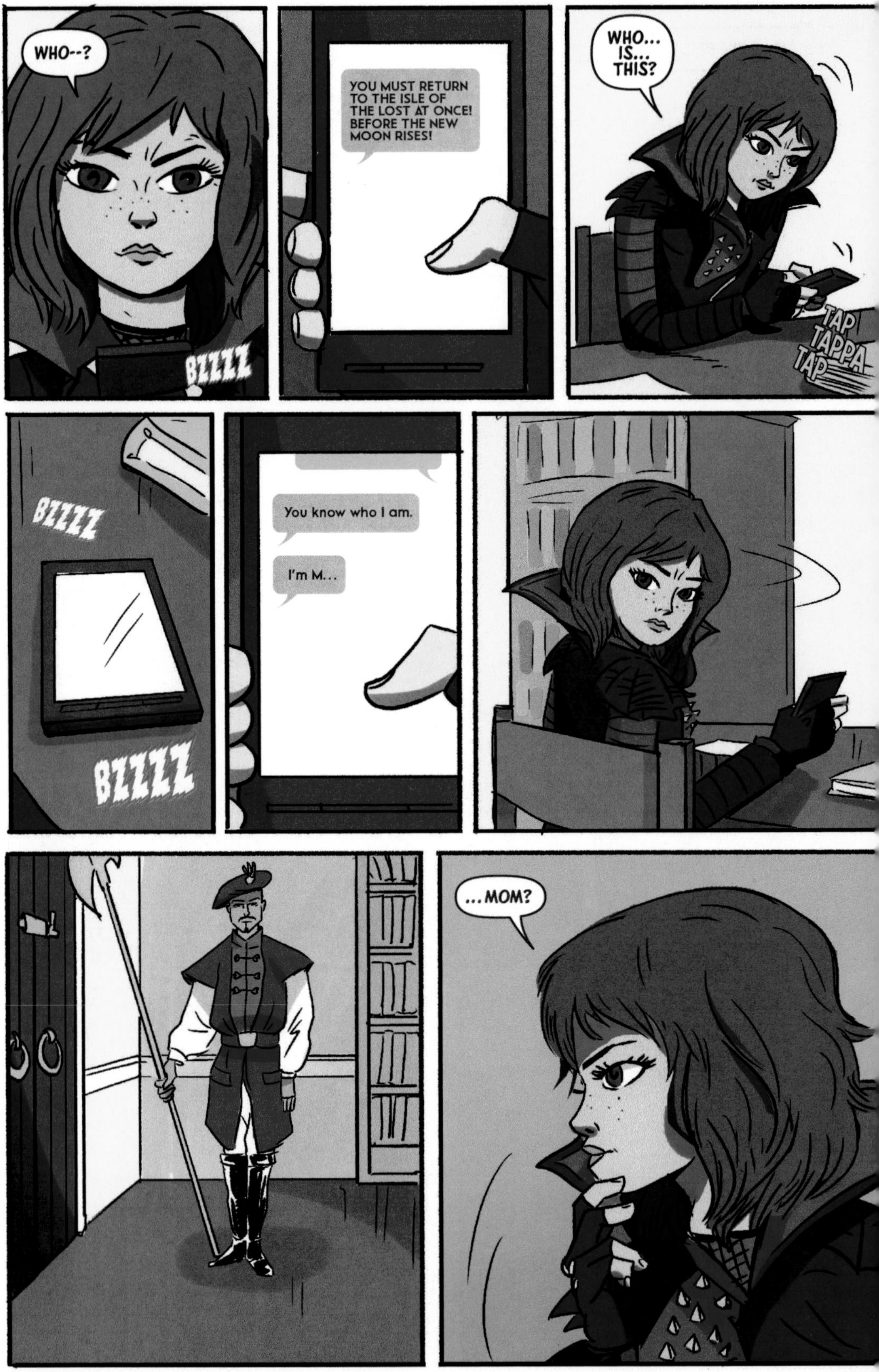
WHO--?
BZZZZ
YOU MUST RETURN TO THE ISLE OF THE LOST AT ONCE! BEFORE THE NEW MOON RISES!
WHO... IS... THIS?
TAP TAPPA TAP
BZZZZ
BZZZZ
You know who I am.
I'm M...
...MOM?

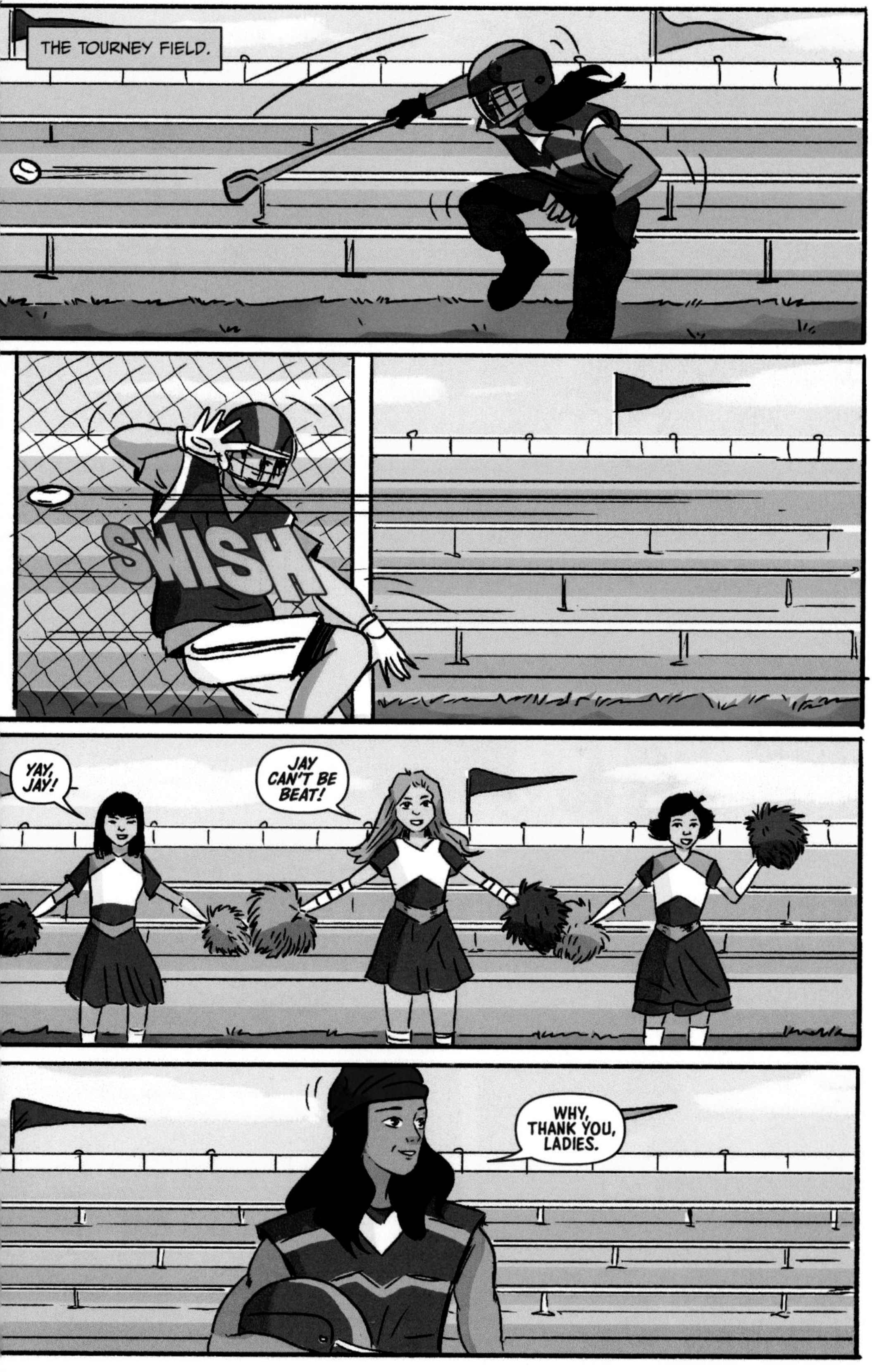
THE TOURNEY FIELD.
SWISH
YAY, JAY!
JAY CAN'T BE BEAT!
WHY, THANK YOU, LADIES.

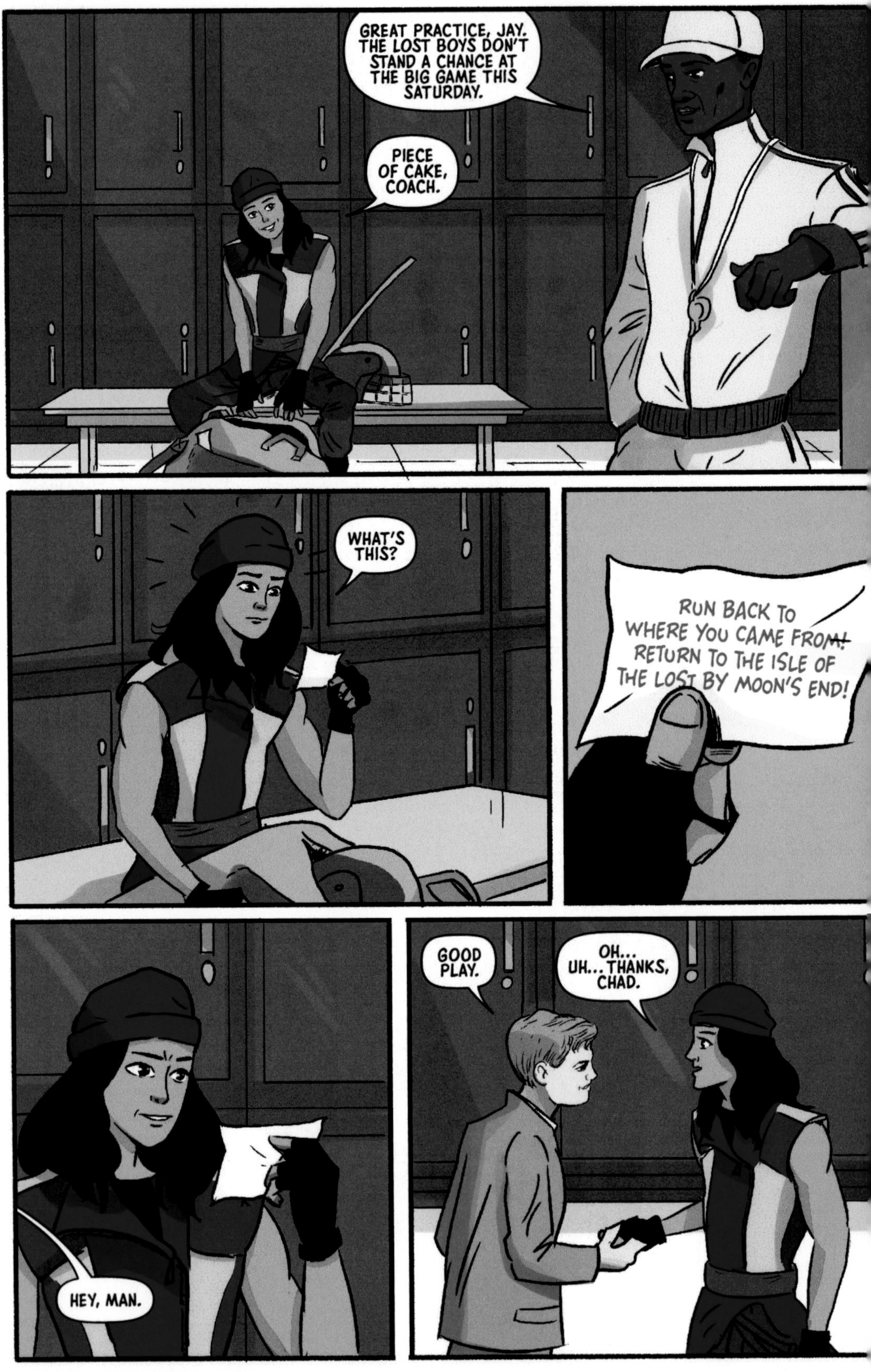
GREAT PRACTICE, JAY. THE LOST BOYS DON'T STAND A CHANCE AT THE BIG GAME THIS SATURDAY.
PIECE OF CAKE, COACH.
WHAT'S THIS?
RUN BACK TO WHERE YOU CAME FROM! RETURN TO THE ISLE OF THE LOST BY MOON'S END!
HEY, MAN.
GOOD PLAY.
OH... UH... THANKS, CHAD.

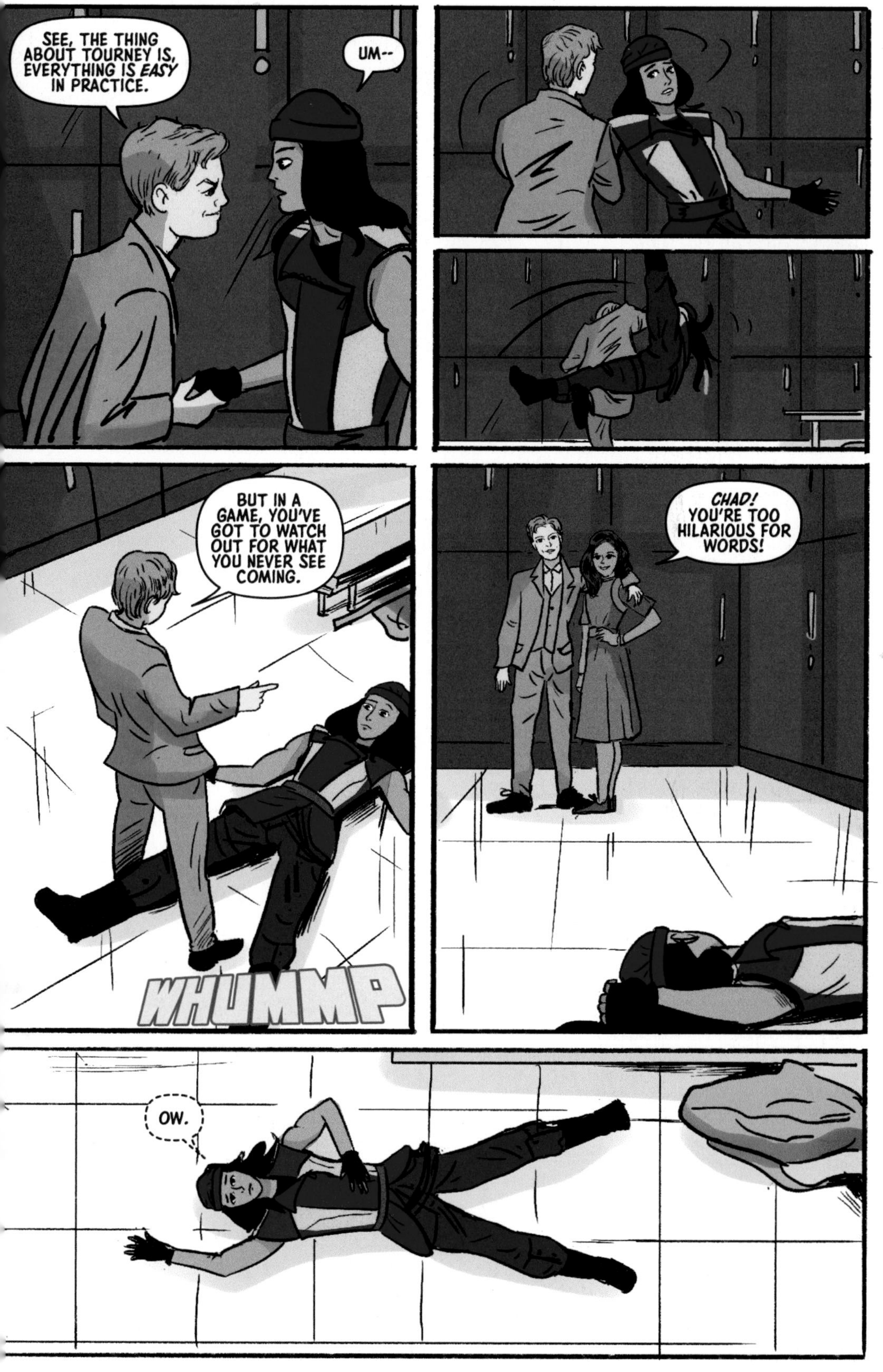
SEE, THE THING ABOUT TOURNEY IS, EVERYTHING IS *EASY* IN PRACTICE.
UM--
BUT IN A GAME, YOU'VE GOT TO WATCH OUT FOR WHAT YOU NEVER SEE COMING.
WHUMMP
CHAD! YOU'RE TOO HILARIOUS FOR WORDS!
OW.

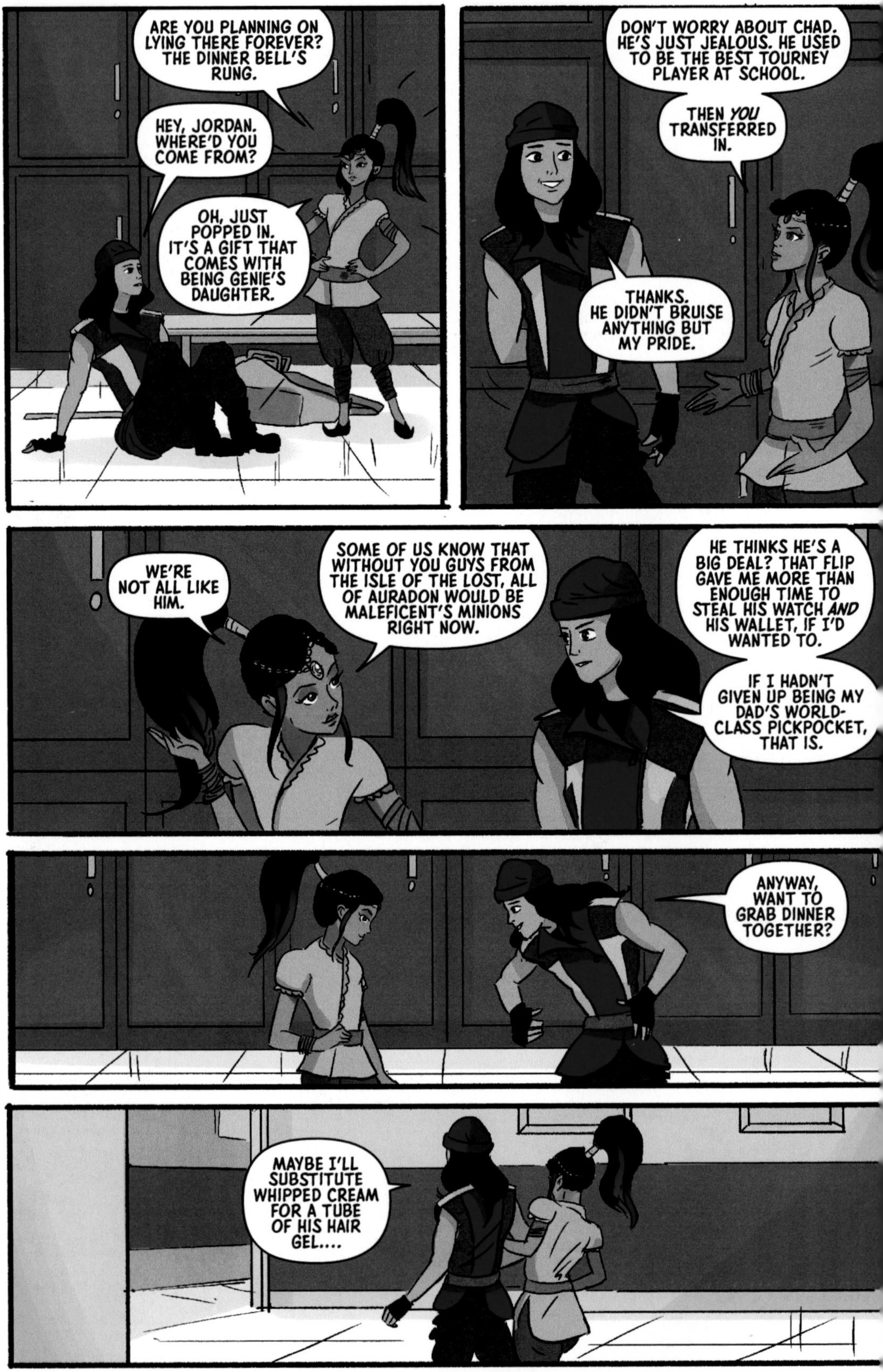
ARE YOU PLANNING ON LYING THERE FOREVER? THE DINNER BELL'S RUNG.
HEY, JORDAN. WHERE'D YOU COME FROM?
OH, JUST POPPED IN. IT'S A GIFT THAT COMES WITH BEING GENIE'S DAUGHTER.
DON'T WORRY ABOUT CHAD. HE'S JUST JEALOUS. HE USED TO BE THE BEST TOURNEY PLAYER AT SCHOOL.
THEN *YOU* TRANSFERRED IN.
THANKS. HE DIDN'T BRUISE ANYTHING BUT MY PRIDE.
WE'RE NOT ALL LIKE HIM.
SOME OF US KNOW THAT WITHOUT YOU GUYS FROM THE ISLE OF THE LOST, ALL OF AURADON WOULD BE MALEFICENT'S MINIONS RIGHT NOW.
HE THINKS HE'S A BIG DEAL? THAT FLIP GAVE ME MORE THAN ENOUGH TIME TO STEAL HIS WATCH *AND* HIS WALLET, IF I'D WANTED TO.
IF I HADN'T GIVEN UP BEING MY DAD'S WORLD-CLASS PICKPOCKET, THAT IS.
ANYWAY, WANT TO GRAB DINNER TOGETHER?
MAYBE I'LL SUBSTITUTE WHIPPED CREAM FOR A TUBE OF HIS HAIR GEL....

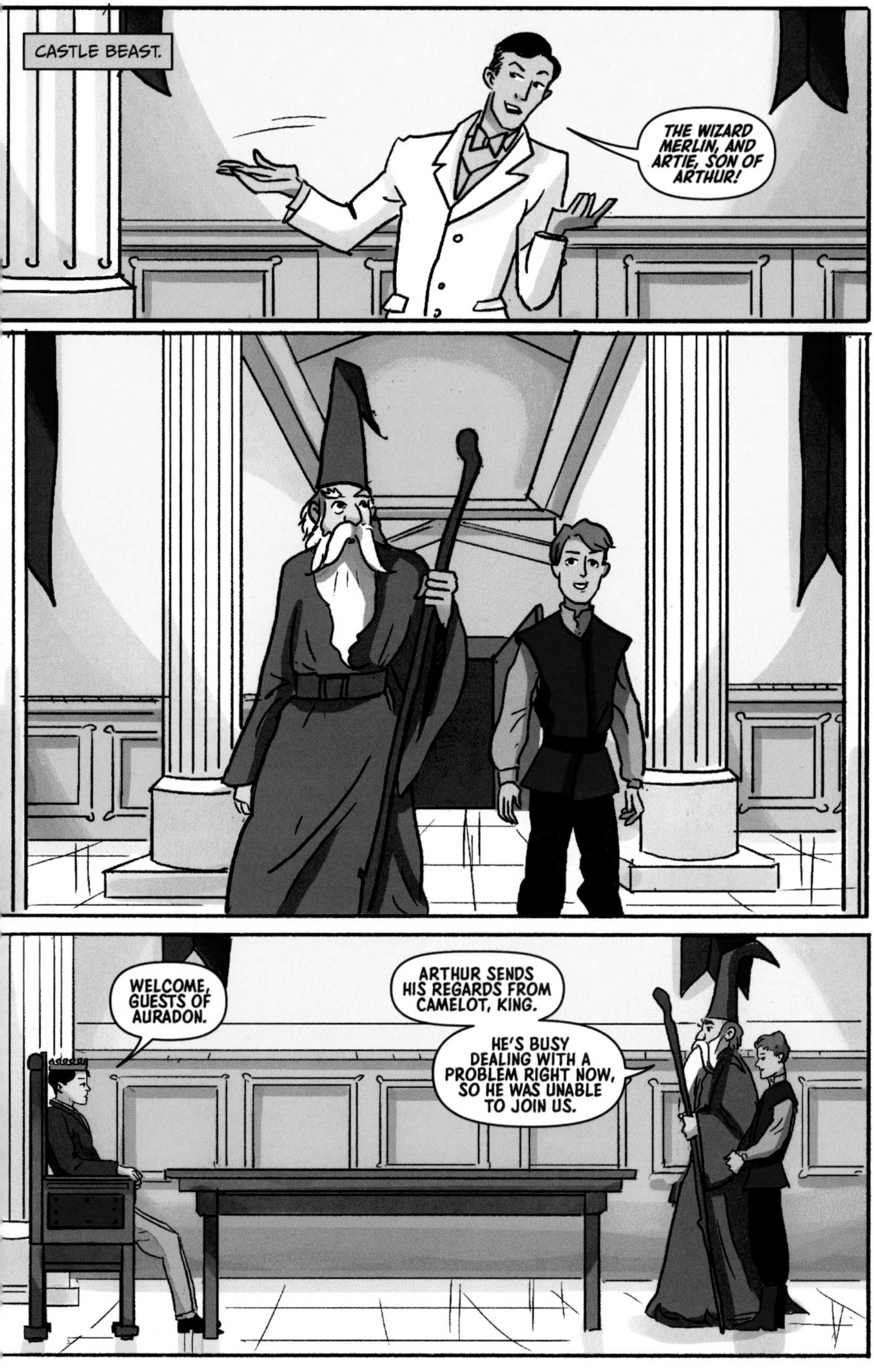
CASTLE BEAST.
THE WIZARD MERLIN, AND ARTIE, SON OF ARTHUR!
WELCOME, GUESTS OF AURADON.
ARTHUR SENDS HIS REGARDS FROM CAMELOT, KING.
HE'S BUSY DEALING WITH A PROBLEM RIGHT NOW, SO HE WAS UNABLE TO JOIN US.

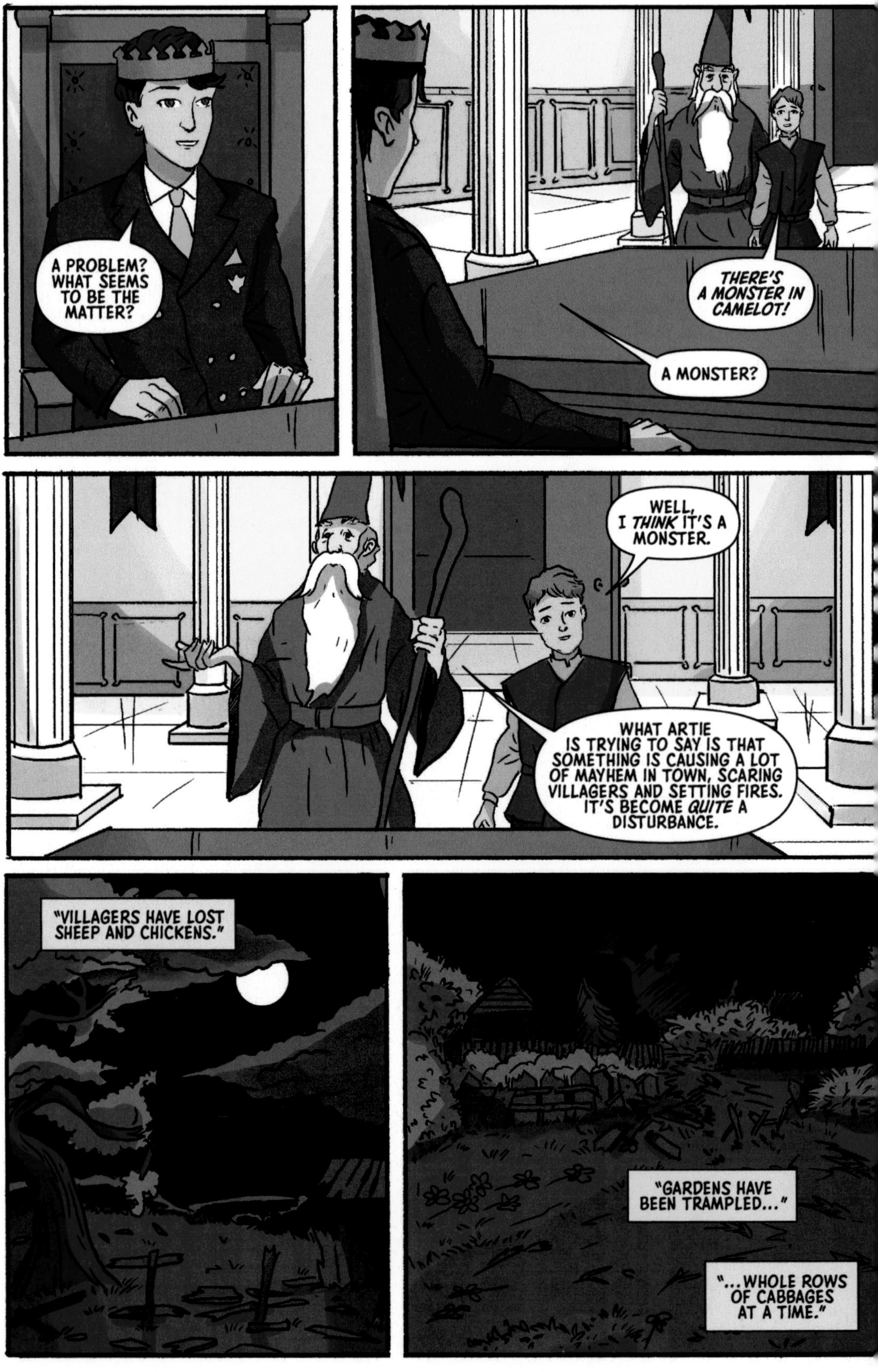
A PROBLEM? WHAT SEEMS TO BE THE MATTER?
THERE'S A MONSTER IN CAMELOT!
A MONSTER?
WELL, I *THINK* IT'S A MONSTER.
WHAT ARTIE IS TRYING TO SAY IS THAT SOMETHING IS CAUSING A LOT OF MAYHEM IN TOWN, SCARING VILLAGERS AND SETTING FIRES. IT'S BECOME *QUITE* A DISTURBANCE.
"VILLAGERS HAVE LOST SHEEP AND CHICKENS."
"GARDENS HAVE BEEN TRAMPLED..."
"...WHOLE ROWS OF CABBAGES AT A TIME."

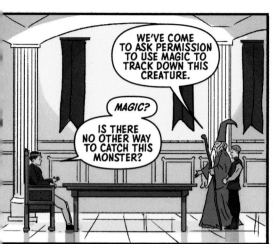

WE'VE COME TO ASK PERMISSION TO USE MAGIC TO TRACK DOWN THIS CREATURE.

MAGIC?

IS THERE NO OTHER WAY TO CATCH THIS MONSTER?

NEED I REMIND YOU THAT I AM THE WIZARD MERLIN?

I WOULDN'T BE HERE IF THERE WAS ANOTHER WAY.

I SEE....

AS THE WIZARD MERLIN, YOU KNOW VERY WELL THAT MAGIC HAS BEEN DISCOURAGED IN AURADON.

THE LAST TIME IT WAS USED, FAIRY GODMOTHER CREATED THE DOME THAT KEPT MAGIC OUT OF THE ISLE OF THE LOST.

AND WE'RE ALL THE BETTER FOR IT. SO FOR NOW, I AM GOING TO REJECT YOUR REQUEST.

BUT SIRE--!

I WILL TRAVEL TO CAMELOT MYSELF TO ASSESS THE SITUATION.

WE WILL LEAVE FIRST THING TOMORROW MORNING.

AS YOU WISH, SIRE.

LET'S HOPE CAMELOT IS STILL STANDING WHEN WE GET THERE.

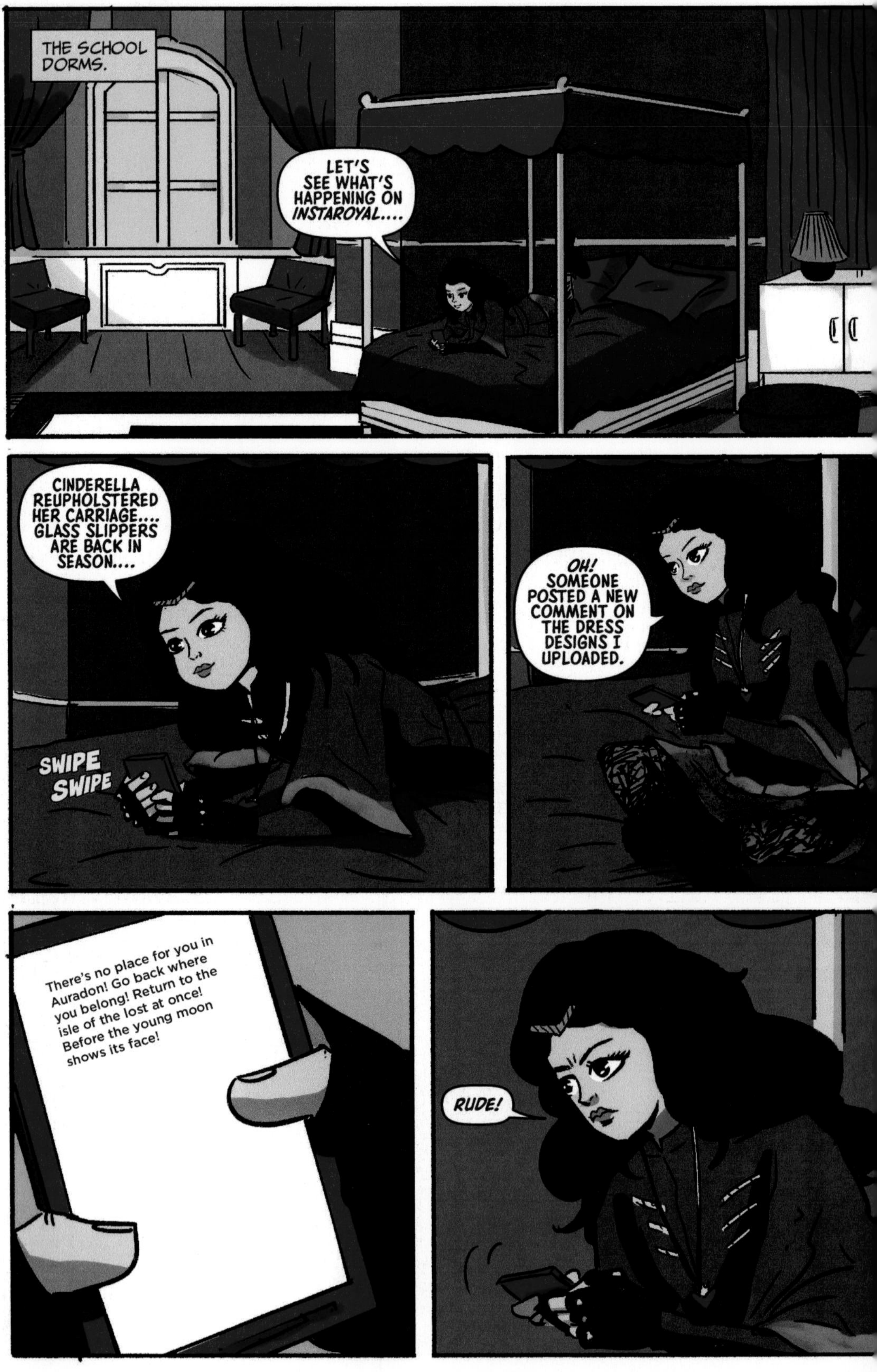
THE SCHOOL DORMS.
LET'S SEE WHAT'S HAPPENING ON INSTAROYAL....
CINDERELLA REUPHOLSTERED HER CARRIAGE.... GLASS SLIPPERS ARE BACK IN SEASON....
SWIPE SWIPE
OH! SOMEONE POSTED A NEW COMMENT ON THE DRESS DESIGNS I UPLOADED.
There's no place for you in Auradon! Go back where you belong! Return to the isle of the lost at once! Before the young moon shows its face!
RUDE!

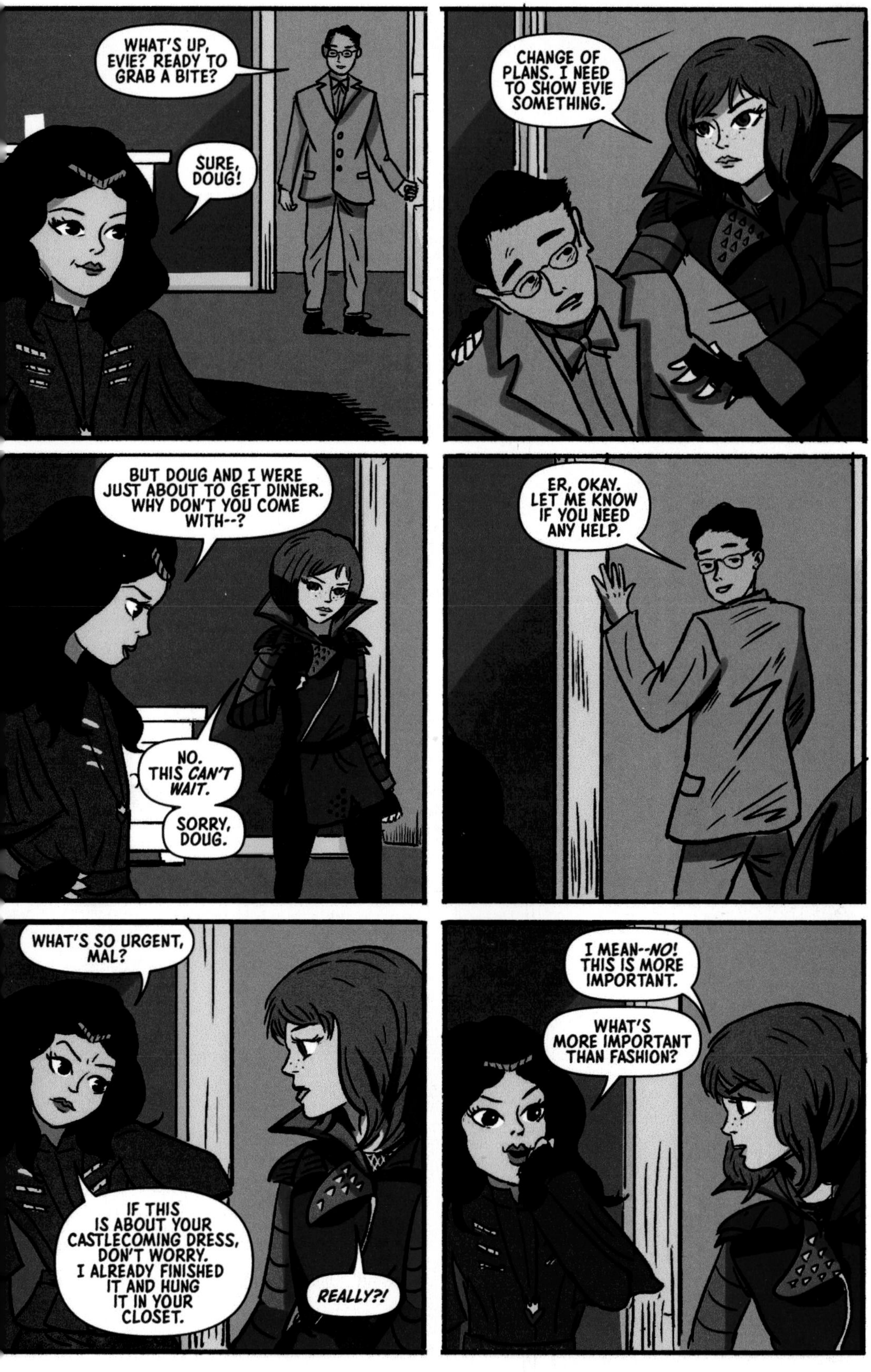
WHAT'S UP, EVIE? READY TO GRAB A BITE?
SURE, DOUG!
CHANGE OF PLANS. I NEED TO SHOW EVIE SOMETHING.
BUT DOUG AND I WERE JUST ABOUT TO GET DINNER. WHY DON'T YOU COME WITH--?
NO. THIS *CAN'T* *WAIT*.
SORRY, DOUG.
ER, OKAY. LET ME KNOW IF YOU NEED ANY HELP.
WHAT'S SO URGENT, MAL?
IF THIS IS ABOUT YOUR CASTLECOMING DRESS, DON'T WORRY. I ALREADY FINISHED IT AND HUNG IT IN YOUR CLOSET.
REALLY?!
I MEAN--*NO!* THIS IS MORE IMPORTANT.
WHAT'S MORE IMPORTANT THAN FASHION?

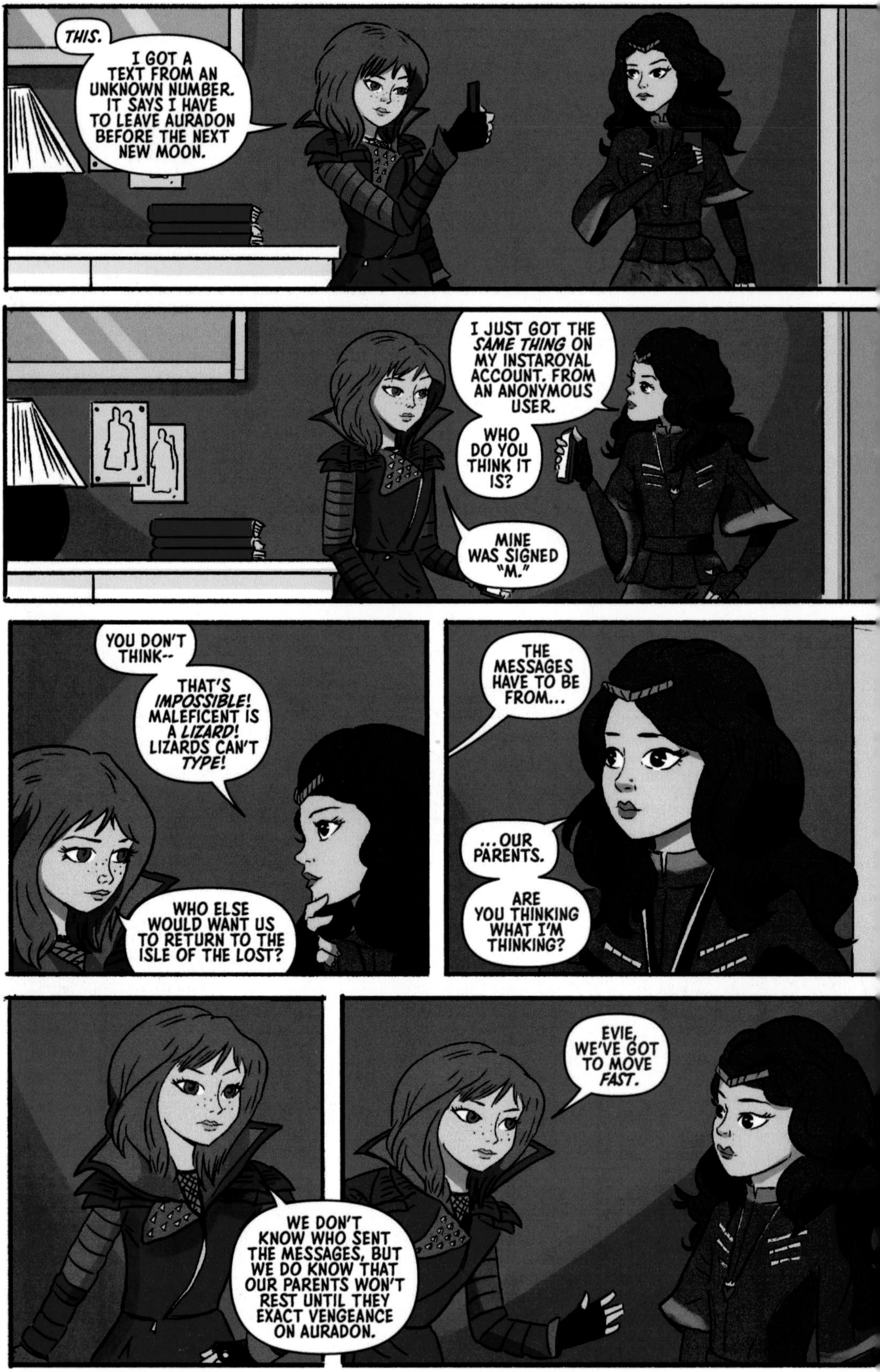
THIS.
I GOT A TEXT FROM AN UNKNOWN NUMBER. IT SAYS I HAVE TO LEAVE AURADON BEFORE THE NEXT NEW MOON.
I JUST GOT THE *SAME THING* ON MY INSTAROYAL ACCOUNT. FROM AN ANONYMOUS USER.
WHO DO YOU THINK IT IS?
MINE WAS SIGNED "M."
YOU DON'T THINK--
THAT'S *IMPOSSIBLE*! MALEFICENT IS A *LIZARD*! LIZARDS CAN'T *TYPE*!
WHO ELSE WOULD WANT US TO RETURN TO THE ISLE OF THE LOST?
THE MESSAGES HAVE TO BE FROM...
...OUR PARENTS.
ARE YOU THINKING WHAT I'M THINKING?
WE DON'T KNOW WHO SENT THE MESSAGES, BUT WE DO KNOW THAT OUR PARENTS WON'T REST UNTIL THEY EXACT VENGEANCE ON AURADON.
EVIE, WE'VE GOT TO MOVE *FAST*.

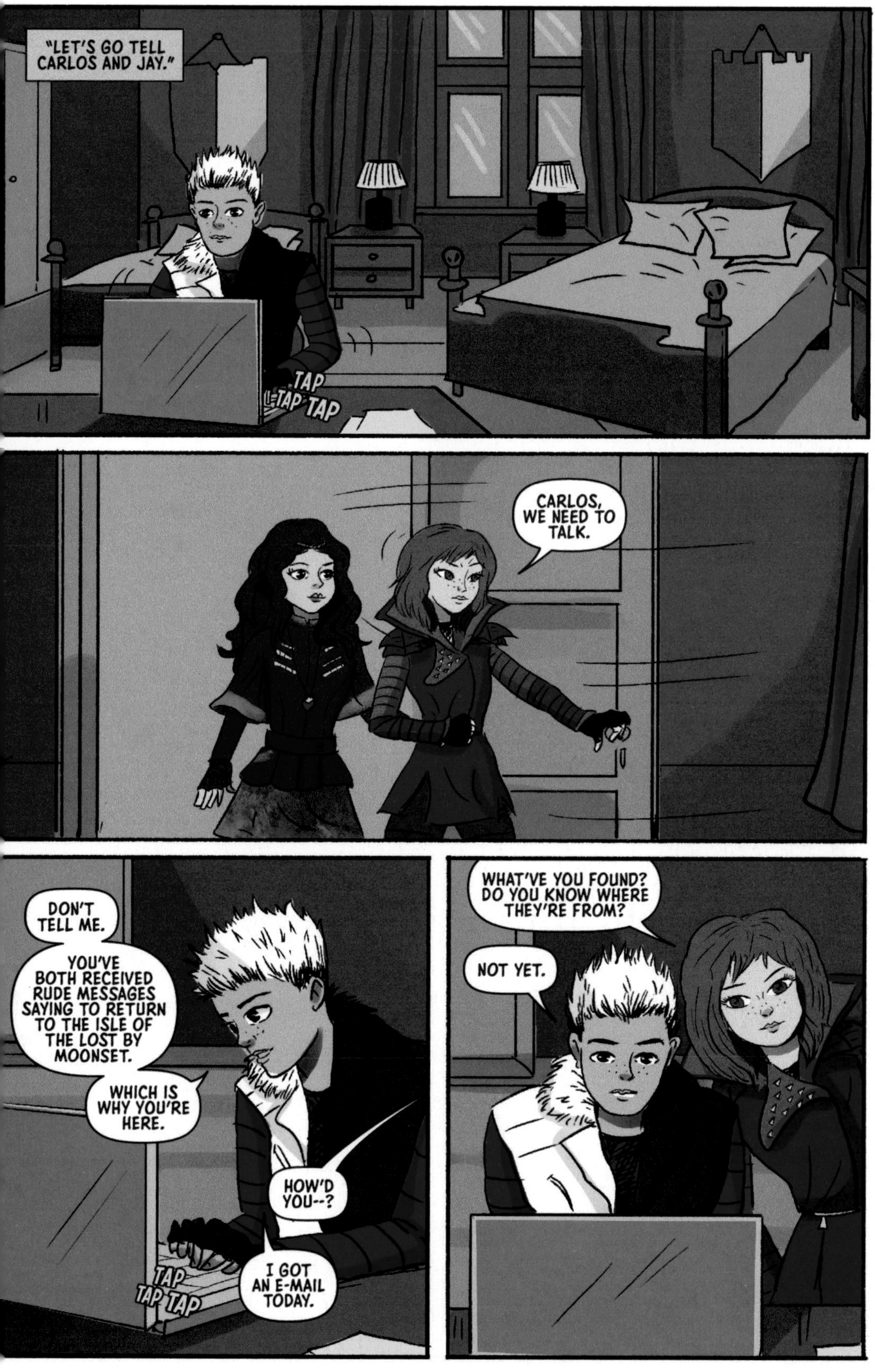
"LET'S GO TELL CARLOS AND JAY."
TAP TAP TAP TAP
CARLOS, WE NEED TO TALK.
DON'T TELL ME.
YOU'VE BOTH RECEIVED RUDE MESSAGES SAYING TO RETURN TO THE ISLE OF THE LOST BY MOONSET.
WHICH IS WHY YOU'RE HERE.
HOW'D YOU--?
I GOT AN E-MAIL TODAY.
TAP TAP TAP
WHAT'VE YOU FOUND? DO YOU KNOW WHERE THEY'RE FROM?
NOT YET.

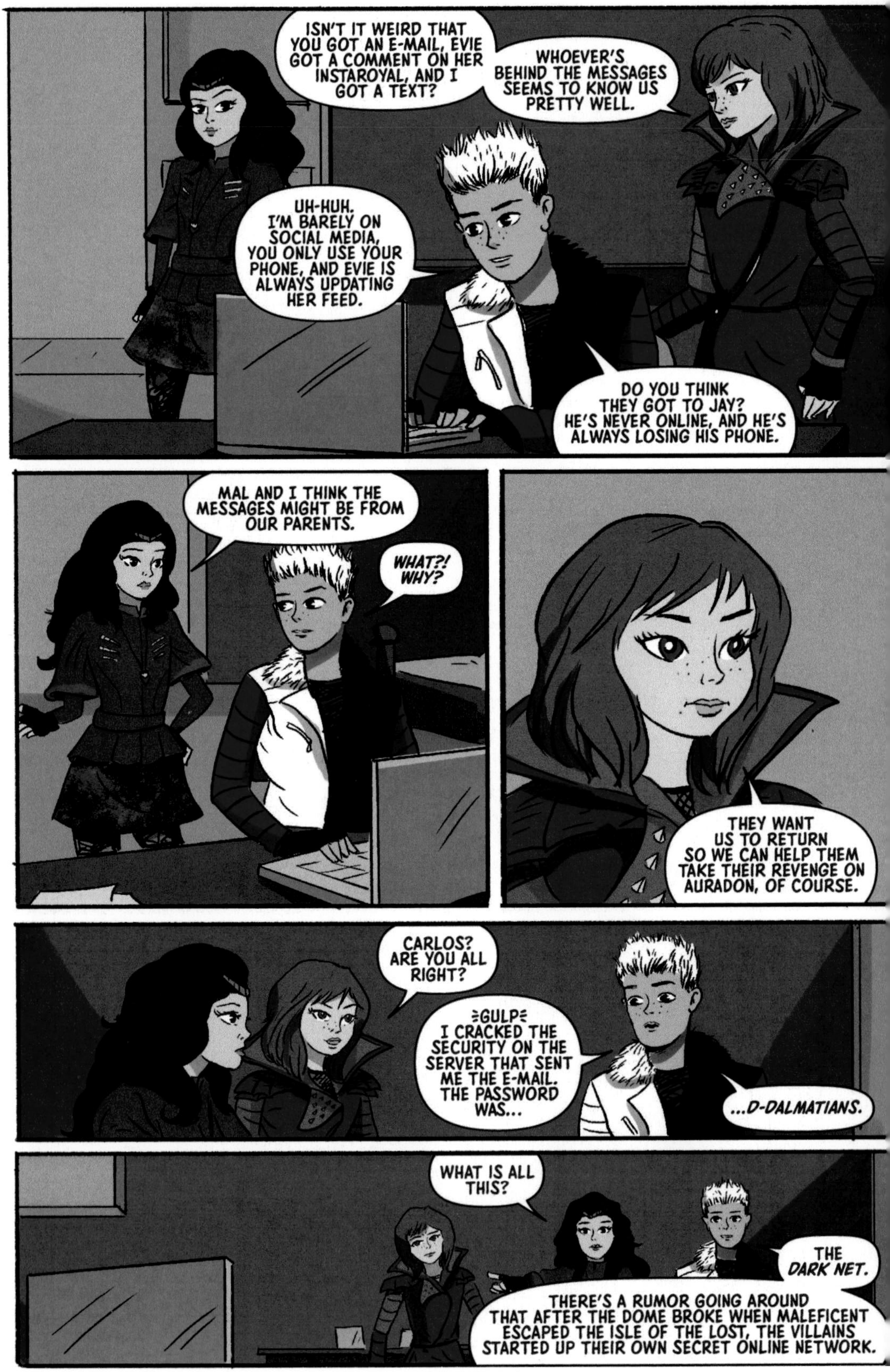

ISN'T IT WEIRD THAT YOU GOT AN E-MAIL, EVIE GOT A COMMENT ON HER INSTAROYAL, AND I GOT A TEXT?
WHOEVER'S BEHIND THE MESSAGES SEEMS TO KNOW US PRETTY WELL.
UH-HUH. I'M BARELY ON SOCIAL MEDIA, YOU ONLY USE YOUR PHONE, AND EVIE IS ALWAYS UPDATING HER FEED.
DO YOU THINK THEY GOT TO JAY? HE'S NEVER ONLINE, AND HE'S ALWAYS LOSING HIS PHONE.
MAL AND I THINK THE MESSAGES MIGHT BE FROM OUR PARENTS.
WHAT?! WHY?
THEY WANT US TO RETURN SO WE CAN HELP THEM TAKE THEIR REVENGE ON AURADON, OF COURSE.
CARLOS? ARE YOU ALL RIGHT?
GULP
I CRACKED THE SECURITY ON THE SERVER THAT SENT ME THE E-MAIL. THE PASSWORD WAS...
...D-DALMATIANS.
WHAT IS ALL THIS?
THE DARK NET.
THERE'S A RUMOR GOING AROUND THAT AFTER THE DOME BROKE WHEN MALEFICENT ESCAPED THE ISLE OF THE LOST, THE VILLAINS STARTED UP THEIR OWN SECRET ONLINE NETWORK.

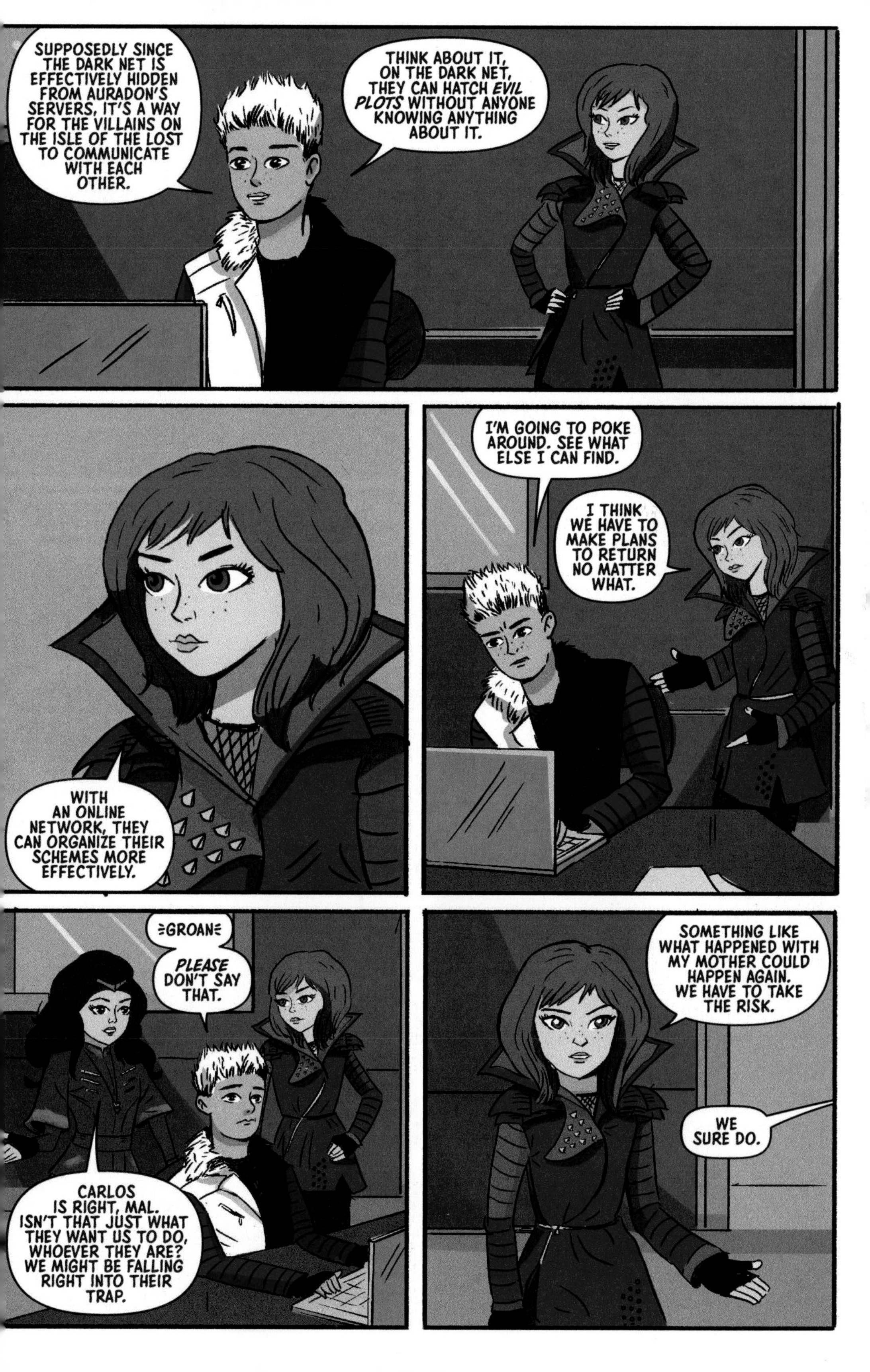
SUPPOSEDLY SINCE THE DARK NET IS EFFECTIVELY HIDDEN FROM AURADON'S SERVERS, IT'S A WAY FOR THE VILLAINS ON THE ISLE OF THE LOST TO COMMUNICATE WITH EACH OTHER.
THINK ABOUT IT, ON THE DARK NET, THEY CAN HATCH *EVIL PLOTS* WITHOUT ANYONE KNOWING ANYTHING ABOUT IT.
WITH AN ONLINE NETWORK, THEY CAN ORGANIZE THEIR SCHEMES MORE EFFECTIVELY.
I'M GOING TO POKE AROUND. SEE WHAT ELSE I CAN FIND.
I THINK WE HAVE TO MAKE PLANS TO RETURN NO MATTER WHAT.
GROAN
PLEASE DON'T SAY THAT.
CARLOS IS RIGHT, MAL. ISN'T THAT JUST WHAT THEY WANT US TO DO, WHOEVER THEY ARE? WE MIGHT BE FALLING RIGHT INTO THEIR TRAP.
SOMETHING LIKE WHAT HAPPENED WITH MY MOTHER COULD HAPPEN AGAIN. WE HAVE TO TAKE THE RISK.
WE SURE DO.

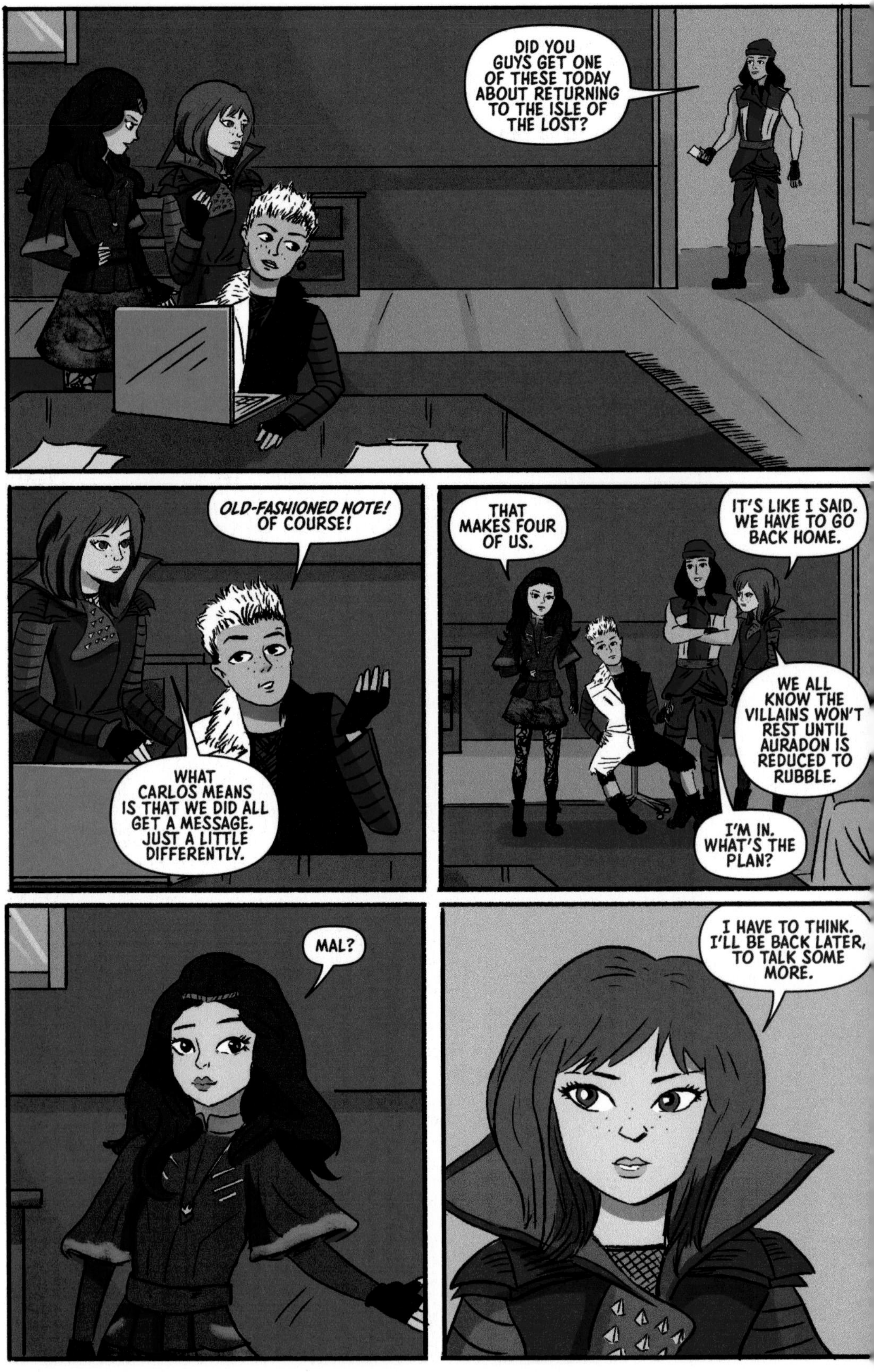
DID YOU GUYS GET ONE OF THESE TODAY ABOUT RETURNING TO THE ISLE OF THE LOST?
OLD-FASHIONED NOTE! OF COURSE!
WHAT CARLOS MEANS IS THAT WE DID ALL GET A MESSAGE. JUST A LITTLE DIFFERENTLY.
THAT MAKES FOUR OF US.
IT'S LIKE I SAID. WE HAVE TO GO BACK HOME.
WE ALL KNOW THE VILLAINS WON'T REST UNTIL AURADON IS REDUCED TO RUBBLE.
I'M IN. WHAT'S THE PLAN?
MAL?
I HAVE TO THINK. I'LL BE BACK LATER, TO TALK SOME MORE.

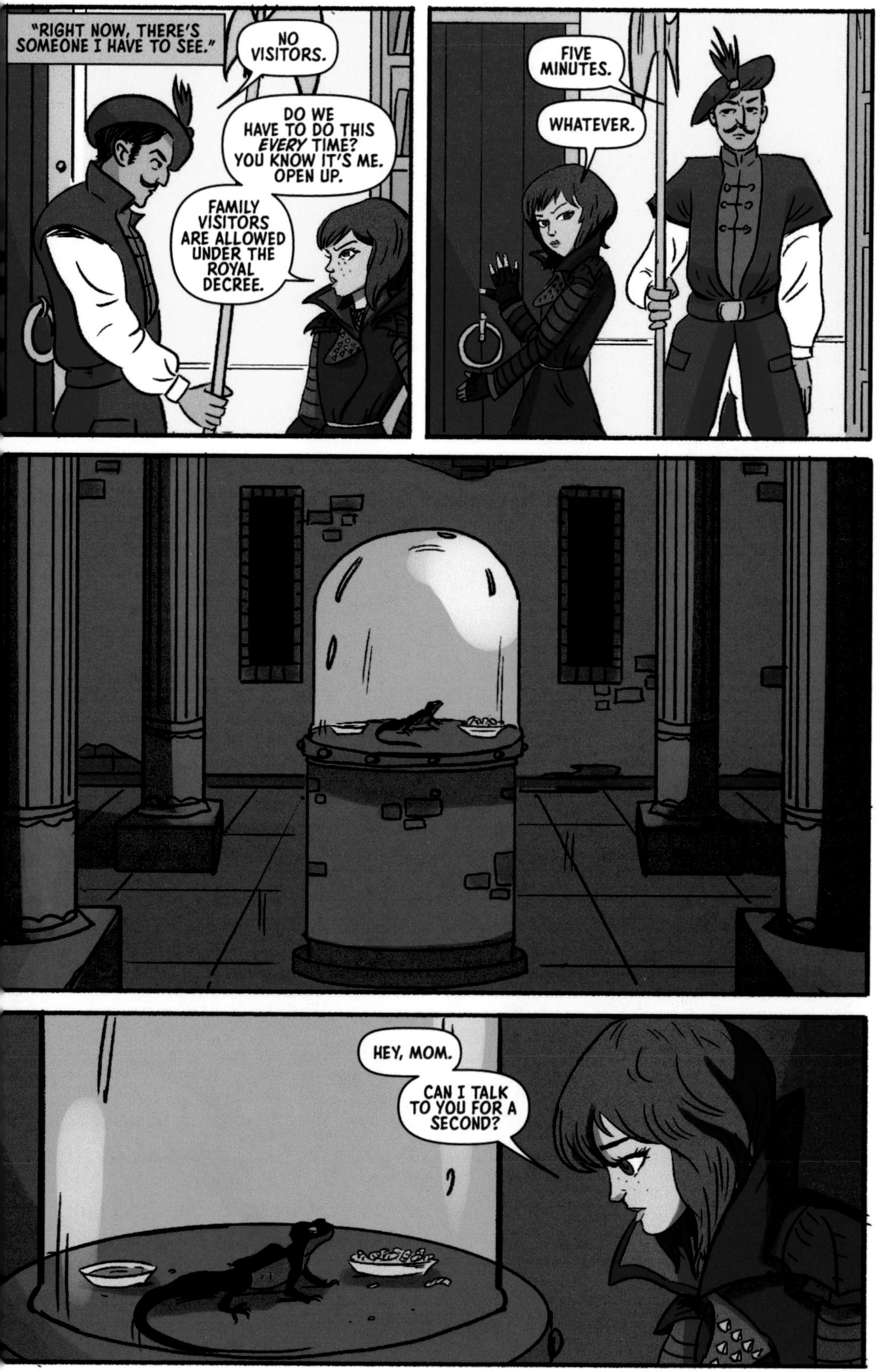
"RIGHT NOW, THERE'S SOMEONE I HAVE TO SEE."
NO VISITORS.
DO WE HAVE TO DO THIS *EVERY* TIME? YOU KNOW IT'S ME. OPEN UP.
FAMILY VISITORS ARE ALLOWED UNDER THE ROYAL DECREE.
FIVE MINUTES.
WHATEVER.
HEY, MOM.
CAN I TALK TO YOU FOR A SECOND?

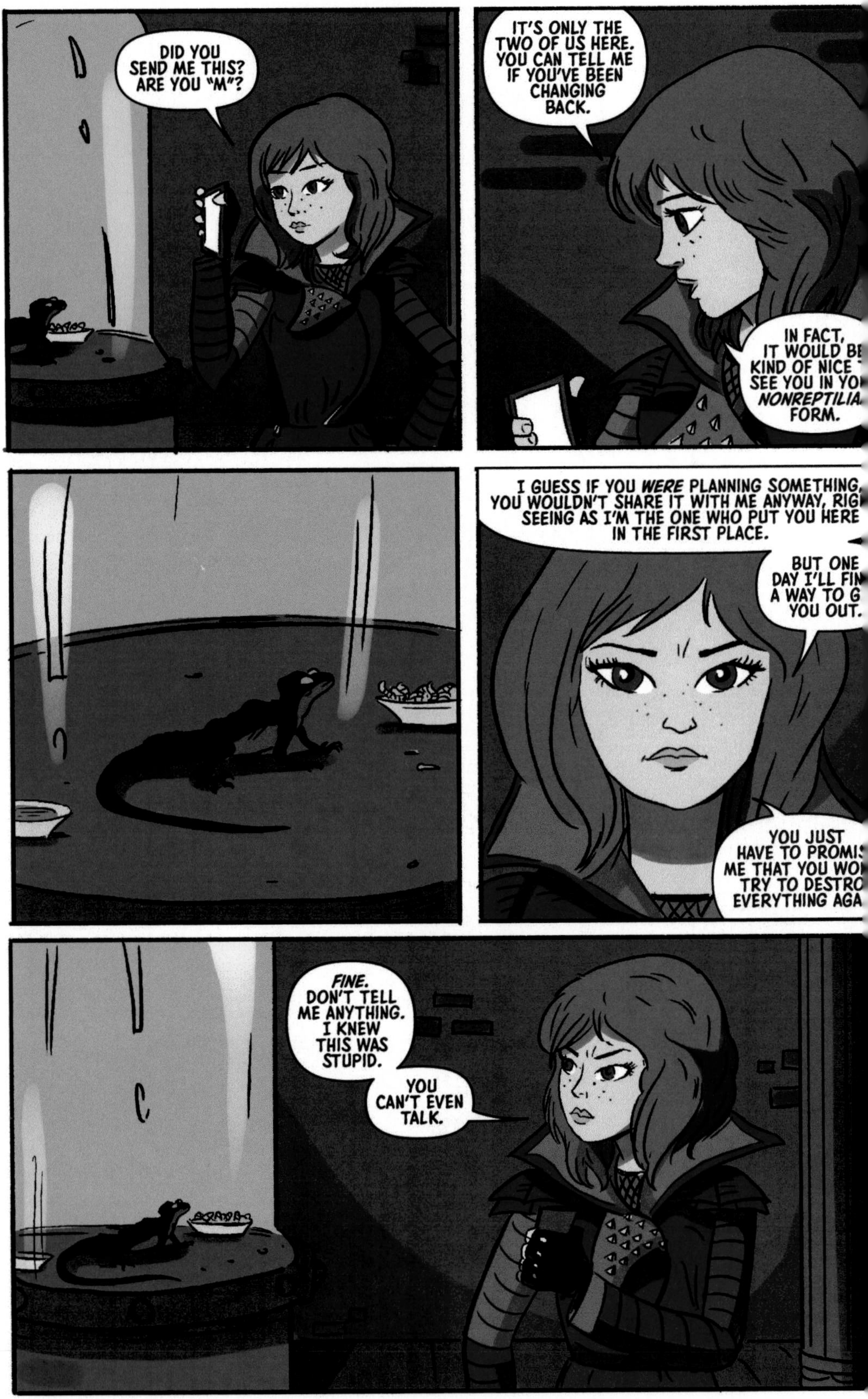
DID YOU SEND ME THIS? ARE YOU "M"?
IT'S ONLY THE TWO OF US HERE. YOU CAN TELL ME IF YOU'VE BEEN CHANGING BACK.
IN FACT, IT WOULD BE KIND OF NICE SEE YOU IN YO NONREPTILIA FORM.
I GUESS IF YOU *WERE* PLANNING SOMETHING, YOU WOULDN'T SHARE IT WITH ME ANYWAY, RIG SEEING AS I'M THE ONE WHO PUT YOU HERE IN THE FIRST PLACE.
BUT ONE DAY I'LL FI A WAY TO G YOU OUT.
YOU JUST HAVE TO PROMIS ME THAT YOU WO TRY TO DESTRO EVERYTHING AGA
FINE. DON'T TELL ME ANYTHING. I KNEW THIS WAS STUPID.
YOU CAN'T EVEN TALK.

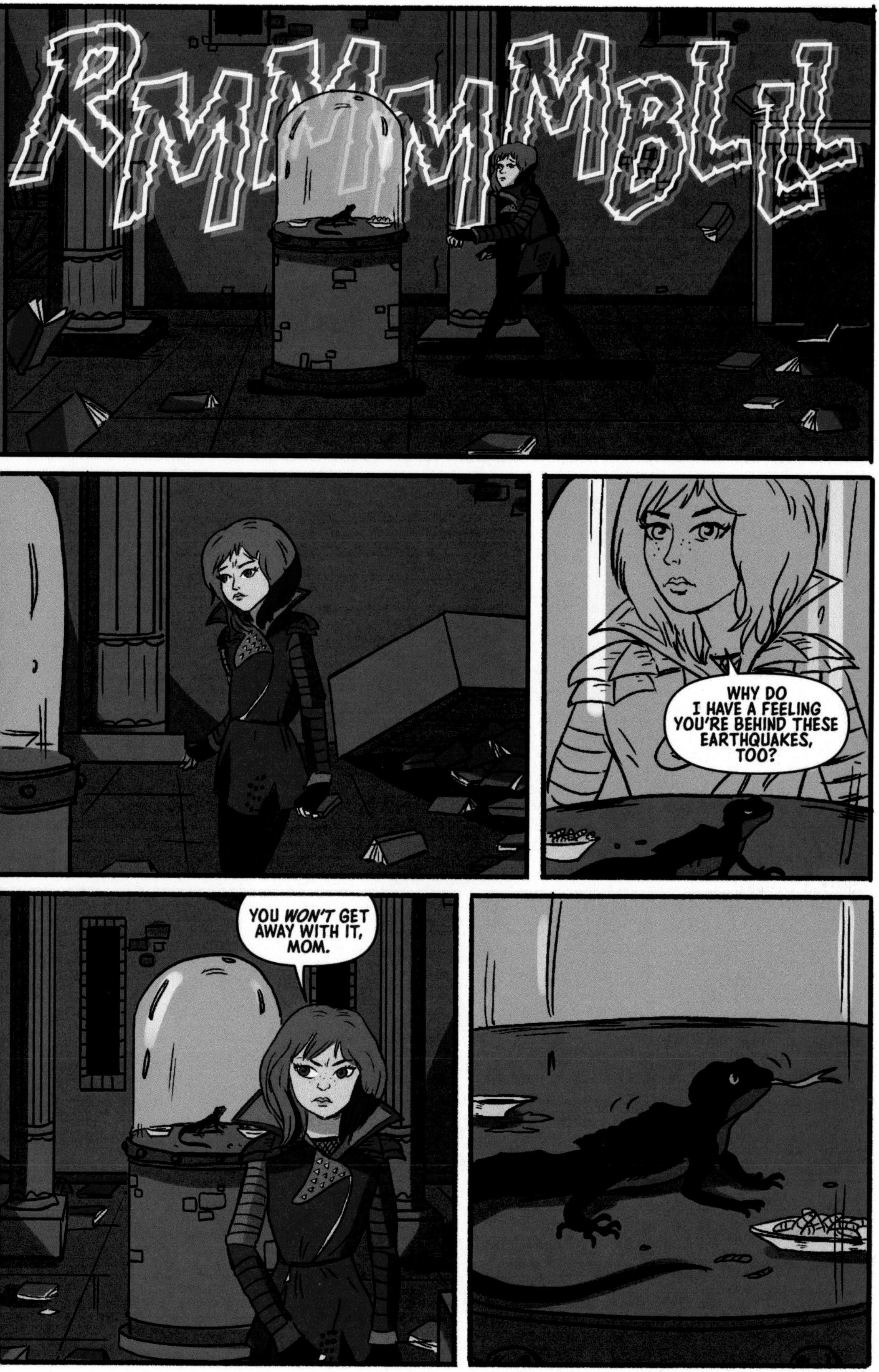
RMMMMBLL
WHY DO I HAVE A FEELING YOU'RE BEHIND THESE EARTHQUAKES, TOO?
YOU *WON'T* GET AWAY WITH IT, MOM.

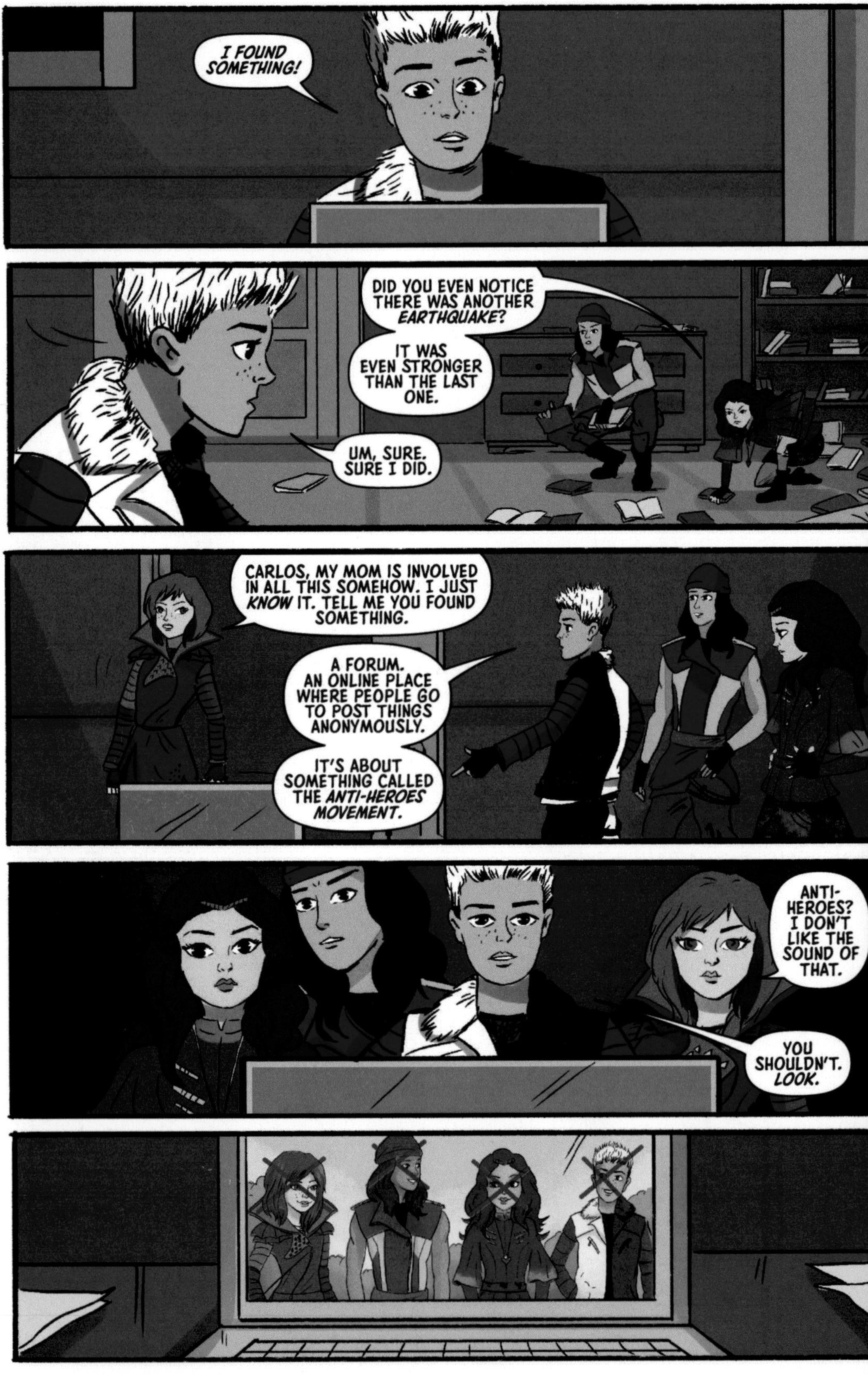
I FOUND SOMETHING!
DID YOU EVEN NOTICE THERE WAS ANOTHER EARTHQUAKE?
IT WAS EVEN STRONGER THAN THE LAST ONE.
UM, SURE. SURE I DID.
CARLOS, MY MOM IS INVOLVED IN ALL THIS SOMEHOW. I JUST KNOW IT. TELL ME YOU FOUND SOMETHING.
A FORUM. AN ONLINE PLACE WHERE PEOPLE GO TO POST THINGS ANONYMOUSLY.
IT'S ABOUT SOMETHING CALLED THE ANTI-HEROES MOVEMENT.
ANTI-HEROES? I DON'T LIKE THE SOUND OF THAT.
YOU SHOULDN'T. LOOK.

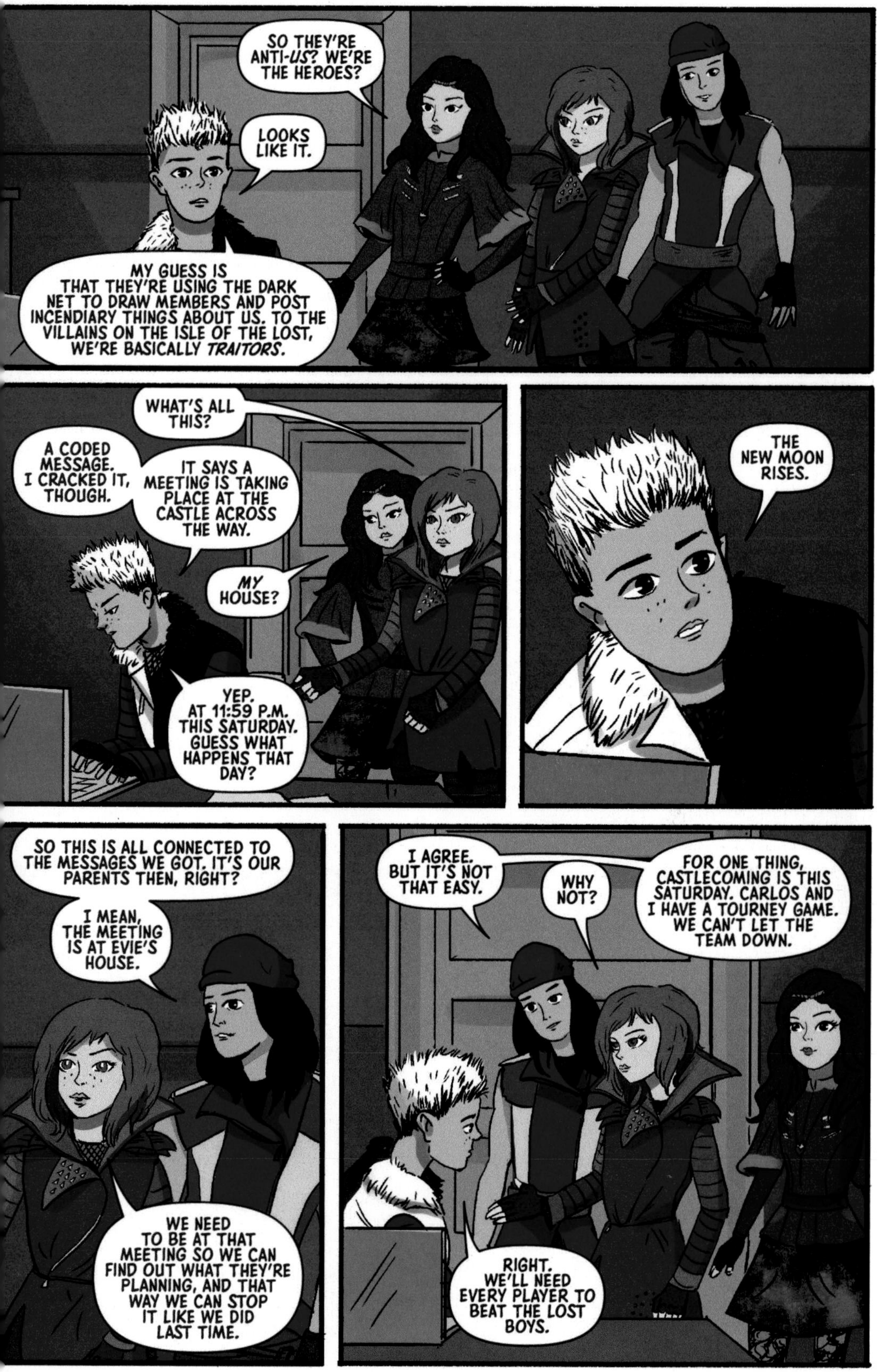
SO THEY'RE ANTI-*US*? WE'RE THE HEROES?
LOOKS LIKE IT.
MY GUESS IS THAT THEY'RE USING THE DARK NET TO DRAW MEMBERS AND POST INCENDIARY THINGS ABOUT US. TO THE VILLAINS ON THE ISLE OF THE LOST, WE'RE BASICALLY *TRAITORS*.
WHAT'S ALL THIS?
A CODED MESSAGE. I CRACKED IT, THOUGH.
IT SAYS A MEETING IS TAKING PLACE AT THE CASTLE ACROSS THE WAY.
MY HOUSE?
YEP. AT 11:59 P.M. THIS SATURDAY. GUESS WHAT HAPPENS THAT DAY?
THE NEW MOON RISES.
SO THIS IS ALL CONNECTED TO THE MESSAGES WE GOT. IT'S OUR PARENTS THEN, RIGHT?
I MEAN, THE MEETING IS AT EVIE'S HOUSE.
WE NEED TO BE AT THAT MEETING SO WE CAN FIND OUT WHAT THEY'RE PLANNING, AND THAT WAY WE CAN STOP IT LIKE WE DID LAST TIME.
I AGREE. BUT IT'S NOT THAT EASY.
WHY NOT?
FOR ONE THING, CASTLECOMING IS THIS SATURDAY. CARLOS AND I HAVE A TOURNEY GAME. WE CAN'T LET THE TEAM DOWN.
RIGHT. WE'LL NEED EVERY PLAYER TO BEAT THE LOST BOYS.

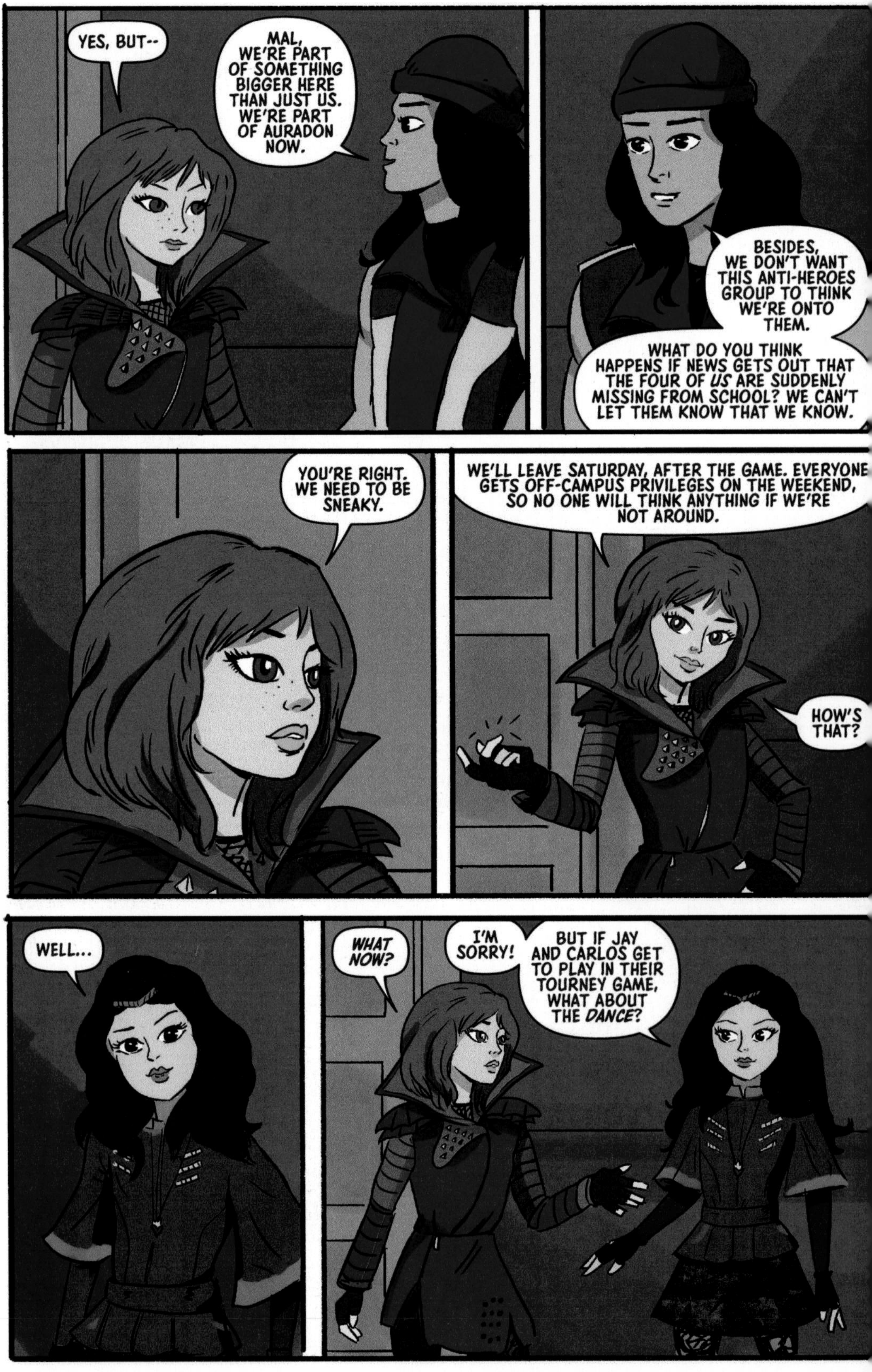
YES, BUT--
MAL, WE'RE PART OF SOMETHING BIGGER HERE THAN JUST US. WE'RE PART OF AURADON NOW.
BESIDES, WE DON'T WANT THIS ANTI-HEROES GROUP TO THINK WE'RE ONTO THEM.
WHAT DO YOU THINK HAPPENS IF NEWS GETS OUT THAT THE FOUR OF *US* ARE SUDDENLY MISSING FROM SCHOOL? WE CAN'T LET THEM KNOW THAT WE KNOW.
YOU'RE RIGHT. WE NEED TO BE SNEAKY.
WE'LL LEAVE SATURDAY, AFTER THE GAME. EVERYONE GETS OFF-CAMPUS PRIVILEGES ON THE WEEKEND, SO NO ONE WILL THINK ANYTHING IF WE'RE NOT AROUND.
HOW'S THAT?
WELL...
WHAT NOW?
I'M SORRY!
BUT IF JAY AND CARLOS GET TO PLAY IN THEIR TOURNEY GAME, WHAT ABOUT THE *DANCE*?

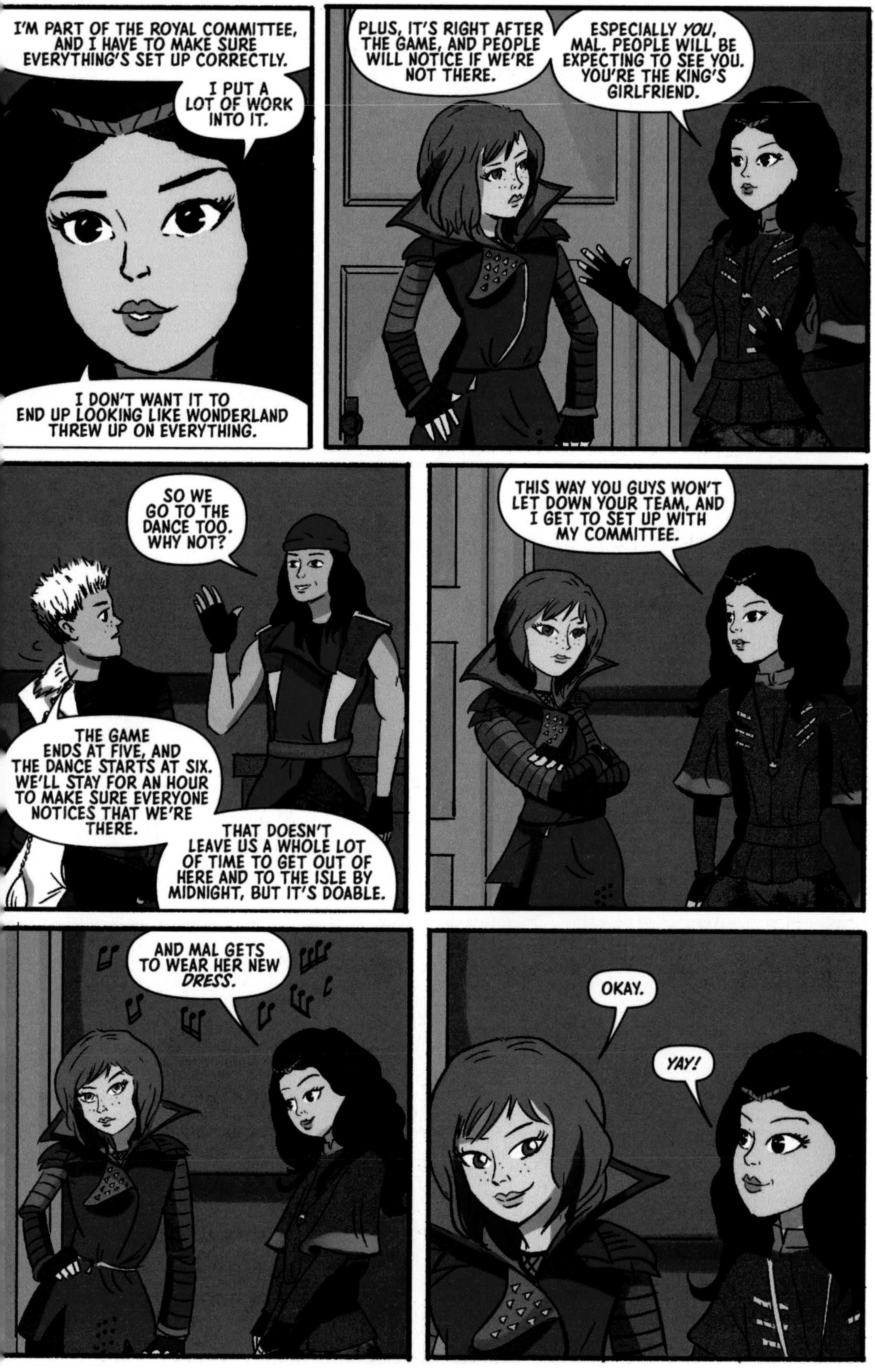
I'M PART OF THE ROYAL COMMITTEE, AND I HAVE TO MAKE SURE EVERYTHING'S SET UP CORRECTLY.
I PUT A LOT OF WORK INTO IT.
I DON'T WANT IT TO END UP LOOKING LIKE WONDERLAND THREW UP ON EVERYTHING.
PLUS, IT'S RIGHT AFTER THE GAME, AND PEOPLE WILL NOTICE IF WE'RE NOT THERE.
ESPECIALLY *YOU*, MAL. PEOPLE WILL BE EXPECTING TO SEE YOU. YOU'RE THE KING'S GIRLFRIEND.
SO WE GO TO THE DANCE TOO. WHY NOT?
THE GAME ENDS AT FIVE, AND THE DANCE STARTS AT SIX. WE'LL STAY FOR AN HOUR TO MAKE SURE EVERYONE NOTICES THAT WE'RE THERE.
THAT DOESN'T LEAVE US A WHOLE LOT OF TIME TO GET OUT OF HERE AND TO THE ISLE BY MIDNIGHT, BUT IT'S DOABLE.
THIS WAY YOU GUYS WON'T LET DOWN YOUR TEAM, AND I GET TO SET UP WITH MY COMMITTEE.
AND MAL GETS TO WEAR HER NEW *DRESS*.
OKAY.
YAY!

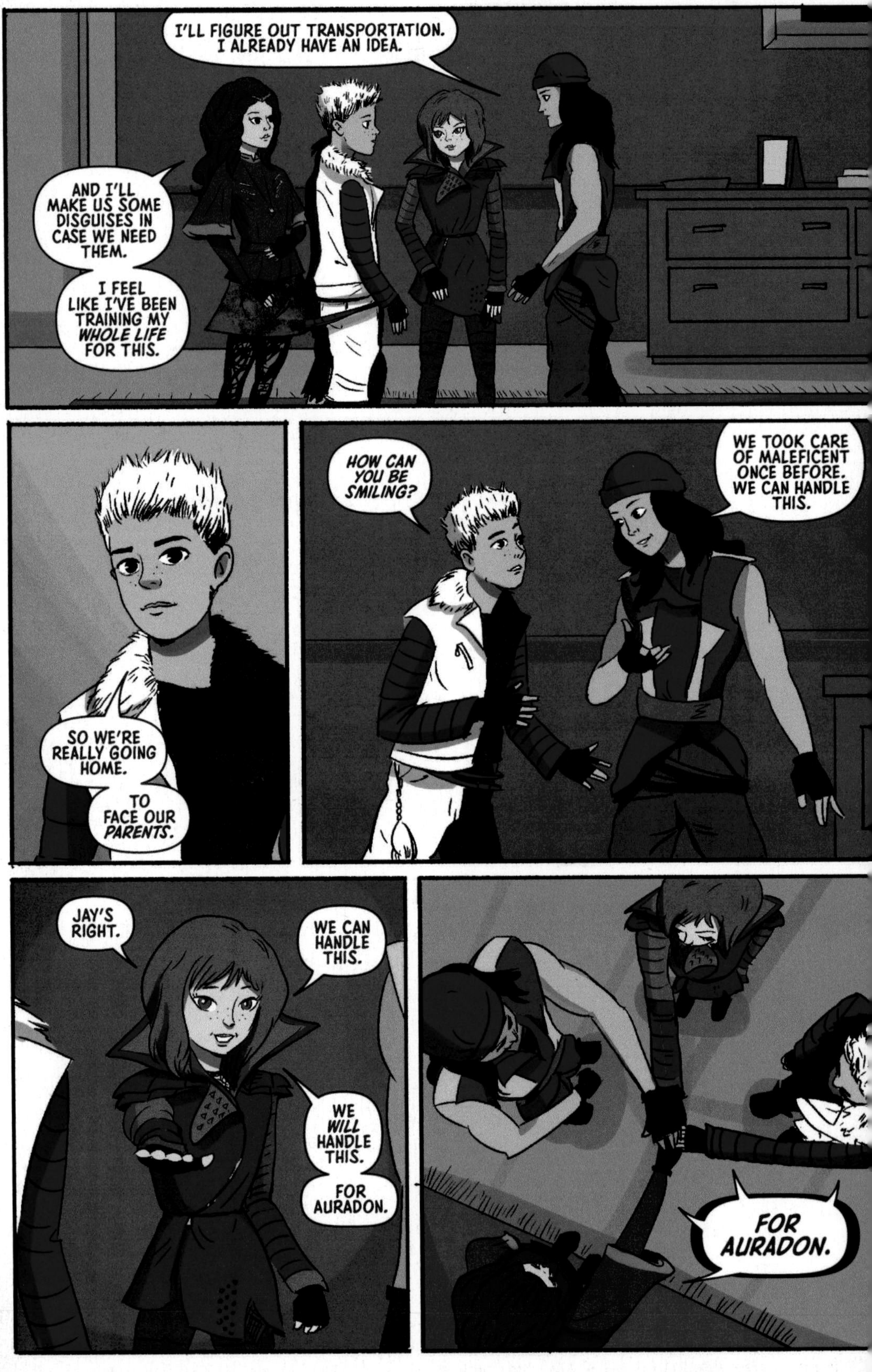
I'LL FIGURE OUT TRANSPORTATION. I ALREADY HAVE AN IDEA.
AND I'LL MAKE US SOME DISGUISES IN CASE WE NEED THEM.
I FEEL LIKE I'VE BEEN TRAINING MY *WHOLE LIFE* FOR THIS.
SO WE'RE REALLY GOING HOME.
TO FACE OUR *PARENTS*.
HOW CAN YOU BE SMILING?
WE TOOK CARE OF MALEFICENT ONCE BEFORE. WE CAN HANDLE THIS.
JAY'S RIGHT.
WE CAN HANDLE THIS.
WE *WILL* HANDLE THIS.
FOR AURADON.
FOR AURADON.

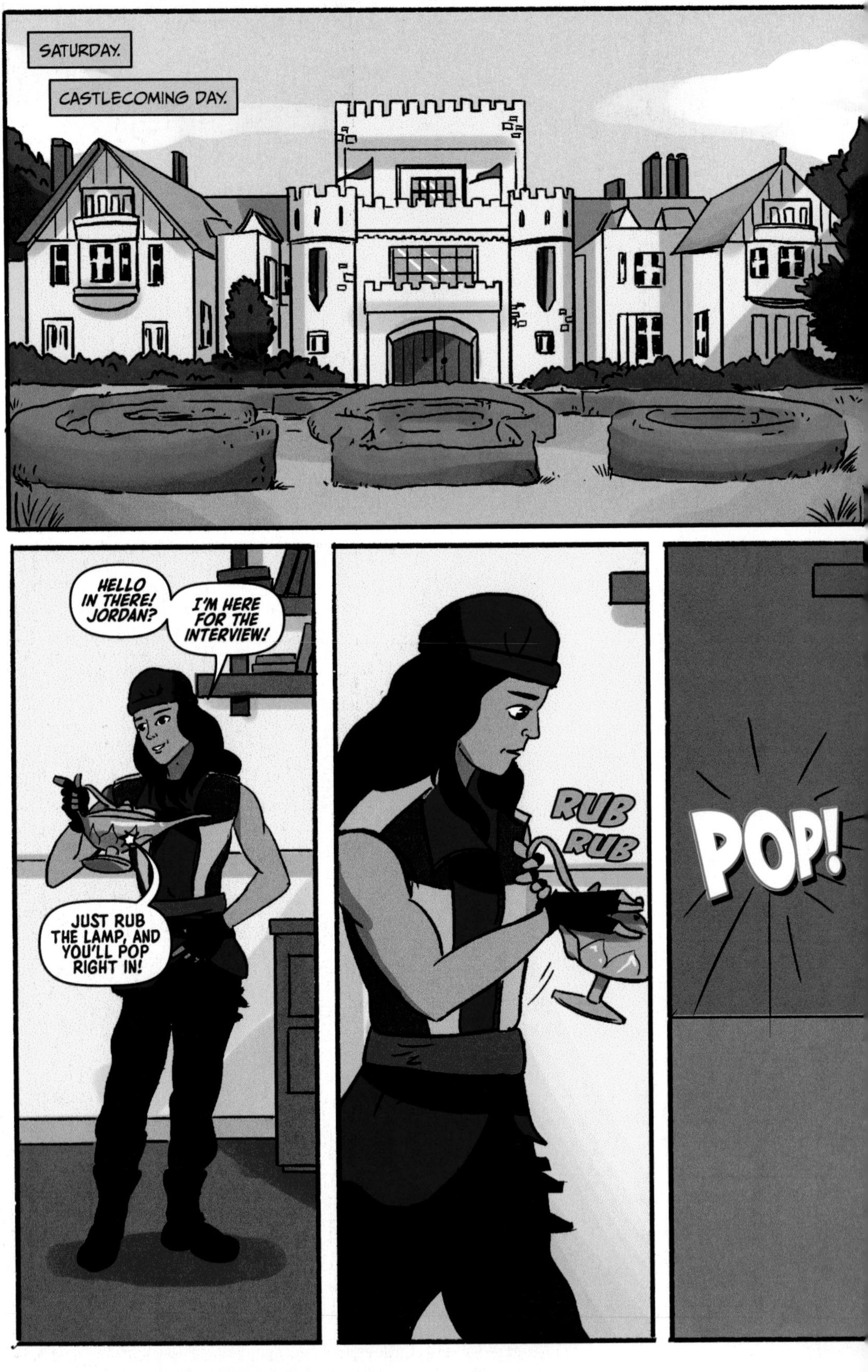
SATURDAY.
CASTLECOMING DAY.
HELLO IN THERE! JORDAN?
I'M HERE FOR THE INTERVIEW!
JUST RUB THE LAMP, AND YOU'LL POP RIGHT IN!
RUB RUB
POP!

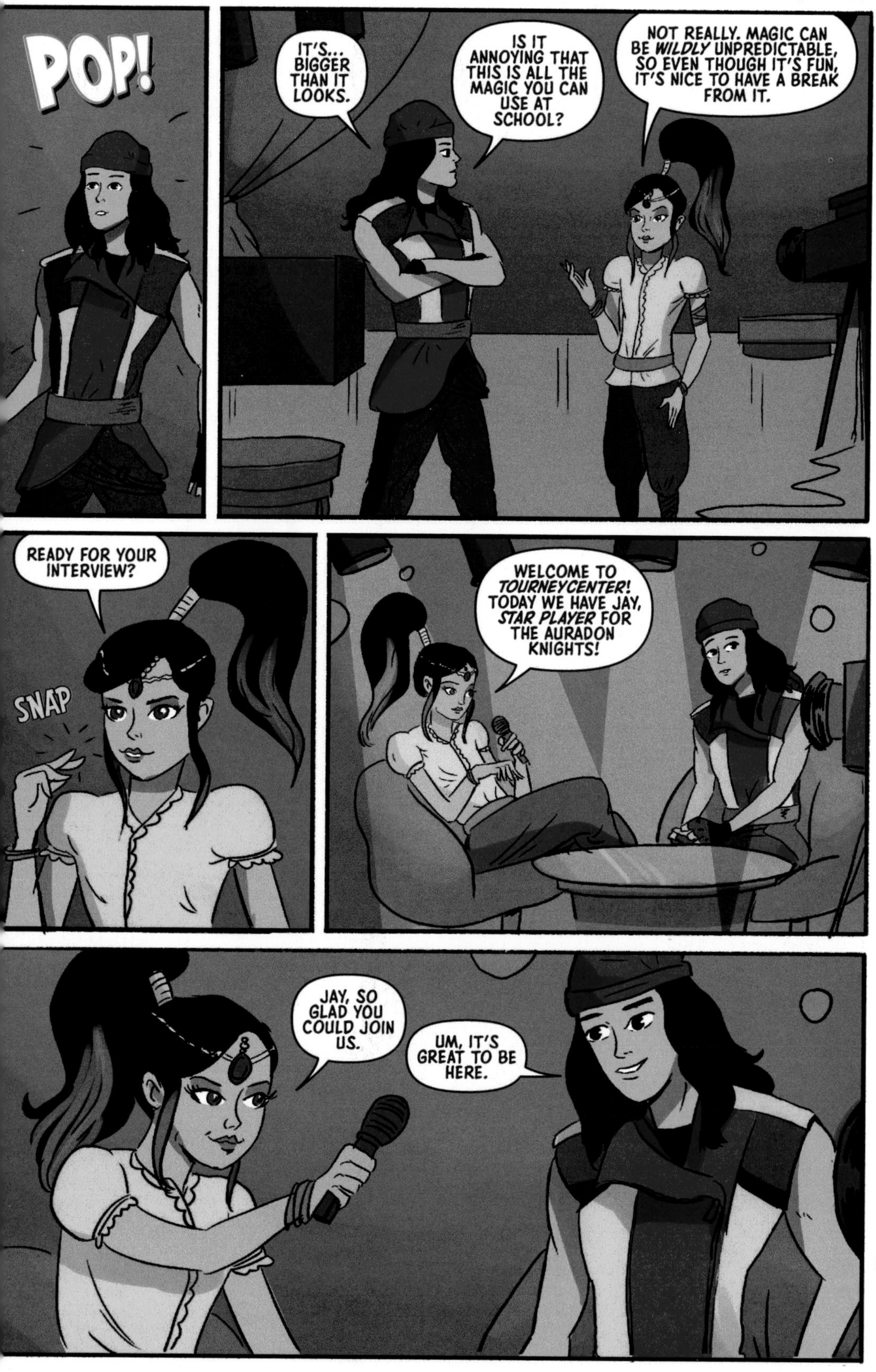
POP!
IT'S... BIGGER THAN IT LOOKS.
IS IT ANNOYING THAT THIS IS ALL THE MAGIC YOU CAN USE AT SCHOOL?
NOT REALLY. MAGIC CAN BE *WILDLY* UNPREDICTABLE, SO EVEN THOUGH IT'S FUN, IT'S NICE TO HAVE A BREAK FROM IT.
READY FOR YOUR INTERVIEW?
SNAP
WELCOME TO *TOURNEYCENTER*! TODAY WE HAVE JAY, *STAR PLAYER* FOR THE AURADON KNIGHTS!
JAY, SO GLAD YOU COULD JOIN US.
UM, IT'S GREAT TO BE HERE.

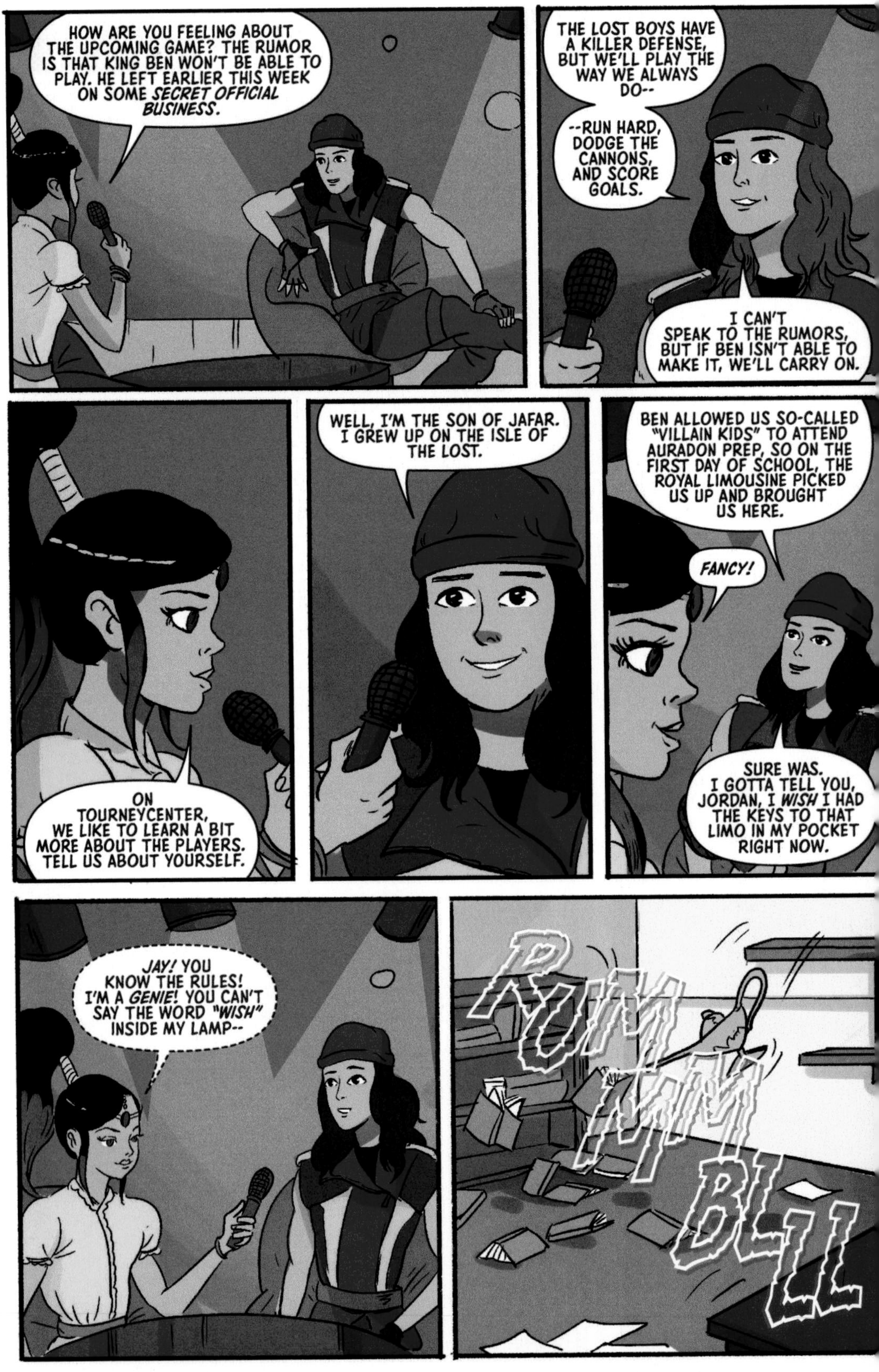
HOW ARE YOU FEELING ABOUT THE UPCOMING GAME? THE RUMOR IS THAT KING BEN WON'T BE ABLE TO PLAY. HE LEFT EARLIER THIS WEEK ON SOME *SECRET OFFICIAL BUSINESS*.
THE LOST BOYS HAVE A KILLER DEFENSE, BUT WE'LL PLAY THE WAY WE ALWAYS DO--
--RUN HARD, DODGE THE CANNONS, AND SCORE GOALS.
I CAN'T SPEAK TO THE RUMORS, BUT IF BEN ISN'T ABLE TO MAKE IT, WE'LL CARRY ON.
ON TOURNEYCENTER, WE LIKE TO LEARN A BIT MORE ABOUT THE PLAYERS. TELL US ABOUT YOURSELF.
WELL, I'M THE SON OF JAFAR. I GREW UP ON THE ISLE OF THE LOST.
BEN ALLOWED US SO-CALLED "VILLAIN KIDS" TO ATTEND AURADON PREP, SO ON THE FIRST DAY OF SCHOOL, THE ROYAL LIMOUSINE PICKED US UP AND BROUGHT US HERE.
FANCY!
SURE WAS. I GOTTA TELL YOU, JORDAN, I *WISH* I HAD THE KEYS TO THAT LIMO IN MY POCKET RIGHT NOW.
JAY! YOU KNOW THE RULES! I'M A *GENIE*! YOU CAN'T SAY THE WORD *"WISH"* INSIDE MY LAMP--
RUMMBLL

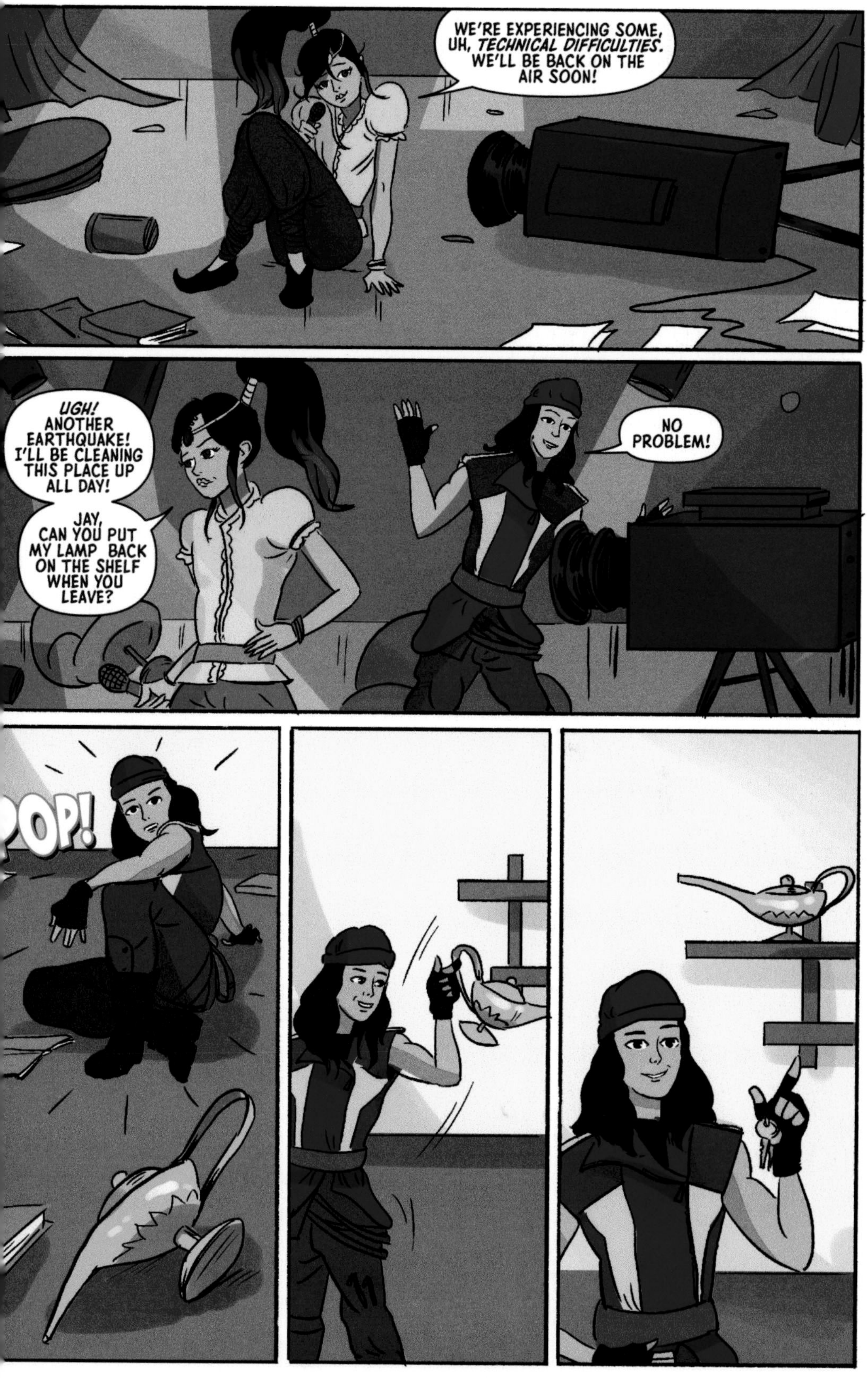
WE'RE EXPERIENCING SOME, UH, *TECHNICAL DIFFICULTIES.* WE'LL BE BACK ON THE AIR SOON!
UGH! ANOTHER EARTHQUAKE! I'LL BE CLEANING THIS PLACE UP ALL DAY!
JAY, CAN YOU PUT MY LAMP BACK ON THE SHELF WHEN YOU LEAVE?
NO PROBLEM!
POP!

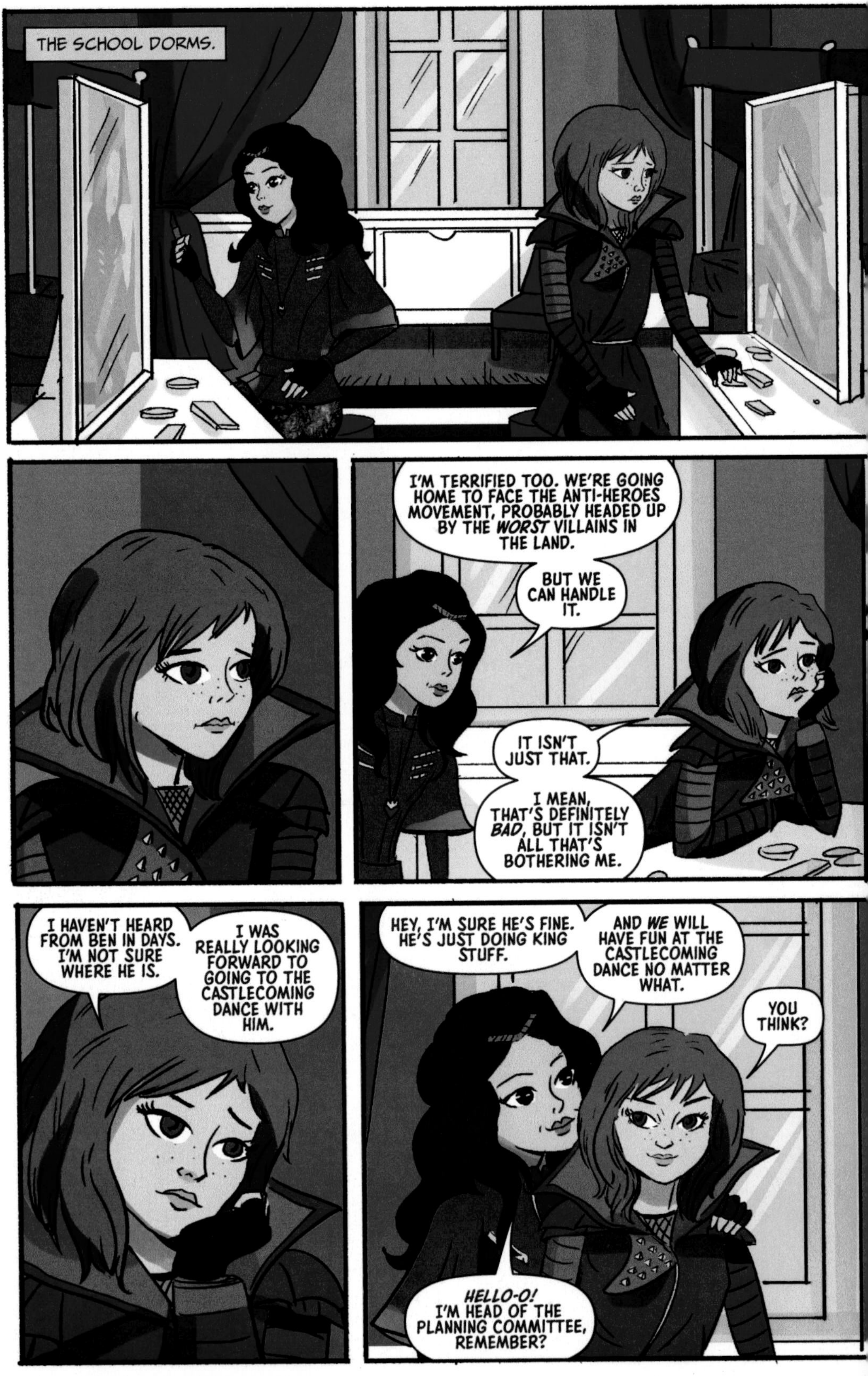
THE SCHOOL DORMS.
I'M TERRIFIED TOO. WE'RE GOING HOME TO FACE THE ANTI-HEROES MOVEMENT, PROBABLY HEADED UP BY THE *WORST* VILLAINS IN THE LAND.
BUT WE CAN HANDLE IT.
IT ISN'T JUST THAT.
I MEAN, THAT'S DEFINITELY *BAD*, BUT IT ISN'T ALL THAT'S BOTHERING ME.
I HAVEN'T HEARD FROM BEN IN DAYS. I'M NOT SURE WHERE HE IS.
I WAS REALLY LOOKING FORWARD TO GOING TO THE CASTLECOMING DANCE WITH HIM.
HEY, I'M SURE HE'S FINE. HE'S JUST DOING KING STUFF.
AND *WE* WILL HAVE FUN AT THE CASTLECOMING DANCE NO MATTER WHAT.
YOU THINK?
HELLO-O! I'M HEAD OF THE PLANNING COMMITTEE, REMEMBER?

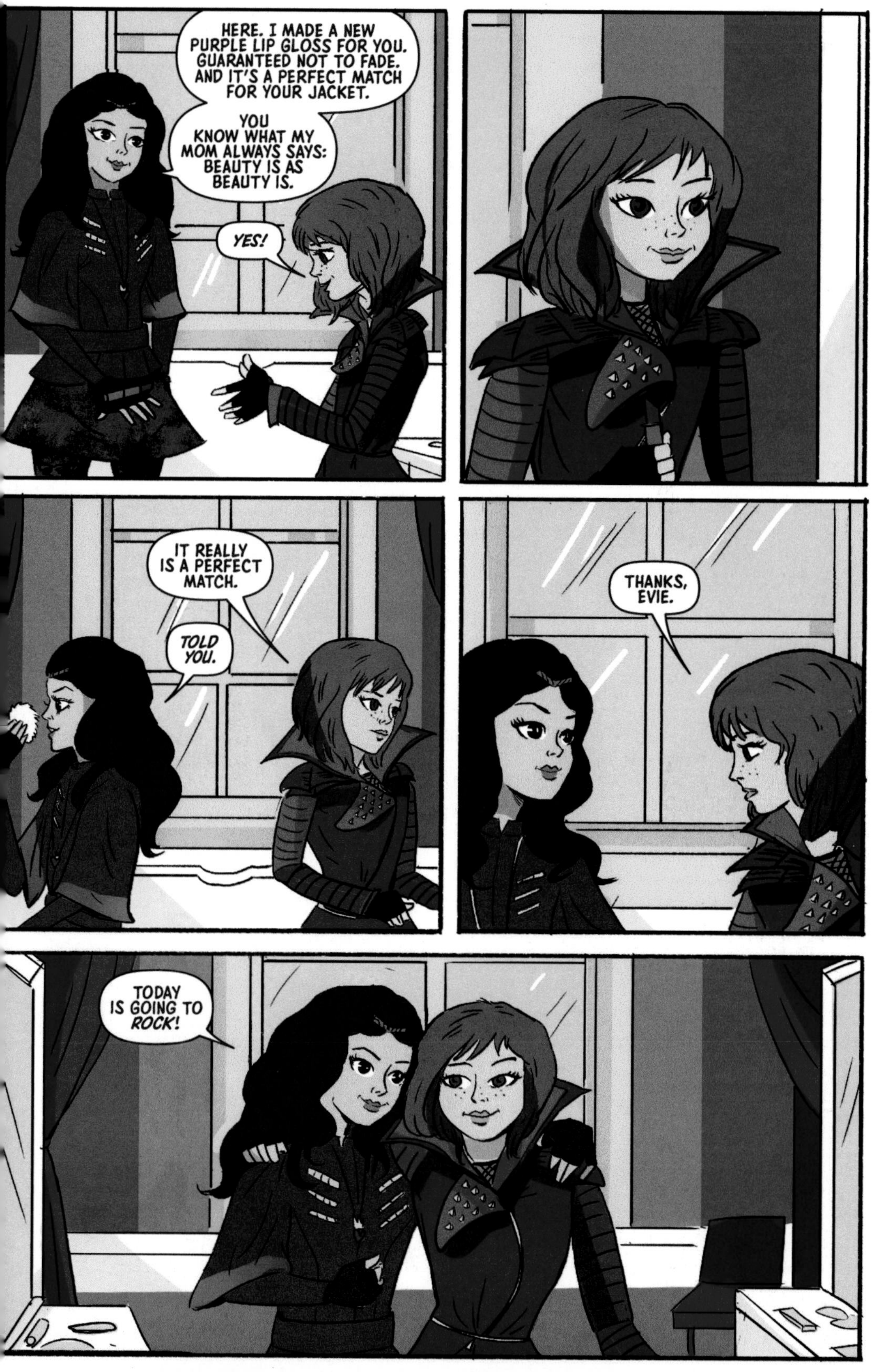
HERE. I MADE A NEW PURPLE LIP GLOSS FOR YOU. GUARANTEED NOT TO FADE. AND IT'S A PERFECT MATCH FOR YOUR JACKET.
YOU KNOW WHAT MY MOM ALWAYS SAYS: BEAUTY IS AS BEAUTY IS.
YES!
IT REALLY IS A PERFECT MATCH.
TOLD YOU.
THANKS, EVIE.
TODAY IS GOING TO ROCK!

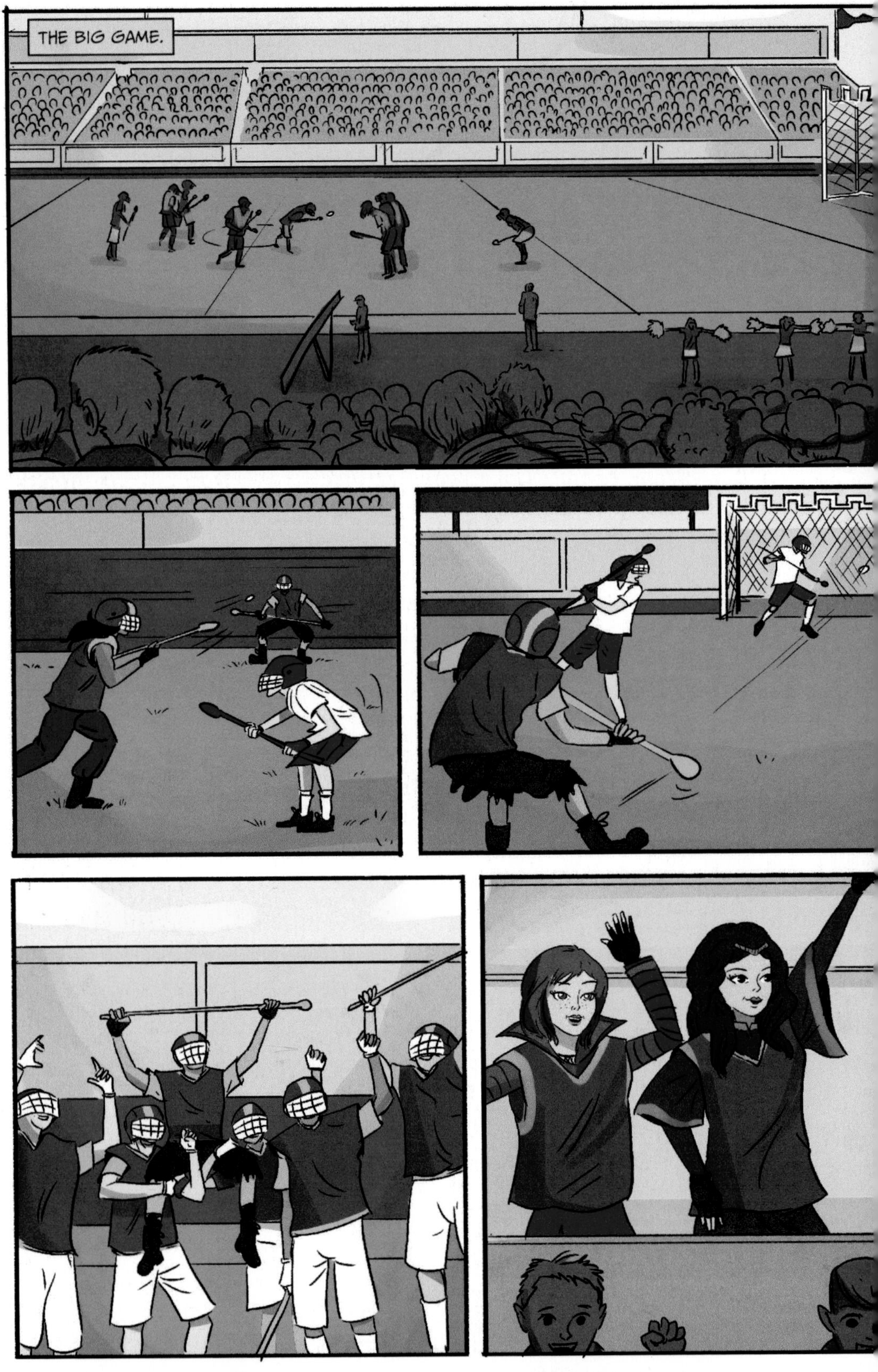
THE BIG GAME.

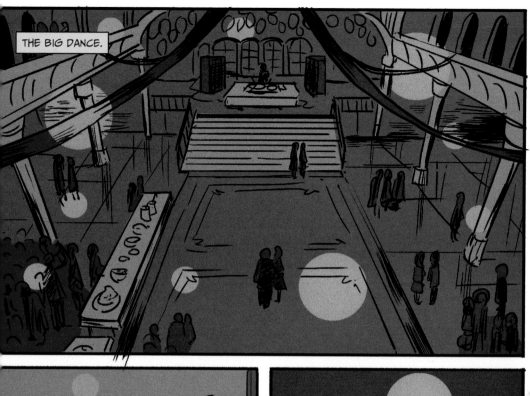

THE BIG DANCE.

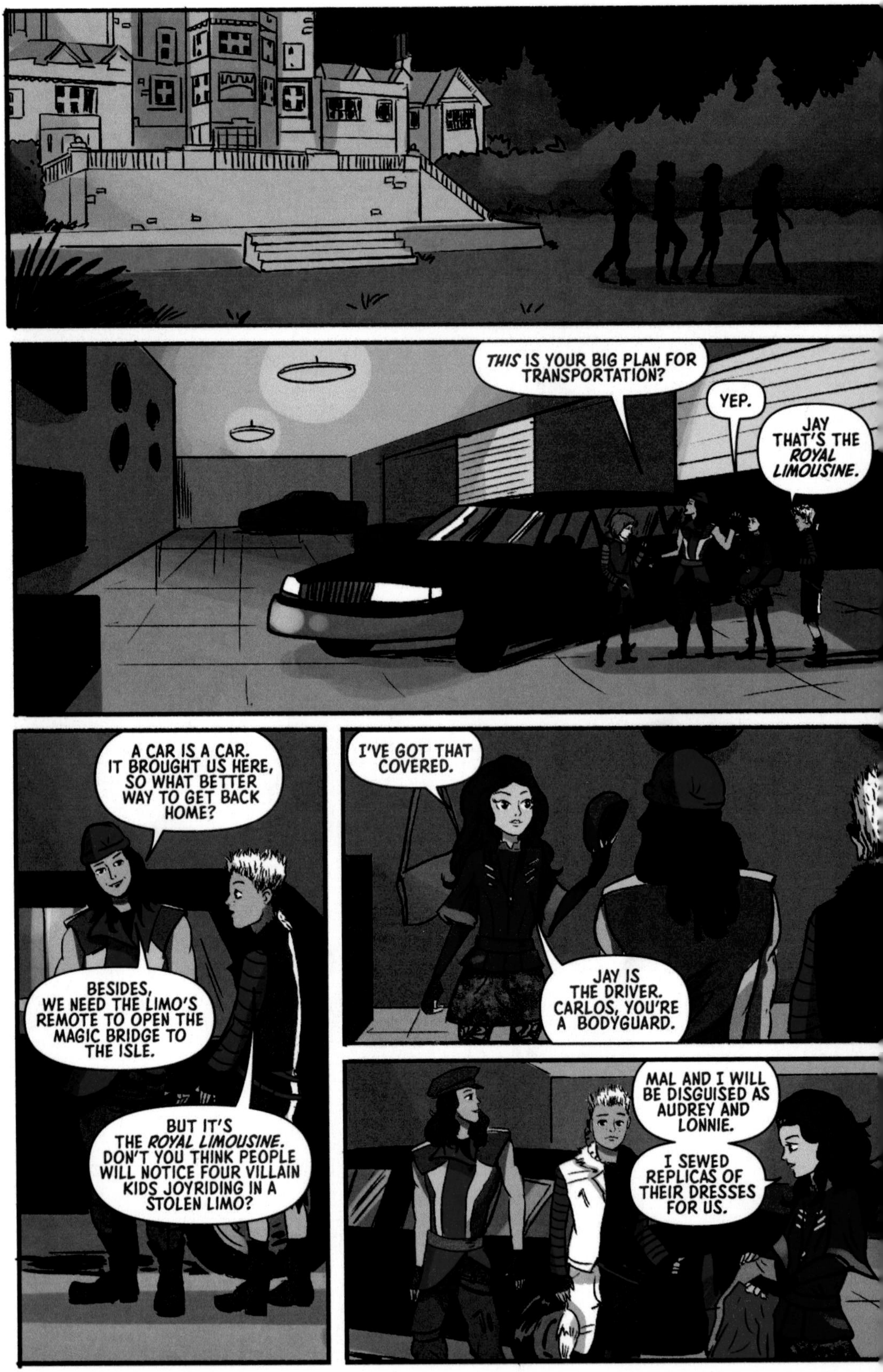
THIS IS YOUR BIG PLAN FOR TRANSPORTATION?
YEP.
JAY THAT'S THE *ROYAL LIMOUSINE.*
A CAR IS A CAR. IT BROUGHT US HERE, SO WHAT BETTER WAY TO GET BACK HOME?
BESIDES, WE NEED THE LIMO'S REMOTE TO OPEN THE MAGIC BRIDGE TO THE ISLE.
BUT IT'S THE *ROYAL LIMOUSINE*. DON'T YOU THINK PEOPLE WILL NOTICE FOUR VILLAIN KIDS JOYRIDING IN A STOLEN LIMO?
I'VE GOT THAT COVERED.
JAY IS THE DRIVER. CARLOS, YOU'RE A BODYGUARD.
MAL AND I WILL BE DISGUISED AS AUDREY AND LONNIE.
I SEWED REPLICAS OF THEIR DRESSES FOR US.

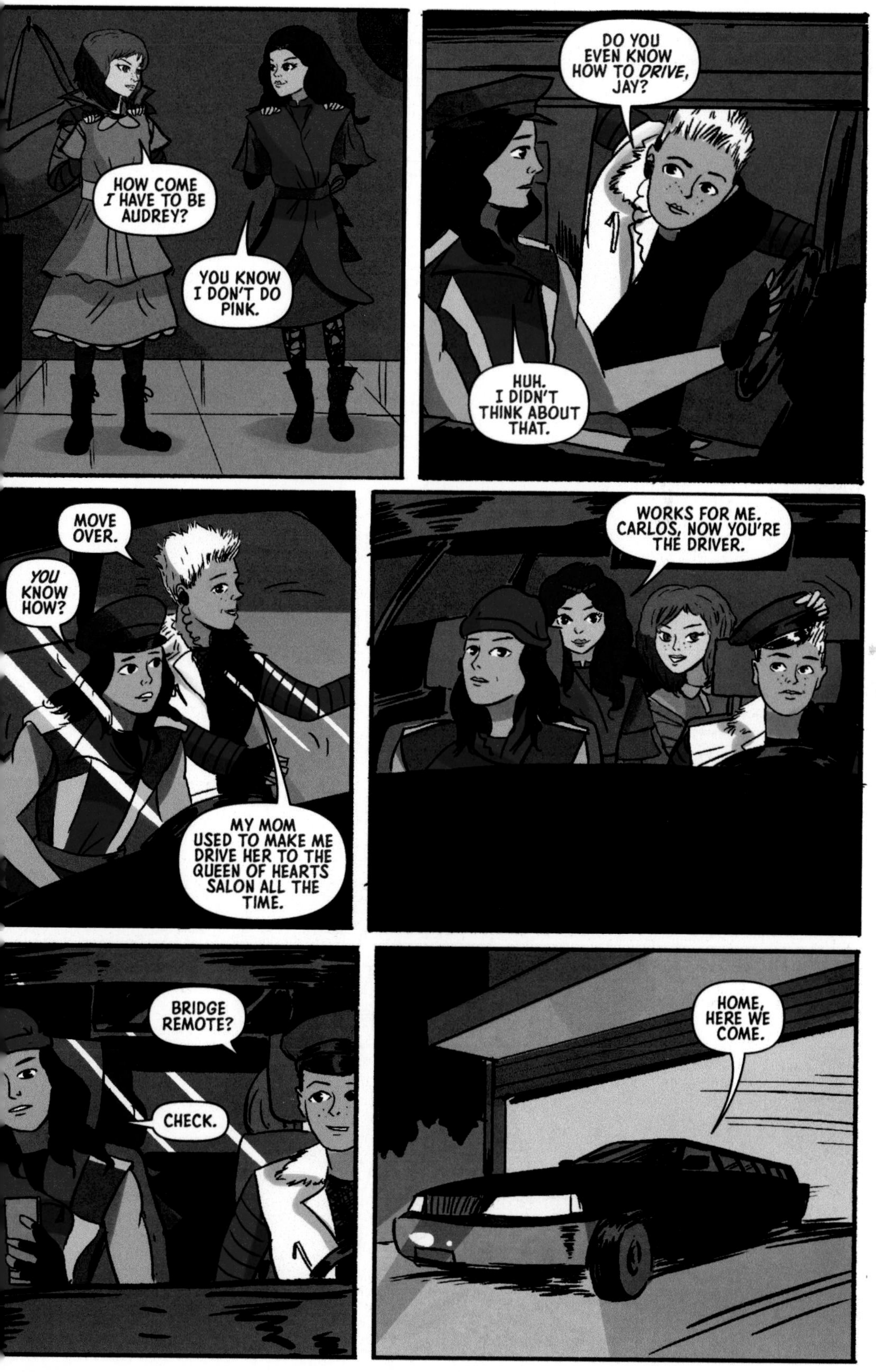
HOW COME *I* HAVE TO BE AUDREY?
YOU KNOW I DON'T DO PINK.
DO YOU EVEN KNOW HOW TO *DRIVE*, JAY?
HUH. I DIDN'T THINK ABOUT THAT.
MOVE OVER.
YOU KNOW HOW?
MY MOM USED TO MAKE ME DRIVE HER TO THE QUEEN OF HEARTS SALON ALL THE TIME.
WORKS FOR ME. CARLOS, NOW YOU'RE THE DRIVER.
BRIDGE REMOTE?
CHECK.
HOME, HERE WE COME.

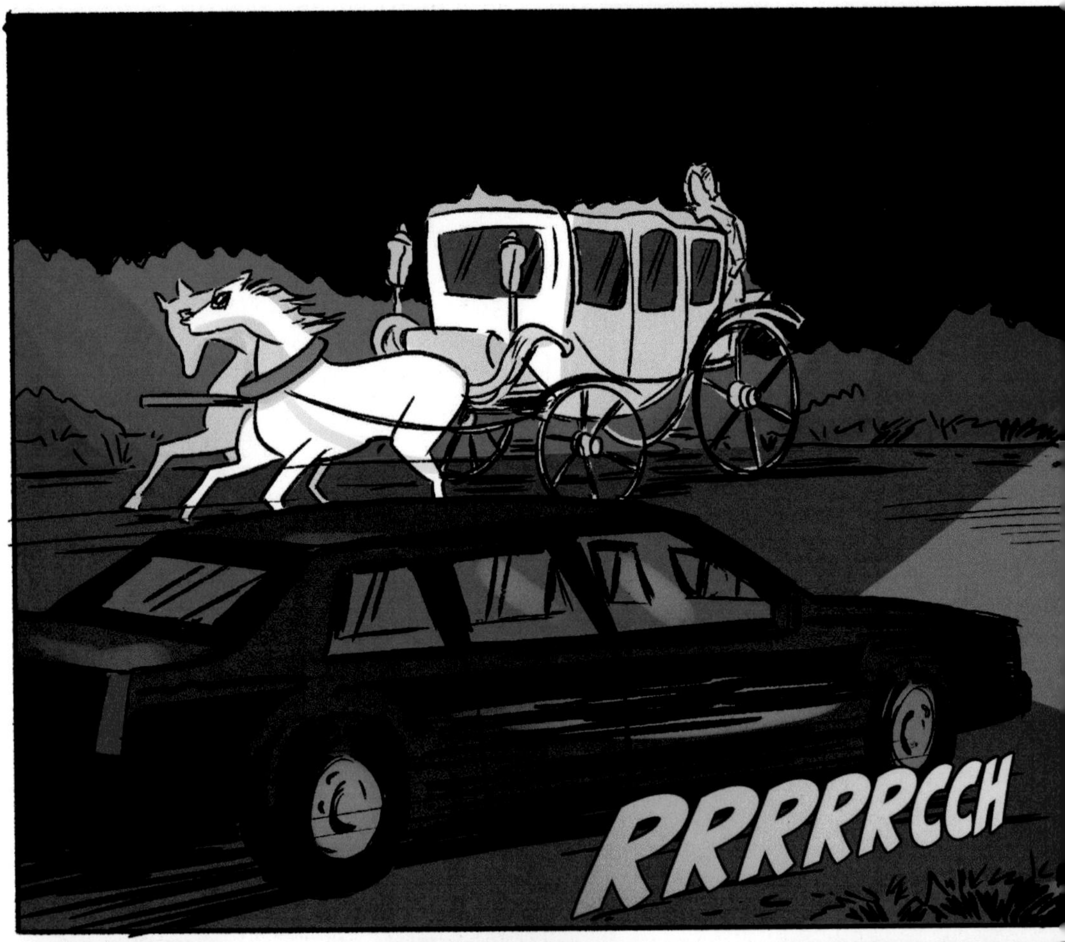
RRRRRCCH

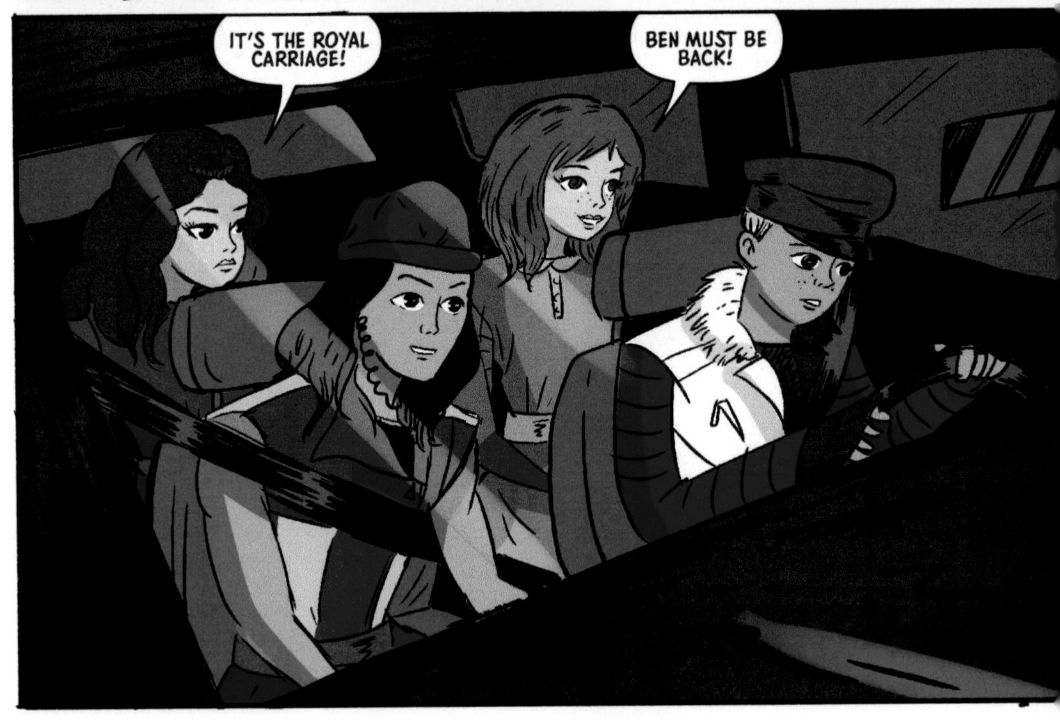
IT'S THE ROYAL CARRIAGE!
BEN MUST BE BACK!

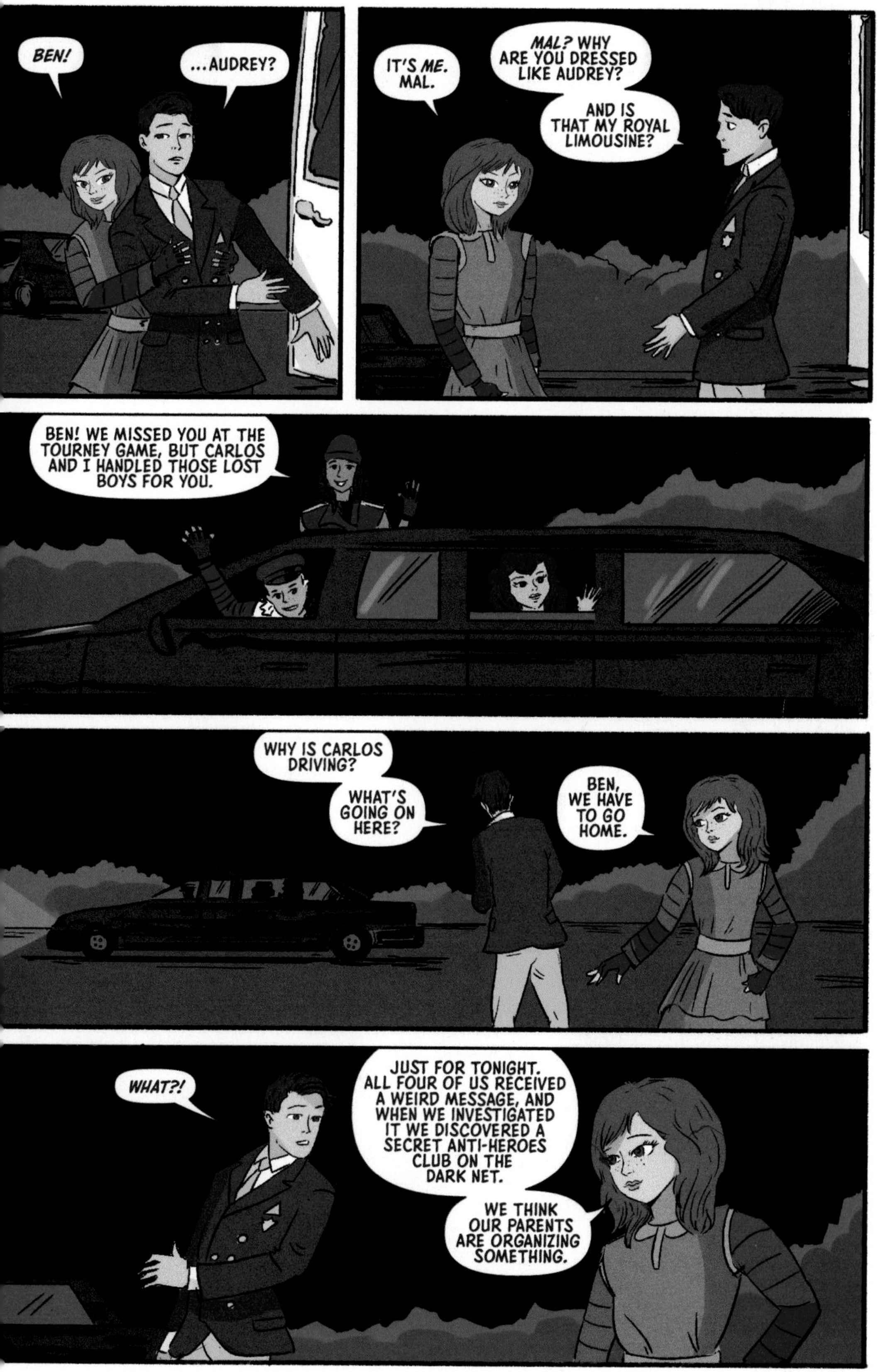
BEN!
...AUDREY?
IT'S ME. MAL.
MAL? WHY ARE YOU DRESSED LIKE AUDREY?
AND IS THAT MY ROYAL LIMOUSINE?
BEN! WE MISSED YOU AT THE TOURNEY GAME, BUT CARLOS AND I HANDLED THOSE LOST BOYS FOR YOU.
WHY IS CARLOS DRIVING?
WHAT'S GOING ON HERE?
BEN, WE HAVE TO GO HOME.
WHAT?!
JUST FOR TONIGHT. ALL FOUR OF US RECEIVED A WEIRD MESSAGE, AND WHEN WE INVESTIGATED IT WE DISCOVERED A SECRET ANTI-HEROES CLUB ON THE DARK NET.
WE THINK OUR PARENTS ARE ORGANIZING SOMETHING.

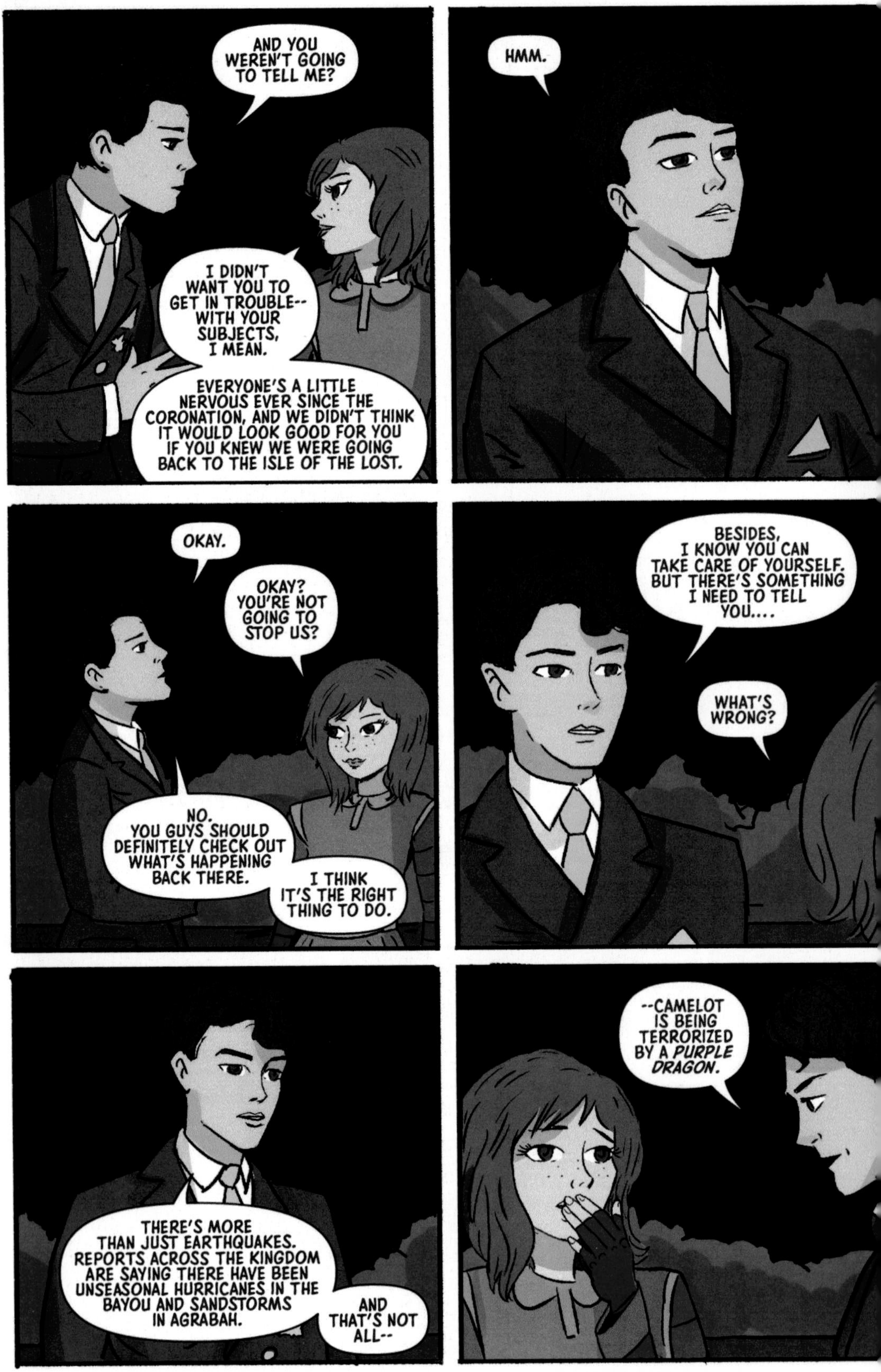
AND YOU WEREN'T GOING TO TELL ME?
I DIDN'T WANT YOU TO GET IN TROUBLE-- WITH YOUR SUBJECTS, I MEAN.
EVERYONE'S A LITTLE NERVOUS EVER SINCE THE CORONATION, AND WE DIDN'T THINK IT WOULD LOOK GOOD FOR YOU IF YOU KNEW WE WERE GOING BACK TO THE ISLE OF THE LOST.
HMM.
OKAY.
OKAY? YOU'RE NOT GOING TO STOP US?
NO. YOU GUYS SHOULD DEFINITELY CHECK OUT WHAT'S HAPPENING BACK THERE.
I THINK IT'S THE RIGHT THING TO DO.
BESIDES, I KNOW YOU CAN TAKE CARE OF YOURSELF. BUT THERE'S SOMETHING I NEED TO TELL YOU....
WHAT'S WRONG?
THERE'S MORE THAN JUST EARTHQUAKES. REPORTS ACROSS THE KINGDOM ARE SAYING THERE HAVE BEEN UNSEASONAL HURRICANES IN THE BAYOU AND SANDSTORMS IN AGRABAH.
AND THAT'S NOT ALL--
--CAMELOT IS BEING TERRORIZED BY A *PURPLE DRAGON*.

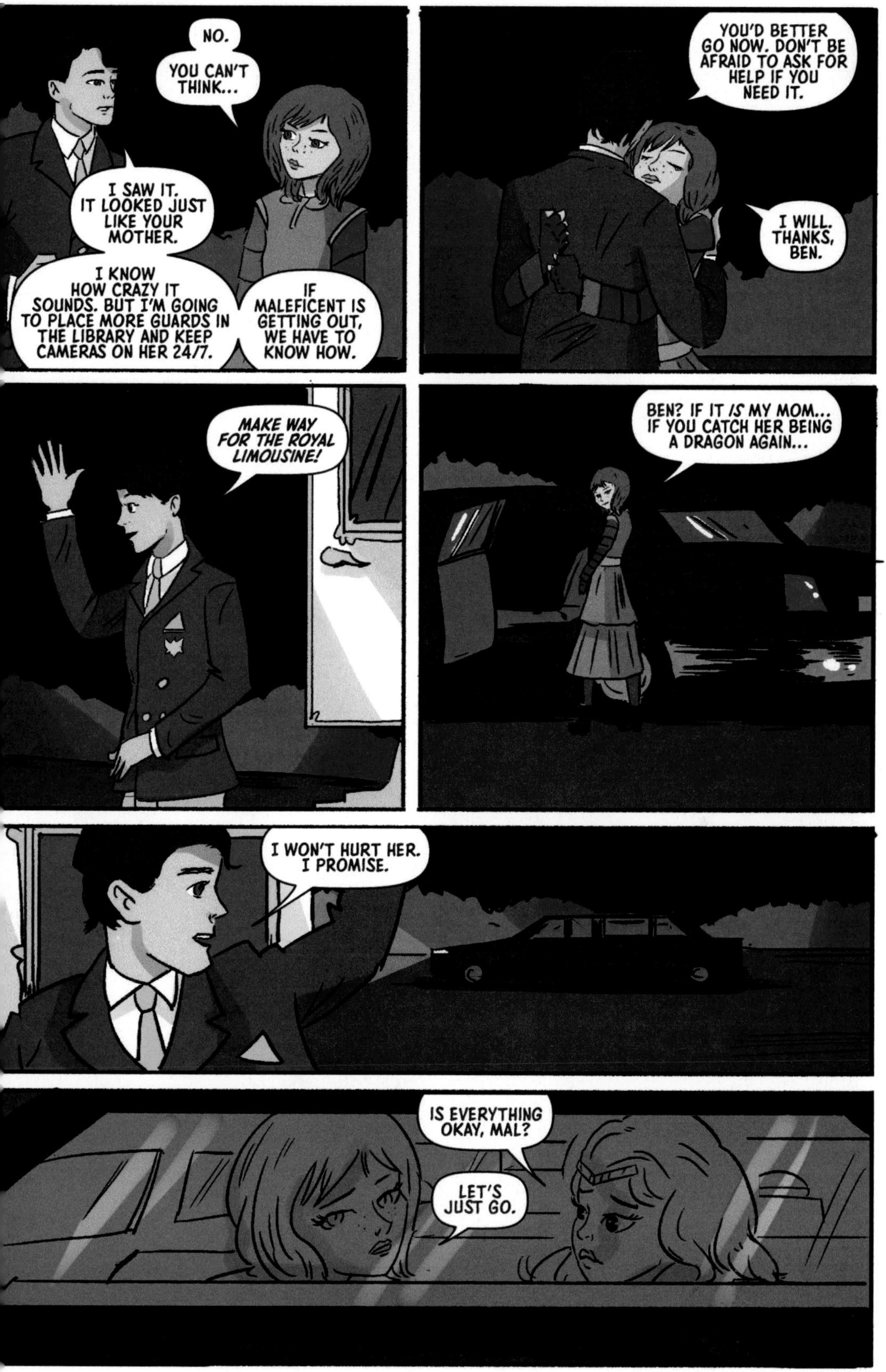
NO.
YOU CAN'T THINK...
I SAW IT. IT LOOKED JUST LIKE YOUR MOTHER.
I KNOW HOW CRAZY IT SOUNDS. BUT I'M GOING TO PLACE MORE GUARDS IN THE LIBRARY AND KEEP CAMERAS ON HER 24/7.
IF MALEFICENT IS GETTING OUT, WE HAVE TO KNOW HOW.
YOU'D BETTER GO NOW. DON'T BE AFRAID TO ASK FOR HELP IF YOU NEED IT.
I WILL. THANKS, BEN.
MAKE WAY FOR THE ROYAL LIMOUSINE!
BEN? IF IT IS MY MOM... IF YOU CATCH HER BEING A DRAGON AGAIN...
I WON'T HURT HER. I PROMISE.
IS EVERYTHING OKAY, MAL?
LET'S JUST GO.

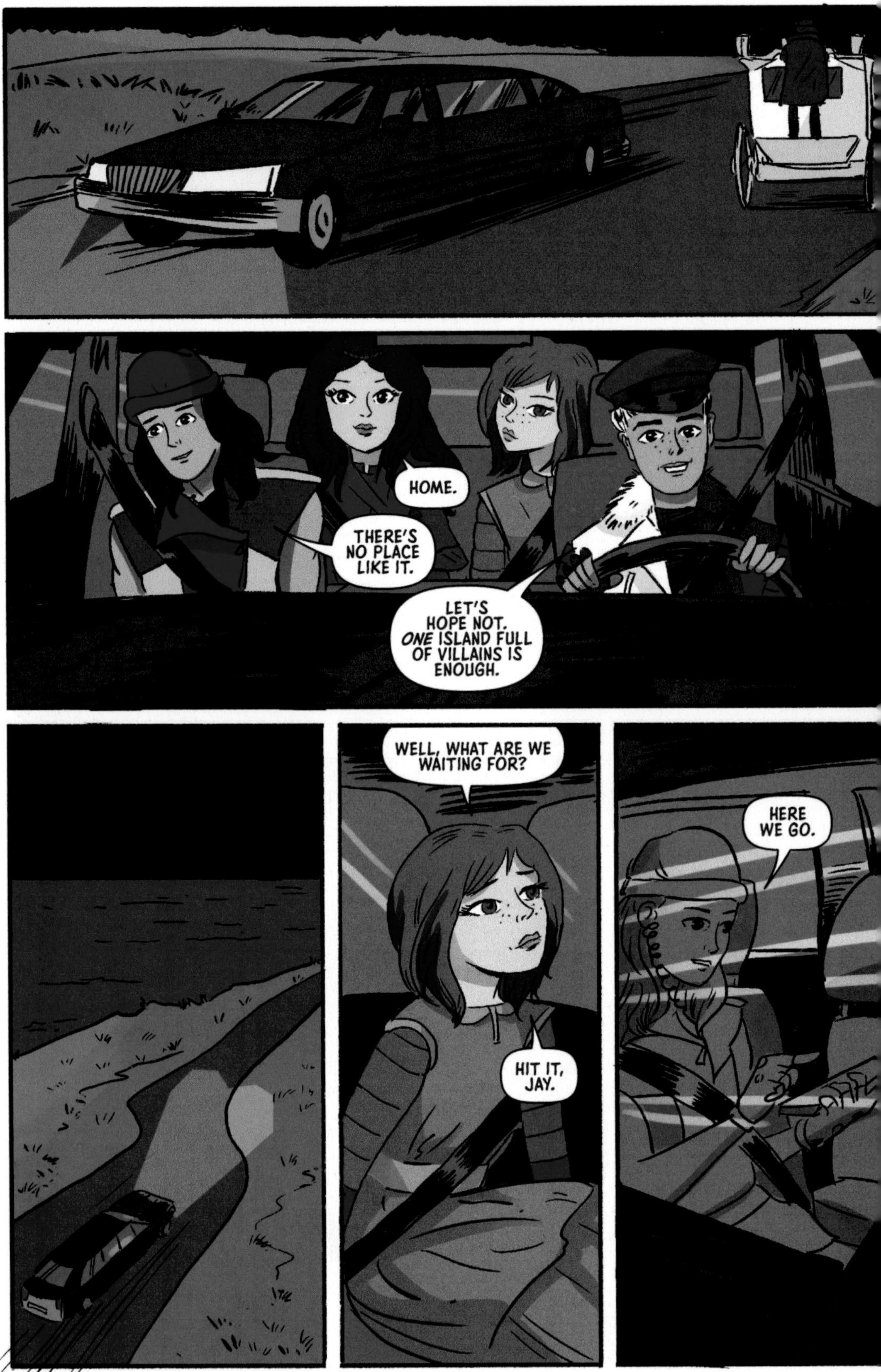
HOME.
THERE'S NO PLACE LIKE IT.
LET'S HOPE NOT. *ONE* ISLAND FULL OF VILLAINS IS ENOUGH.
WELL, WHAT ARE WE WAITING FOR?
HIT IT, JAY.
HERE WE GO.

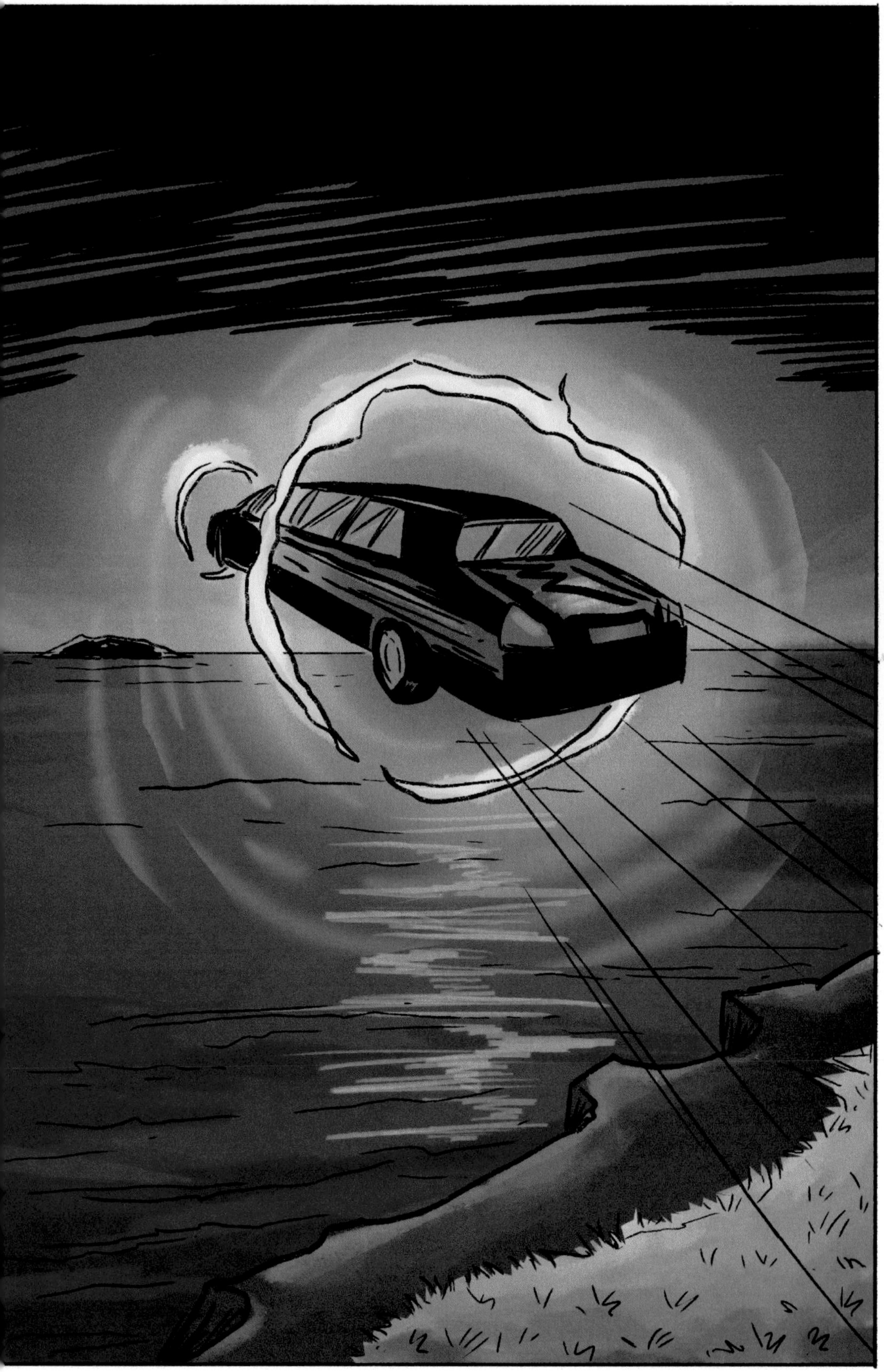

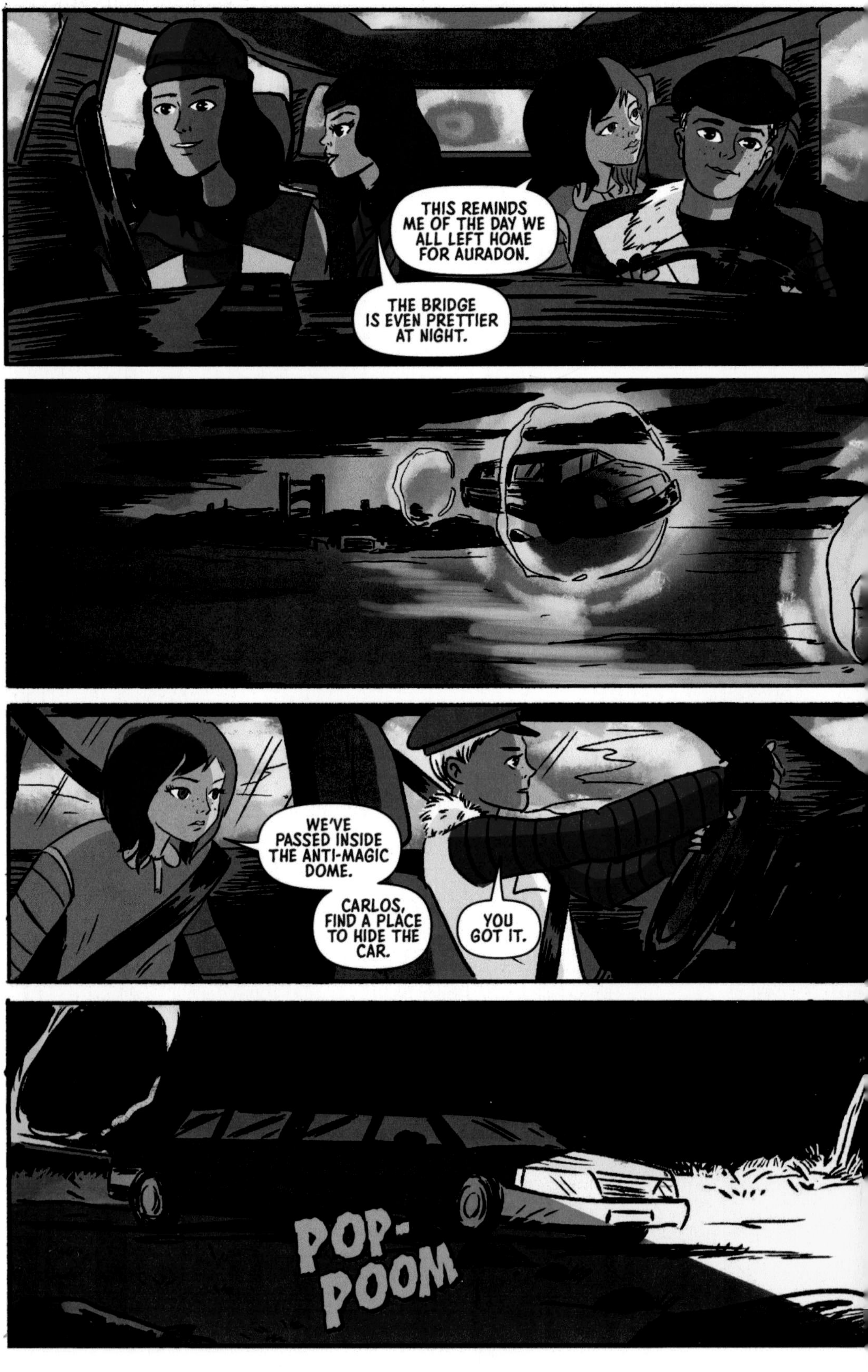
THIS REMINDS ME OF THE DAY WE ALL LEFT HOME FOR AURADON.
THE BRIDGE IS EVEN PRETTIER AT NIGHT.
WE'VE PASSED INSIDE THE ANTI-MAGIC DOME.
CARLOS, FIND A PLACE TO HIDE THE CAR.
YOU GOT IT.
POP-POOM

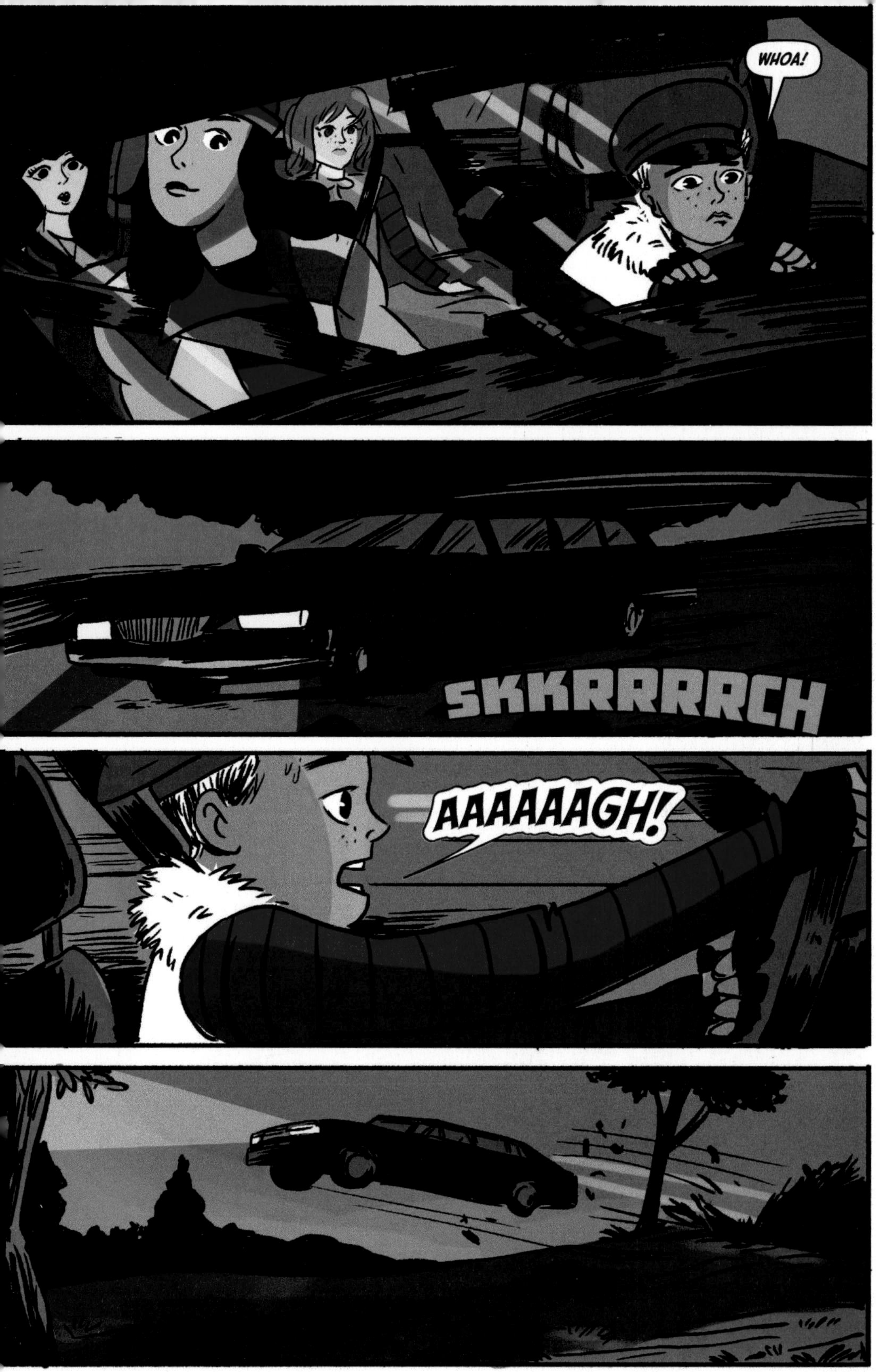
WHOA!
SKKRRRRRCH
AAAAAAGH!

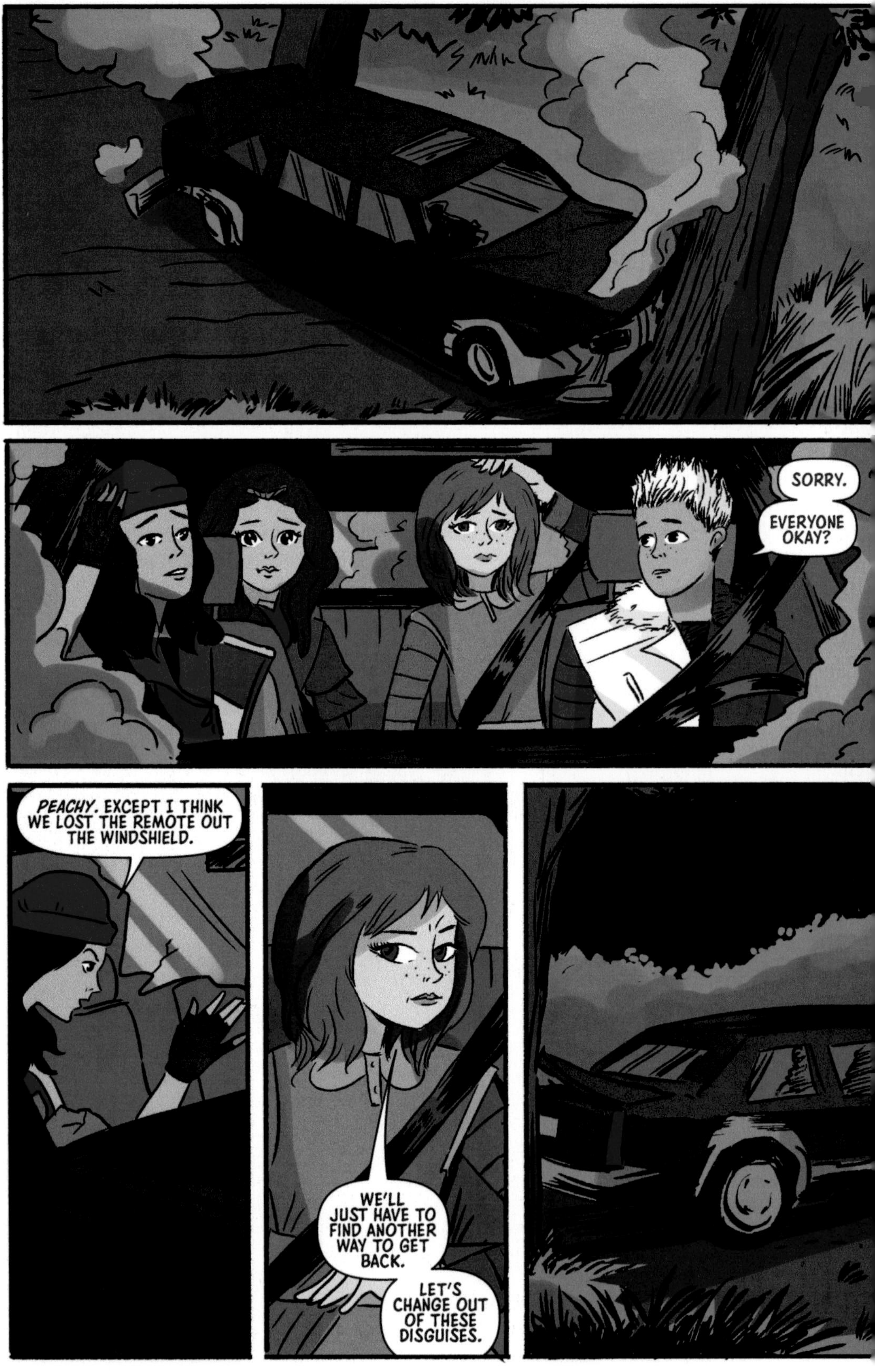
SORRY.
EVERYONE OKAY?
PEACHY. EXCEPT I THINK WE LOST THE REMOTE OUT THE WINDSHIELD.
WE'LL JUST HAVE TO FIND ANOTHER WAY TO GET BACK.
LET'S CHANGE OUT OF THESE DISGUISES.

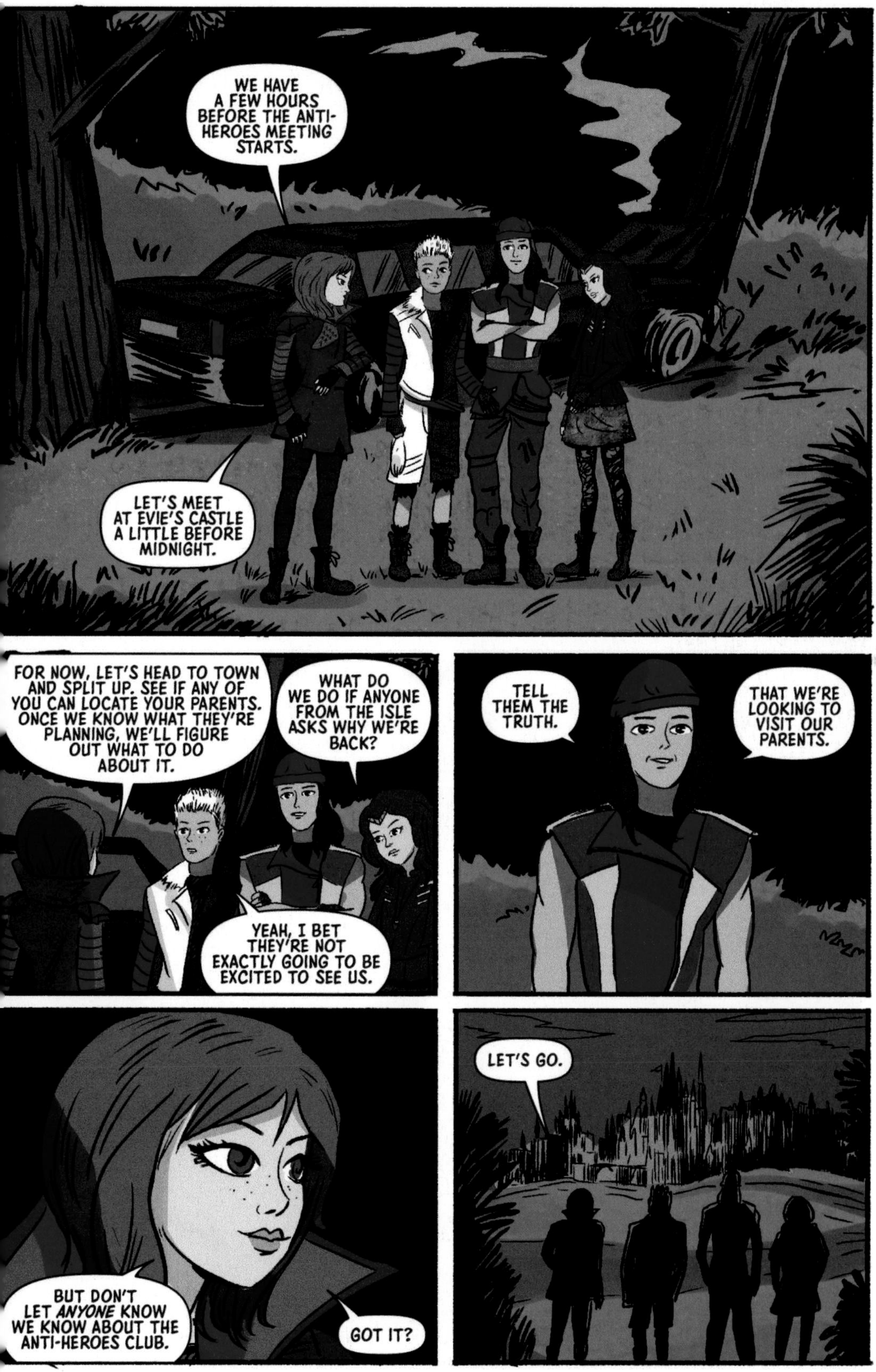
WE HAVE A FEW HOURS BEFORE THE ANTI-HEROES MEETING STARTS.
LET'S MEET AT EVIE'S CASTLE A LITTLE BEFORE MIDNIGHT.
FOR NOW, LET'S HEAD TO TOWN AND SPLIT UP. SEE IF ANY OF YOU CAN LOCATE YOUR PARENTS. ONCE WE KNOW WHAT THEY'RE PLANNING, WE'LL FIGURE OUT WHAT TO DO ABOUT IT.
WHAT DO WE DO IF ANYONE FROM THE ISLE ASKS WHY WE'RE BACK?
YEAH, I BET THEY'RE NOT EXACTLY GOING TO BE EXCITED TO SEE US.
TELL THEM THE TRUTH.
THAT WE'RE LOOKING TO VISIT OUR PARENTS.
BUT DON'T LET *ANYONE* KNOW WE KNOW ABOUT THE ANTI-HEROES CLUB.
GOT IT?
LET'S GO.

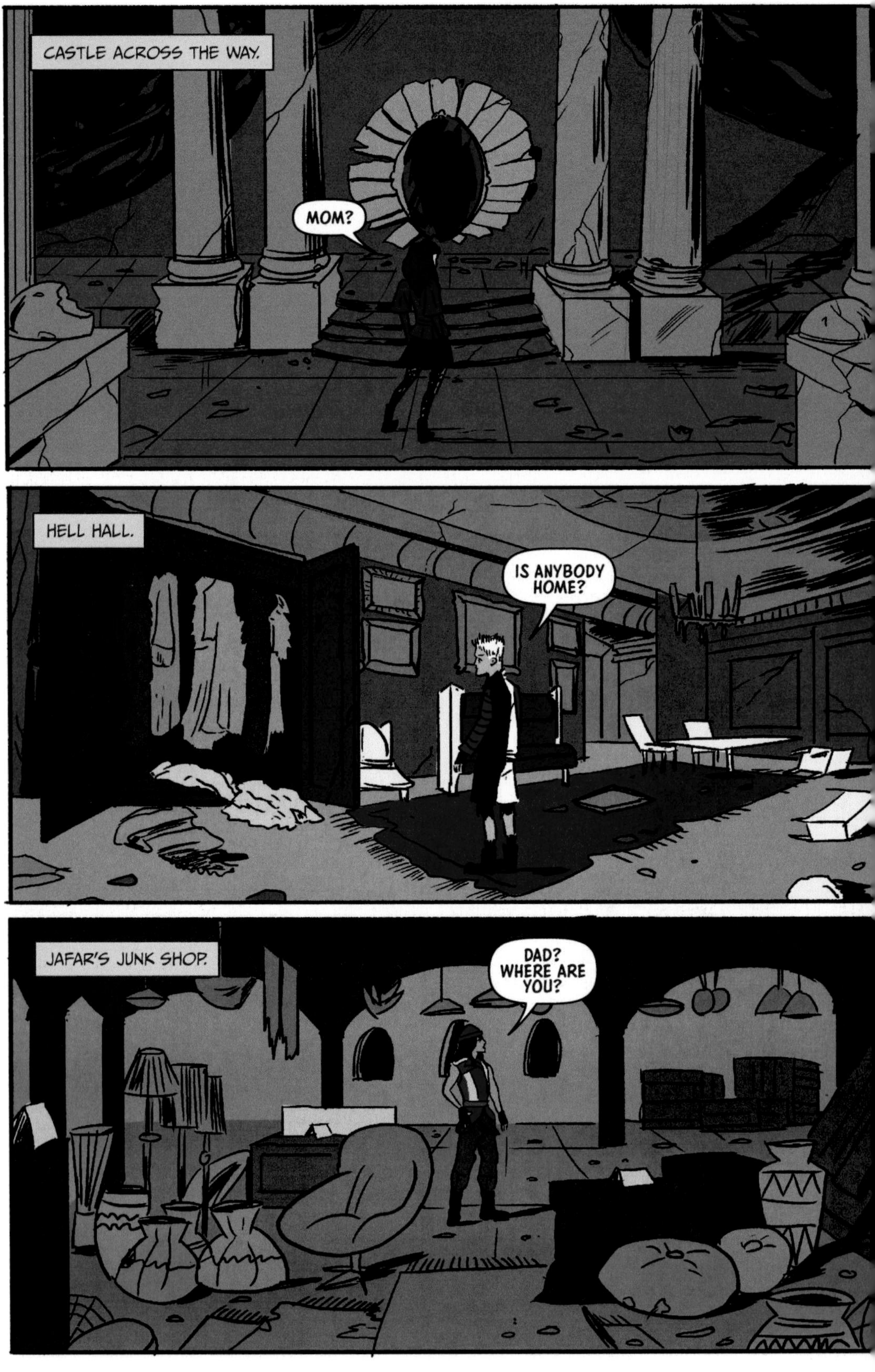

CASTLE ACROSS THE WAY.
MOM?
HELL HALL.
IS ANYBODY HOME?
JAFAR'S JUNK SHOP.
DAD? WHERE ARE YOU?

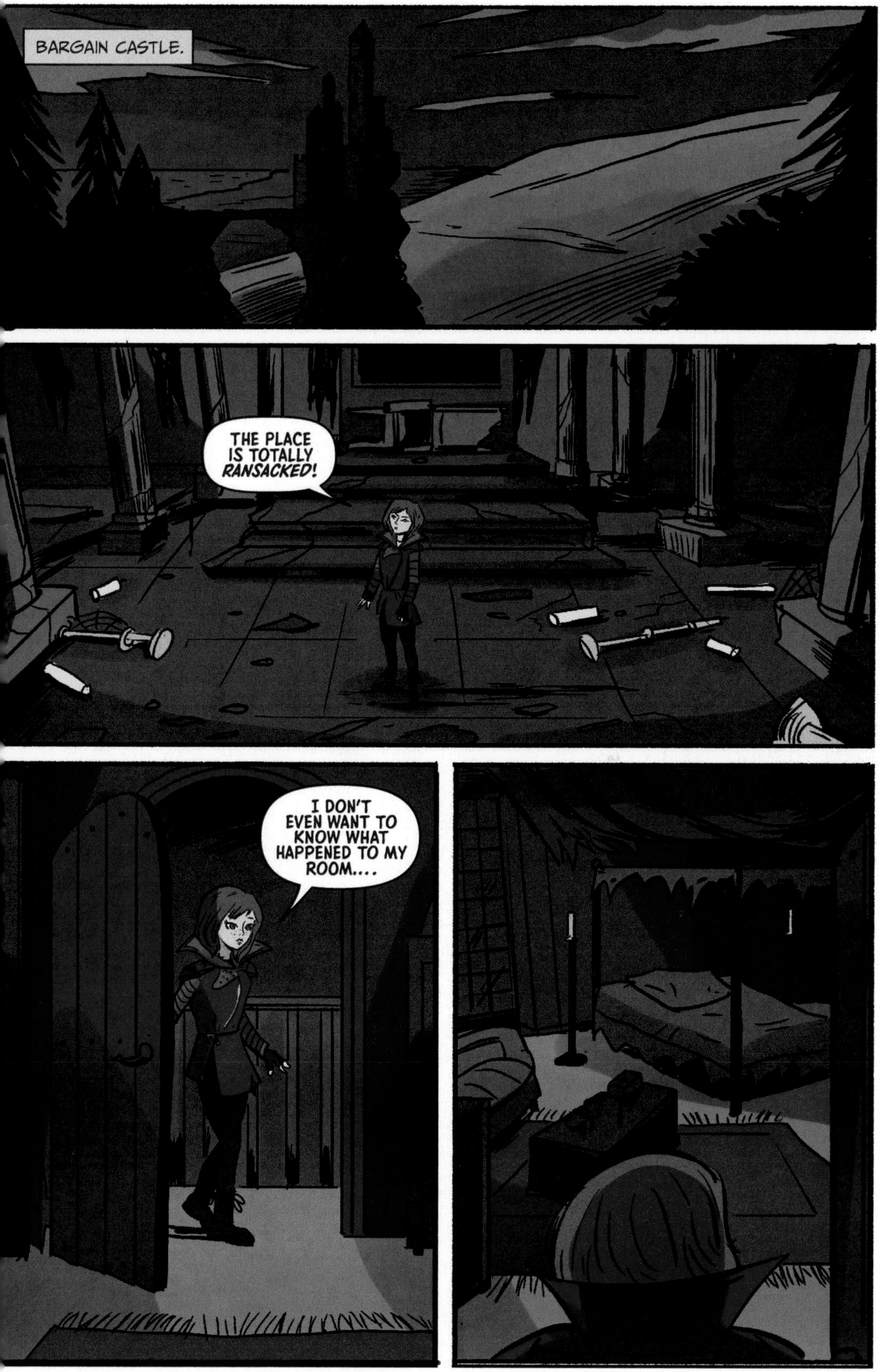
BARGAIN CASTLE.
THE PLACE IS TOTALLY *RANSACKED!*
I DON'T EVEN WANT TO KNOW WHAT HAPPENED TO MY ROOM....

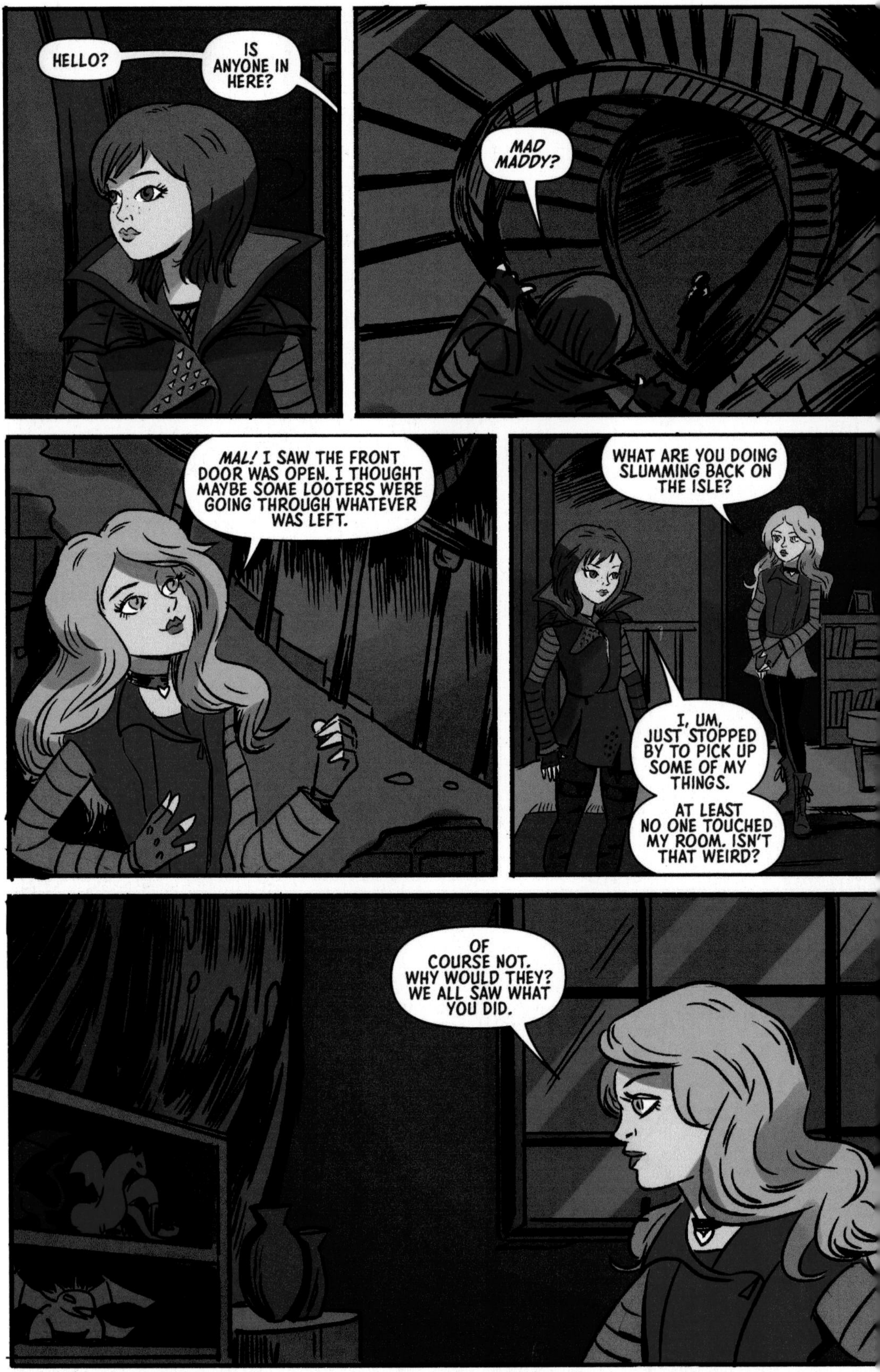
HELLO?
IS ANYONE IN HERE?
MAD MADDY?
MAL! I SAW THE FRONT DOOR WAS OPEN. I THOUGHT MAYBE SOME LOOTERS WERE GOING THROUGH WHATEVER WAS LEFT.
WHAT ARE YOU DOING SLUMMING BACK ON THE ISLE?
I, UM, JUST STOPPED BY TO PICK UP SOME OF MY THINGS.
AT LEAST NO ONE TOUCHED MY ROOM. ISN'T THAT WEIRD?
OF COURSE NOT. WHY WOULD THEY? WE ALL SAW WHAT YOU DID.

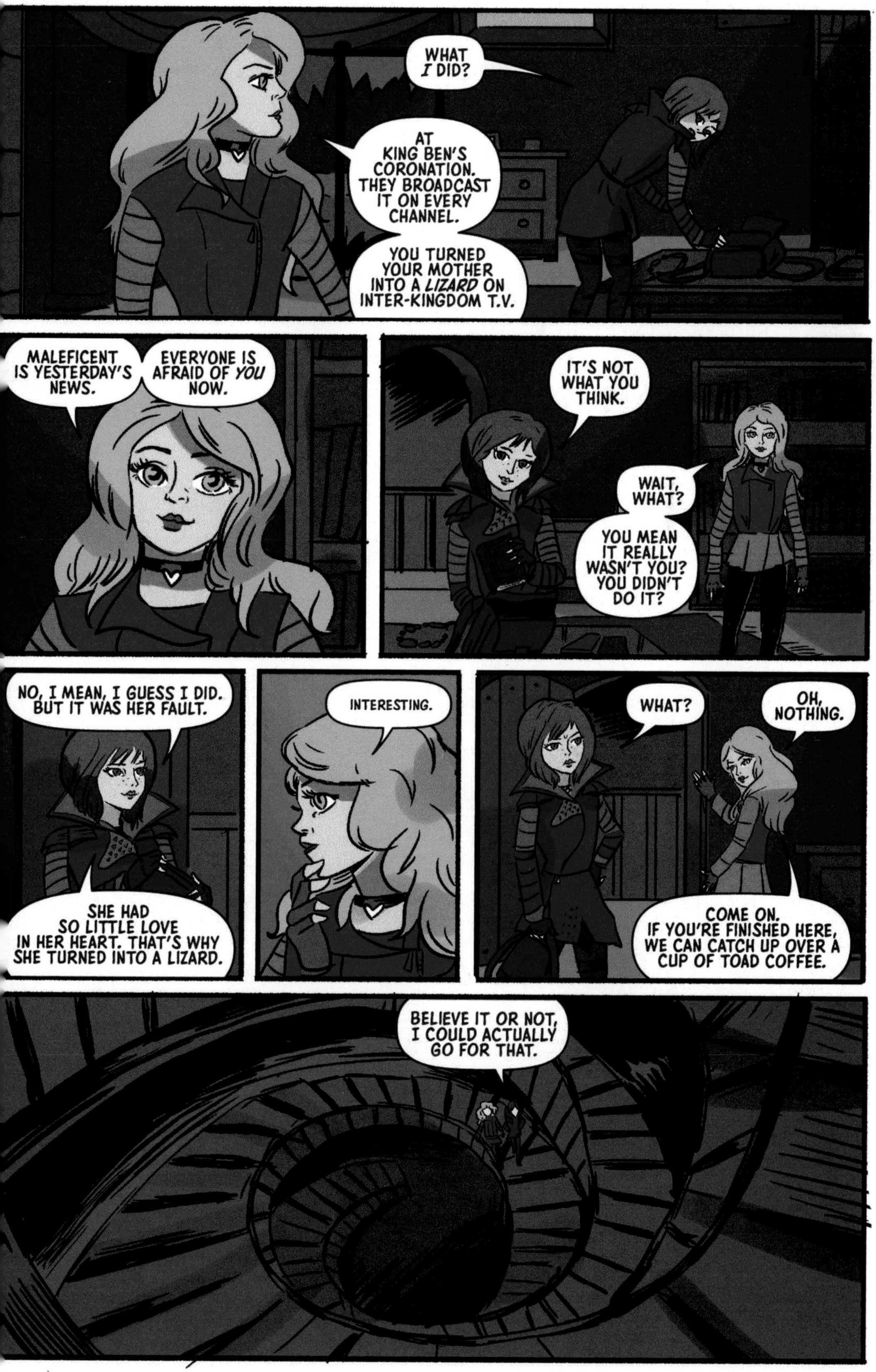
WHAT *I* DID?
AT KING BEN'S CORONATION. THEY BROADCAST IT ON EVERY CHANNEL.
YOU TURNED YOUR MOTHER INTO A *LIZARD* ON INTER-KINGDOM T.V.
MALEFICENT IS YESTERDAY'S NEWS.
EVERYONE IS AFRAID OF *YOU* NOW.
IT'S NOT WHAT YOU THINK.
WAIT, WHAT?
YOU MEAN IT REALLY WASN'T YOU? YOU DIDN'T DO IT?
NO, I MEAN, I GUESS I DID. BUT IT WAS HER FAULT.
SHE HAD SO LITTLE LOVE IN HER HEART. THAT'S WHY SHE TURNED INTO A LIZARD.
INTERESTING.
WHAT?
OH, NOTHING.
COME ON. IF YOU'RE FINISHED HERE, WE CAN CATCH UP OVER A CUP OF TOAD COFFEE.
BELIEVE IT OR NOT, I COULD ACTUALLY GO FOR THAT.

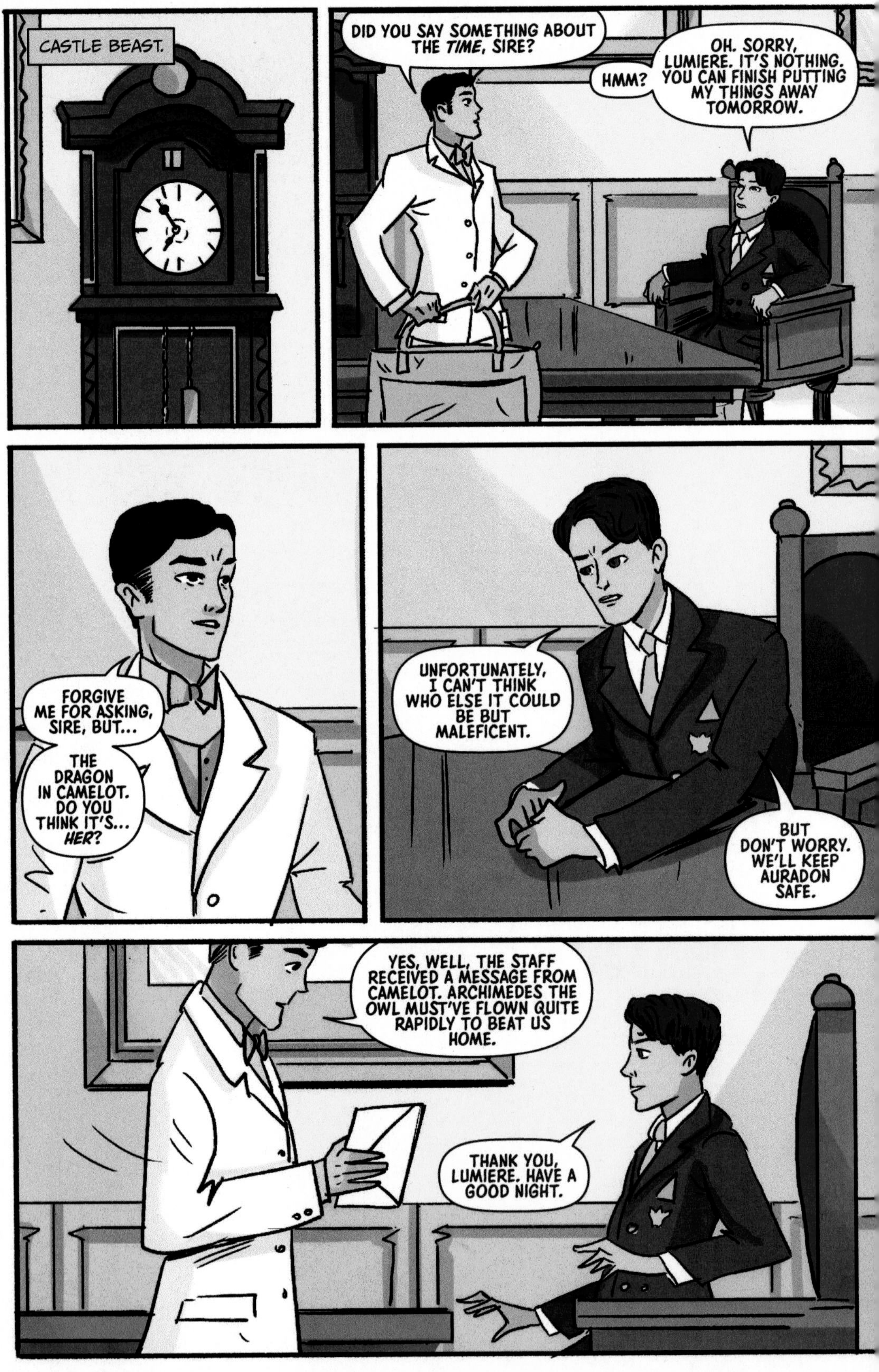
CASTLE BEAST.
DID YOU SAY SOMETHING ABOUT THE *TIME*, SIRE?
HMM?
OH. SORRY, LUMIERE. IT'S NOTHING. YOU CAN FINISH PUTTING MY THINGS AWAY TOMORROW.
FORGIVE ME FOR ASKING, SIRE, BUT...
THE DRAGON IN CAMELOT. DO YOU THINK IT'S... *HER*?
UNFORTUNATELY, I CAN'T THINK WHO ELSE IT COULD BE BUT MALEFICENT.
BUT DON'T WORRY. WE'LL KEEP AURADON SAFE.
YES, WELL, THE STAFF RECEIVED A MESSAGE FROM CAMELOT. ARCHIMEDES THE OWL MUST'VE FLOWN QUITE RAPIDLY TO BEAT US HOME.
THANK YOU, LUMIERE. HAVE A GOOD NIGHT.

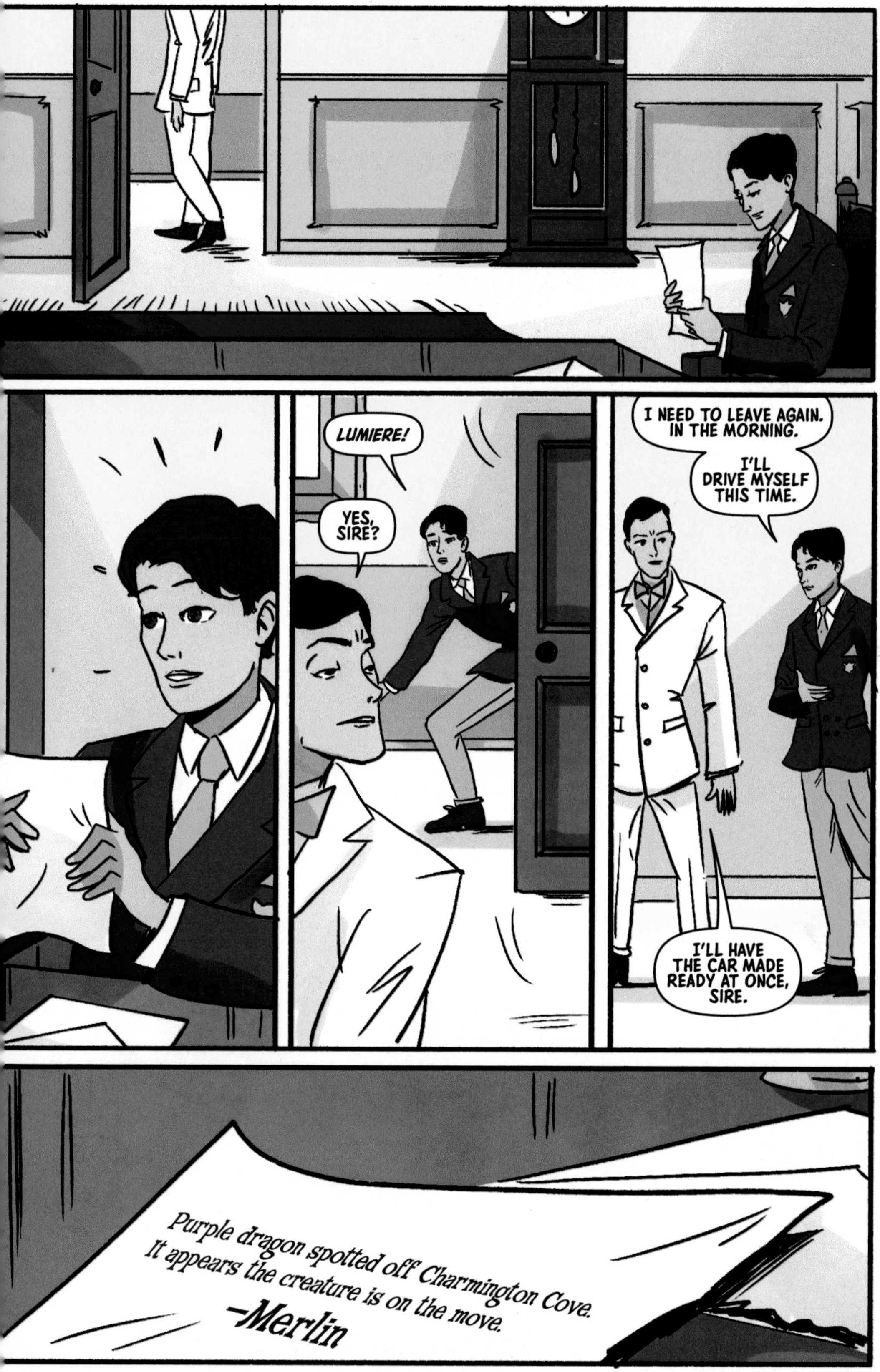
LUMIERE!
YES, SIRE?
I NEED TO LEAVE AGAIN. IN THE MORNING.
I'LL DRIVE MYSELF THIS TIME.
I'LL HAVE THE CAR MADE READY AT ONCE, SIRE.
Purple dragon spotted off Charmington Cove.
It appears the creature is on the move.
–Merlin

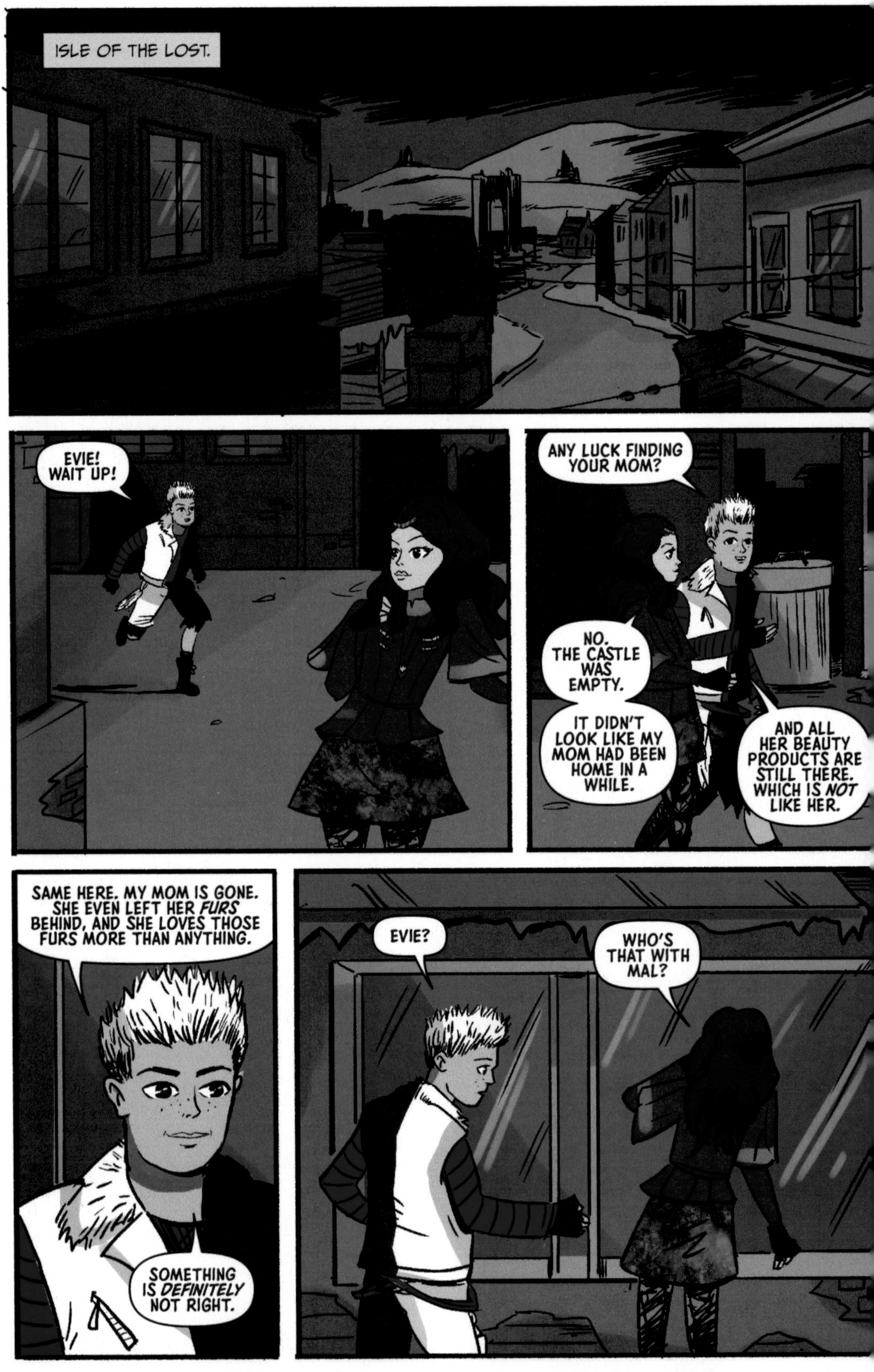
ISLE OF THE LOST.
EVIE! WAIT UP!
ANY LUCK FINDING YOUR MOM?
NO. THE CASTLE WAS EMPTY.
IT DIDN'T LOOK LIKE MY MOM HAD BEEN HOME IN A WHILE.
AND ALL HER BEAUTY PRODUCTS ARE STILL THERE. WHICH IS *NOT* LIKE HER.
SAME HERE. MY MOM IS GONE. SHE EVEN LEFT HER *FURS* BEHIND, AND SHE LOVES THOSE FURS MORE THAN ANYTHING.
SOMETHING IS *DEFINITELY* NOT RIGHT.
EVIE?
WHO'S THAT WITH MAL?

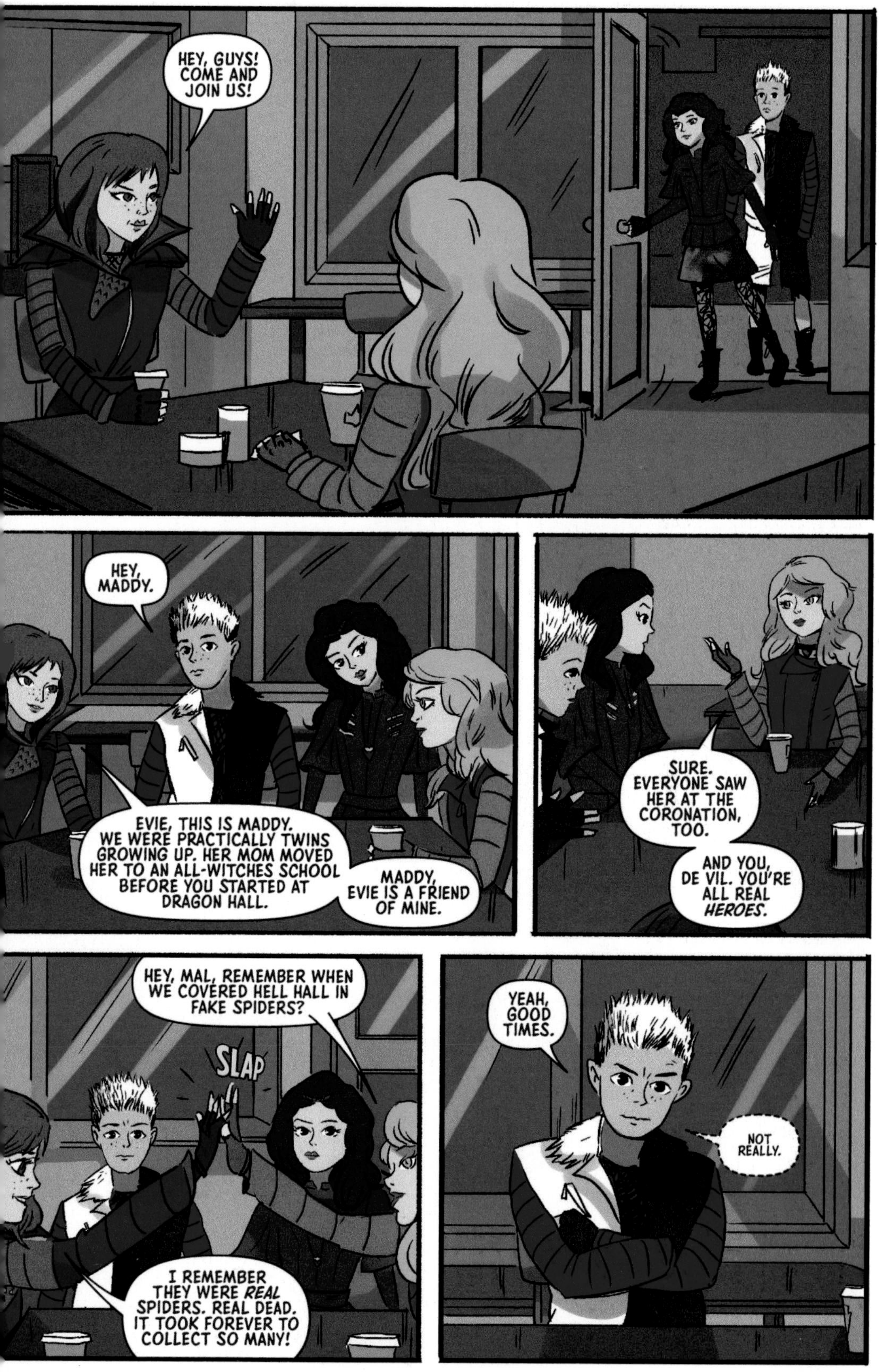
HEY, GUYS! COME AND JOIN US!
HEY, MADDY.
EVIE, THIS IS MADDY. WE WERE PRACTICALLY TWINS GROWING UP. HER MOM MOVED HER TO AN ALL-WITCHES SCHOOL BEFORE YOU STARTED AT DRAGON HALL.
MADDY, EVIE IS A FRIEND OF MINE.
SURE. EVERYONE SAW HER AT THE CORONATION, TOO.
AND YOU, DE VIL. YOU'RE ALL REAL *HEROES*.
HEY, MAL, REMEMBER WHEN WE COVERED HELL HALL IN FAKE SPIDERS?
SLAP
I REMEMBER THEY WERE *REAL* SPIDERS. REAL DEAD. IT TOOK FOREVER TO COLLECT SO MANY!
YEAH, GOOD TIMES.
NOT REALLY.

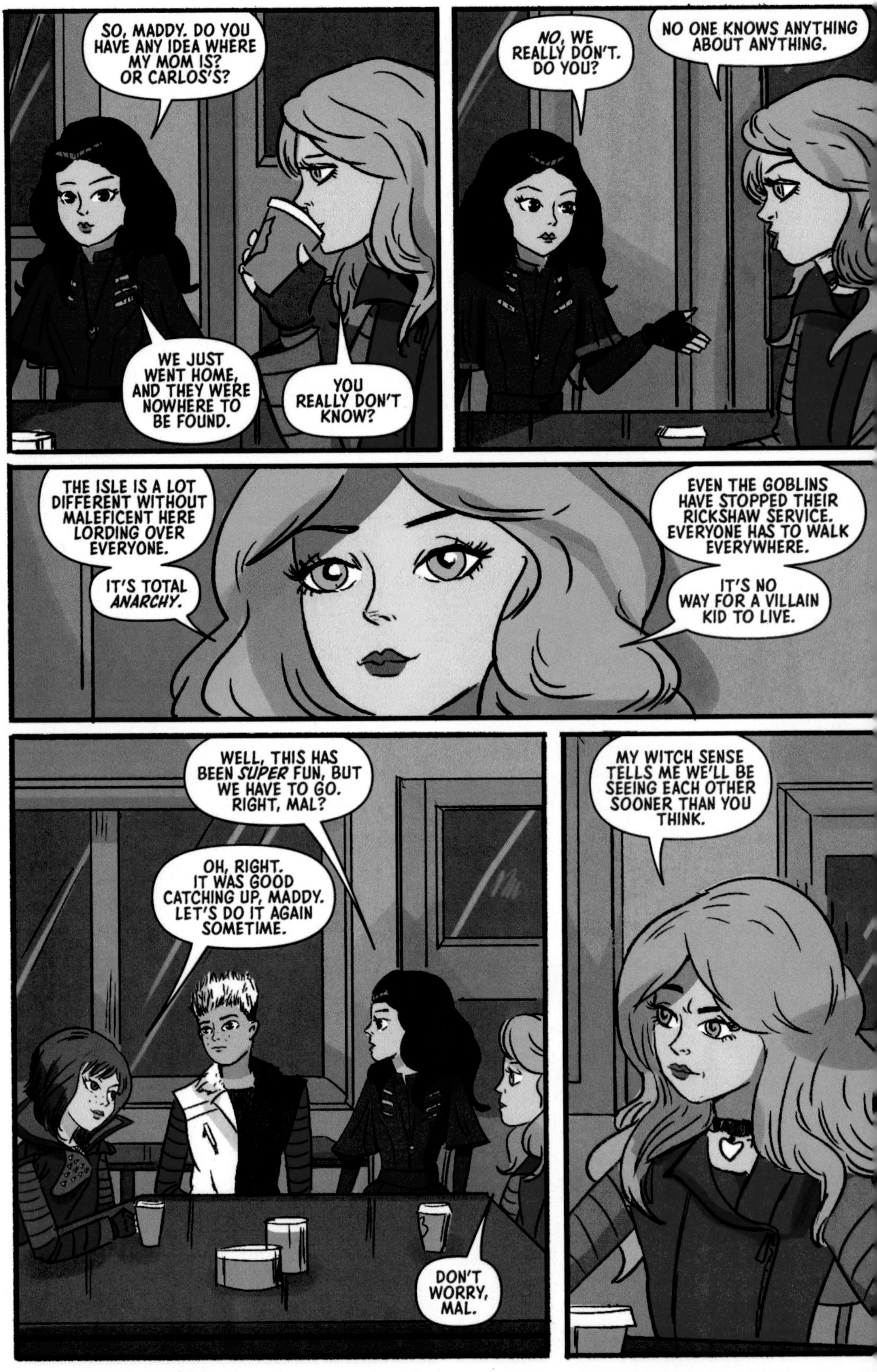
SO, MADDY. DO YOU HAVE ANY IDEA WHERE MY MOM IS? OR CARLOS'S?
WE JUST WENT HOME, AND THEY WERE NOWHERE TO BE FOUND.
YOU REALLY DON'T KNOW?
NO, WE REALLY DON'T. DO YOU?
NO ONE KNOWS ANYTHING ABOUT ANYTHING.
THE ISLE IS A LOT DIFFERENT WITHOUT MALEFICENT HERE LORDING OVER EVERYONE.
IT'S TOTAL *ANARCHY*.
EVEN THE GOBLINS HAVE STOPPED THEIR RICKSHAW SERVICE. EVERYONE HAS TO WALK EVERYWHERE.
IT'S NO WAY FOR A VILLAIN KID TO LIVE.
WELL, THIS HAS BEEN *SUPER* FUN, BUT WE HAVE TO GO. RIGHT, MAL?
OH, RIGHT. IT WAS GOOD CATCHING UP, MADDY. LET'S DO IT AGAIN SOMETIME.
DON'T WORRY, MAL.
MY WITCH SENSE TELLS ME WE'LL BE SEEING EACH OTHER SOONER THAN YOU THINK.

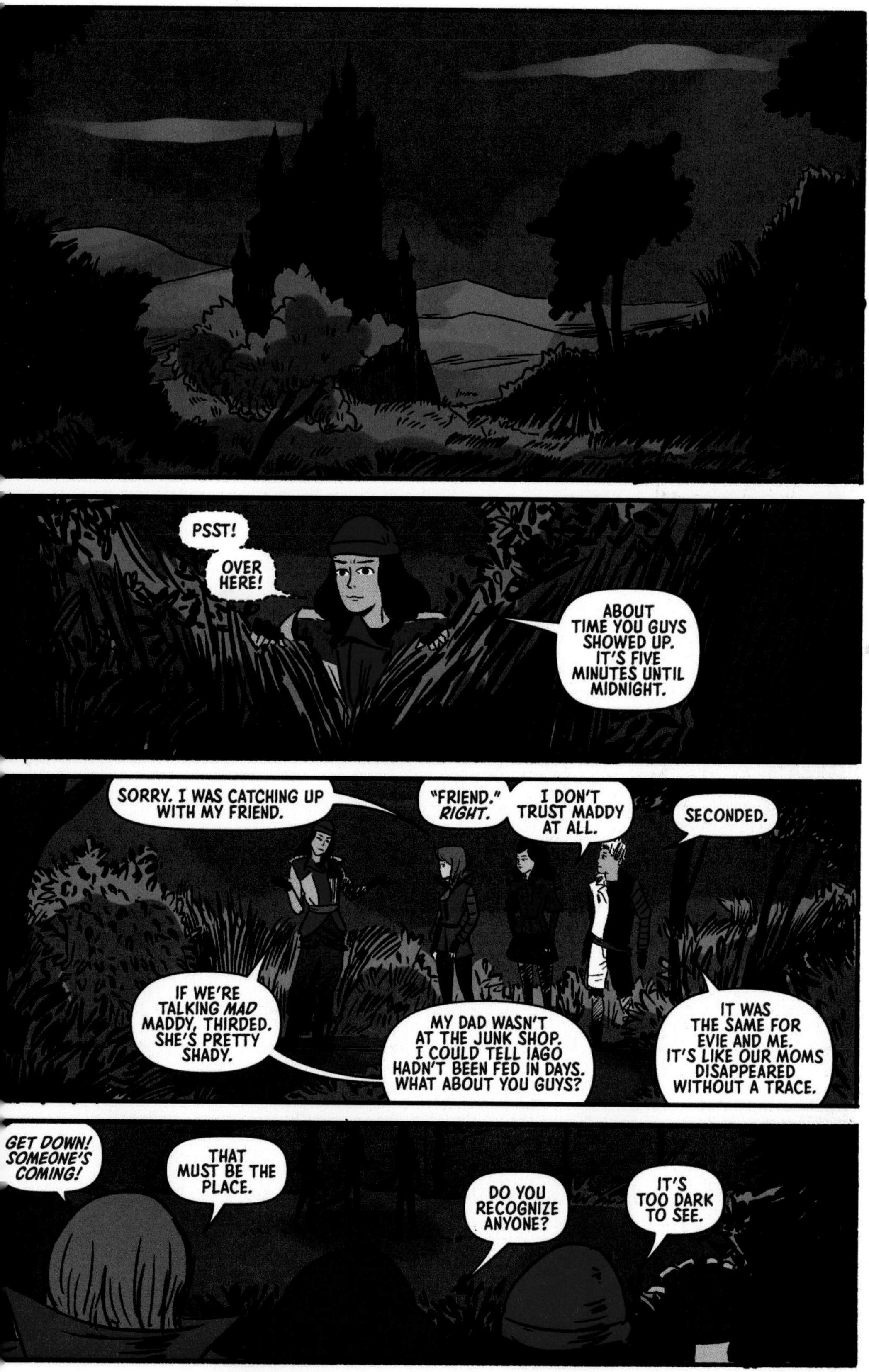
PSST!
OVER HERE!
ABOUT TIME YOU GUYS SHOWED UP. IT'S FIVE MINUTES UNTIL MIDNIGHT.
SORRY. I WAS CATCHING UP WITH MY FRIEND.
"FRIEND." *RIGHT.*
I DON'T TRUST MADDY AT ALL.
SECONDED.
IF WE'RE TALKING *MAD* MADDY, THIRDED. SHE'S PRETTY SHADY.
MY DAD WASN'T AT THE JUNK SHOP. I COULD TELL IAGO HADN'T BEEN FED IN DAYS. WHAT ABOUT YOU GUYS?
IT WAS THE SAME FOR EVIE AND ME. IT'S LIKE OUR MOMS DISAPPEARED WITHOUT A TRACE.
GET DOWN! SOMEONE'S COMING!
THAT MUST BE THE PLACE.
DO YOU RECOGNIZE ANYONE?
IT'S TOO DARK TO SEE.

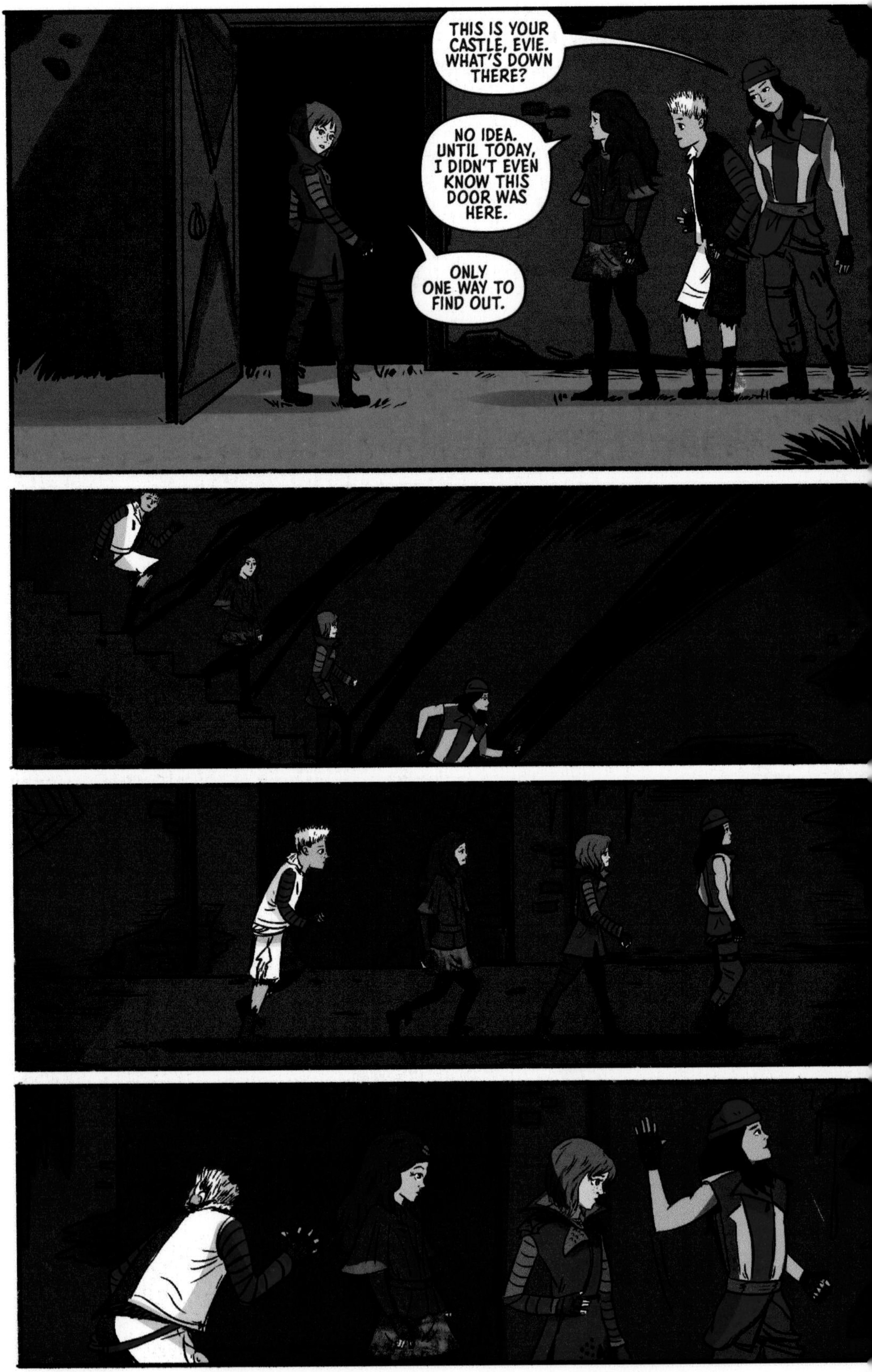
THIS IS YOUR CASTLE, EVIE. WHAT'S DOWN THERE?
NO IDEA. UNTIL TODAY, I DIDN'T EVEN KNOW THIS DOOR WAS HERE.
ONLY ONE WAY TO FIND OUT.

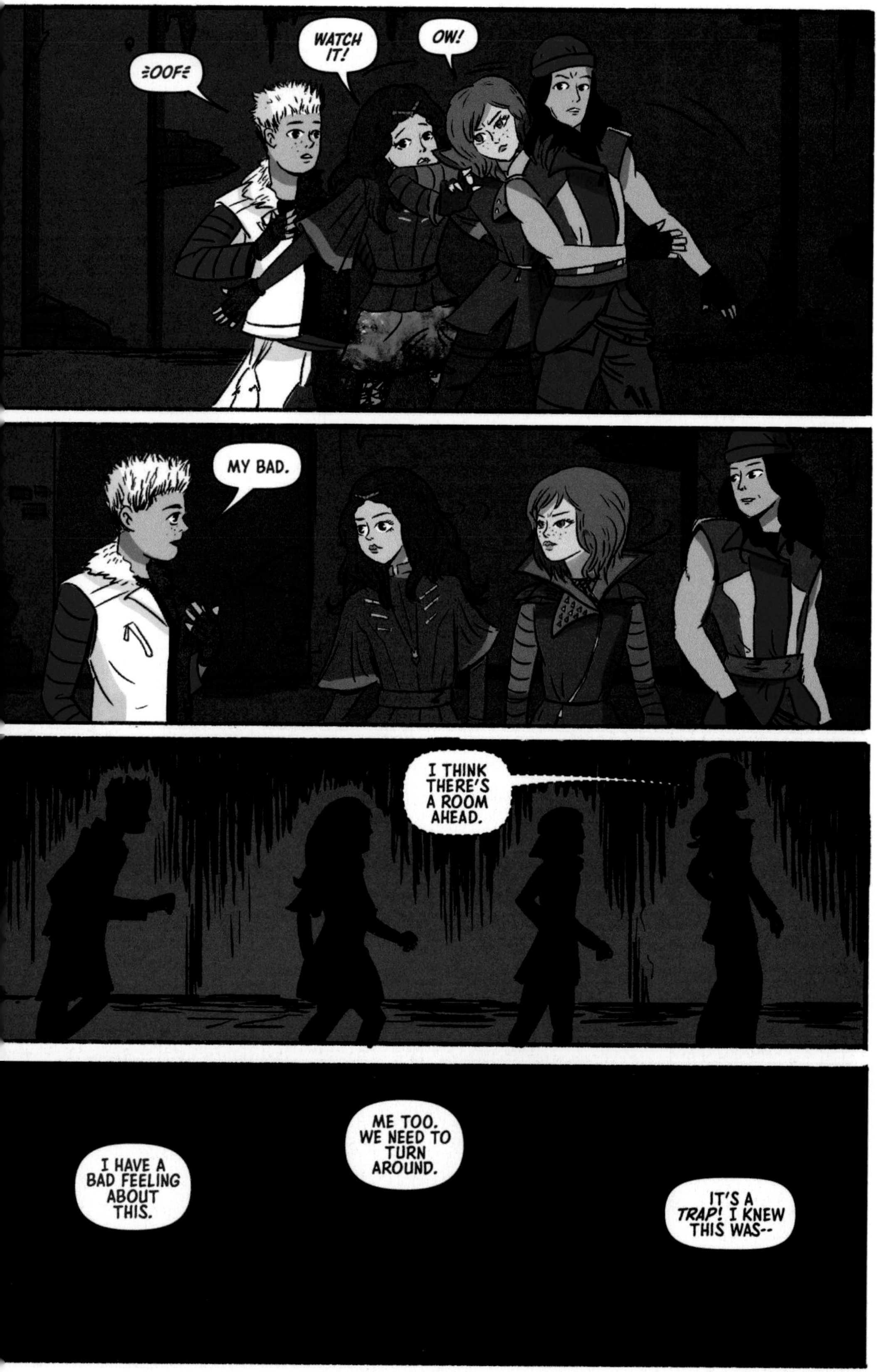
OOF
WATCH IT!
OW!
MY BAD.
I THINK THERE'S A ROOM AHEAD.
I HAVE A BAD FEELING ABOUT THIS.
ME TOO. WE NEED TO TURN AROUND.
IT'S A *TRAP!* I KNEW THIS WAS--

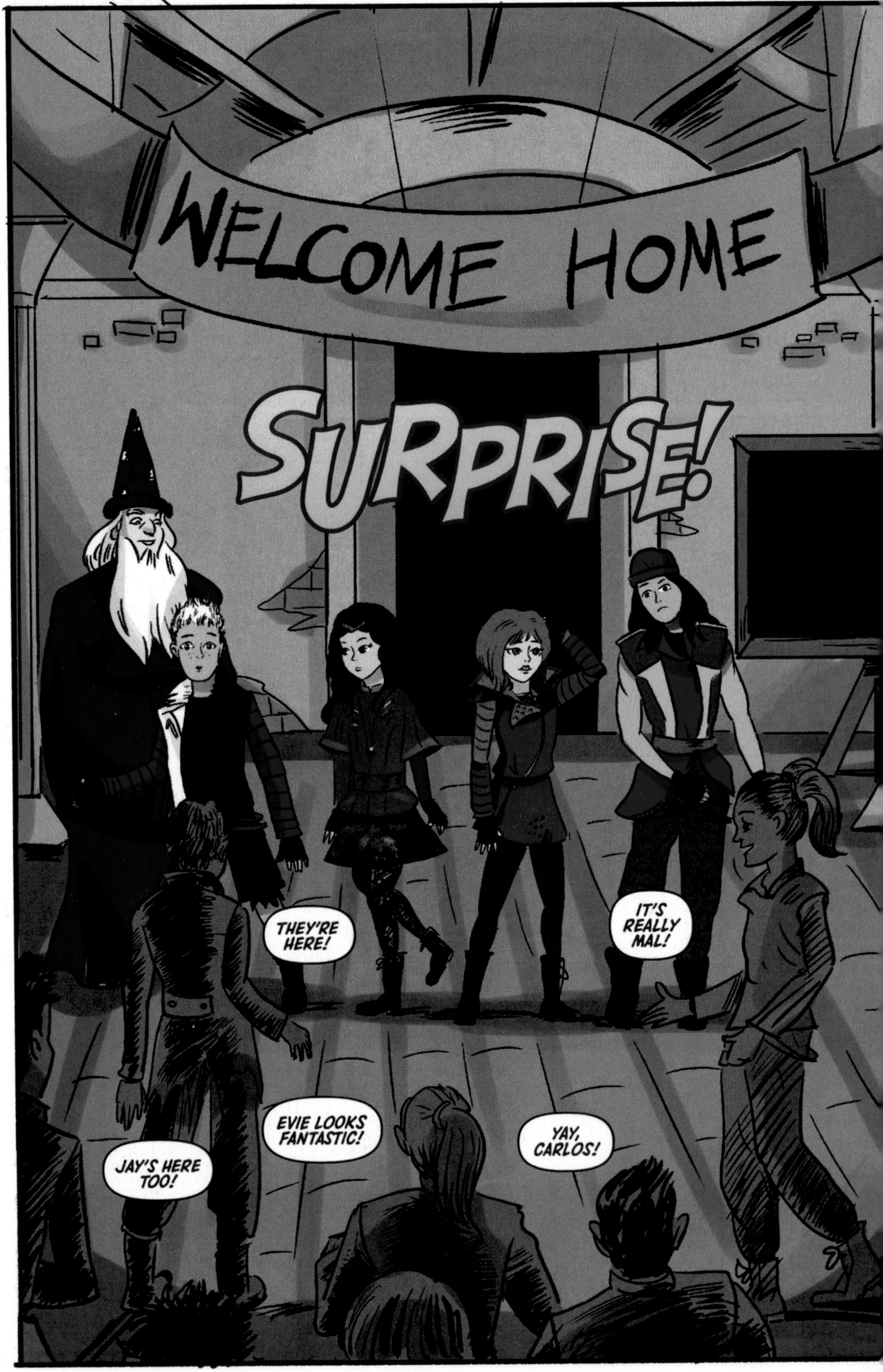
WELCOME HOME
SURPRISE!
THEY'RE HERE!
IT'S REALLY MAL!
EVIE LOOKS FANTASTIC!
YAY, CARLOS!
JAY'S HERE TOO!

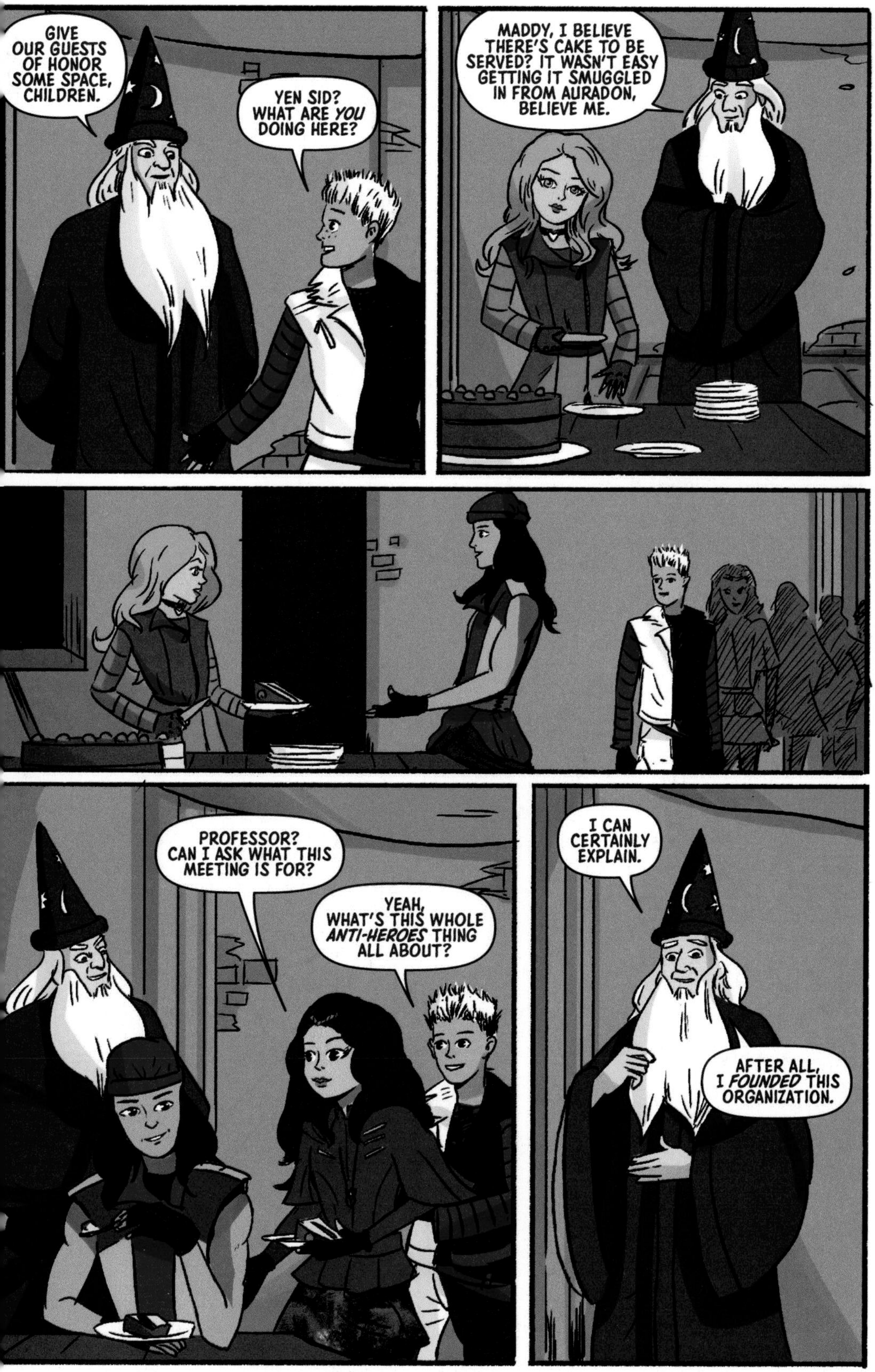
GIVE OUR GUESTS OF HONOR SOME SPACE, CHILDREN.
YEN SID? WHAT ARE *YOU* DOING HERE?
MADDY, I BELIEVE THERE'S CAKE TO BE SERVED? IT WASN'T EASY GETTING IT SMUGGLED IN FROM AURADON, BELIEVE ME.
PROFESSOR? CAN I ASK WHAT THIS MEETING IS FOR?
YEAH, WHAT'S THIS WHOLE *ANTI-HEROES* THING ALL ABOUT?
I CAN CERTAINLY EXPLAIN.
AFTER ALL, I *FOUNDED* THIS ORGANIZATION.

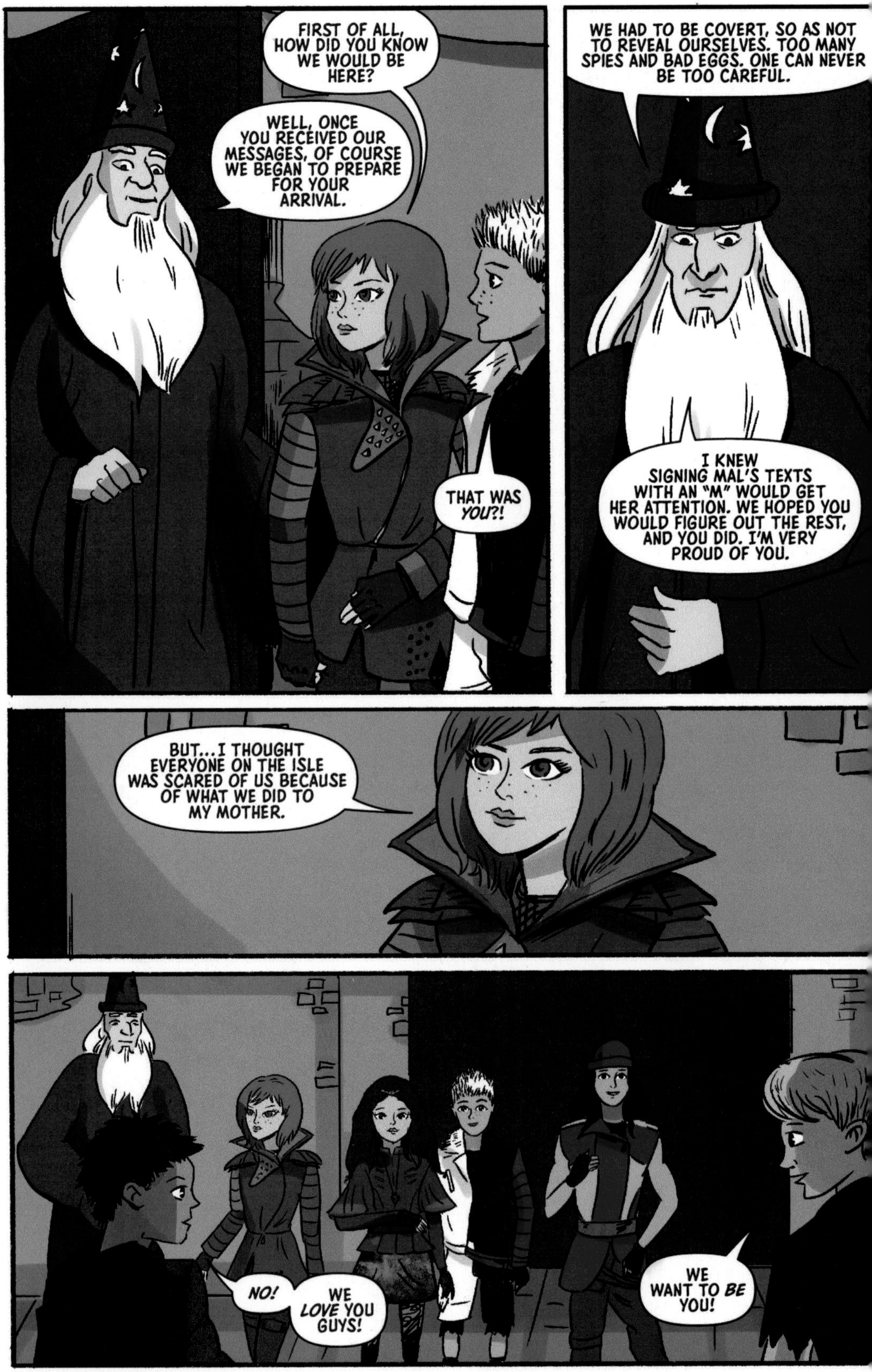
FIRST OF ALL, HOW DID YOU KNOW WE WOULD BE HERE?
WELL, ONCE YOU RECEIVED OUR MESSAGES, OF COURSE WE BEGAN TO PREPARE FOR YOUR ARRIVAL.
THAT WAS *YOU*?!
WE HAD TO BE COVERT, SO AS NOT TO REVEAL OURSELVES. TOO MANY SPIES AND BAD EGGS. ONE CAN NEVER BE TOO CAREFUL.
I KNEW SIGNING MAL'S TEXTS WITH AN "M" WOULD GET HER ATTENTION. WE HOPED YOU WOULD FIGURE OUT THE REST, AND YOU DID. I'M VERY PROUD OF YOU.
BUT...I THOUGHT EVERYONE ON THE ISLE WAS *SCARED* OF US BECAUSE OF WHAT WE DID TO MY MOTHER.
NO!
WE *LOVE* YOU GUYS!
WE WANT TO *BE* YOU!

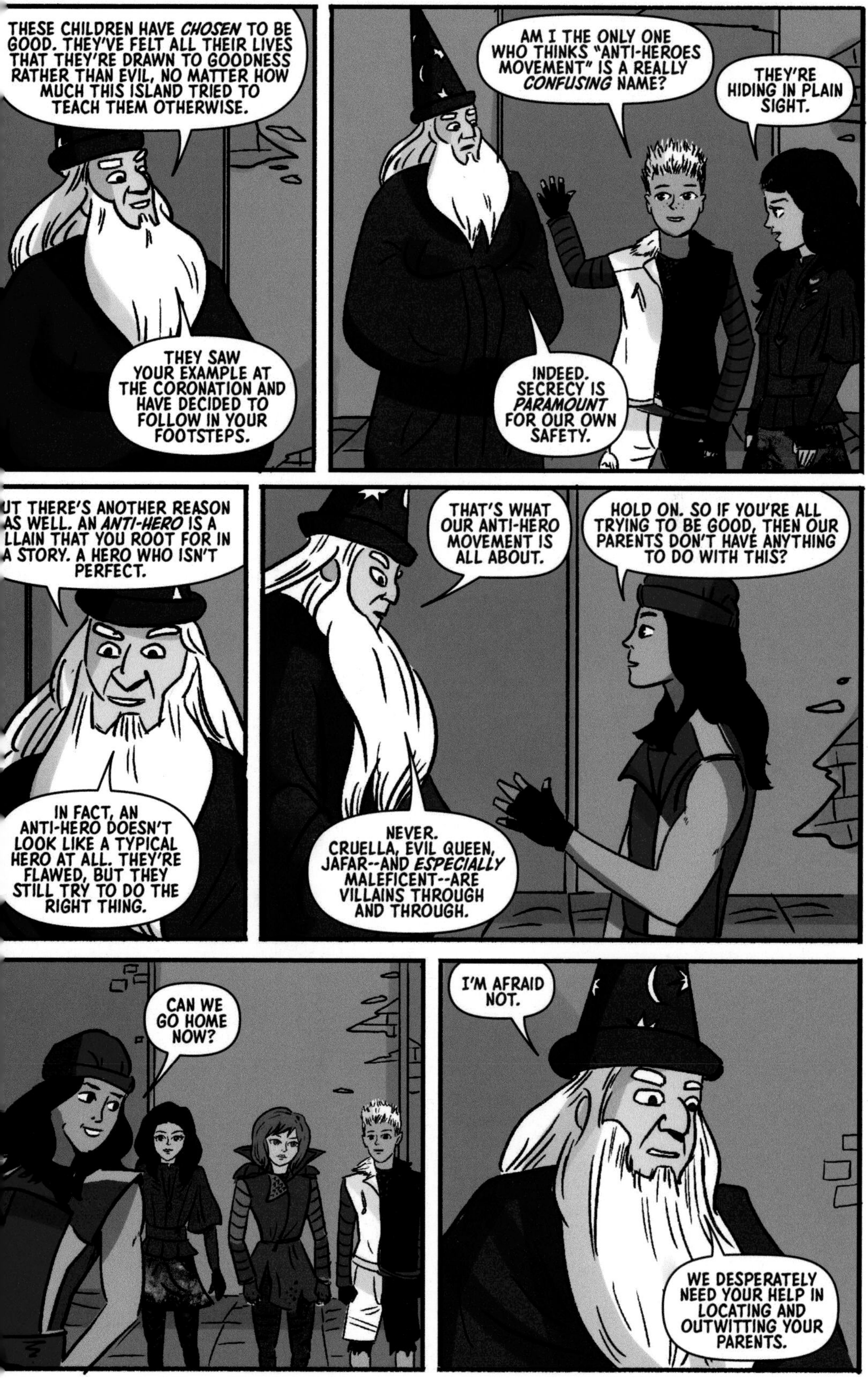
THESE CHILDREN HAVE *CHOSEN* TO BE GOOD. THEY'VE FELT ALL THEIR LIVES THAT THEY'RE DRAWN TO GOODNESS RATHER THAN EVIL, NO MATTER HOW MUCH THIS ISLAND TRIED TO TEACH THEM OTHERWISE.
THEY SAW YOUR EXAMPLE AT THE CORONATION AND HAVE DECIDED TO FOLLOW IN YOUR FOOTSTEPS.
AM I THE ONLY ONE WHO THINKS "ANTI-HEROES MOVEMENT" IS A REALLY *CONFUSING* NAME?
THEY'RE HIDING IN PLAIN SIGHT.
INDEED. SECRECY IS *PARAMOUNT* FOR OUR OWN SAFETY.
UT THERE'S ANOTHER REASON AS WELL. AN *ANTI-HERO* IS A LLAIN THAT YOU ROOT FOR IN A STORY. A HERO WHO ISN'T PERFECT.
IN FACT, AN ANTI-HERO DOESN'T LOOK LIKE A TYPICAL HERO AT ALL. THEY'RE FLAWED, BUT THEY STILL TRY TO DO THE RIGHT THING.
THAT'S WHAT OUR ANTI-HERO MOVEMENT IS ALL ABOUT.
HOLD ON. SO IF YOU'RE ALL TRYING TO BE GOOD, THEN OUR PARENTS DON'T HAVE ANYTHING TO DO WITH THIS?
NEVER. CRUELLA, EVIL QUEEN, JAFAR--AND *ESPECIALLY* MALEFICENT--ARE VILLAINS THROUGH AND THROUGH.
CAN WE GO HOME NOW?
I'M AFRAID NOT.
WE DESPERATELY NEED YOUR HELP IN LOCATING AND OUTWITTING YOUR PARENTS.

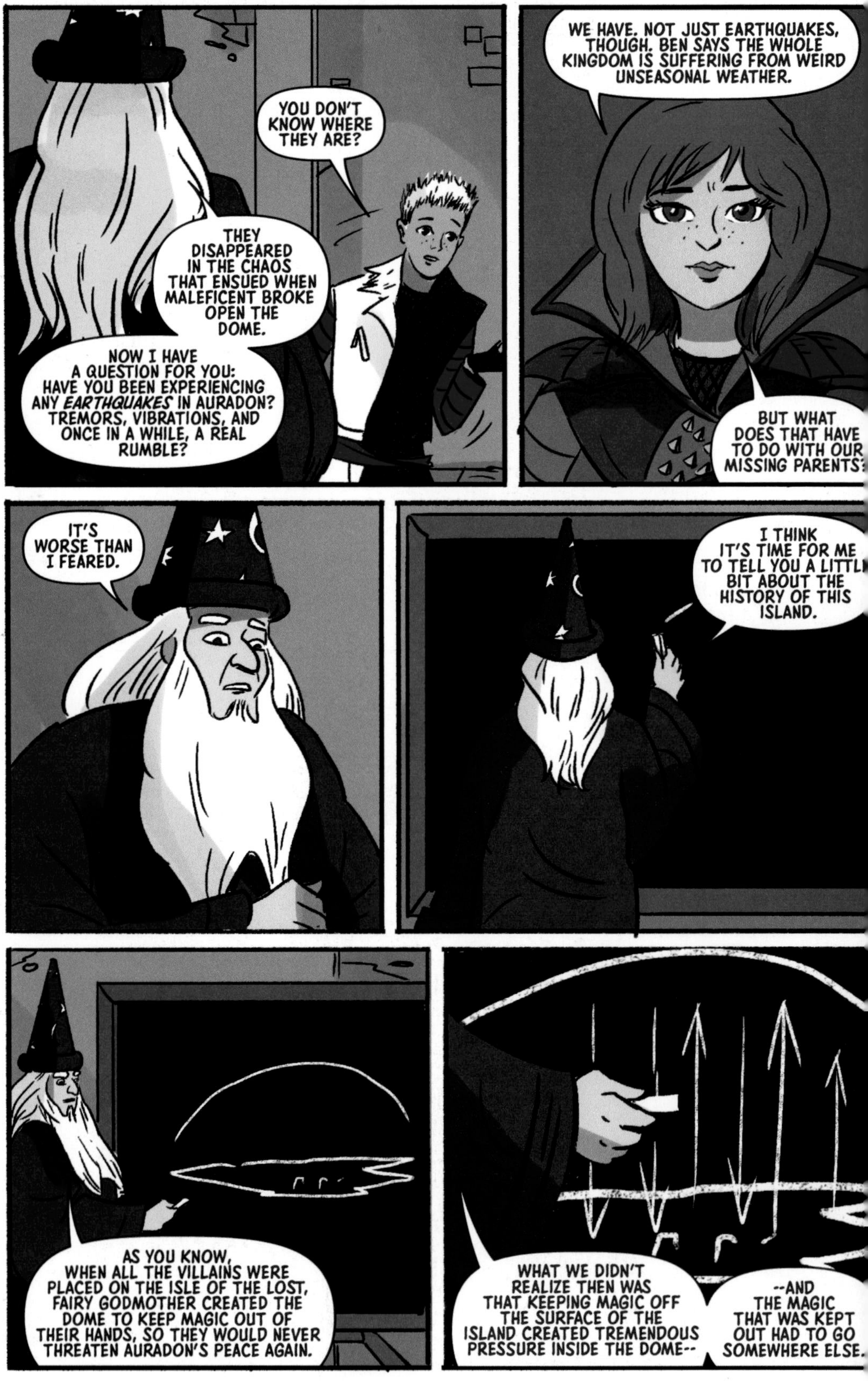
YOU DON'T KNOW WHERE THEY ARE?
THEY DISAPPEARED IN THE CHAOS THAT ENSUED WHEN MALEFICENT BROKE OPEN THE DOME.
NOW I HAVE A QUESTION FOR YOU: HAVE YOU BEEN EXPERIENCING ANY *EARTHQUAKES* IN AURADON? TREMORS, VIBRATIONS, AND ONCE IN A WHILE, A REAL RUMBLE?
WE HAVE. NOT JUST EARTHQUAKES, THOUGH. BEN SAYS THE WHOLE KINGDOM IS SUFFERING FROM WEIRD UNSEASONAL WEATHER.
BUT WHAT DOES THAT HAVE TO DO WITH OUR MISSING PARENTS?
IT'S WORSE THAN I FEARED.
I THINK IT'S TIME FOR ME TO TELL YOU A LITTL BIT ABOUT THE HISTORY OF THIS ISLAND.
AS YOU KNOW, WHEN ALL THE VILLAINS WERE PLACED ON THE ISLE OF THE LOST, FAIRY GODMOTHER CREATED THE DOME TO KEEP MAGIC OUT OF THEIR HANDS, SO THEY WOULD NEVER THREATEN AURADON'S PEACE AGAIN.
WHAT WE DIDN'T REALIZE THEN WAS THAT KEEPING MAGIC OFF THE SURFACE OF THE ISLAND CREATED TREMENDOUS PRESSURE INSIDE THE DOME--
--AND THE MAGIC THAT WAS KEPT OUT HAD TO GO SOMEWHERE ELSE.

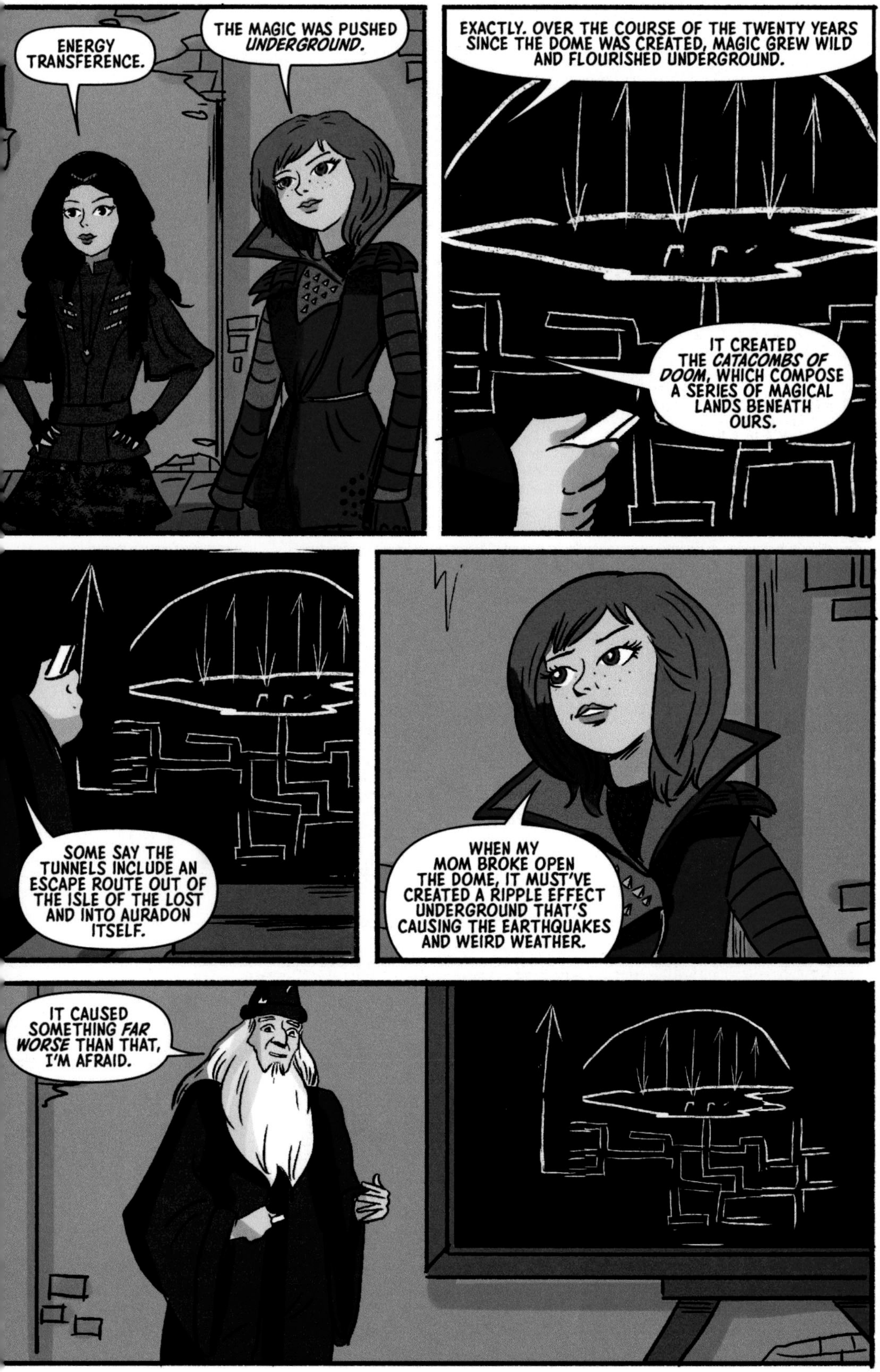
ENERGY TRANSFERENCE.
THE MAGIC WAS PUSHED *UNDERGROUND.*
EXACTLY. OVER THE COURSE OF THE TWENTY YEARS SINCE THE DOME WAS CREATED, MAGIC GREW WILD AND FLOURISHED UNDERGROUND.
IT CREATED THE *CATACOMBS OF DOOM*, WHICH COMPOSE A SERIES OF MAGICAL LANDS BENEATH OURS.
SOME SAY THE TUNNELS INCLUDE AN ESCAPE ROUTE OUT OF THE ISLE OF THE LOST AND INTO AURADON ITSELF.
WHEN MY MOM BROKE OPEN THE DOME, IT MUST'VE CREATED A RIPPLE EFFECT UNDERGROUND THAT'S CAUSING THE EARTHQUAKES AND WEIRD WEATHER.
IT CAUSED SOMETHING *FAR WORSE* THAN THAT, I'M AFRAID.

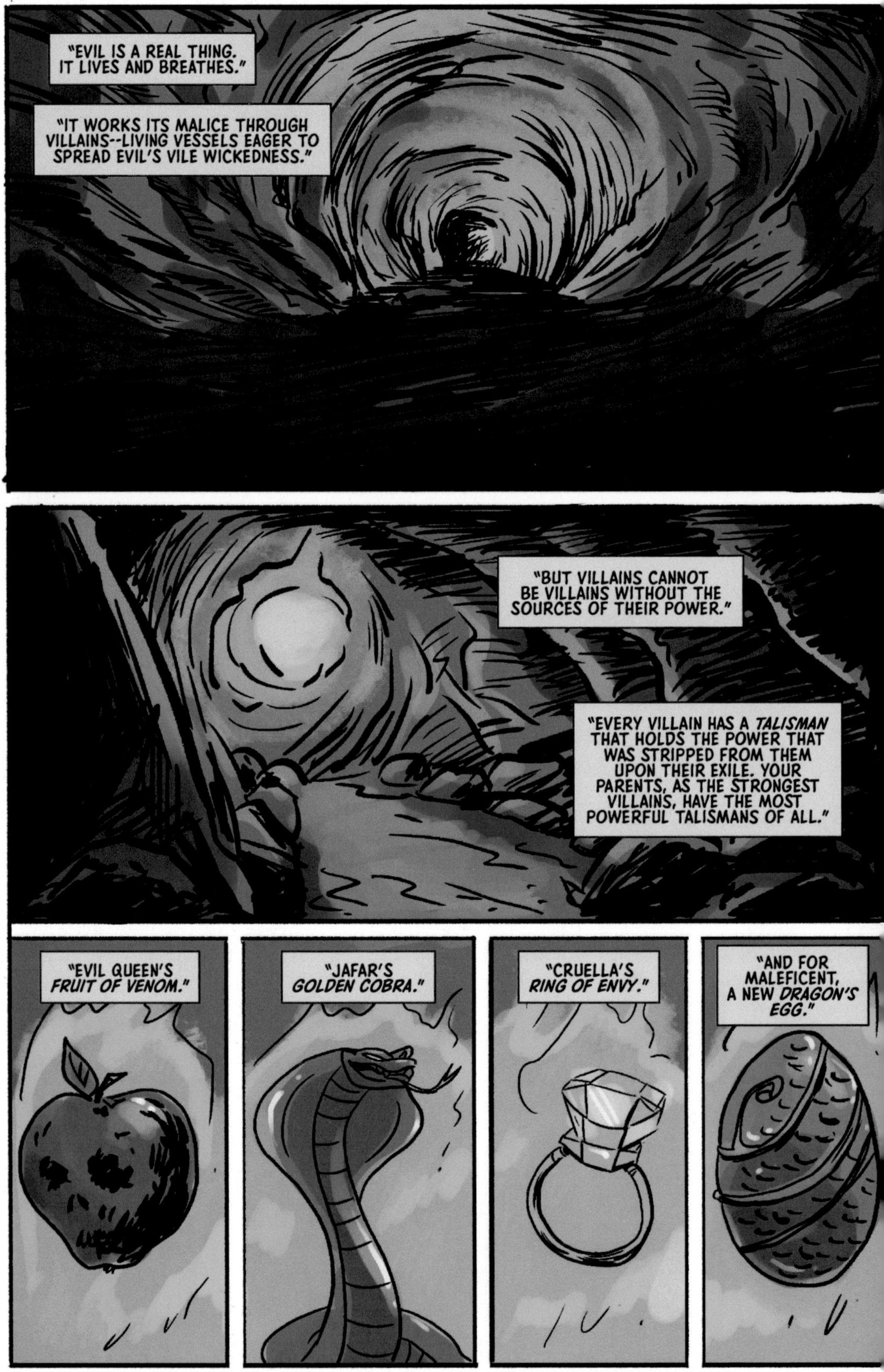
"EVIL IS A REAL THING. IT LIVES AND BREATHES."
"IT WORKS ITS MALICE THROUGH VILLAINS--LIVING VESSELS EAGER TO SPREAD EVIL'S VILE WICKEDNESS."
"BUT VILLAINS CANNOT BE VILLAINS WITHOUT THE SOURCES OF THEIR POWER."
"EVERY VILLAIN HAS A *TALISMAN* THAT HOLDS THE POWER THAT WAS STRIPPED FROM THEM UPON THEIR EXILE. YOUR PARENTS, AS THE STRONGEST VILLAINS, HAVE THE MOST POWERFUL TALISMANS OF ALL."
"EVIL QUEEN'S *FRUIT OF VENOM.*"
"JAFAR'S *GOLDEN COBRA.*"
"CRUELLA'S *RING OF ENVY.*"
"AND FOR MALEFICENT, A NEW *DRAGON'S EGG.*"

THE TALISMANS WANT TO BE FOUND. THEY HAVE ALREADY SEDUCED YOUR PARENTS INTO LOOKING FOR THEM, AND SOON THEY WILL DRAW OTHERS TO THEIR SIDE.

USED TOGETHER, IN YOUR PARENTS' HANDS, THESE FOUR EVIL TALISMANS CAN OVERCOME THE POWER OF GOOD ONCE AND FOR ALL.

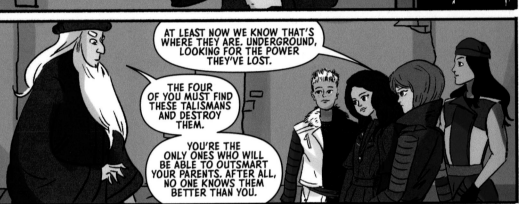

AT LEAST NOW WE KNOW THAT'S WHERE THEY ARE. UNDERGROUND, LOOKING FOR THE POWER THEY'VE LOST.

THE FOUR OF YOU MUST FIND THESE TALISMANS AND DESTROY THEM.

YOU'RE THE ONLY ONES WHO WILL BE ABLE TO OUTSMART YOUR PARENTS. AFTER ALL, NO ONE KNOWS THEM BETTER THAN YOU.

GREAT, LET'S GO.

WE MUST FIND THE ENTRANCE TO THE CATACOMBS FIRST.

THE REST OF THE ANTI-HEROES WILL HELP.

BUT FIRST, I HAVE ADVICE FOR EACH OF YOU. ACQUIRING THESE TALISMANS WILL BE VERY DANGEROUS. EVIL IS SEDUCTIVE. YOU MUST REMAIN STRONG AND NOT FALL PREY TO ITS TEMPTATIONS.

CARLOS DE VIL, YOU POSSESS A KEEN INTELLECT.

HOWEVER, DO NOT LET YOUR HEAD RULE YOUR HEART.

LEARN TO SEE WHAT IS *TRULY* IN FRONT OF YOU.

EVIE, REMEMBER THAT EVEN WHEN YOU BELIEVE YOU ARE ALONE IN THE WORLD, YOU ARE FAR FROM FRIENDLESS.

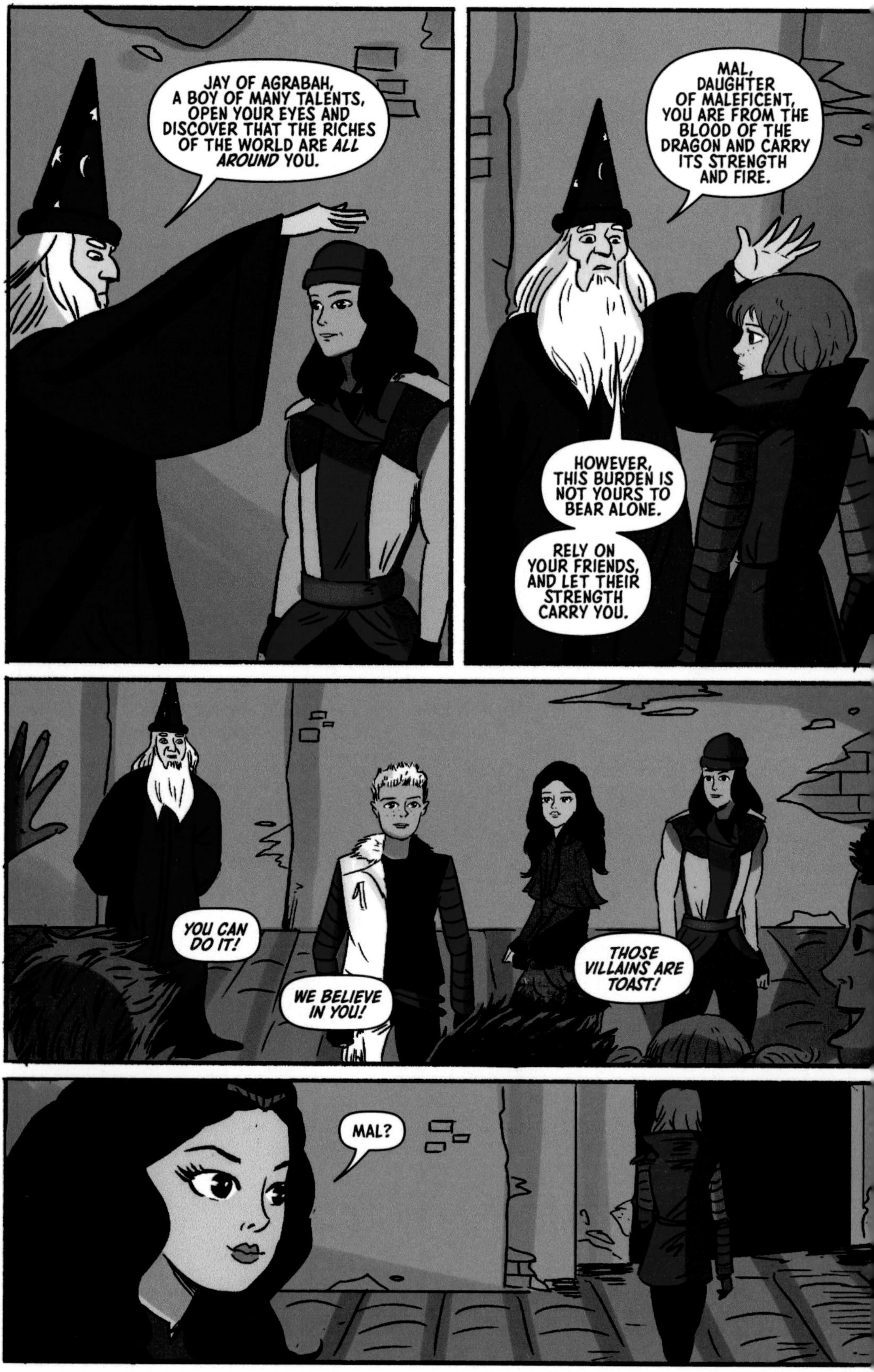
JAY OF AGRABAH, A BOY OF MANY TALENTS, OPEN YOUR EYES AND DISCOVER THAT THE RICHES OF THE WORLD ARE *ALL AROUND* YOU.
MAL, DAUGHTER OF MALEFICENT, YOU ARE FROM THE BLOOD OF THE DRAGON AND CARRY ITS STRENGTH AND FIRE.
HOWEVER, THIS BURDEN IS NOT YOURS TO BEAR ALONE.
RELY ON YOUR FRIENDS, AND LET THEIR STRENGTH CARRY YOU.
YOU CAN DO IT!
WE BELIEVE IN YOU!
THOSE VILLAINS ARE TOAST!
MAL?

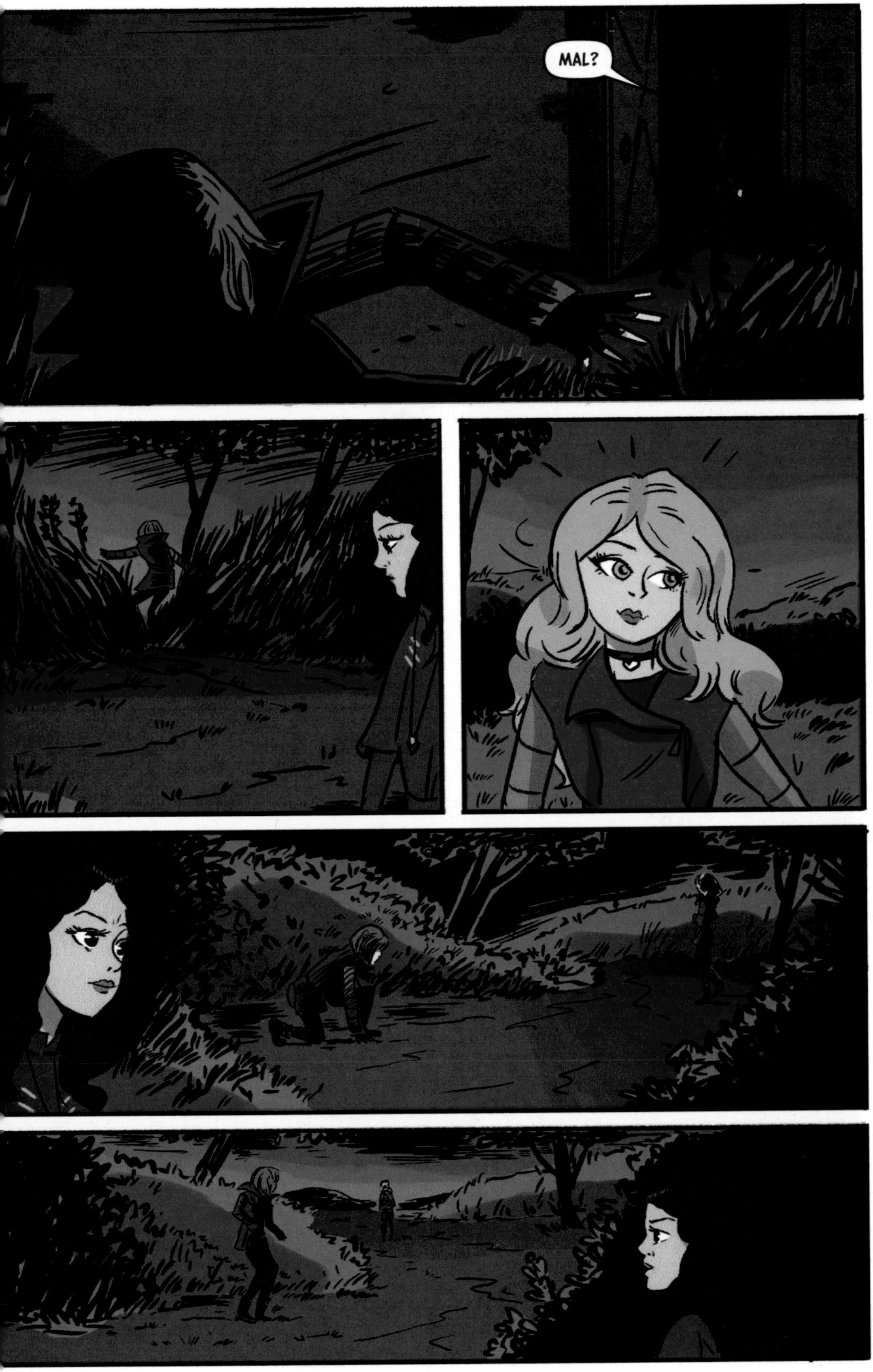
MAL?

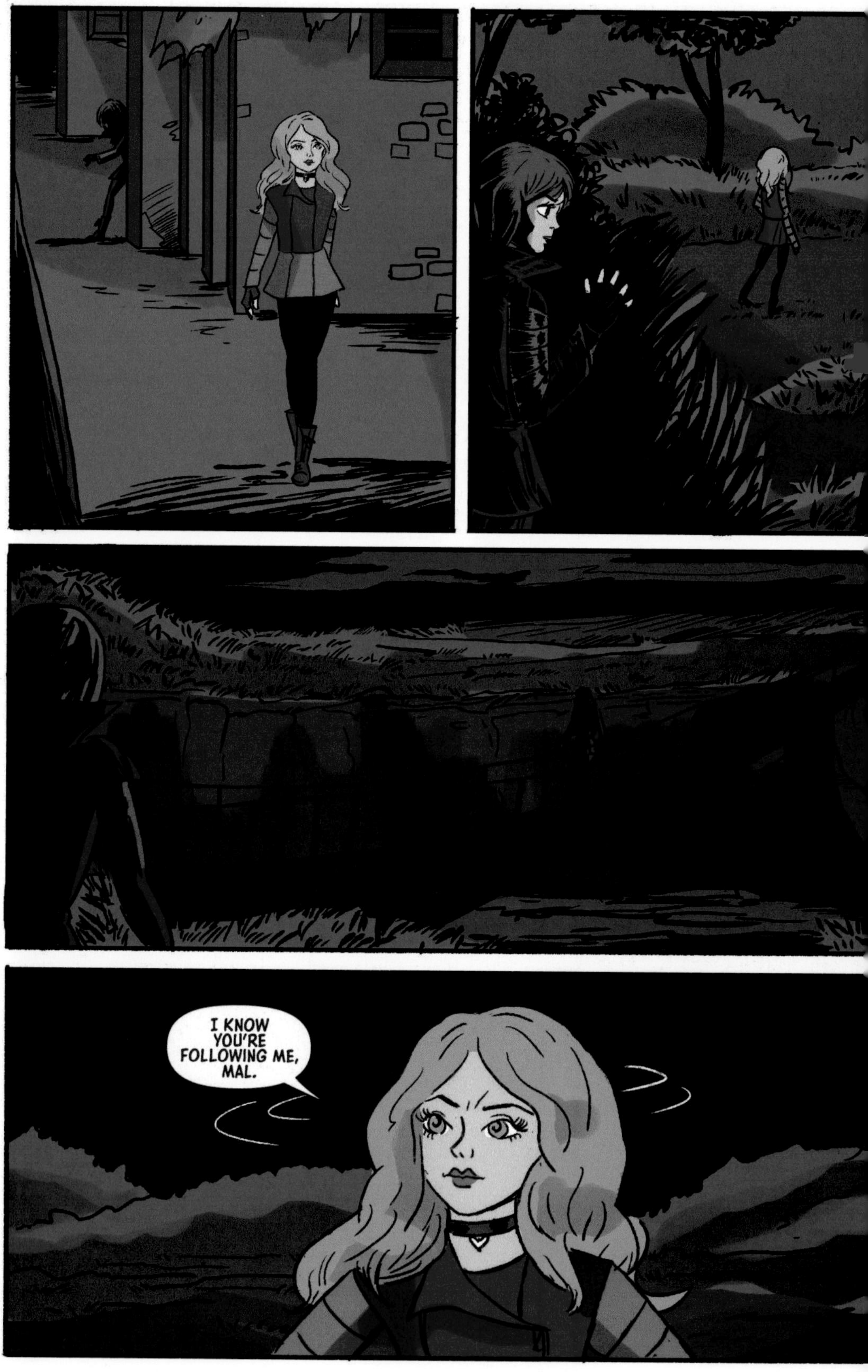
I KNOW YOU'RE FOLLOWING ME, MAL.

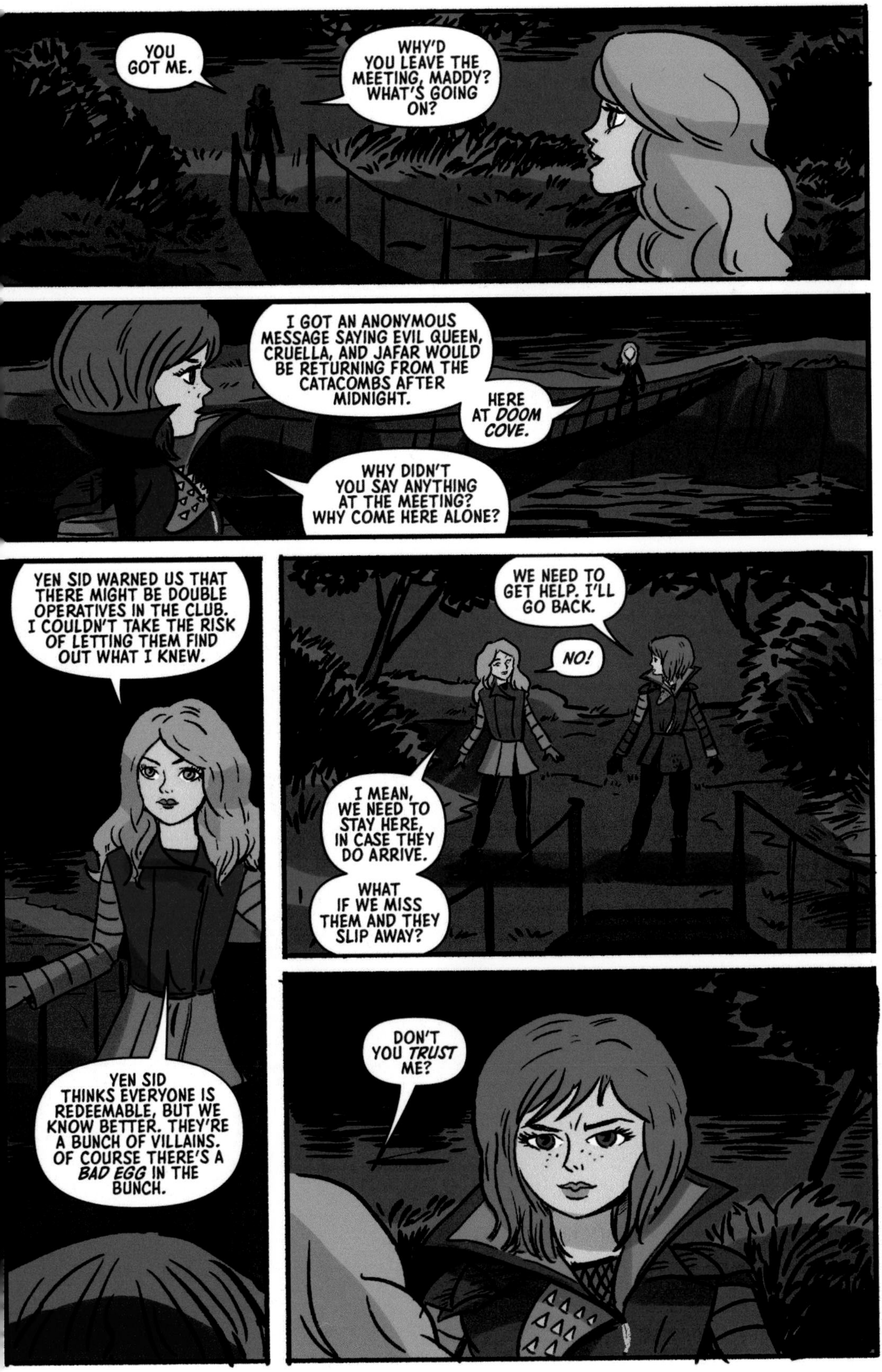
YOU GOT ME.
WHY'D YOU LEAVE THE MEETING, MADDY? WHAT'S GOING ON?
I GOT AN ANONYMOUS MESSAGE SAYING EVIL QUEEN, CRUELLA, AND JAFAR WOULD BE RETURNING FROM THE CATACOMBS AFTER MIDNIGHT.
HERE AT DOOM COVE.
WHY DIDN'T YOU SAY ANYTHING AT THE MEETING? WHY COME HERE ALONE?
YEN SID WARNED US THAT THERE MIGHT BE DOUBLE OPERATIVES IN THE CLUB. I COULDN'T TAKE THE RISK OF LETTING THEM FIND OUT WHAT I KNEW.
YEN SID THINKS EVERYONE IS REDEEMABLE, BUT WE KNOW BETTER. THEY'RE A BUNCH OF VILLAINS. OF COURSE THERE'S A BAD EGG IN THE BUNCH.
WE NEED TO GET HELP. I'LL GO BACK.
NO!
I MEAN, WE NEED TO STAY HERE, IN CASE THEY DO ARRIVE.
WHAT IF WE MISS THEM AND THEY SLIP AWAY?
DON'T YOU TRUST ME?

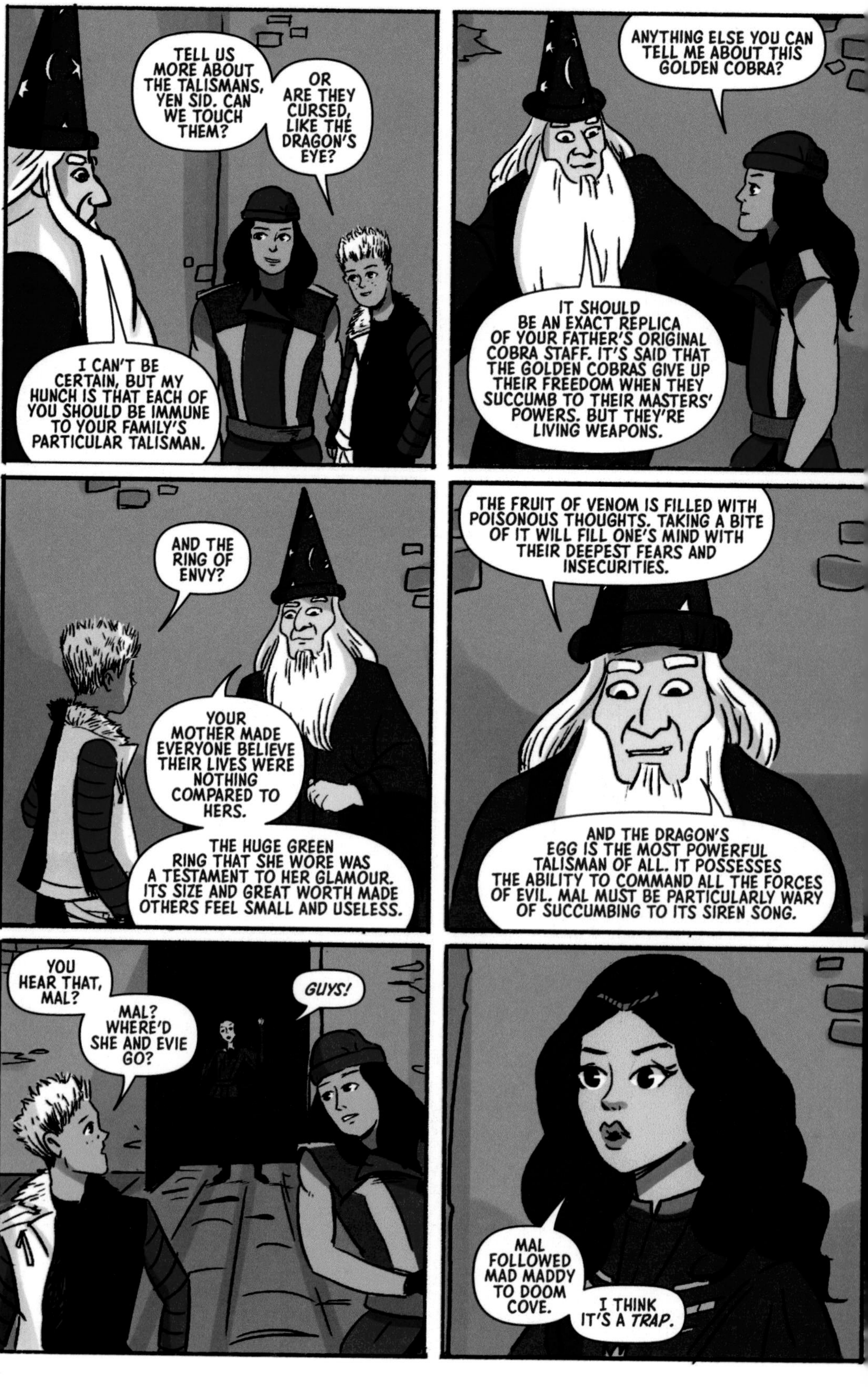
TELL US MORE ABOUT THE TALISMANS, YEN SID. CAN WE TOUCH THEM?
OR ARE THEY CURSED, LIKE THE DRAGON'S EYE?
I CAN'T BE CERTAIN, BUT MY HUNCH IS THAT EACH OF YOU SHOULD BE IMMUNE TO YOUR FAMILY'S PARTICULAR TALISMAN.
ANYTHING ELSE YOU CAN TELL ME ABOUT THIS GOLDEN COBRA?
IT SHOULD BE AN EXACT REPLICA OF YOUR FATHER'S ORIGINAL COBRA STAFF. IT'S SAID THAT THE GOLDEN COBRAS GIVE UP THEIR FREEDOM WHEN THEY SUCCUMB TO THEIR MASTERS' POWERS. BUT THEY'RE LIVING WEAPONS.
AND THE RING OF ENVY?
YOUR MOTHER MADE EVERYONE BELIEVE THEIR LIVES WERE NOTHING COMPARED TO HERS.
THE HUGE GREEN RING THAT SHE WORE WAS A TESTAMENT TO HER GLAMOUR. ITS SIZE AND GREAT WORTH MADE OTHERS FEEL SMALL AND USELESS.
THE FRUIT OF VENOM IS FILLED WITH POISONOUS THOUGHTS. TAKING A BITE OF IT WILL FILL ONE'S MIND WITH THEIR DEEPEST FEARS AND INSECURITIES.
AND THE DRAGON'S EGG IS THE MOST POWERFUL TALISMAN OF ALL. IT POSSESSES THE ABILITY TO COMMAND ALL THE FORCES OF EVIL. MAL MUST BE PARTICULARLY WARY OF SUCCUMBING TO ITS SIREN SONG.
YOU HEAR THAT, MAL?
MAL? WHERE'D SHE AND EVIE GO?
GUYS!
MAL FOLLOWED MAD MADDY TO DOOM COVE.
I THINK IT'S A *TRAP*.

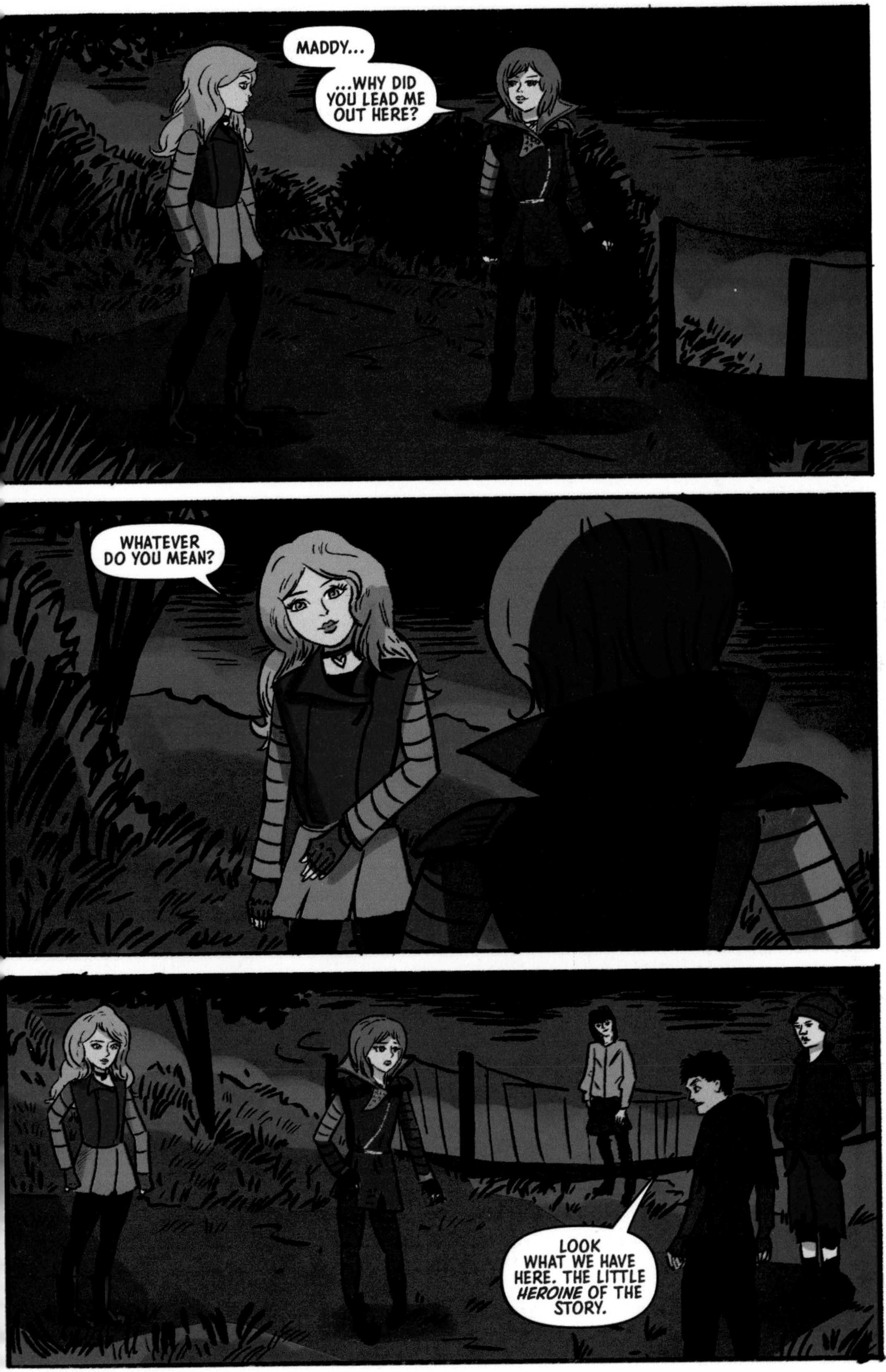

MADDY...
...WHY DID YOU LEAD ME OUT HERE?
WHATEVER DO YOU MEAN?
LOOK WHAT WE HAVE HERE. THE LITTLE *HEROINE* OF THE STORY.

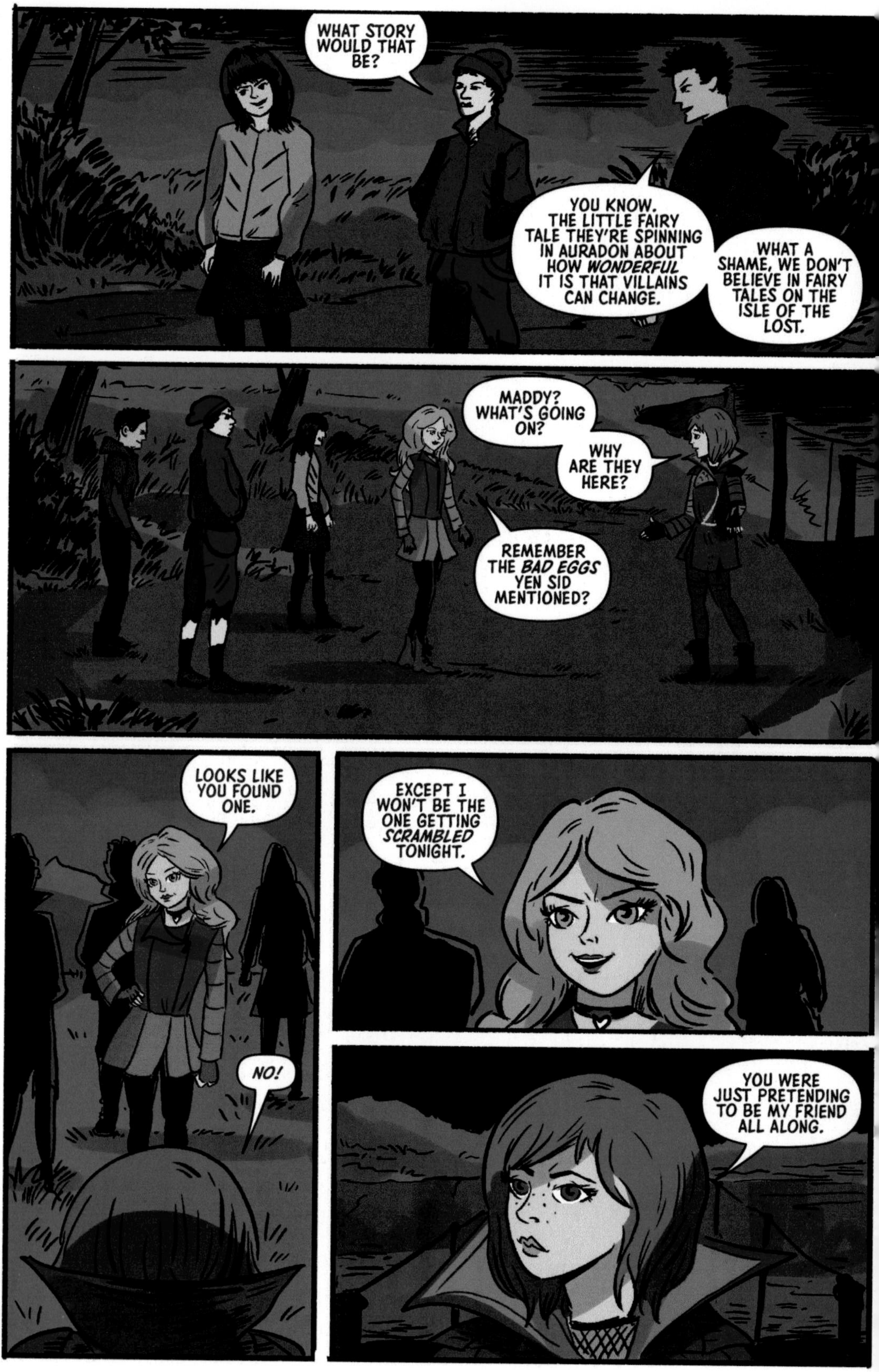
WHAT STORY WOULD THAT BE?
YOU KNOW. THE LITTLE FAIRY TALE THEY'RE SPINNING IN AURADON ABOUT HOW *WONDERFUL* IT IS THAT VILLAINS CAN CHANGE.
WHAT A SHAME, WE DON'T BELIEVE IN FAIRY TALES ON THE ISLE OF THE LOST.
MADDY? WHAT'S GOING ON?
WHY ARE THEY HERE?
REMEMBER THE *BAD EGGS* YEN SID MENTIONED?
LOOKS LIKE YOU FOUND ONE.
NO!
EXCEPT I WON'T BE THE ONE GETTING *SCRAMBLED* TONIGHT.
YOU WERE JUST PRETENDING TO BE MY FRIEND ALL ALONG.

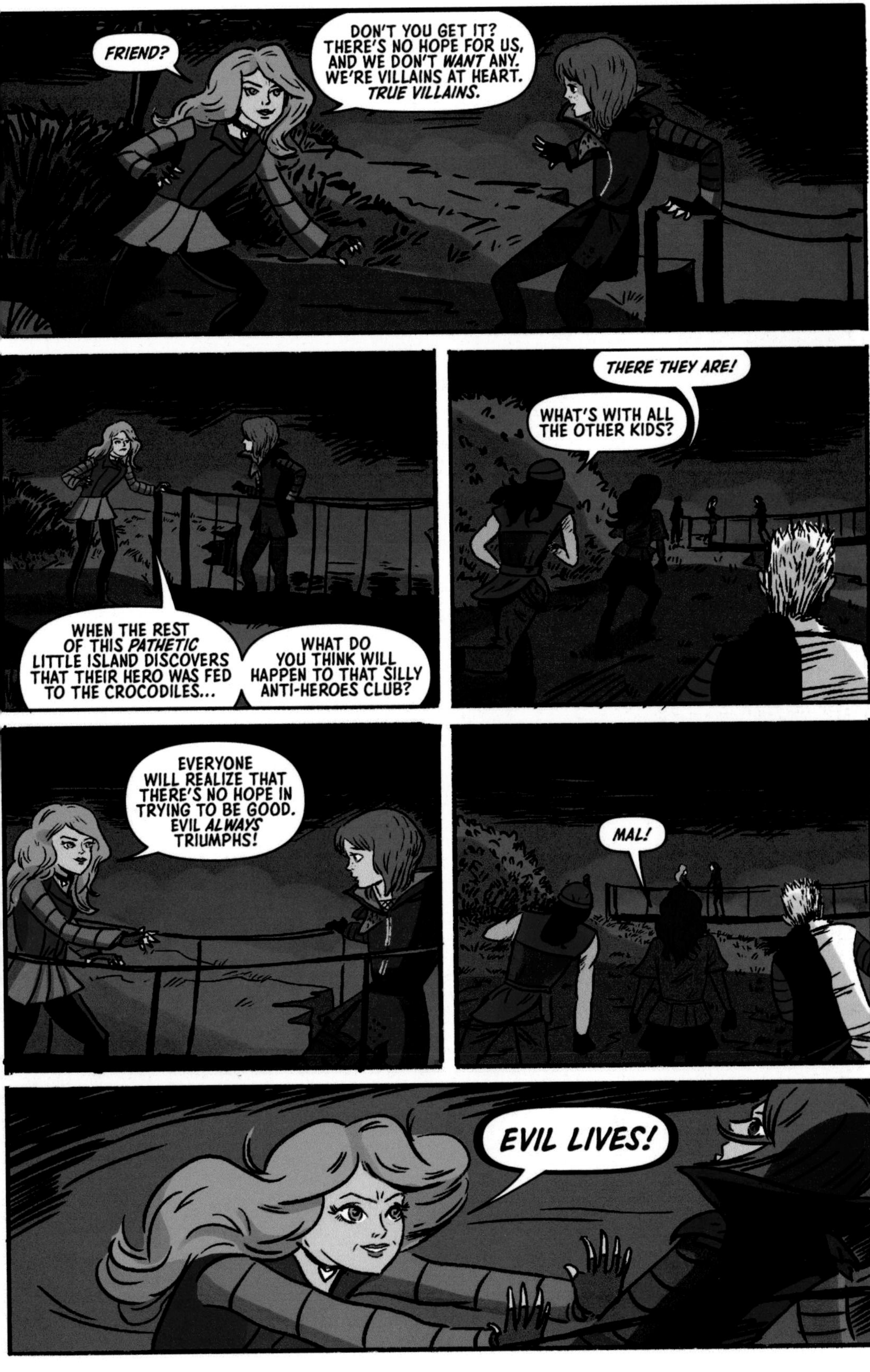
FRIEND?
DON'T YOU GET IT? THERE'S NO HOPE FOR US, AND WE DON'T *WANT* ANY. WE'RE VILLAINS AT HEART. *TRUE VILLAINS.*
WHEN THE REST OF THIS *PATHETIC* LITTLE ISLAND DISCOVERS THAT THEIR HERO WAS FED TO THE CROCODILES...
WHAT DO YOU THINK WILL HAPPEN TO THAT SILLY ANTI-HEROES CLUB?
THERE THEY ARE!
WHAT'S WITH ALL THE OTHER KIDS?
EVERYONE WILL REALIZE THAT THERE'S NO HOPE IN TRYING TO BE GOOD. EVIL *ALWAYS* TRIUMPHS!
MAL!
EVIL LIVES!

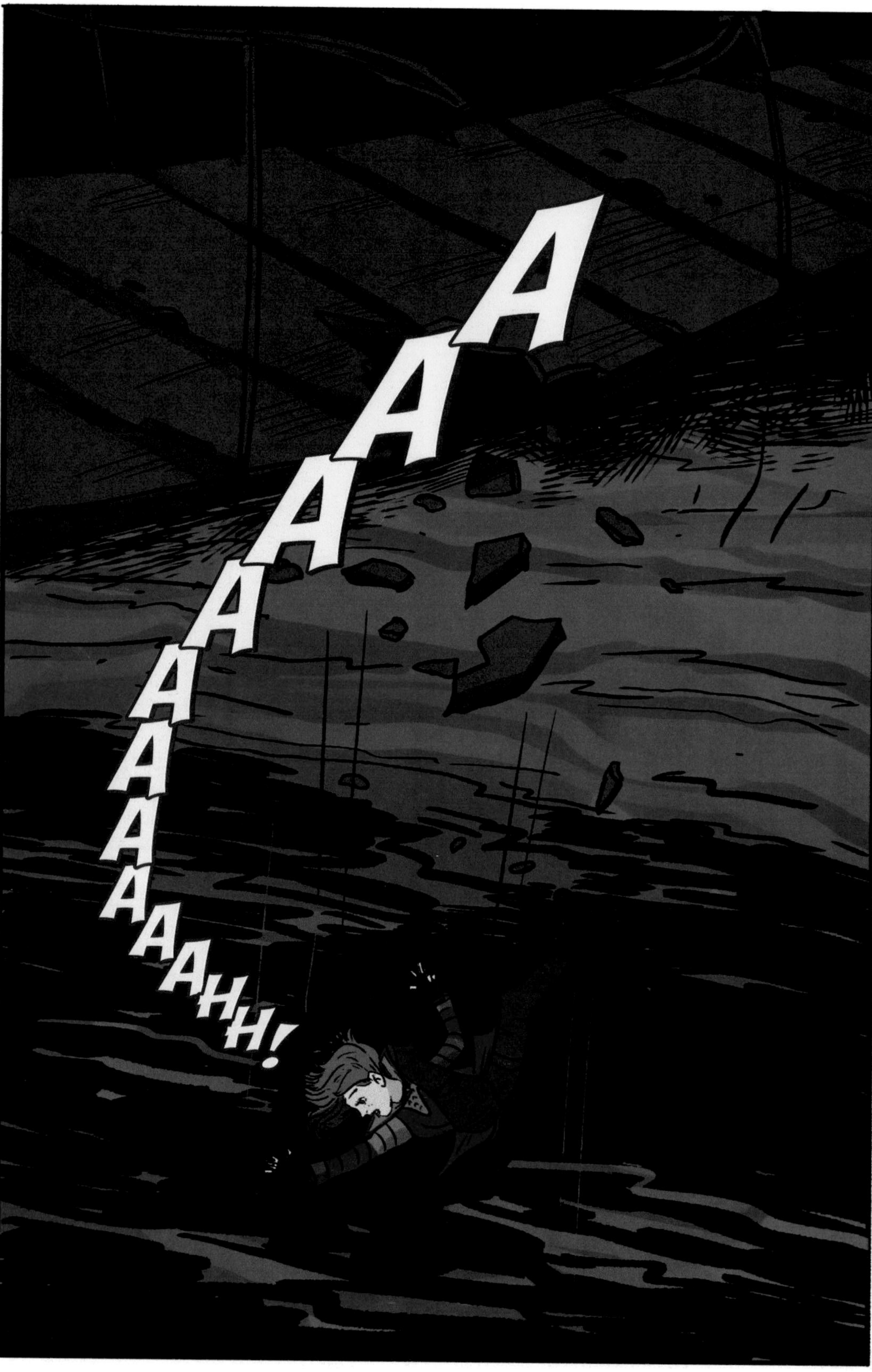
AAAAAAAAAAAHH!

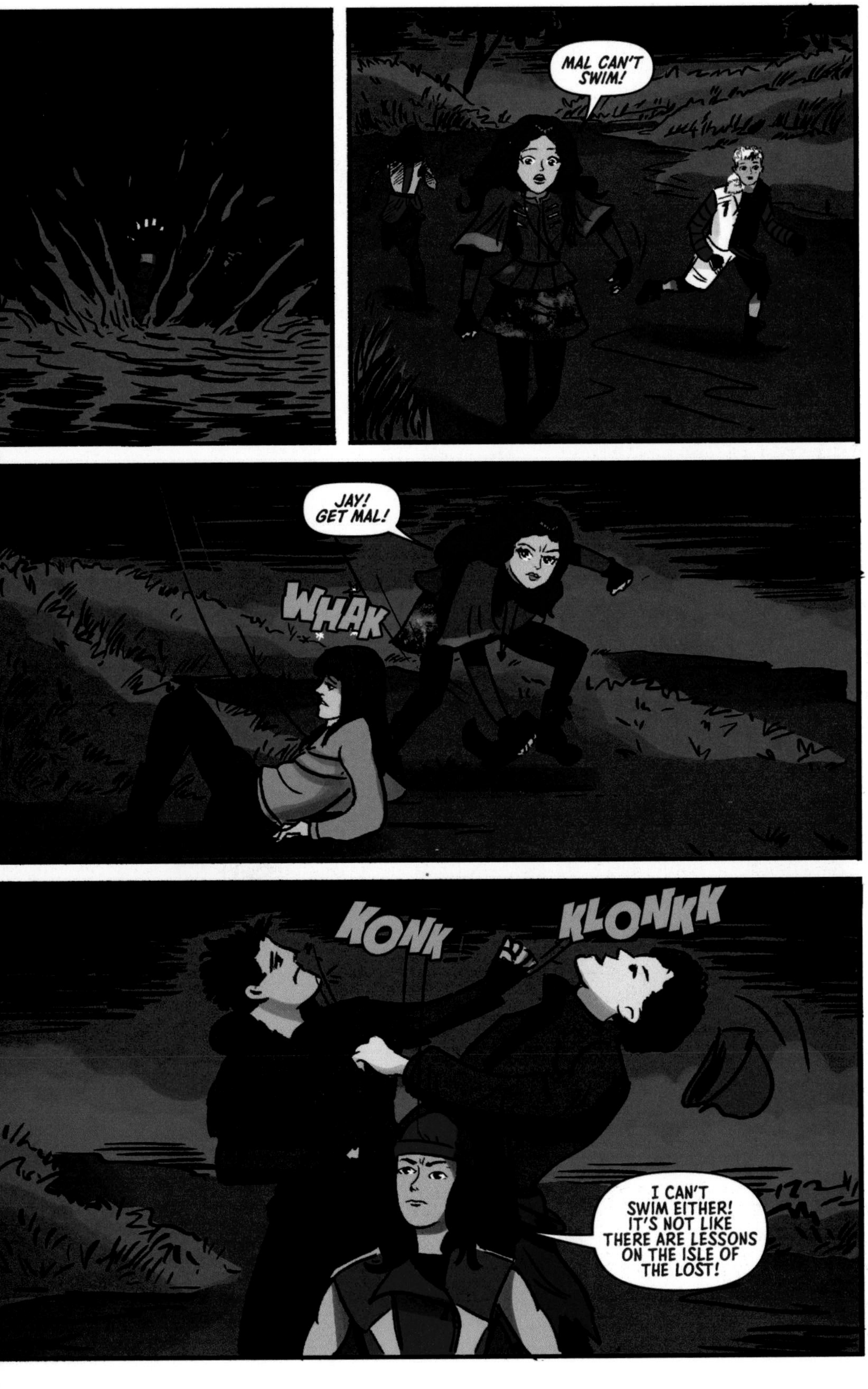
MAL CAN'T SWIM!
JAY! GET MAL!
WHAK
KONK
KLONKK
I CAN'T SWIM EITHER! IT'S NOT LIKE THERE ARE LESSONS ON THE ISLE OF THE LOST!

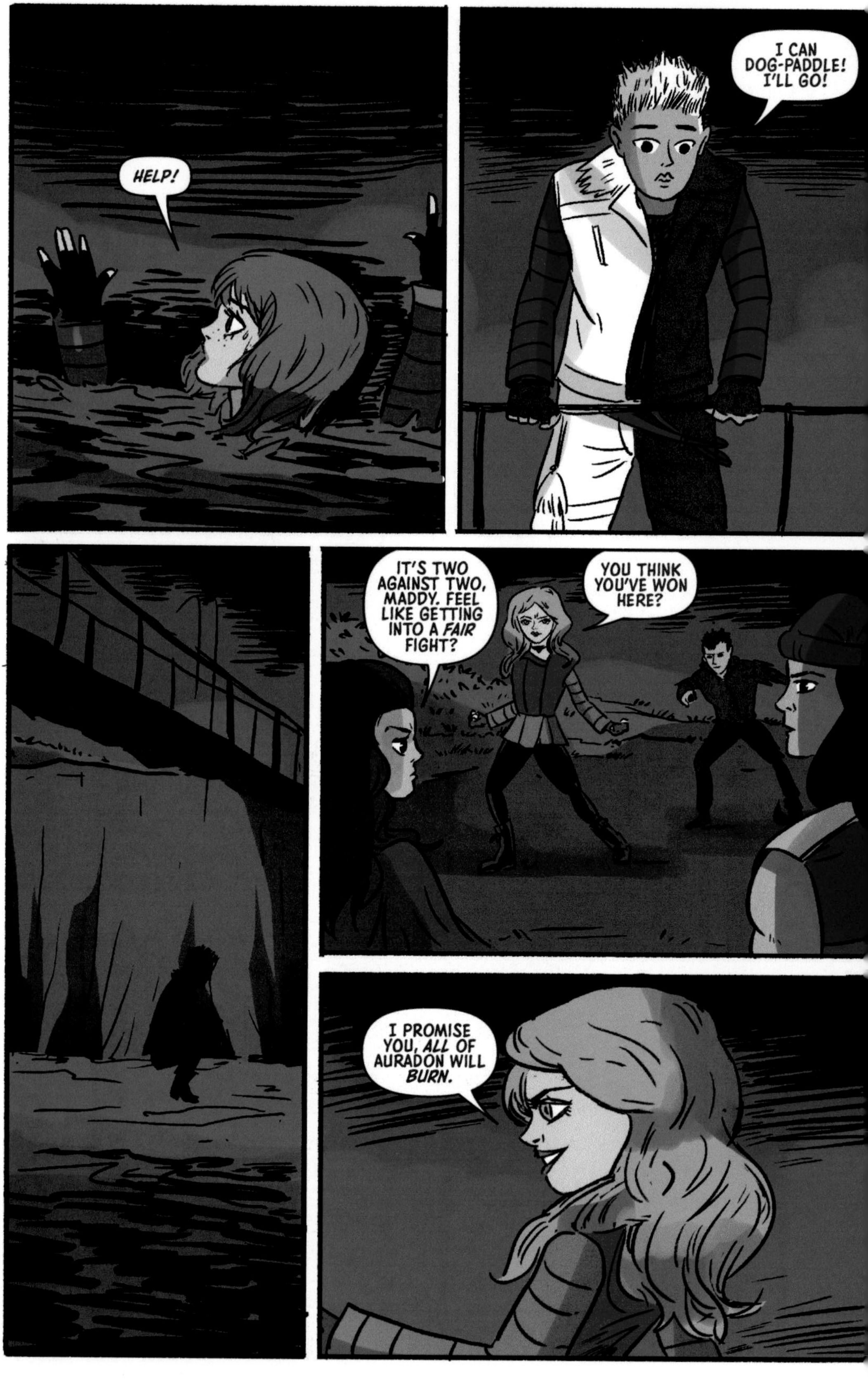
HELP!
I CAN DOG-PADDLE! I'LL GO!
IT'S TWO AGAINST TWO, MADDY. FEEL LIKE GETTING INTO A *FAIR* FIGHT?
YOU THINK YOU'VE WON HERE?
I PROMISE YOU, *ALL* OF AURADON WILL *BURN*.

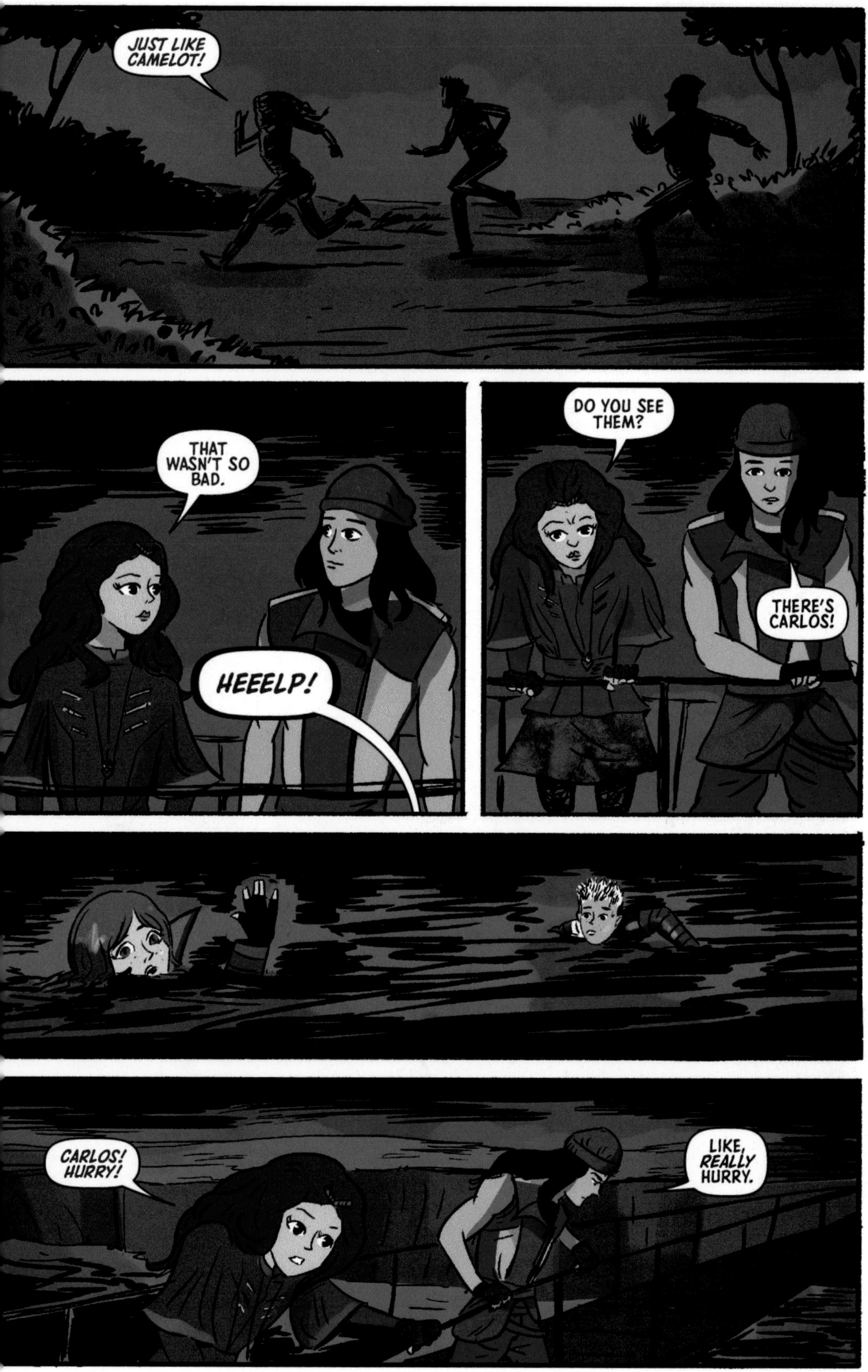
JUST LIKE CAMELOT!
THAT WASN'T SO BAD.
HEEELP!
DO YOU SEE THEM?
THERE'S CARLOS!
CARLOS! HURRY!
LIKE, REALLY HURRY.

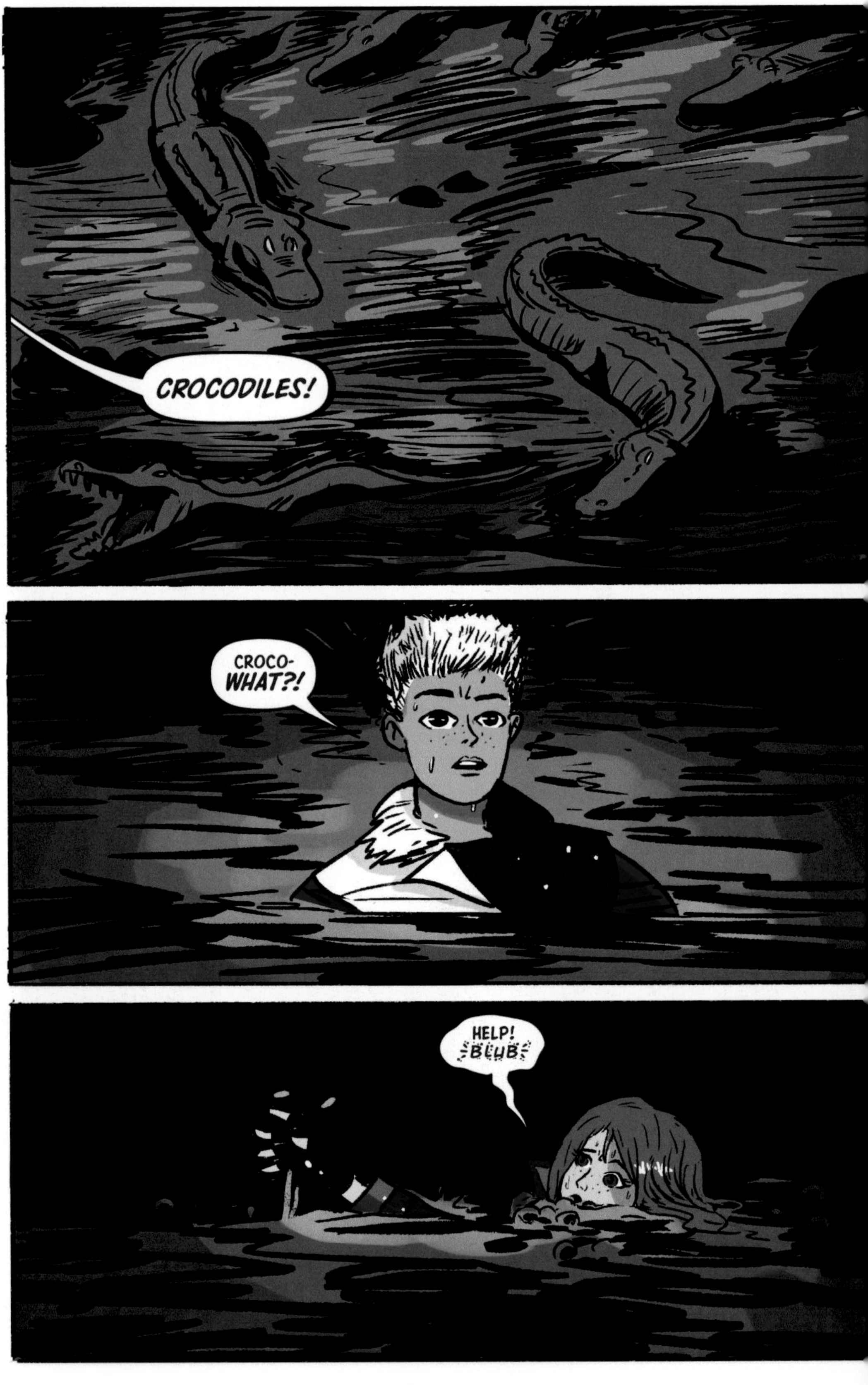
CROCODILES!
CROCO-WHAT?!
HELP! BLUB

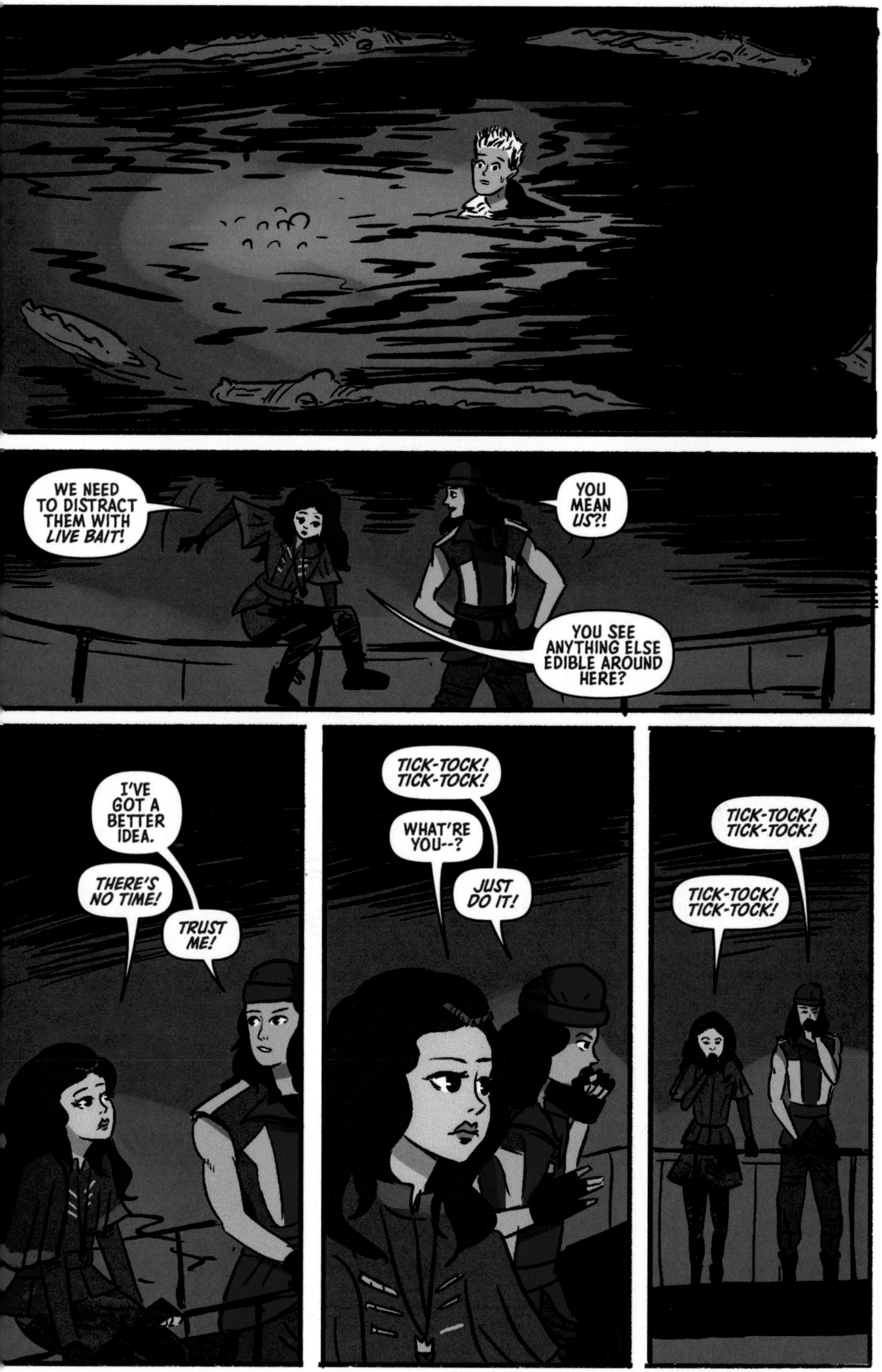
WE NEED TO DISTRACT THEM WITH LIVE BAIT!
YOU MEAN US?!
YOU SEE ANYTHING ELSE EDIBLE AROUND HERE?
I'VE GOT A BETTER IDEA.
THERE'S NO TIME!
TRUST ME!
TICK-TOCK! TICK-TOCK!
WHAT'RE YOU--?
JUST DO IT!
TICK-TOCK! TICK-TOCK!
TICK-TOCK! TICK-TOCK!

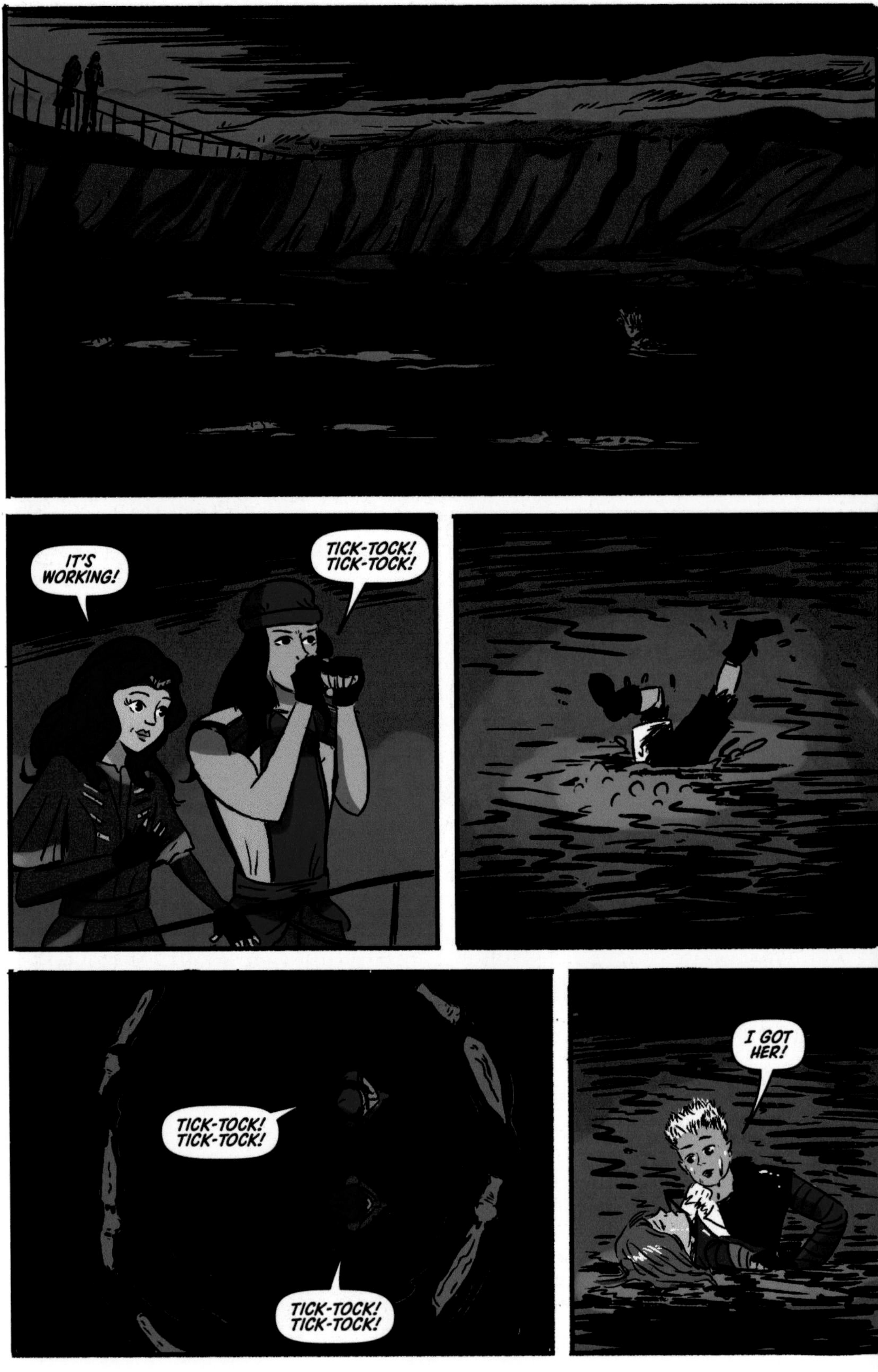
IT'S WORKING!
TICK-TOCK! TICK-TOCK!
TICK-TOCK! TICK-TOCK!
TICK-TOCK! TICK-TOCK!
I GOT HER!

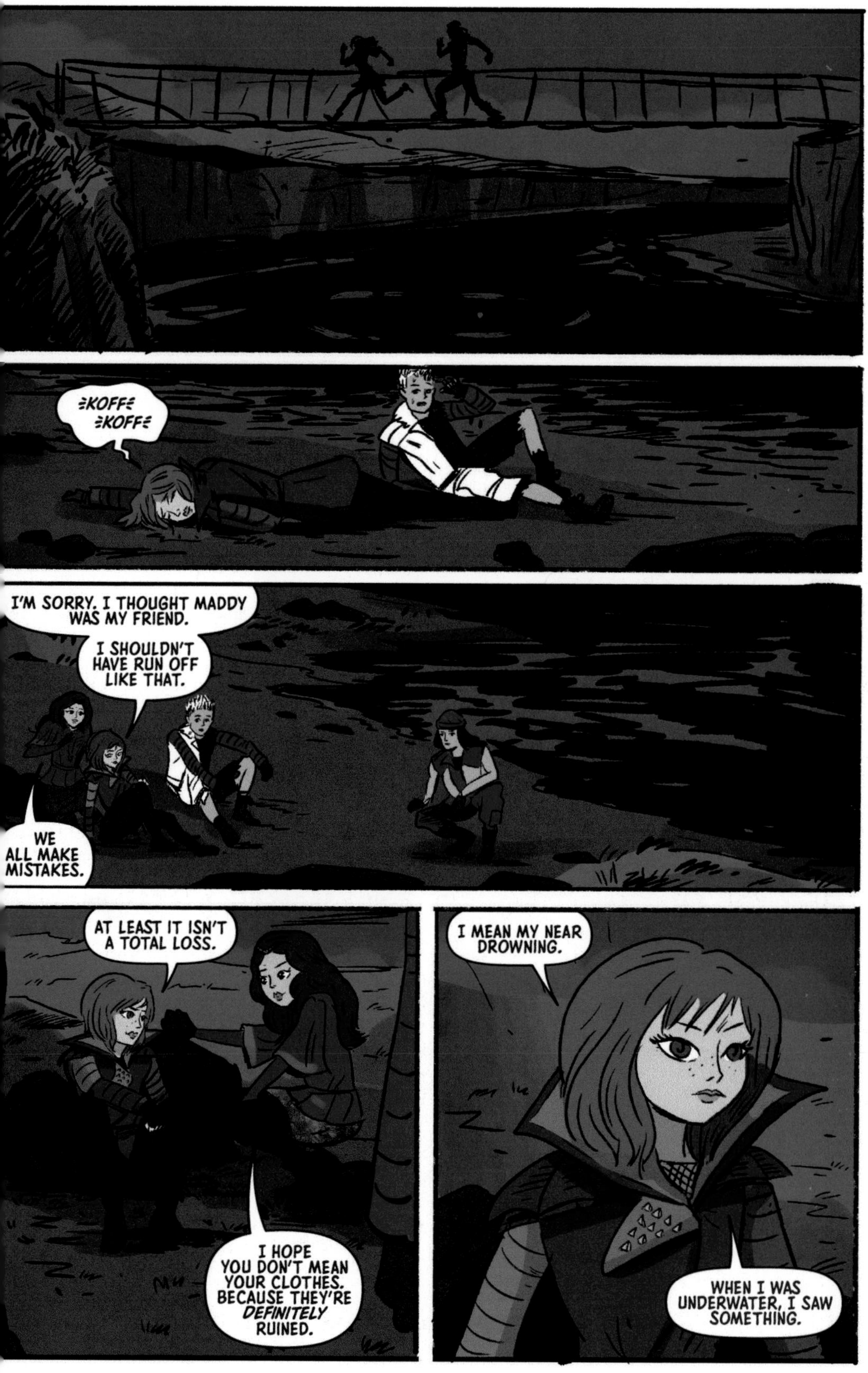
KOFF KOFF
I'M SORRY. I THOUGHT MADDY WAS MY FRIEND.
I SHOULDN'T HAVE RUN OFF LIKE THAT.
WE ALL MAKE MISTAKES.
AT LEAST IT ISN'T A TOTAL LOSS.
I HOPE YOU DON'T MEAN YOUR CLOTHES. BECAUSE THEY'RE *DEFINITELY* RUINED.
I MEAN MY NEAR DROWNING.
WHEN I WAS UNDERWATER, I SAW SOMETHING.

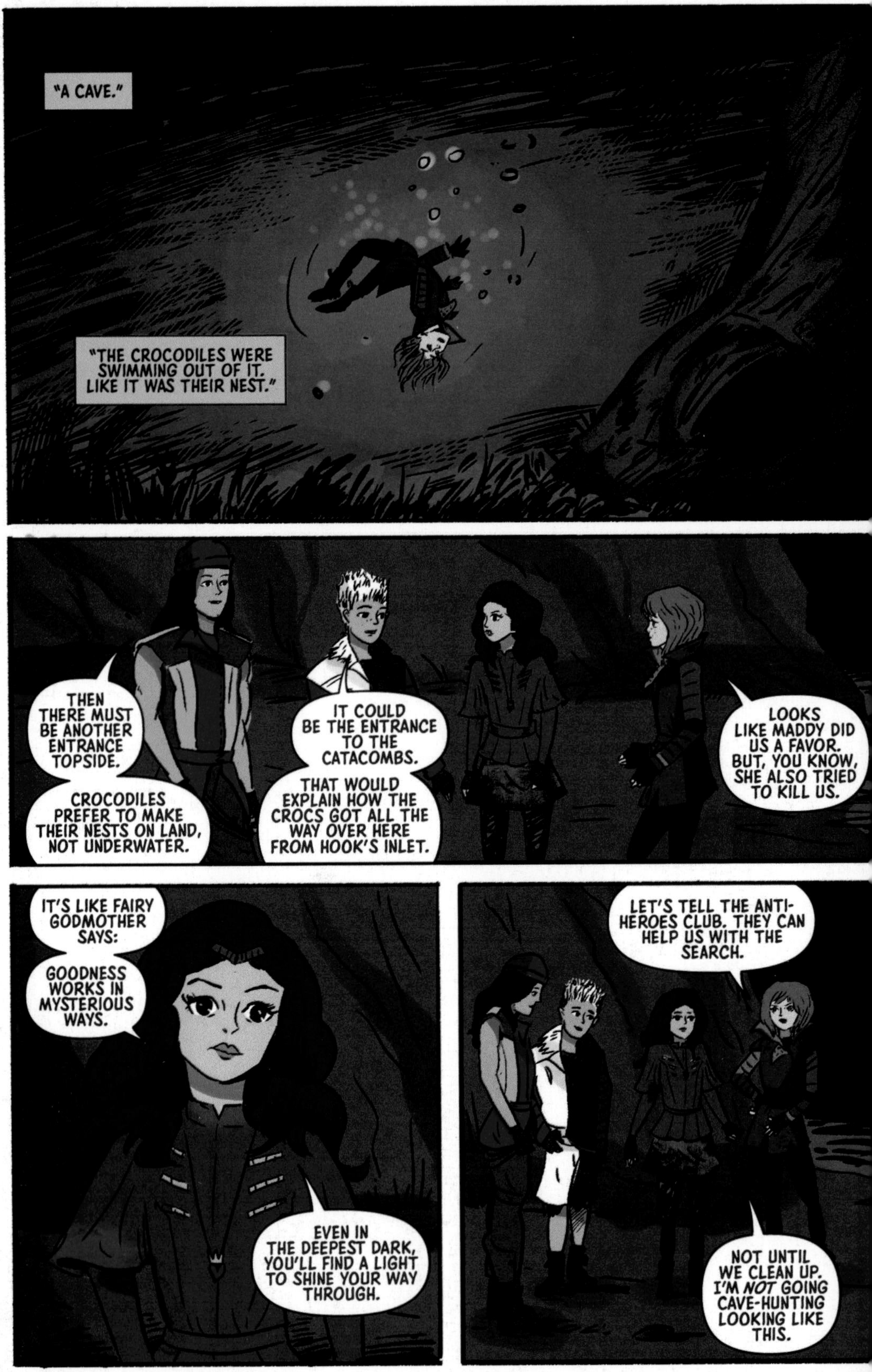
"A CAVE."
"THE CROCODILES WERE SWIMMING OUT OF IT. LIKE IT WAS THEIR NEST."
THEN THERE MUST BE ANOTHER ENTRANCE TOPSIDE.
CROCODILES PREFER TO MAKE THEIR NESTS ON LAND, NOT UNDERWATER.
IT COULD BE THE ENTRANCE TO THE CATACOMBS.
THAT WOULD EXPLAIN HOW THE CROCS GOT ALL THE WAY OVER HERE FROM HOOK'S INLET.
LOOKS LIKE MADDY DID US A FAVOR. BUT, YOU KNOW, SHE ALSO TRIED TO KILL US.
IT'S LIKE FAIRY GODMOTHER SAYS:
GOODNESS WORKS IN MYSTERIOUS WAYS.
EVEN IN THE DEEPEST DARK, YOU'LL FIND A LIGHT TO SHINE YOUR WAY THROUGH.
LET'S TELL THE ANTI-HEROES CLUB. THEY CAN HELP US WITH THE SEARCH.
NOT UNTIL WE CLEAN UP. I'M *NOT* GOING CAVE-HUNTING LOOKING LIKE THIS.

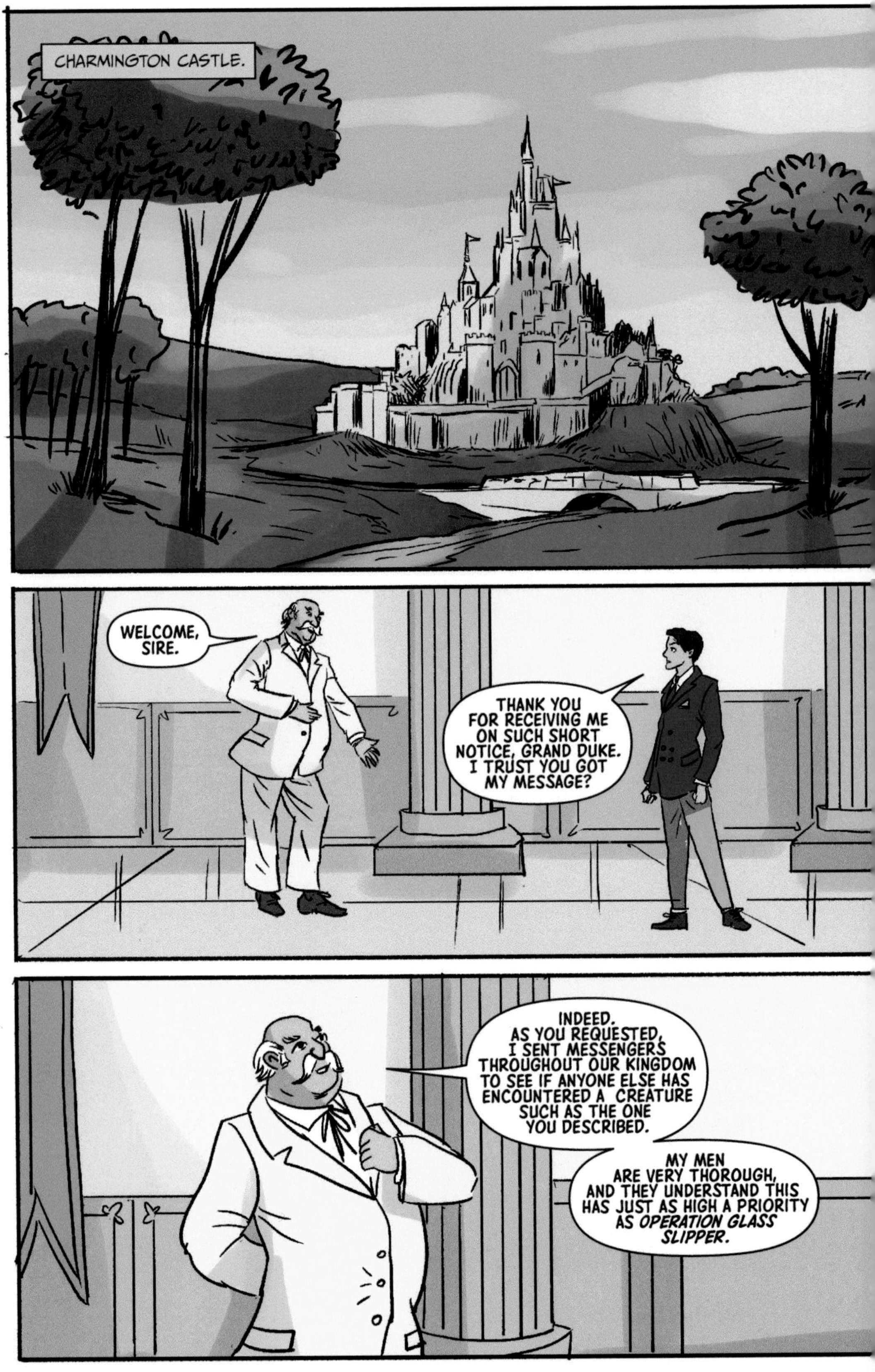
CHARMINGTON CASTLE.
WELCOME, SIRE.
THANK YOU FOR RECEIVING ME ON SUCH SHORT NOTICE, GRAND DUKE. I TRUST YOU GOT MY MESSAGE?
INDEED. AS YOU REQUESTED, I SENT MESSENGERS THROUGHOUT OUR KINGDOM TO SEE IF ANYONE ELSE HAS ENCOUNTERED A CREATURE SUCH AS THE ONE YOU DESCRIBED.
MY MEN ARE VERY THOROUGH, AND THEY UNDERSTAND THIS HAS JUST AS HIGH A PRIORITY AS *OPERATION GLASS SLIPPER*.

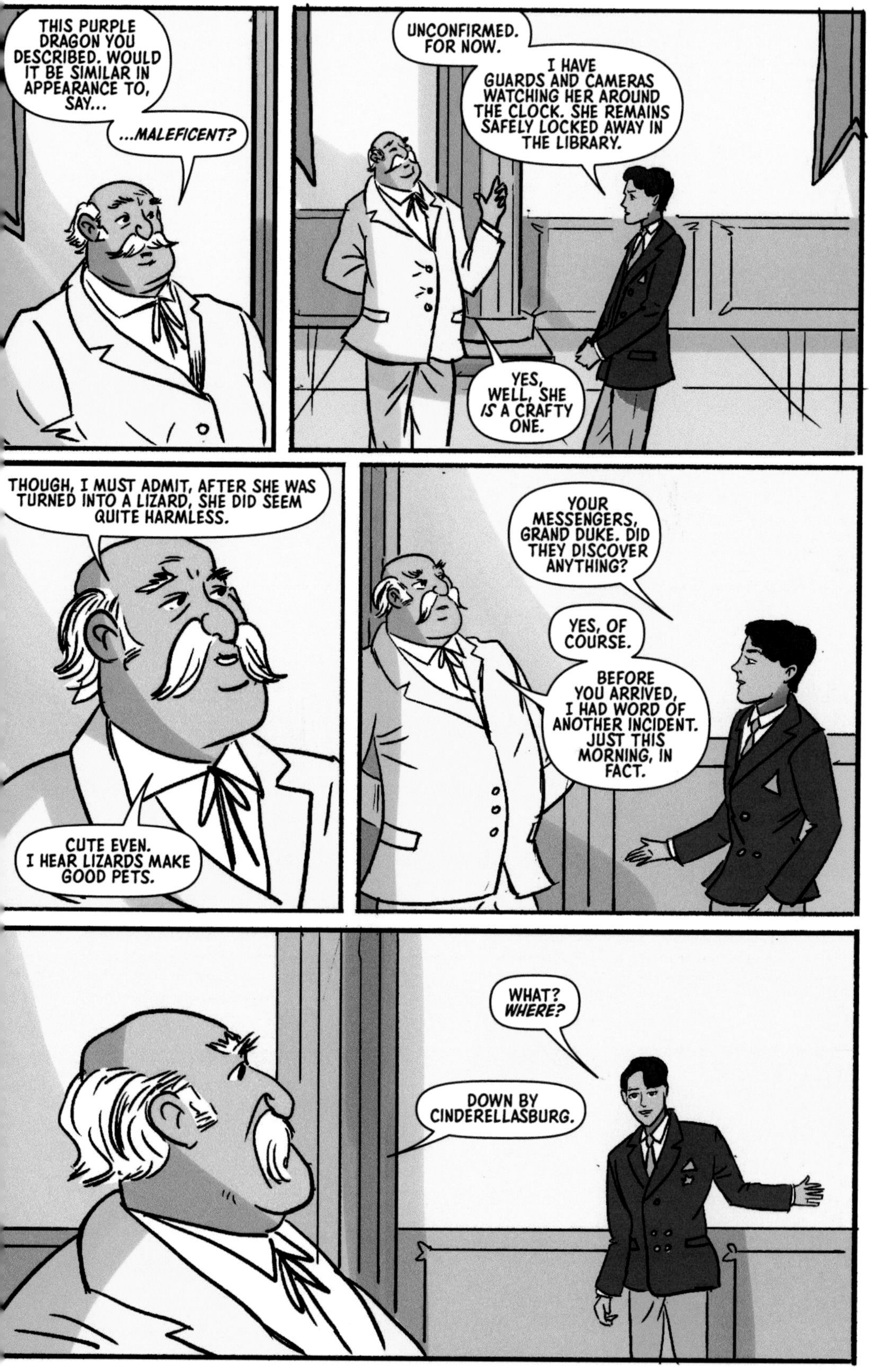
THIS PURPLE DRAGON YOU DESCRIBED. WOULD IT BE SIMILAR IN APPEARANCE TO, SAY...
...*MALEFICENT?*
UNCONFIRMED. FOR NOW.
I HAVE GUARDS AND CAMERAS WATCHING HER AROUND THE CLOCK. SHE REMAINS SAFELY LOCKED AWAY IN THE LIBRARY.
YES, WELL, SHE *IS* A CRAFTY ONE.
THOUGH, I MUST ADMIT, AFTER SHE WAS TURNED INTO A LIZARD, SHE DID SEEM QUITE HARMLESS.
CUTE EVEN. I HEAR LIZARDS MAKE GOOD PETS.
YOUR MESSENGERS, GRAND DUKE. DID THEY DISCOVER ANYTHING?
YES, OF COURSE.
BEFORE YOU ARRIVED, I HAD WORD OF ANOTHER INCIDENT. JUST THIS MORNING, IN FACT.
WHAT? *WHERE?*
DOWN BY CINDERELLASBURG.

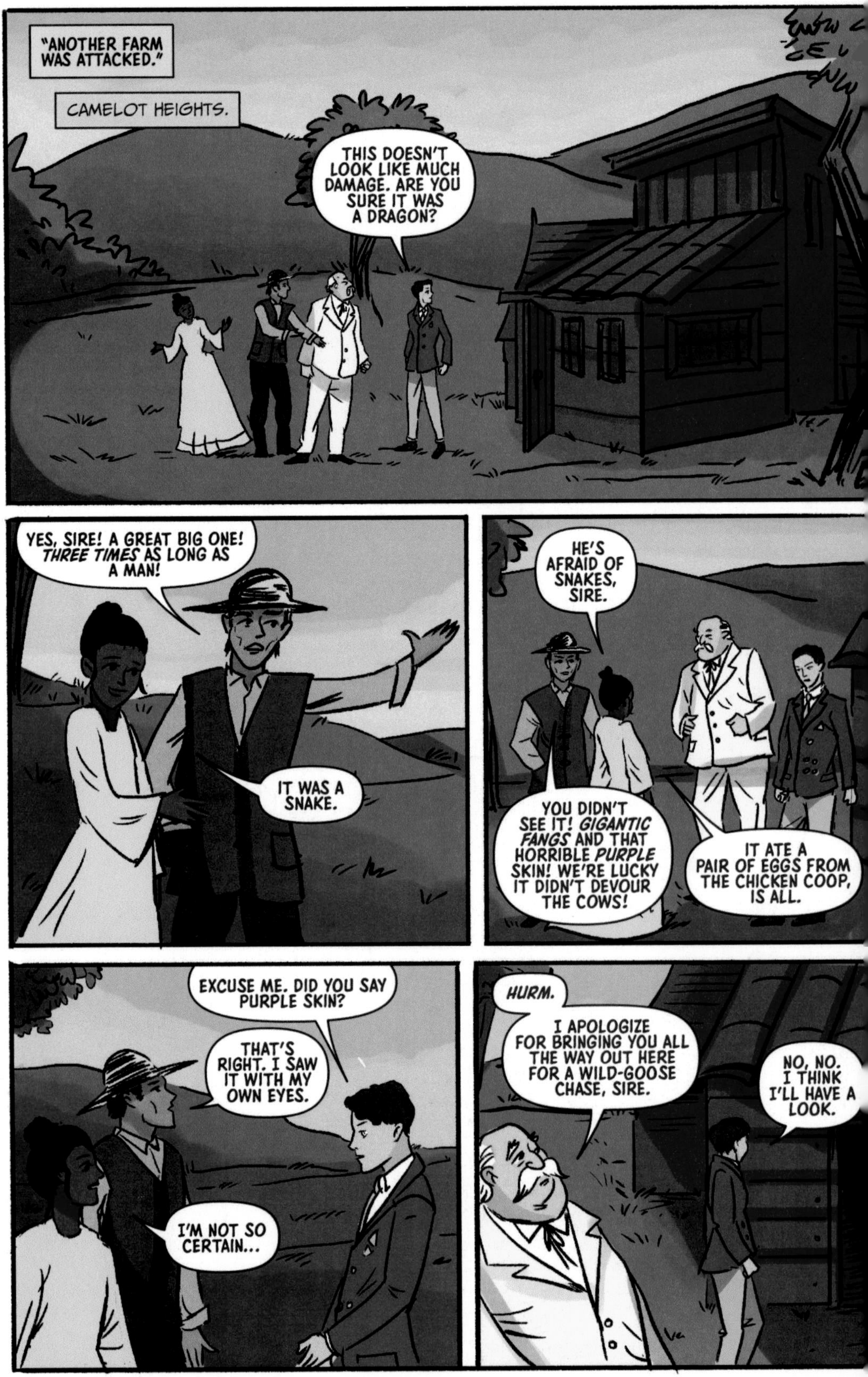
"ANOTHER FARM WAS ATTACKED."
CAMELOT HEIGHTS.
THIS DOESN'T LOOK LIKE MUCH DAMAGE. ARE YOU SURE IT WAS A DRAGON?
YES, SIRE! A GREAT BIG ONE! *THREE TIMES* AS LONG AS A MAN!
IT WAS A SNAKE.
HE'S AFRAID OF SNAKES, SIRE.
YOU DIDN'T SEE IT! *GIGANTIC FANGS* AND THAT HORRIBLE *PURPLE* SKIN! WE'RE LUCKY IT DIDN'T DEVOUR THE COWS!
IT ATE A PAIR OF EGGS FROM THE CHICKEN COOP, IS ALL.
EXCUSE ME. DID YOU SAY PURPLE SKIN?
THAT'S RIGHT. I SAW IT WITH MY OWN EYES.
I'M NOT SO CERTAIN...
HURM.
I APOLOGIZE FOR BRINGING YOU ALL THE WAY OUT HERE FOR A WILD-GOOSE CHASE, SIRE.
NO, NO. I THINK I'LL HAVE A LOOK.

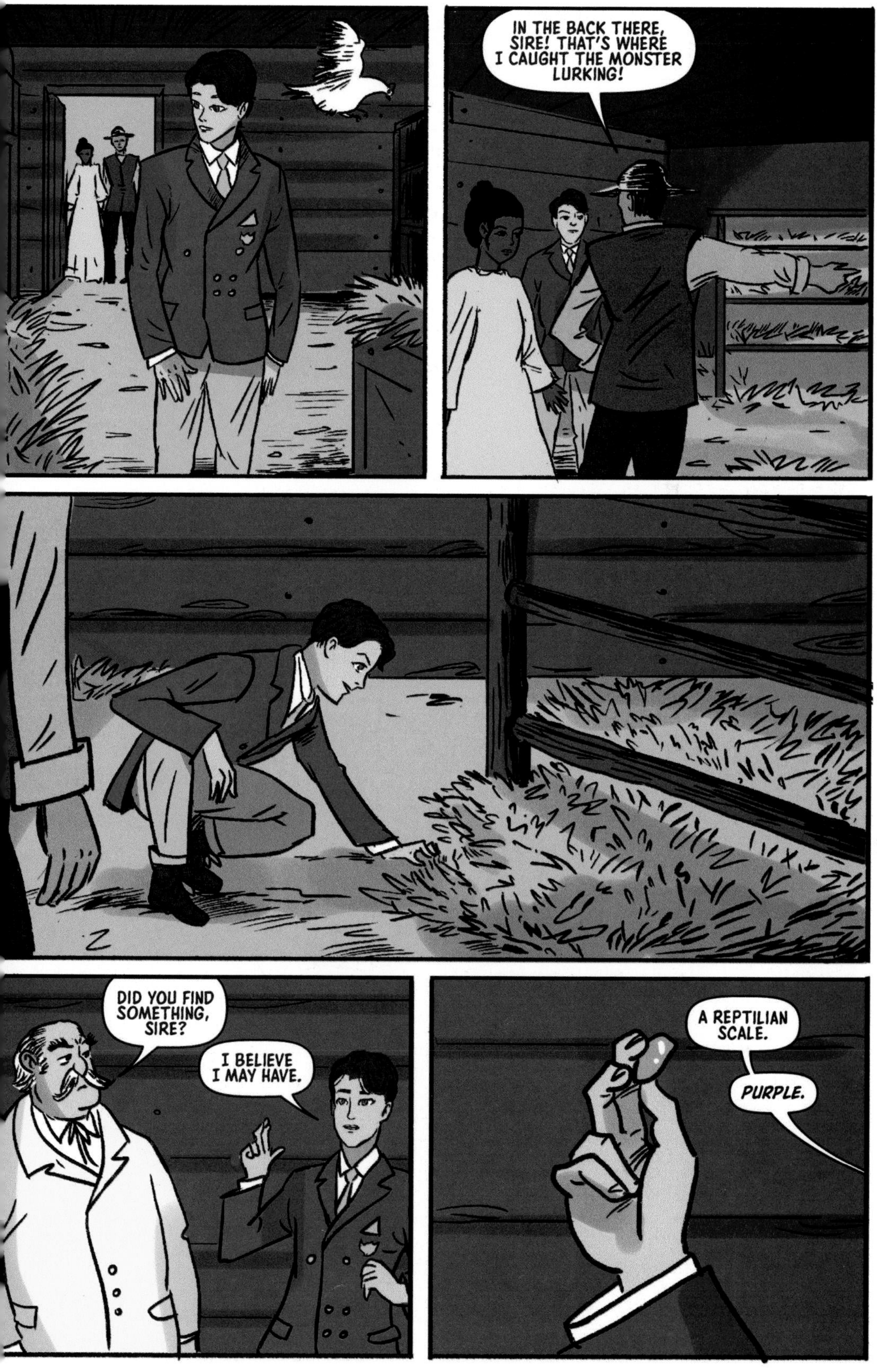
IN THE BACK THERE, SIRE! THAT'S WHERE I CAUGHT THE MONSTER LURKING!
DID YOU FIND SOMETHING, SIRE?
I BELIEVE I MAY HAVE.
A REPTILIAN SCALE.
PURPLE.

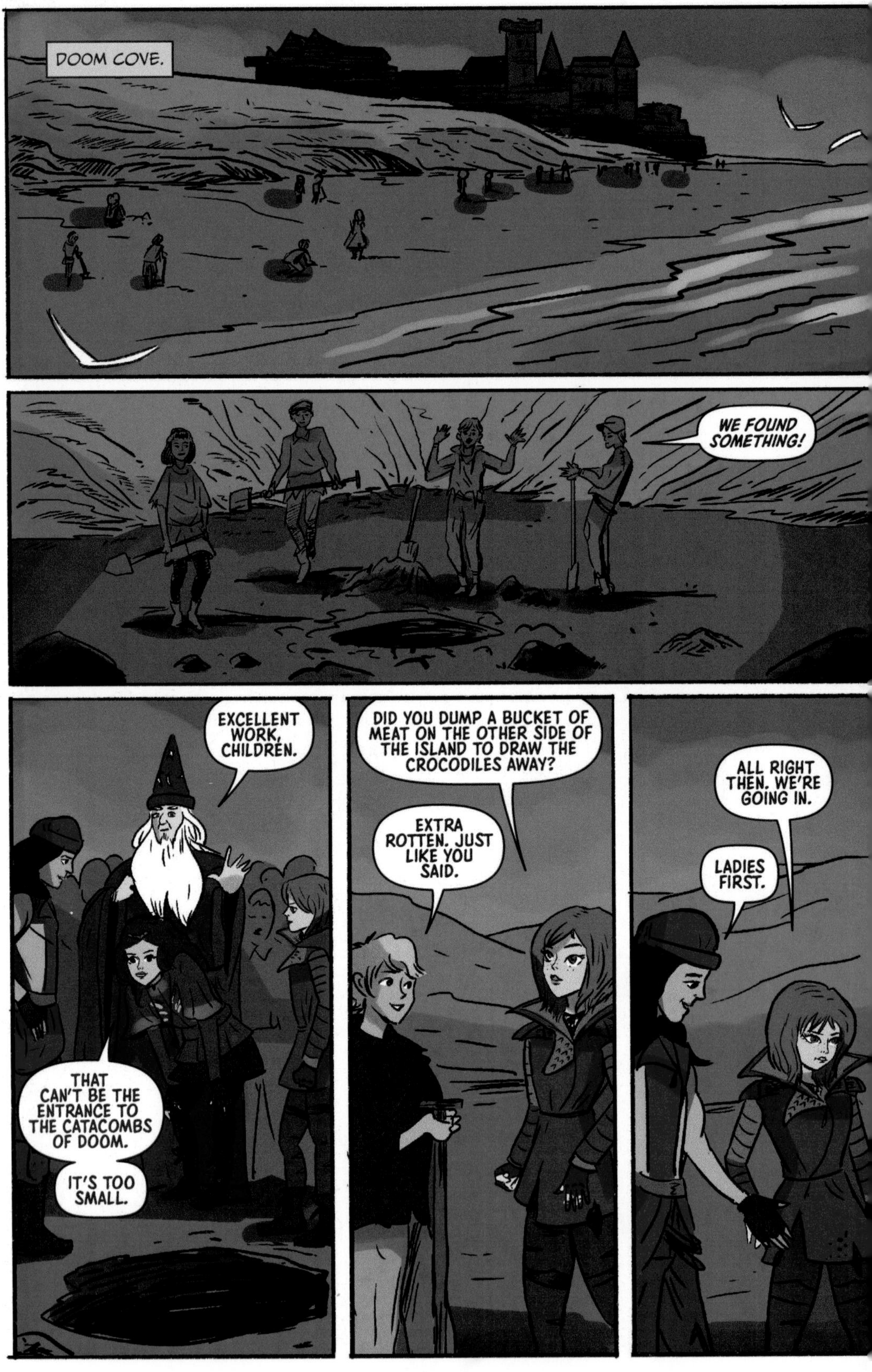
DOOM COVE.
WE FOUND SOMETHING!
EXCELLENT WORK, CHILDREN.
THAT CAN'T BE THE ENTRANCE TO THE CATACOMBS OF DOOM.
IT'S TOO SMALL.
DID YOU DUMP A BUCKET OF MEAT ON THE OTHER SIDE OF THE ISLAND TO DRAW THE CROCODILES AWAY?
EXTRA ROTTEN. JUST LIKE YOU SAID.
ALL RIGHT THEN. WE'RE GOING IN.
LADIES FIRST.

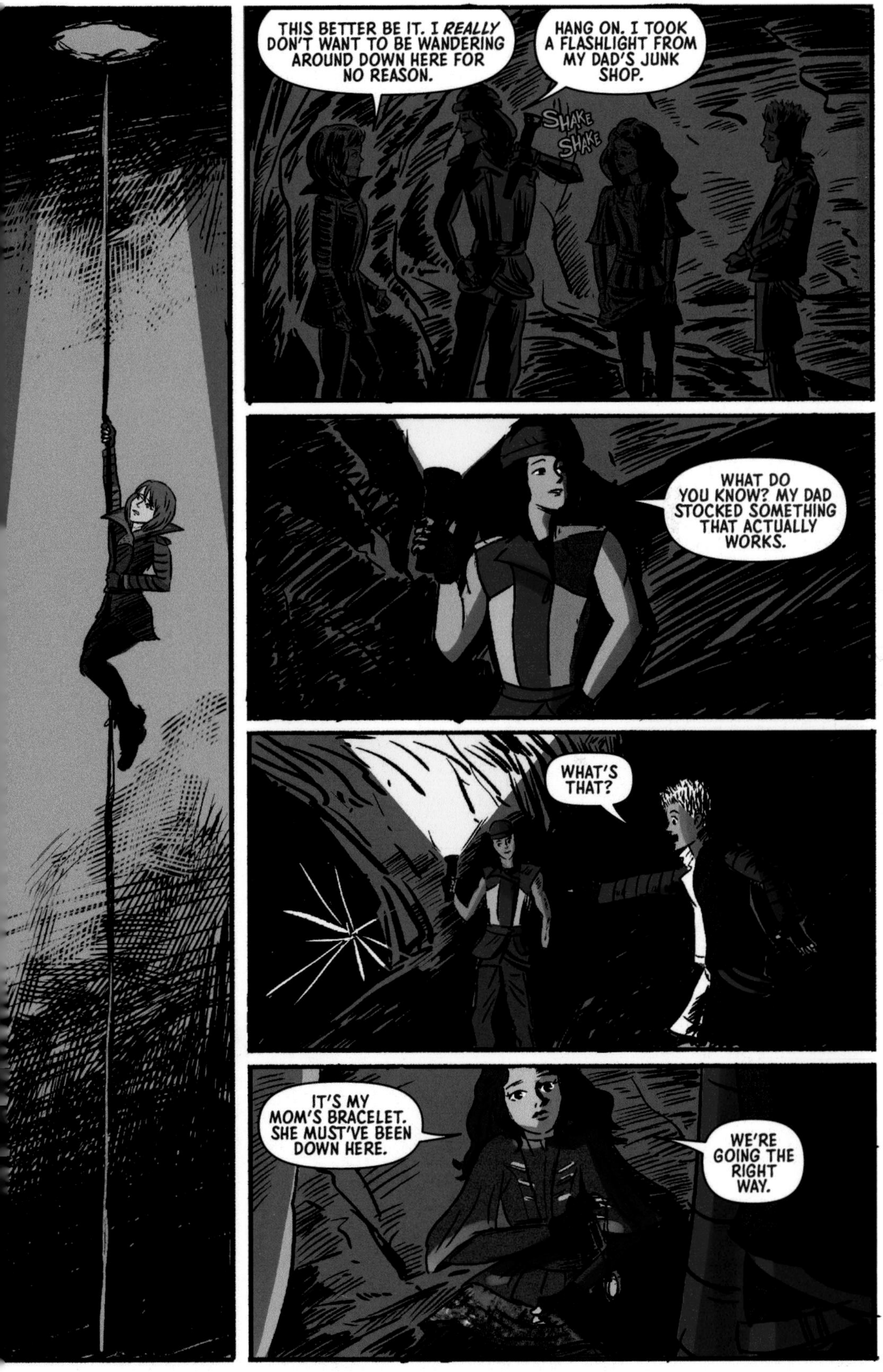
THIS BETTER BE IT. I *REALLY* DON'T WANT TO BE WANDERING AROUND DOWN HERE FOR NO REASON.
HANG ON. I TOOK A FLASHLIGHT FROM MY DAD'S JUNK SHOP.
SHAKE SHAKE
WHAT DO YOU KNOW? MY DAD STOCKED SOMETHING THAT ACTUALLY WORKS.
WHAT'S THAT?
IT'S MY MOM'S BRACELET. SHE MUST'VE BEEN DOWN HERE.
WE'RE GOING THE RIGHT WAY.

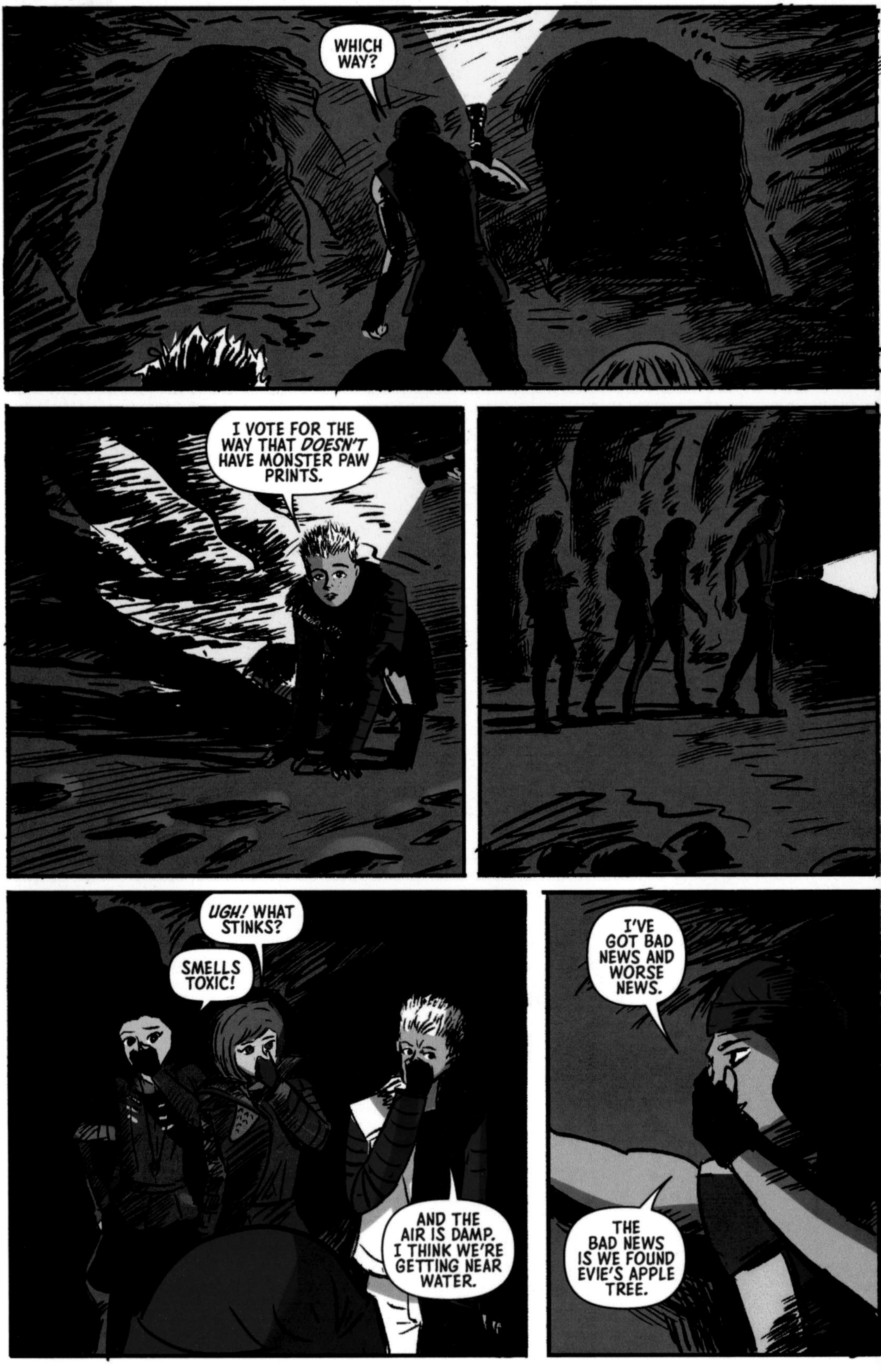
WHICH WAY?
I VOTE FOR THE WAY THAT *DOESN'T* HAVE MONSTER PAW PRINTS.
UGH! WHAT STINKS?
SMELLS TOXIC!
AND THE AIR IS DAMP. I THINK WE'RE GETTING NEAR WATER.
I'VE GOT BAD NEWS AND WORSE NEWS.
THE BAD NEWS IS WE FOUND EVIE'S APPLE TREE.

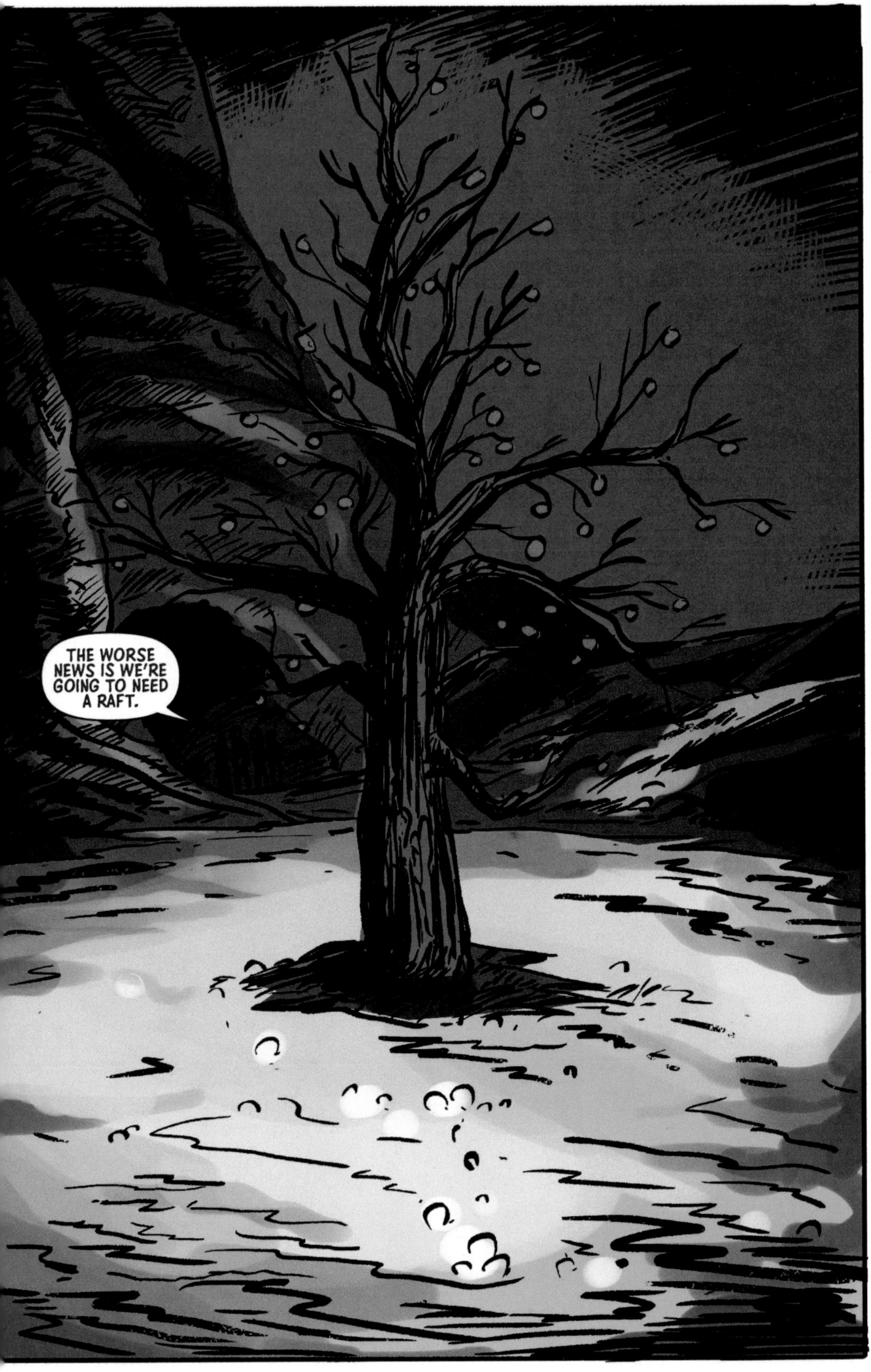
THE WORSE NEWS IS WE'RE GOING TO NEED A RAFT.

AN ISLAND WITHIN AN ISLAND, AND UNDERWATER TOO.

YEN SID IS RIGHT—THE MAGIC DOWN HERE IS *WILD*.

THERE'S NOTHING HERE TO MAKE A RAFT.

WE'LL HAVE TO FIND ANOTHER WAY ACROSS.

GUYS, WATCH THIS.

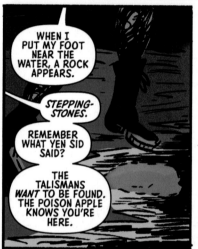

WHEN I PUT MY FOOT NEAR THE WATER, A ROCK APPEARS.

STEPPING-STONES.

REMEMBER WHAT YEN SID SAID?

THE TALISMANS *WANT* TO BE FOUND. THE POISON APPLE KNOWS YOU'RE HERE.

DON'T LET THE WATER TOUCH YOU. MOM TAUGHT ME A LOT ABOUT POISONS.

THIS STUFF WILL MELT US LIKE SUGAR CUBES IN A HOT CUP OF TEA.

SWEET.

IT'S A LOT BIGGER UP CLOSE.

WELL, EVIE, START CLIMBING.

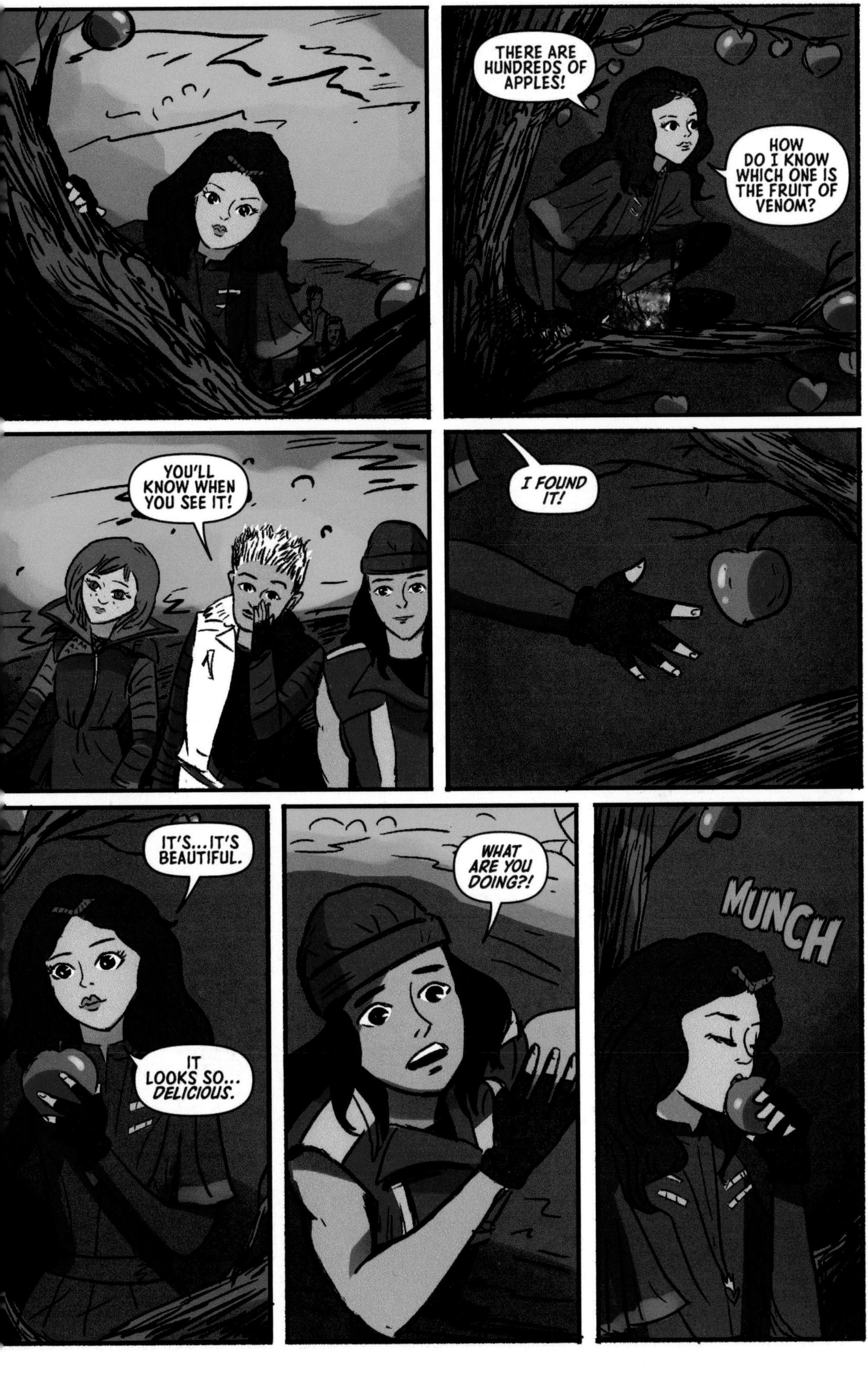
THERE ARE HUNDREDS OF APPLES!
HOW DO I KNOW WHICH ONE IS THE FRUIT OF VENOM?
YOU'LL KNOW WHEN YOU SEE IT!
I FOUND IT!
IT'S...IT'S BEAUTIFUL.
IT LOOKS SO... DELICIOUS.
WHAT ARE YOU DOING?!
MUNCH

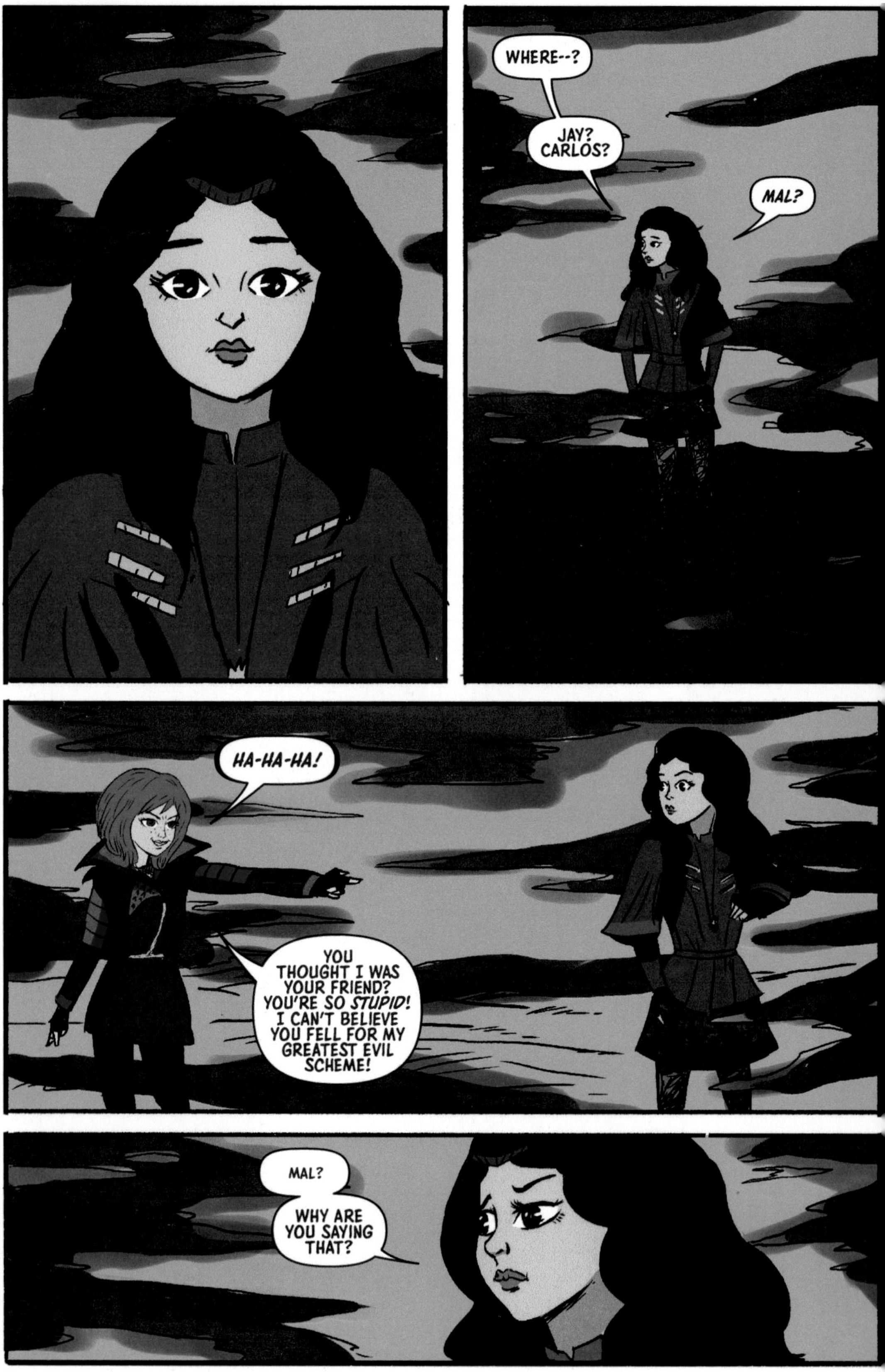
WHERE--?
JAY? CARLOS?
MAL?
HA-HA-HA!
YOU THOUGHT I WAS YOUR FRIEND? YOU'RE SO *STUPID*! I CAN'T BELIEVE YOU FELL FOR MY GREATEST EVIL SCHEME!
MAL?
WHY ARE YOU SAYING THAT?

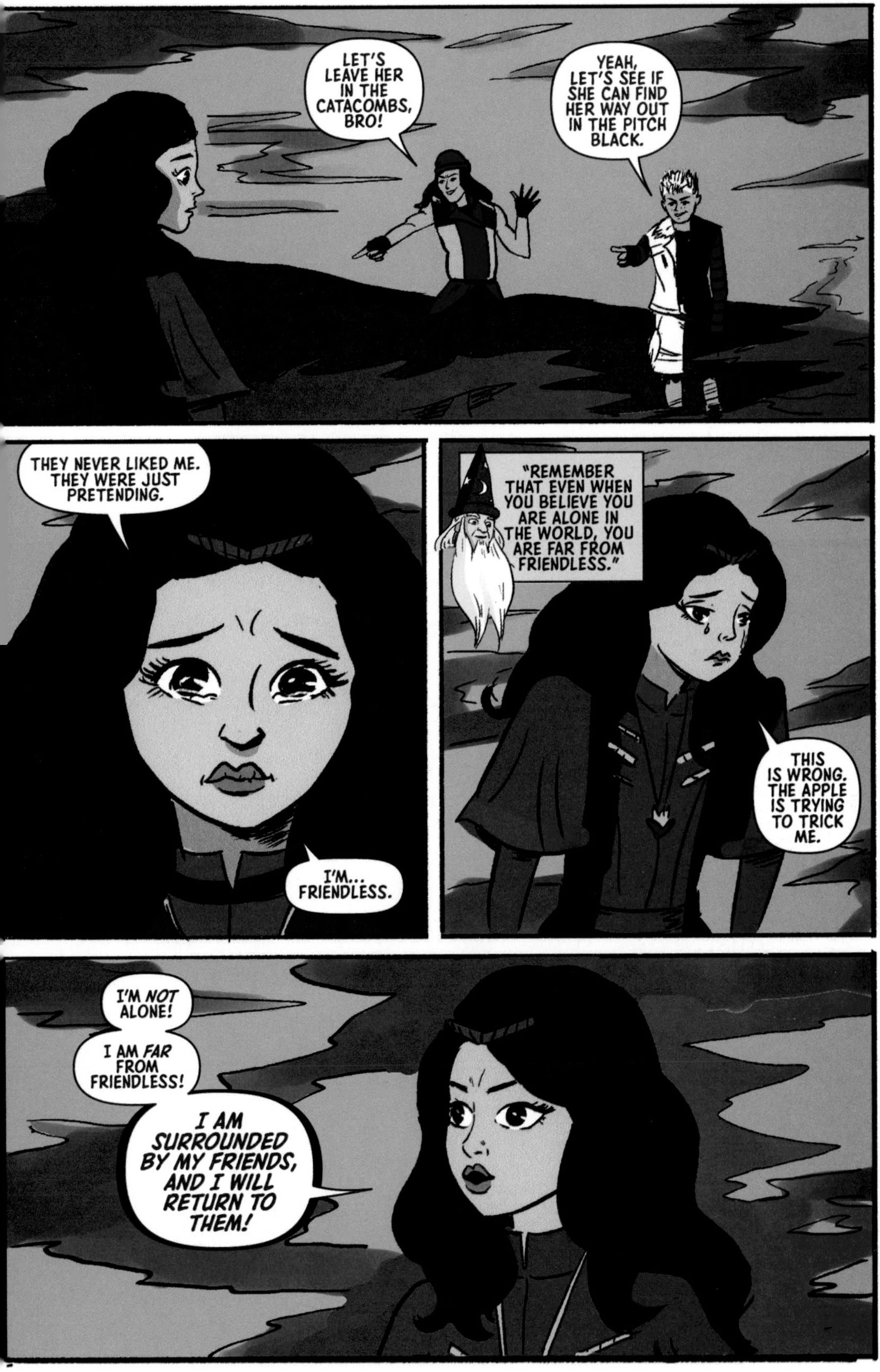
LET'S LEAVE HER IN THE CATACOMBS, BRO!
YEAH, LET'S SEE IF SHE CAN FIND HER WAY OUT IN THE PITCH BLACK.
THEY NEVER LIKED ME. THEY WERE JUST PRETENDING.
I'M... FRIENDLESS.
"REMEMBER THAT EVEN WHEN YOU BELIEVE YOU ARE ALONE IN THE WORLD, YOU ARE FAR FROM FRIENDLESS."
THIS IS WRONG. THE APPLE IS TRYING TO TRICK ME.
I'M *NOT* ALONE!
I AM *FAR* FROM FRIENDLESS!
I AM SURROUNDED BY MY FRIENDS, AND I WILL RETURN TO THEM!

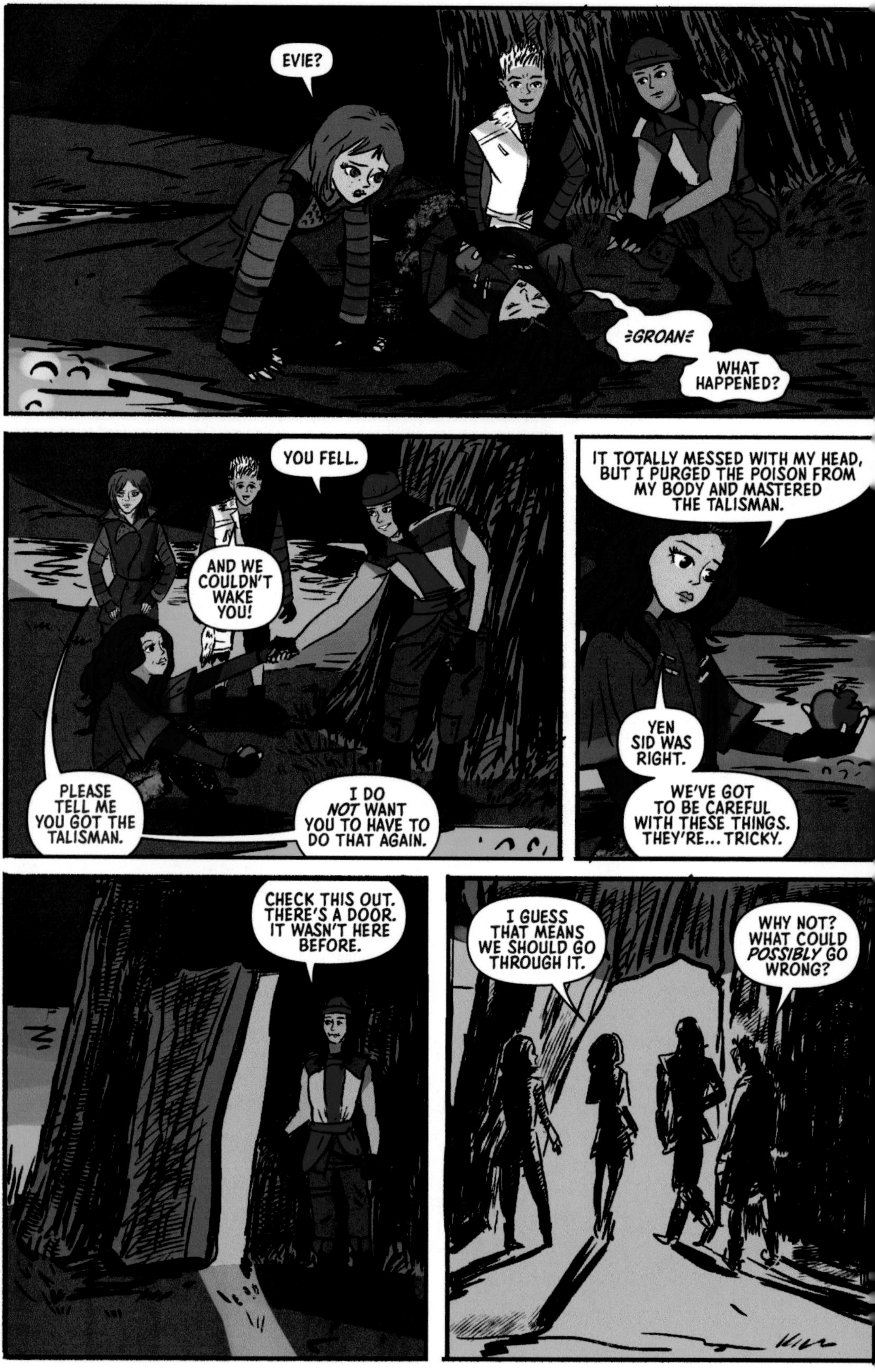
EVIE?
≡GROAN≡
WHAT HAPPENED?
YOU FELL.
AND WE COULDN'T WAKE YOU!
PLEASE TELL ME YOU GOT THE TALISMAN.
I DO *NOT* WANT YOU TO HAVE TO DO THAT AGAIN.
IT TOTALLY MESSED WITH MY HEAD, BUT I PURGED THE POISON FROM MY BODY AND MASTERED THE TALISMAN.
YEN SID WAS RIGHT.
WE'VE GOT TO BE CAREFUL WITH THESE THINGS. THEY'RE... TRICKY.
CHECK THIS OUT. THERE'S A DOOR. IT WASN'T HERE BEFORE.
I GUESS THAT MEANS WE SHOULD GO THROUGH IT.
WHY NOT? WHAT COULD *POSSIBLY* GO WRONG?

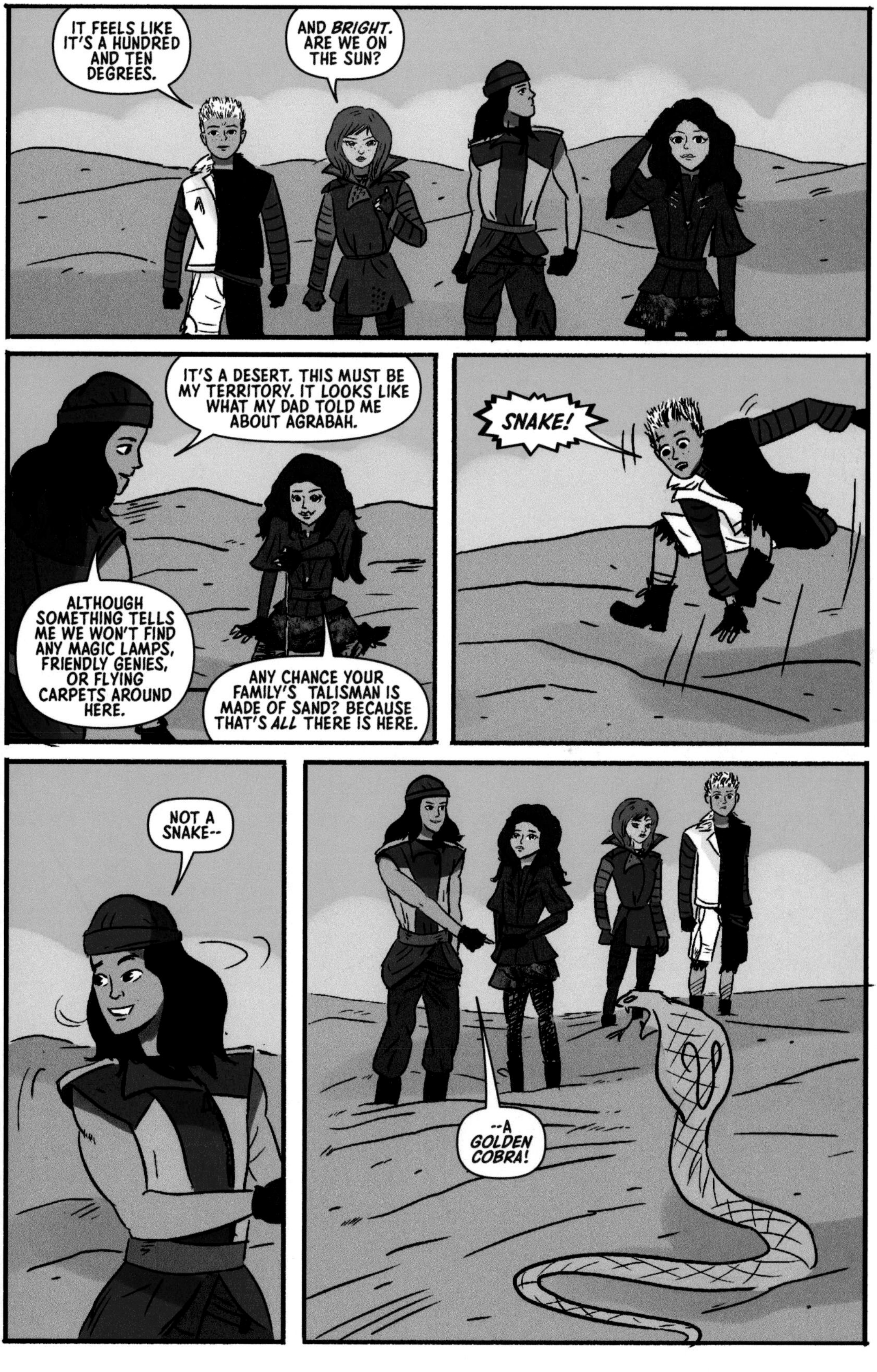
IT FEELS LIKE IT'S A HUNDRED AND TEN DEGREES.
AND *BRIGHT*. ARE WE ON THE SUN?
IT'S A DESERT. THIS MUST BE MY TERRITORY. IT LOOKS LIKE WHAT MY DAD TOLD ME ABOUT AGRABAH.
ALTHOUGH SOMETHING TELLS ME WE WON'T FIND ANY MAGIC LAMPS, FRIENDLY GENIES, OR FLYING CARPETS AROUND HERE.
ANY CHANCE YOUR FAMILY'S TALISMAN IS MADE OF SAND? BECAUSE THAT'S *ALL* THERE IS HERE.
SNAKE!
NOT A SNAKE--
--A *GOLDEN COBRA!*

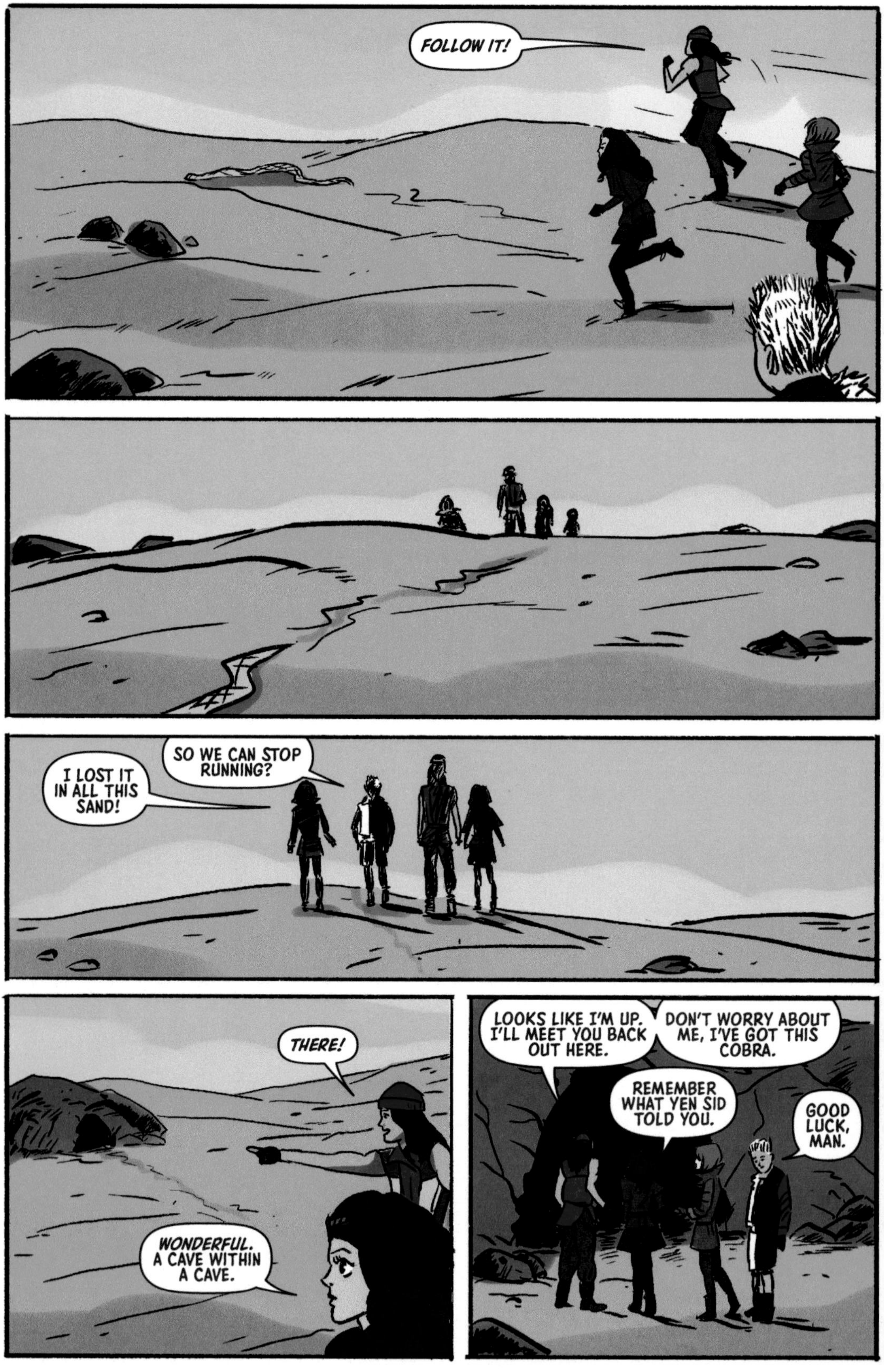
FOLLOW IT!
I LOST IT IN ALL THIS SAND!
SO WE CAN STOP RUNNING?
THERE!
WONDERFUL. A CAVE WITHIN A CAVE.
LOOKS LIKE I'M UP. I'LL MEET YOU BACK OUT HERE.
DON'T WORRY ABOUT ME, I'VE GOT THIS COBRA.
REMEMBER WHAT YEN SID TOLD YOU.
GOOD LUCK, MAN.

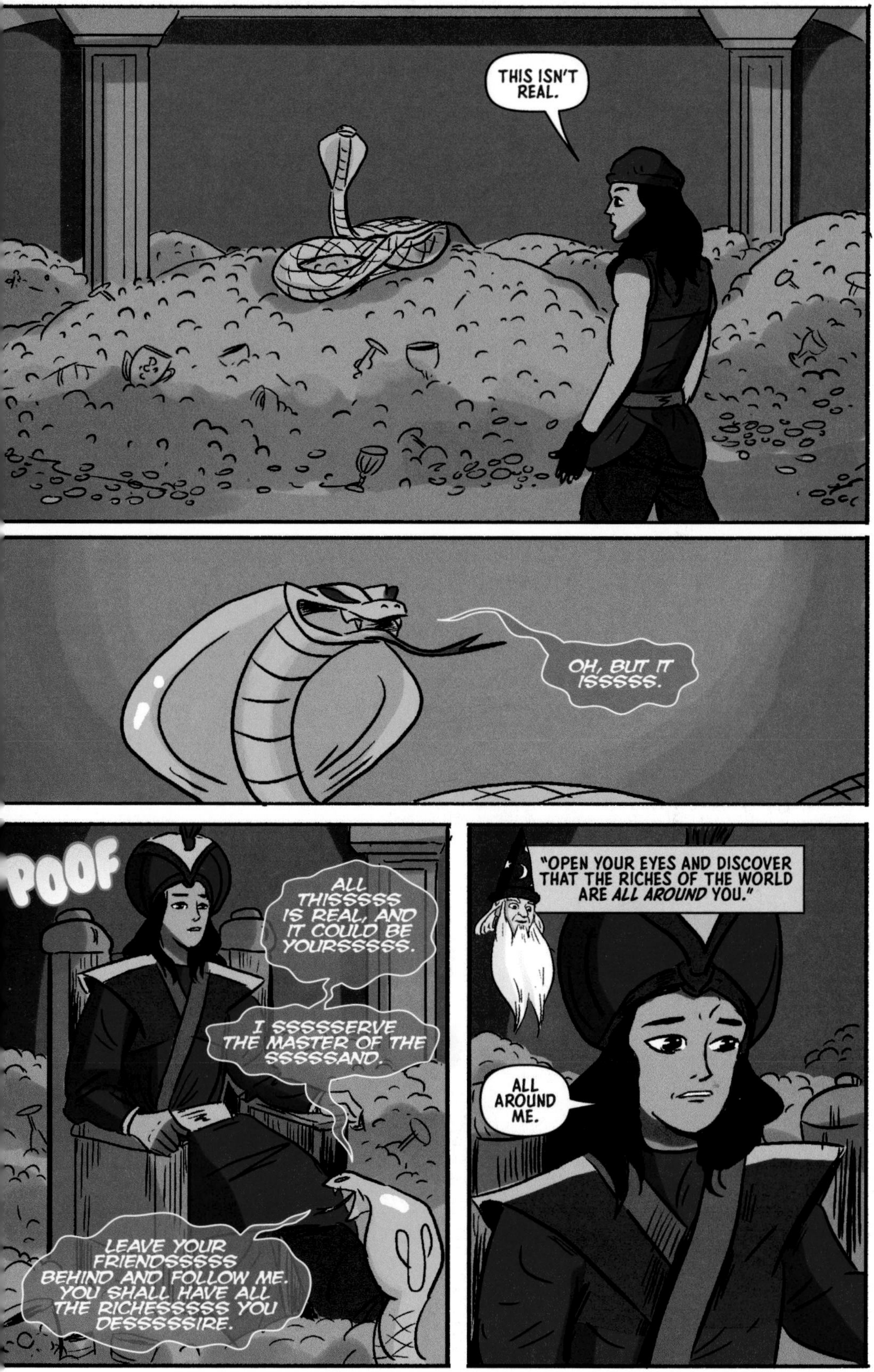
THIS ISN'T REAL.
OH, BUT IT ISSSSS.
POOF
ALL THISSSSS IS REAL, AND IT COULD BE YOURSSSSS.
I SSSSSERVE THE MASTER OF THE SSSSSAND.
LEAVE YOUR FRIENDSSSSS BEHIND AND FOLLOW ME. YOU SHALL HAVE ALL THE RICHESSSSS YOU DESSSSSIRE.
"OPEN YOUR EYES AND DISCOVER THAT THE RICHES OF THE WORLD ARE *ALL AROUND* YOU."
ALL AROUND ME.

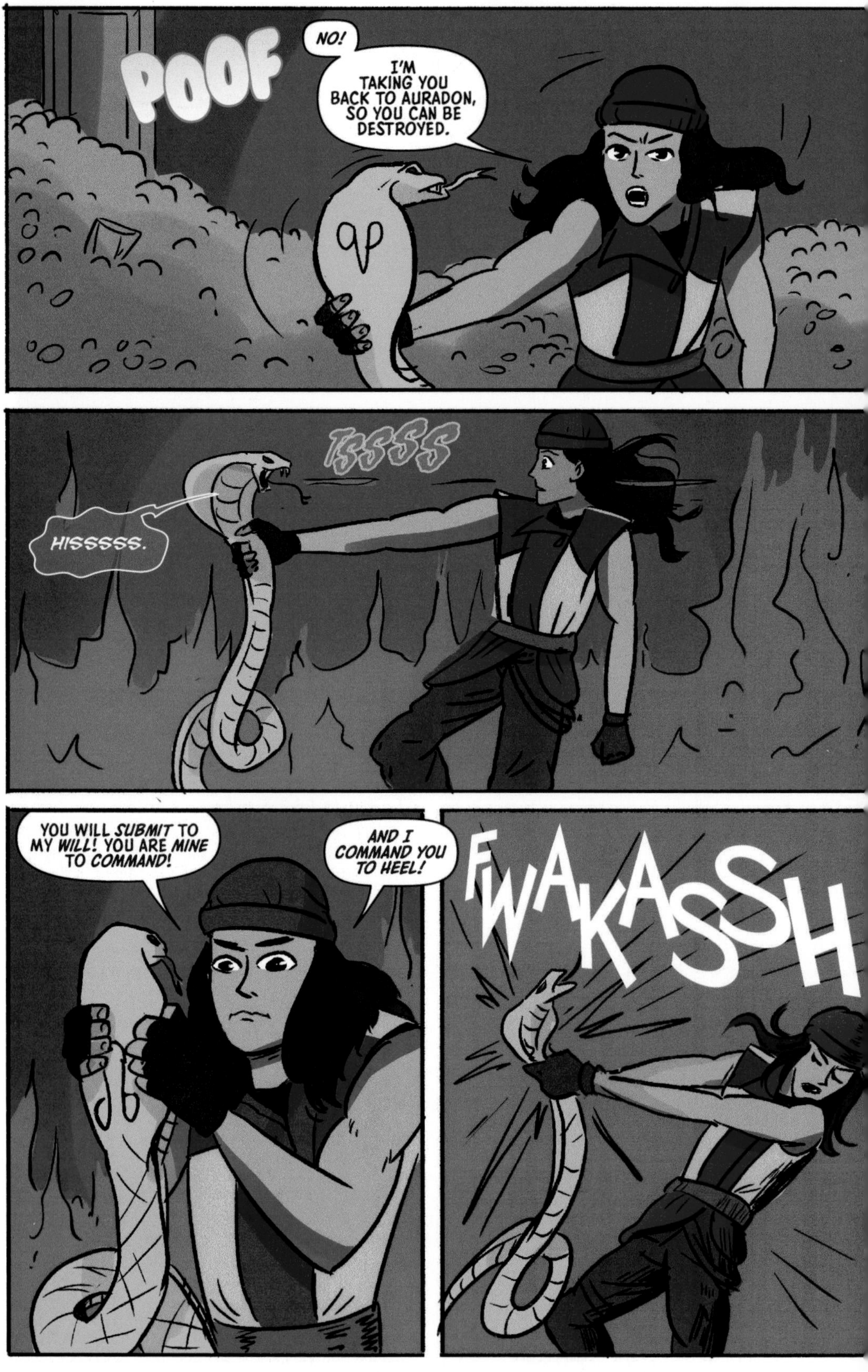
POOF
NO!
I'M TAKING YOU BACK TO AURADON, SO YOU CAN BE DESTROYED.
TSSSS
HISSSSS.
YOU WILL SUBMIT TO MY WILL! YOU ARE MINE TO COMMAND!
AND I COMMAND YOU TO HEEL!
FWAKASSH

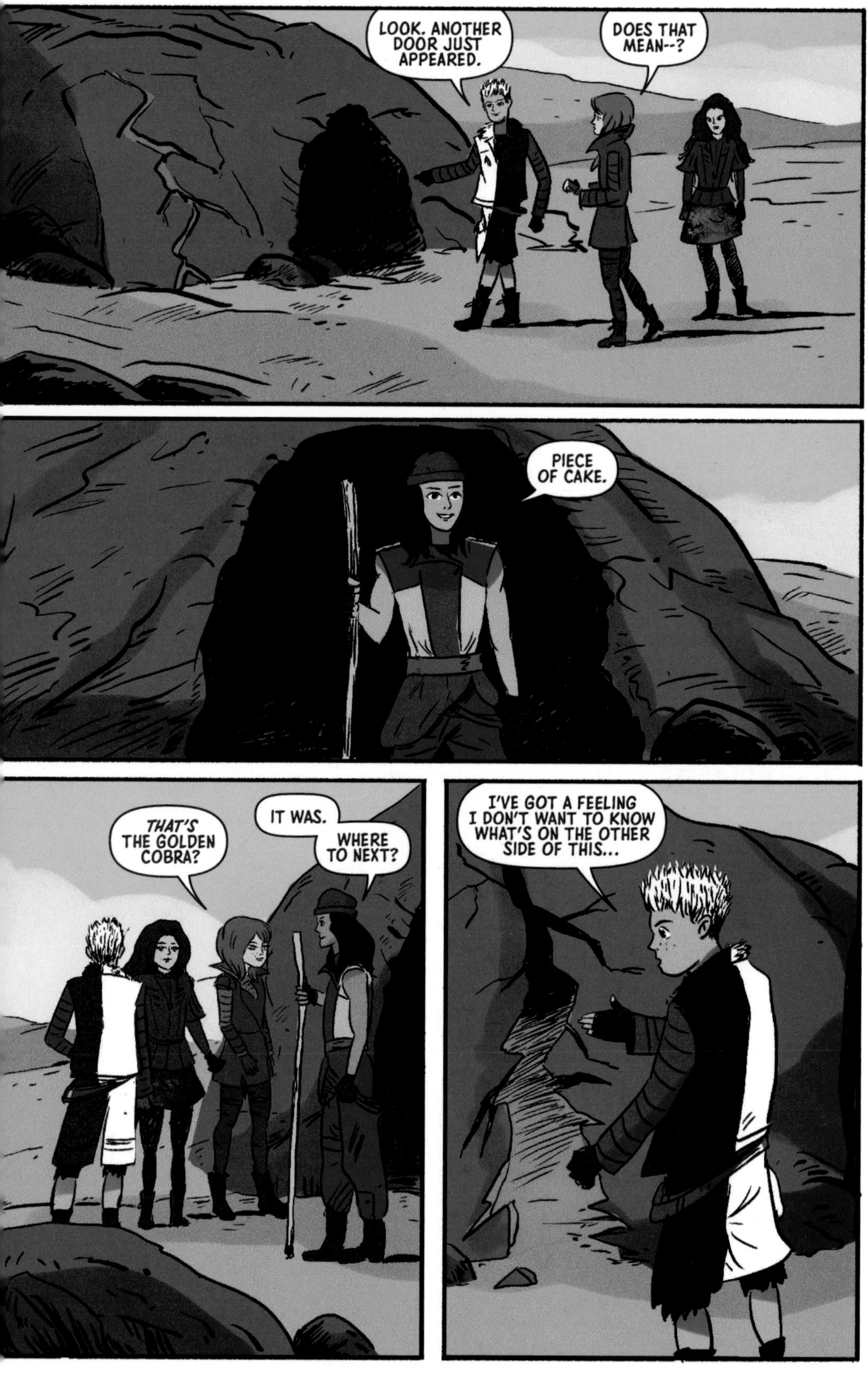
LOOK. ANOTHER DOOR JUST APPEARED.
DOES THAT MEAN--?
PIECE OF CAKE.
THAT'S THE GOLDEN COBRA?
IT WAS.
WHERE TO NEXT?
I'VE GOT A FEELING I DON'T WANT TO KNOW WHAT'S ON THE OTHER SIDE OF THIS...

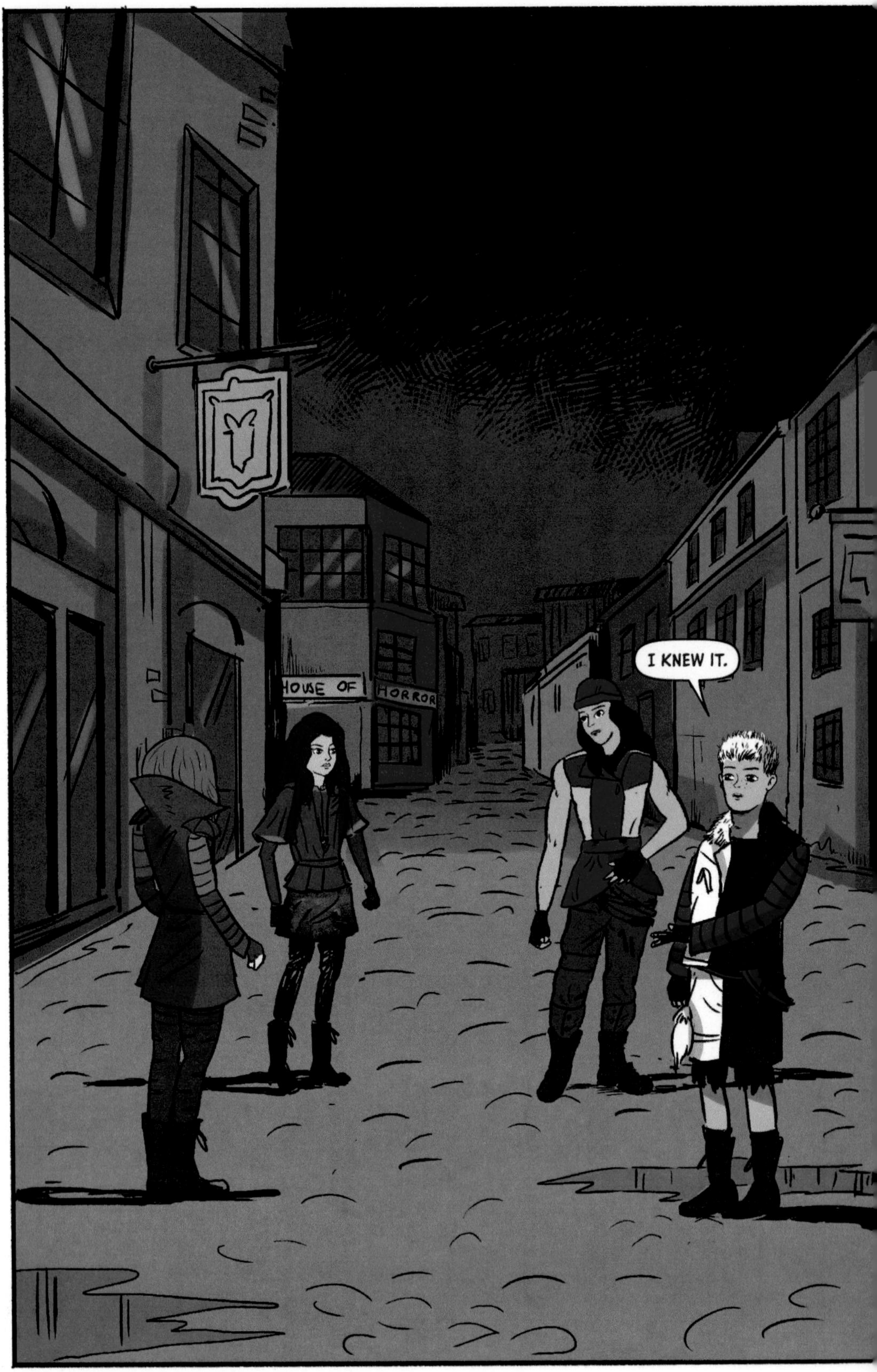
HOUSE OF
HORROR
I KNEW IT.

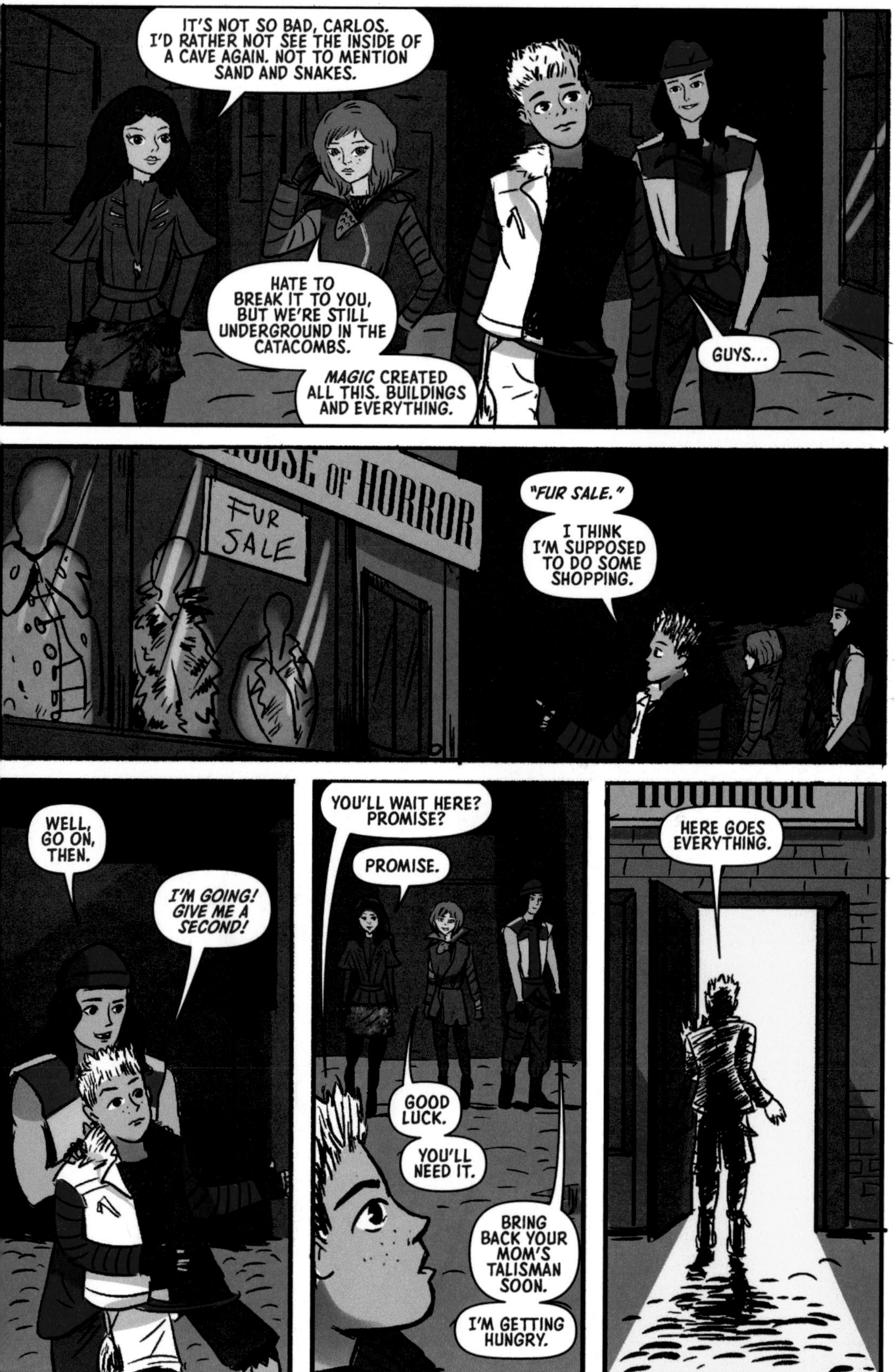
IT'S NOT SO BAD, CARLOS. I'D RATHER NOT SEE THE INSIDE OF A CAVE AGAIN. NOT TO MENTION SAND AND SNAKES.
HATE TO BREAK IT TO YOU, BUT WE'RE STILL UNDERGROUND IN THE CATACOMBS.
MAGIC CREATED ALL THIS. BUILDINGS AND EVERYTHING.
GUYS...
HOUSE OF HORROR
FUR SALE
"FUR SALE."
I THINK I'M SUPPOSED TO DO SOME SHOPPING.
WELL, GO ON, THEN.
I'M GOING! GIVE ME A SECOND!
YOU'LL WAIT HERE? PROMISE?
PROMISE.
GOOD LUCK.
YOU'LL NEED IT.
BRING BACK YOUR MOM'S TALISMAN SOON.
I'M GETTING HUNGRY.
HERE GOES EVERYTHING.

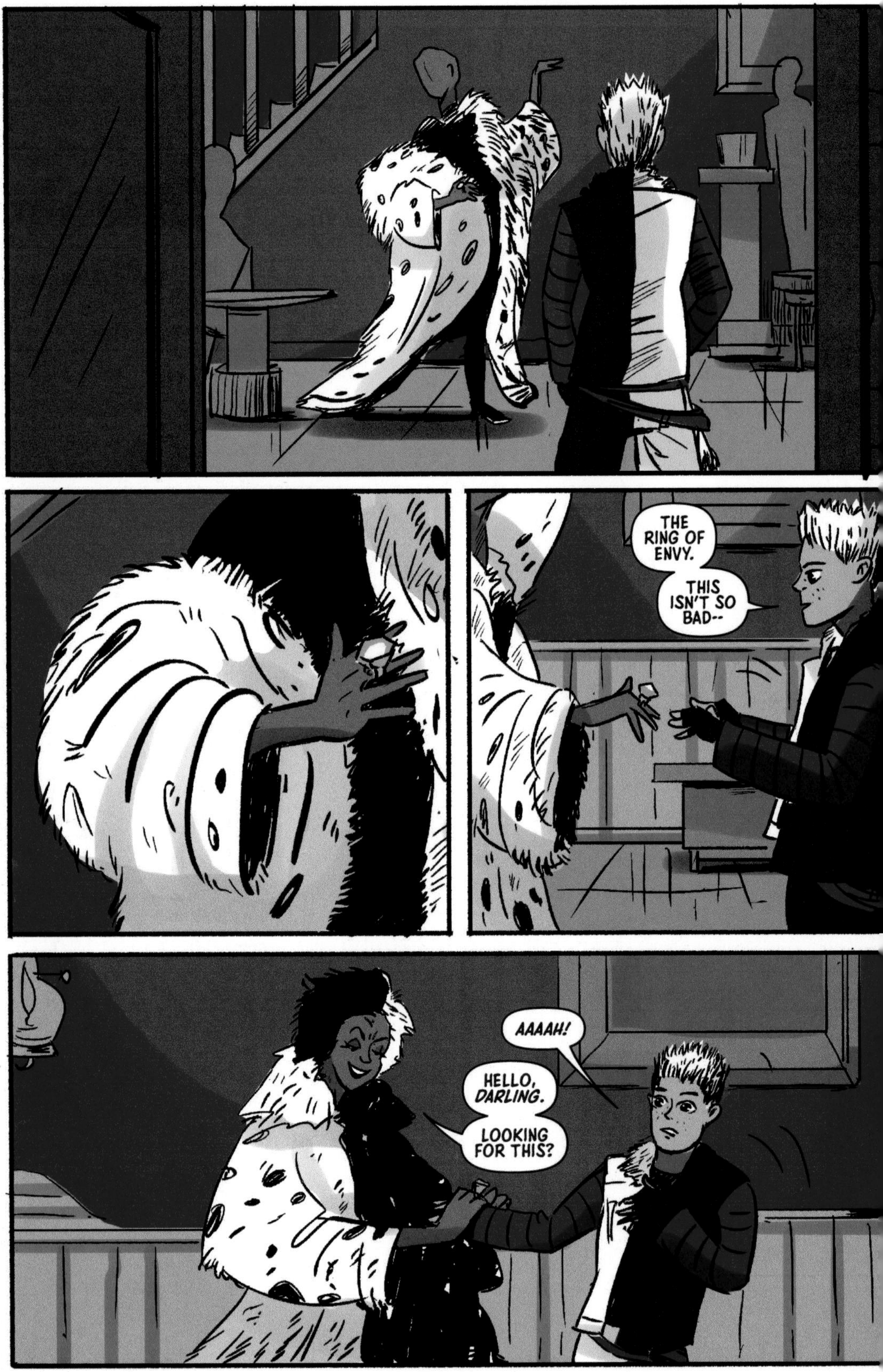
THE RING OF ENVY.
THIS ISN'T SO BAD--
AAAAH!
HELLO, *DARLING*.
LOOKING FOR THIS?

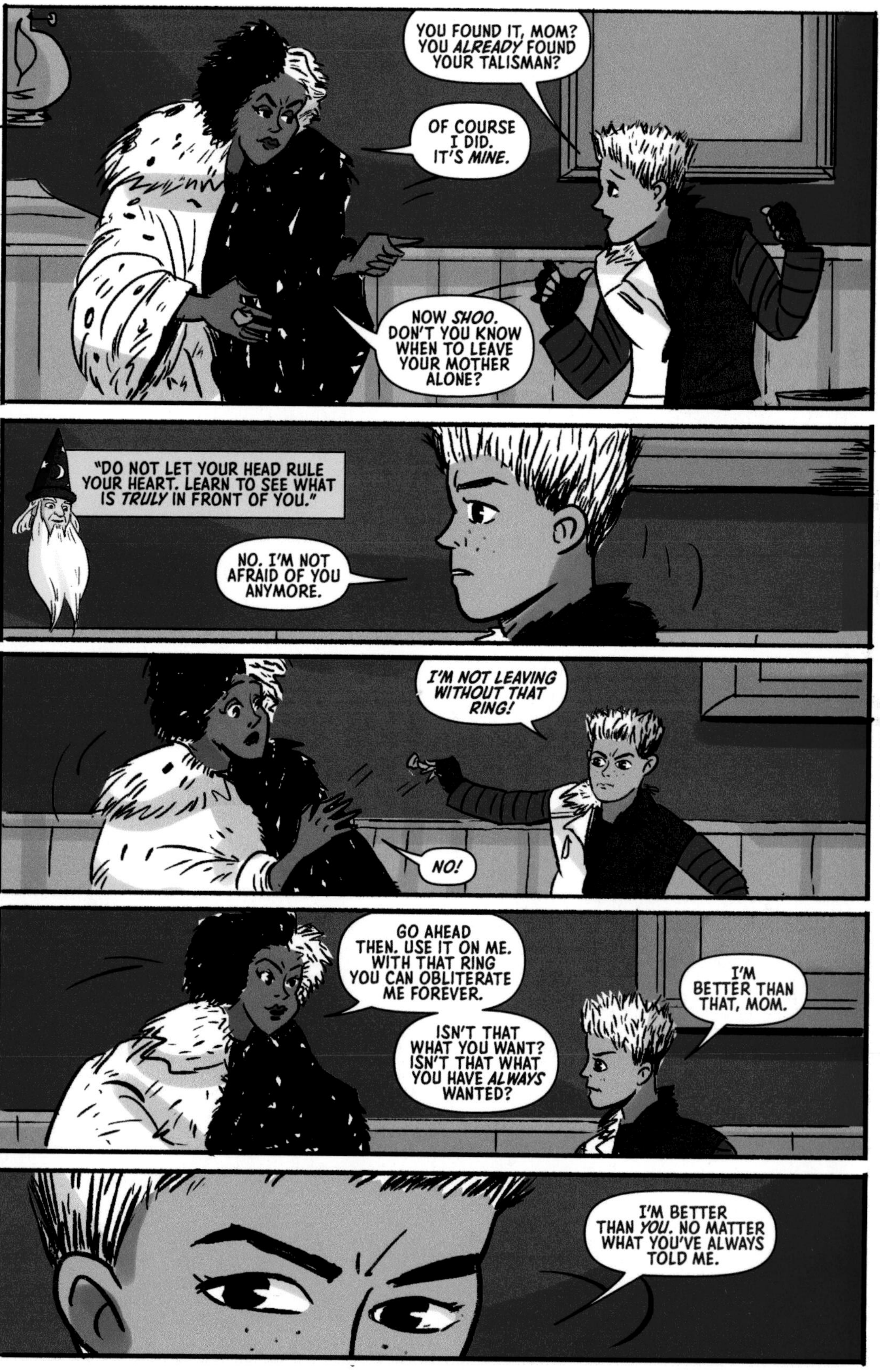
YOU FOUND IT, MOM? YOU *ALREADY* FOUND YOUR TALISMAN?
OF COURSE I DID. IT'S *MINE*.
NOW *SHOO*. DON'T YOU KNOW WHEN TO LEAVE YOUR MOTHER ALONE?
"DO NOT LET YOUR HEAD RULE YOUR HEART. LEARN TO SEE WHAT IS *TRULY* IN FRONT OF YOU."
NO. I'M NOT AFRAID OF YOU ANYMORE.
I'M NOT LEAVING WITHOUT THAT RING!
NO!
GO AHEAD THEN. USE IT ON ME. WITH THAT RING YOU CAN OBLITERATE ME FOREVER.
ISN'T THAT WHAT YOU WANT? ISN'T THAT WHAT YOU HAVE *ALWAYS* WANTED?
I'M BETTER THAN THAT, MOM.
I'M BETTER THAN *YOU*. NO MATTER WHAT YOU'VE ALWAYS TOLD ME.

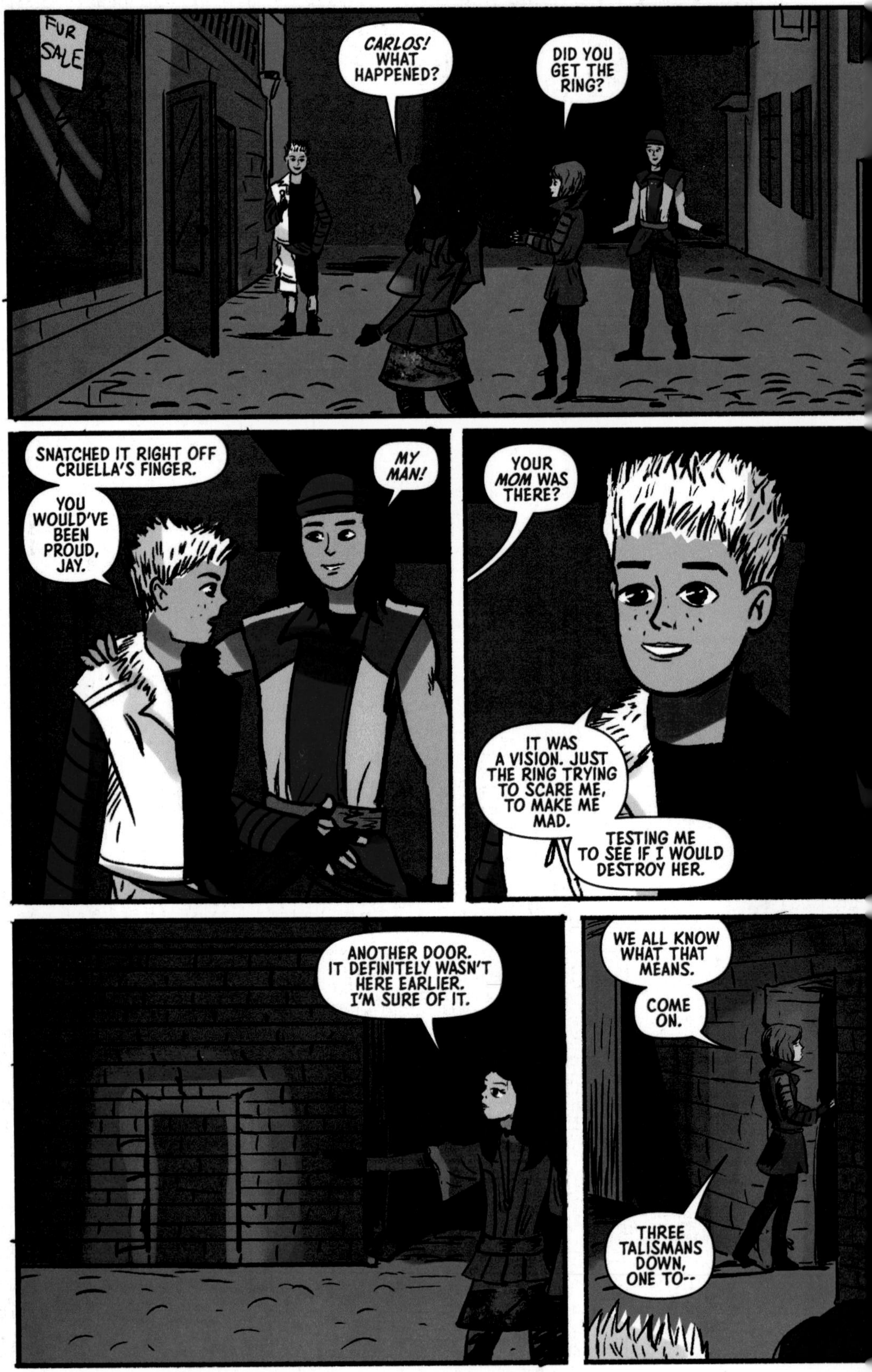
FUR SALE
CARLOS! WHAT HAPPENED?
DID YOU GET THE RING?
SNATCHED IT RIGHT OFF CRUELLA'S FINGER.
YOU WOULD'VE BEEN PROUD, JAY.
MY MAN!
YOUR MOM WAS THERE?
IT WAS A VISION. JUST THE RING TRYING TO SCARE ME, TO MAKE ME MAD.
TESTING ME TO SEE IF I WOULD DESTROY HER.
ANOTHER DOOR. IT DEFINITELY WASN'T HERE EARLIER. I'M SURE OF IT.
WE ALL KNOW WHAT THAT MEANS.
COME ON.
THREE TALISMANS DOWN, ONE TO--

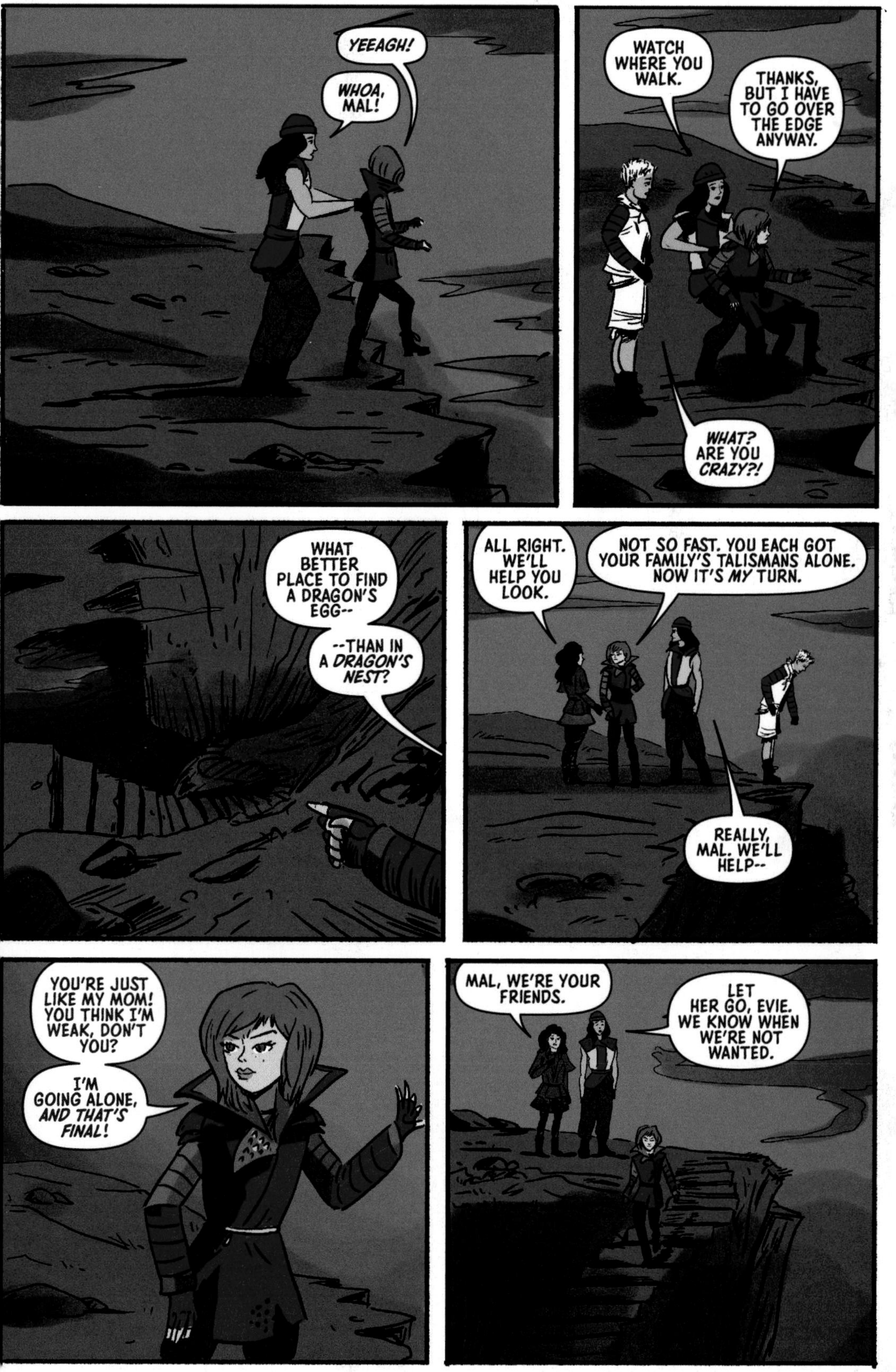
YEEAGH!
WHOA, MAL!
WATCH WHERE YOU WALK.
THANKS, BUT I HAVE TO GO OVER THE EDGE ANYWAY.
WHAT? ARE YOU CRAZY?!
WHAT BETTER PLACE TO FIND A DRAGON'S EGG--
--THAN IN A DRAGON'S NEST?
ALL RIGHT. WE'LL HELP YOU LOOK.
NOT SO FAST. YOU EACH GOT YOUR FAMILY'S TALISMANS ALONE. NOW IT'S MY TURN.
REALLY, MAL. WE'LL HELP--
YOU'RE JUST LIKE MY MOM! YOU THINK I'M WEAK, DON'T YOU?
I'M GOING ALONE, AND THAT'S FINAL!
MAL, WE'RE YOUR FRIENDS.
LET HER GO, EVIE. WE KNOW WHEN WE'RE NOT WANTED.

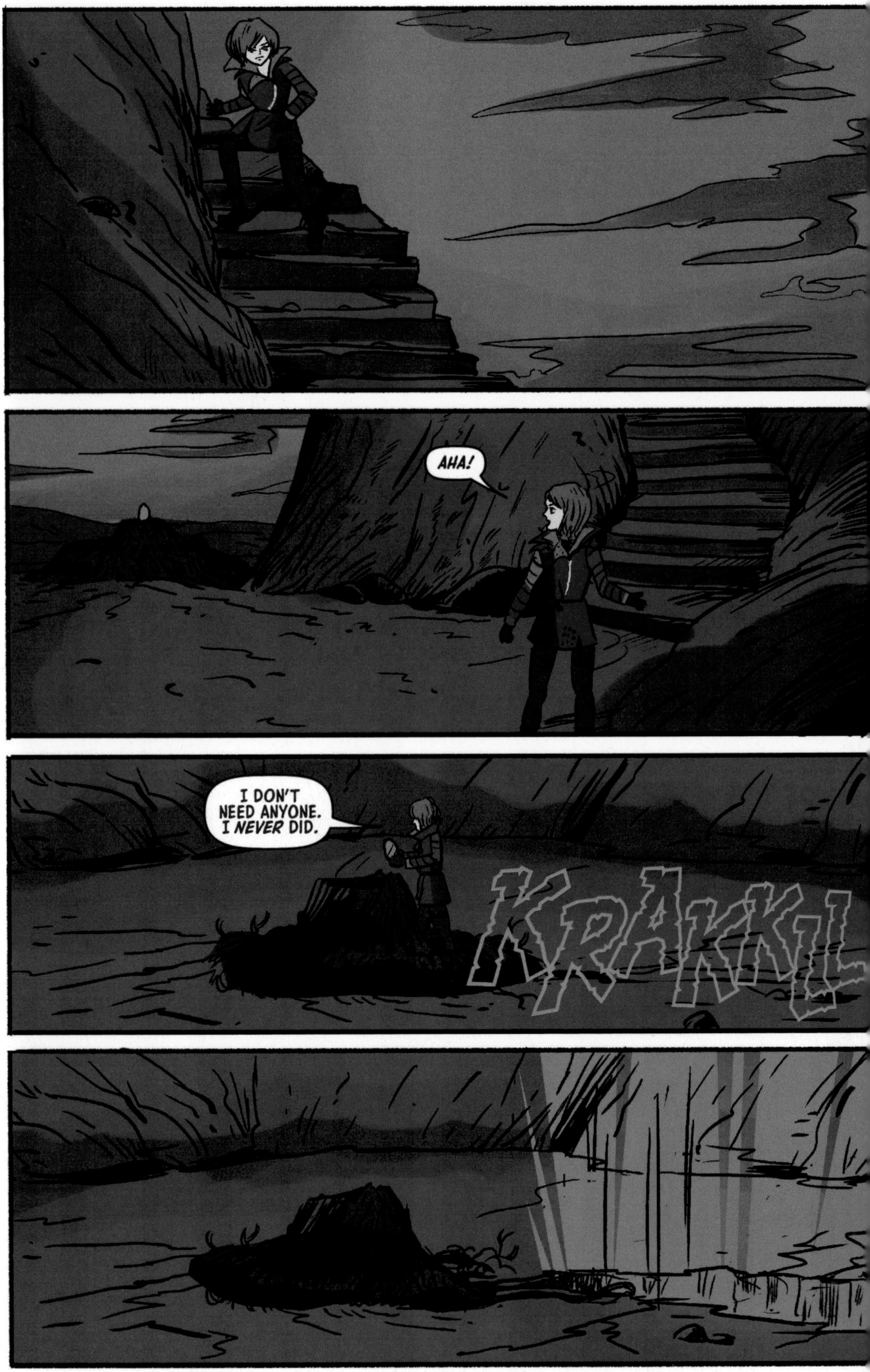
AHA!
I DON'T NEED ANYONE. I *NEVER* DID.
KRAKKL

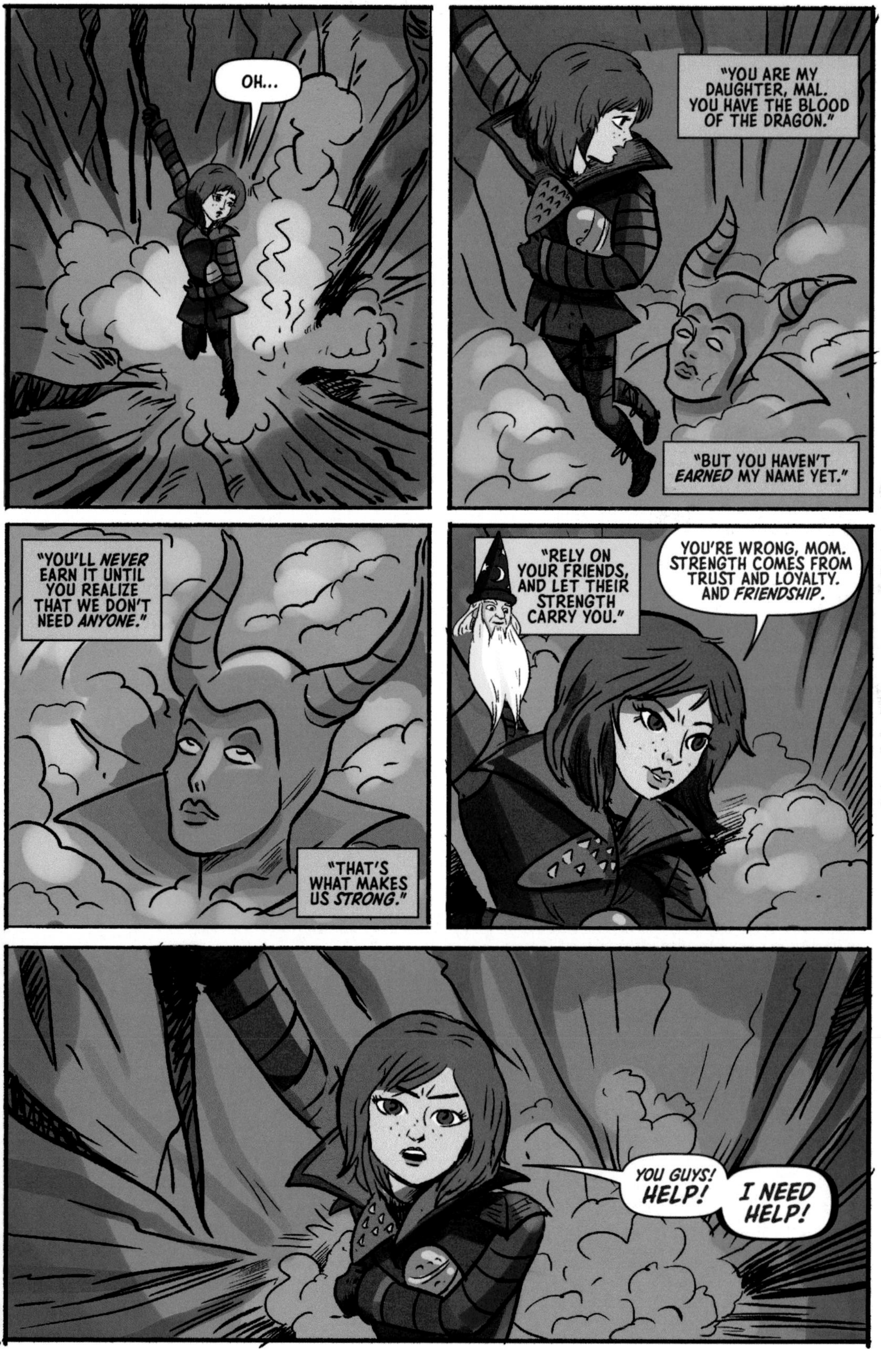
OH...
"YOU ARE MY DAUGHTER, MAL. YOU HAVE THE BLOOD OF THE DRAGON."
"BUT YOU HAVEN'T *EARNED* MY NAME YET."
"YOU'LL *NEVER* EARN IT UNTIL YOU REALIZE THAT WE DON'T NEED *ANYONE*."
"THAT'S WHAT MAKES US *STRONG*."
"RELY ON YOUR FRIENDS, AND LET THEIR STRENGTH CARRY YOU."
YOU'RE WRONG, MOM. STRENGTH COMES FROM TRUST AND LOYALTY. AND *FRIENDSHIP*.
YOU GUYS! HELP!
I NEED HELP!

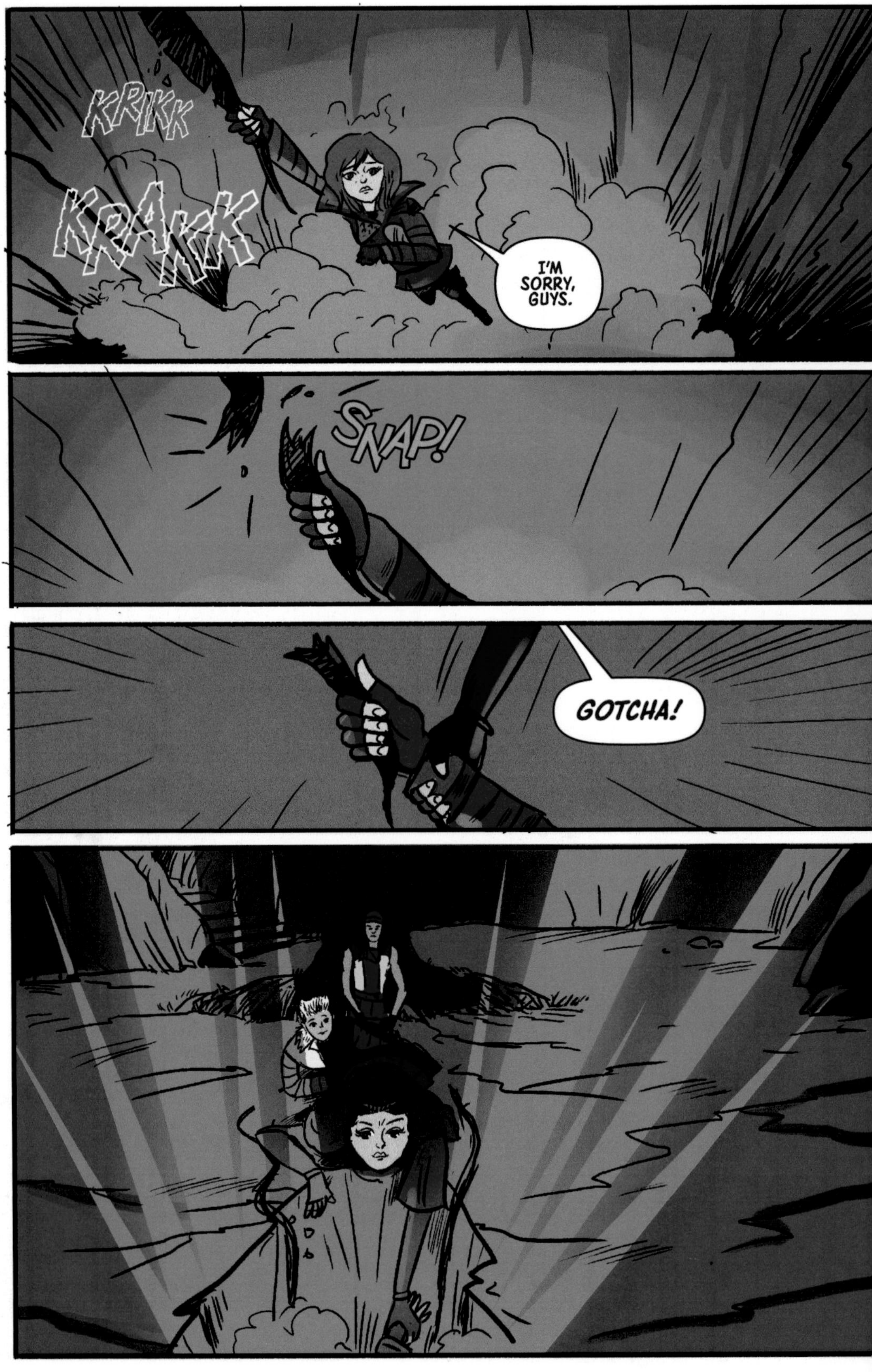
KRIKK
KRAKK
I'M SORRY, GUYS.
SNAP!
GOTCHA!

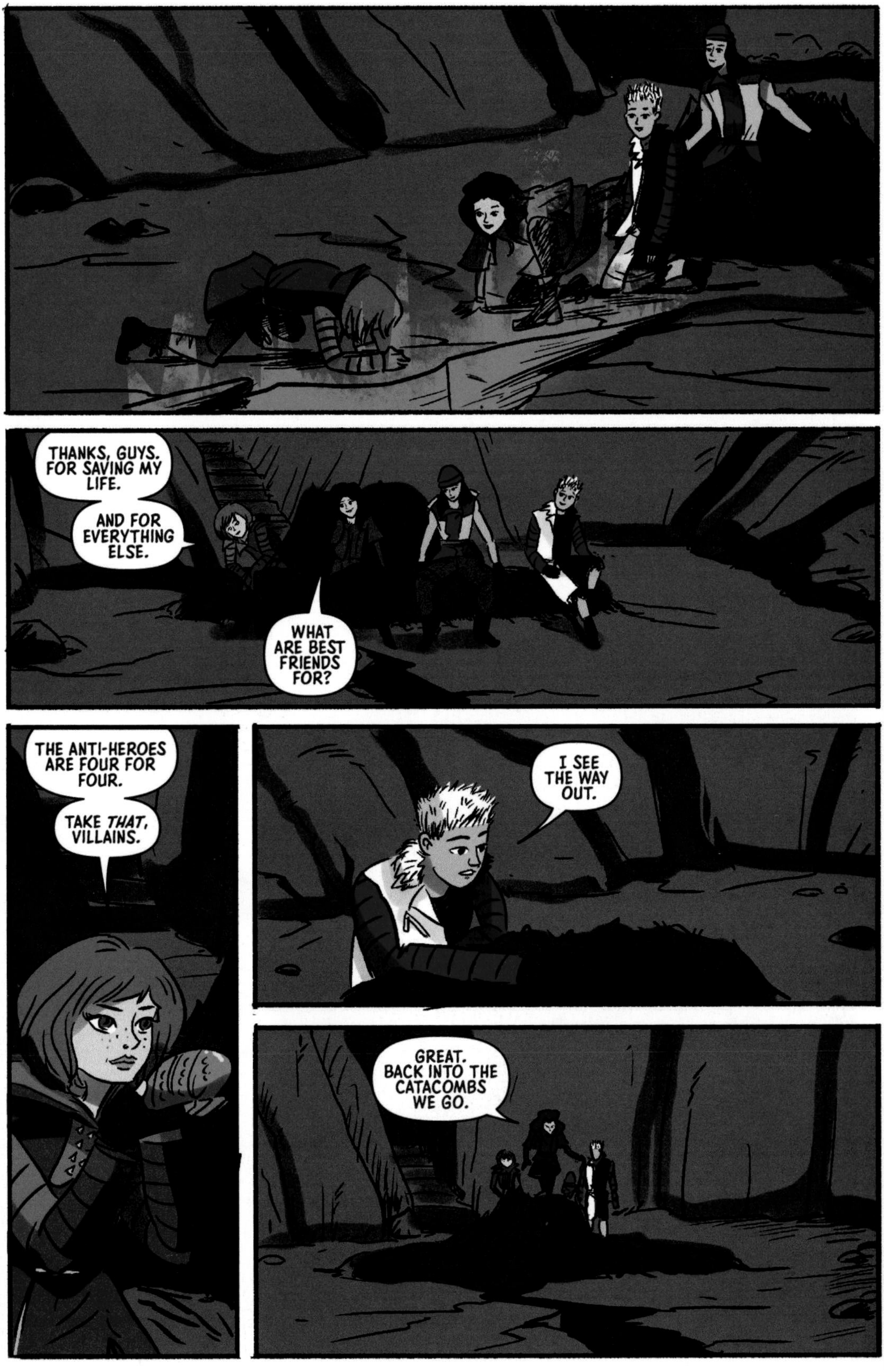
THANKS, GUYS. FOR SAVING MY LIFE.
AND FOR EVERYTHING ELSE.
WHAT ARE BEST FRIENDS FOR?
THE ANTI-HEROES ARE FOUR FOR FOUR.
TAKE *THAT*, VILLAINS.
I SEE THE WAY OUT.
GREAT. BACK INTO THE CATACOMBS WE GO.

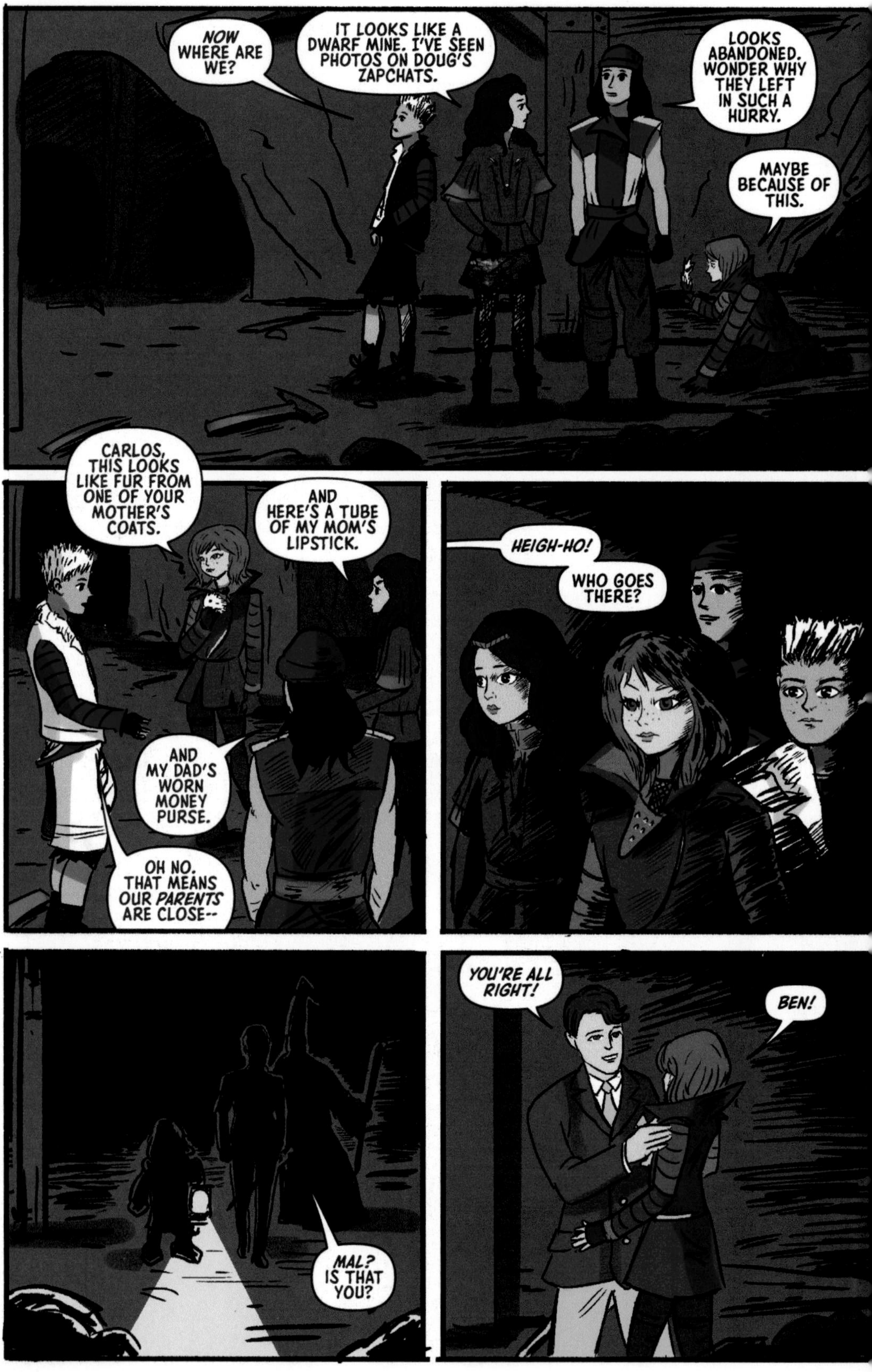
NOW WHERE ARE WE?
IT LOOKS LIKE A DWARF MINE. I'VE SEEN PHOTOS ON DOUG'S ZAPCHATS.
LOOKS ABANDONED. WONDER WHY THEY LEFT IN SUCH A HURRY.
MAYBE BECAUSE OF THIS.
CARLOS, THIS LOOKS LIKE FUR FROM ONE OF YOUR MOTHER'S COATS.
AND HERE'S A TUBE OF MY MOM'S LIPSTICK.
AND MY DAD'S WORN MONEY PURSE.
OH NO. THAT MEANS OUR *PARENTS* ARE CLOSE--
HEIGH-HO!
WHO GOES THERE?
MAL? IS THAT YOU?
YOU'RE ALL RIGHT!
BEN!

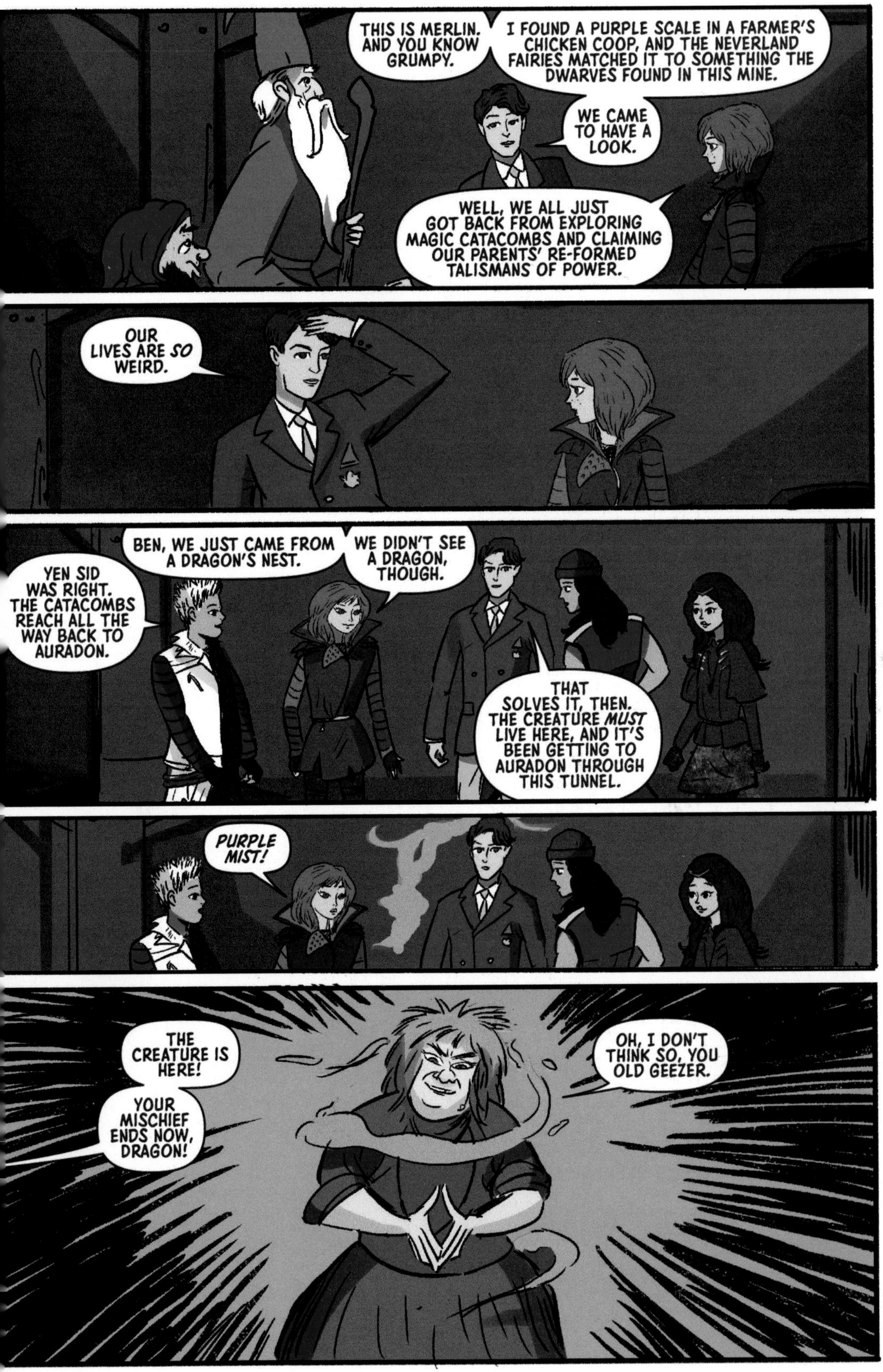
THIS IS MERLIN. AND YOU KNOW GRUMPY.
I FOUND A PURPLE SCALE IN A FARMER'S CHICKEN COOP, AND THE NEVERLAND FAIRIES MATCHED IT TO SOMETHING THE DWARVES FOUND IN THIS MINE.
WE CAME TO HAVE A LOOK.
WELL, WE ALL JUST GOT BACK FROM EXPLORING MAGIC CATACOMBS AND CLAIMING OUR PARENTS' RE-FORMED TALISMANS OF POWER.
OUR LIVES ARE *SO* WEIRD.
YEN SID WAS RIGHT. THE CATACOMBS REACH ALL THE WAY BACK TO AURADON.
BEN, WE JUST CAME FROM A DRAGON'S NEST.
WE DIDN'T SEE A DRAGON, THOUGH.
THAT SOLVES IT, THEN. THE CREATURE *MUST* LIVE HERE, AND IT'S BEEN GETTING TO AURADON THROUGH THIS TUNNEL.
PURPLE MIST!
THE CREATURE IS HERE!
YOUR MISCHIEF ENDS NOW, DRAGON!
OH, I DON'T THINK SO, YOU OLD GEEZER.

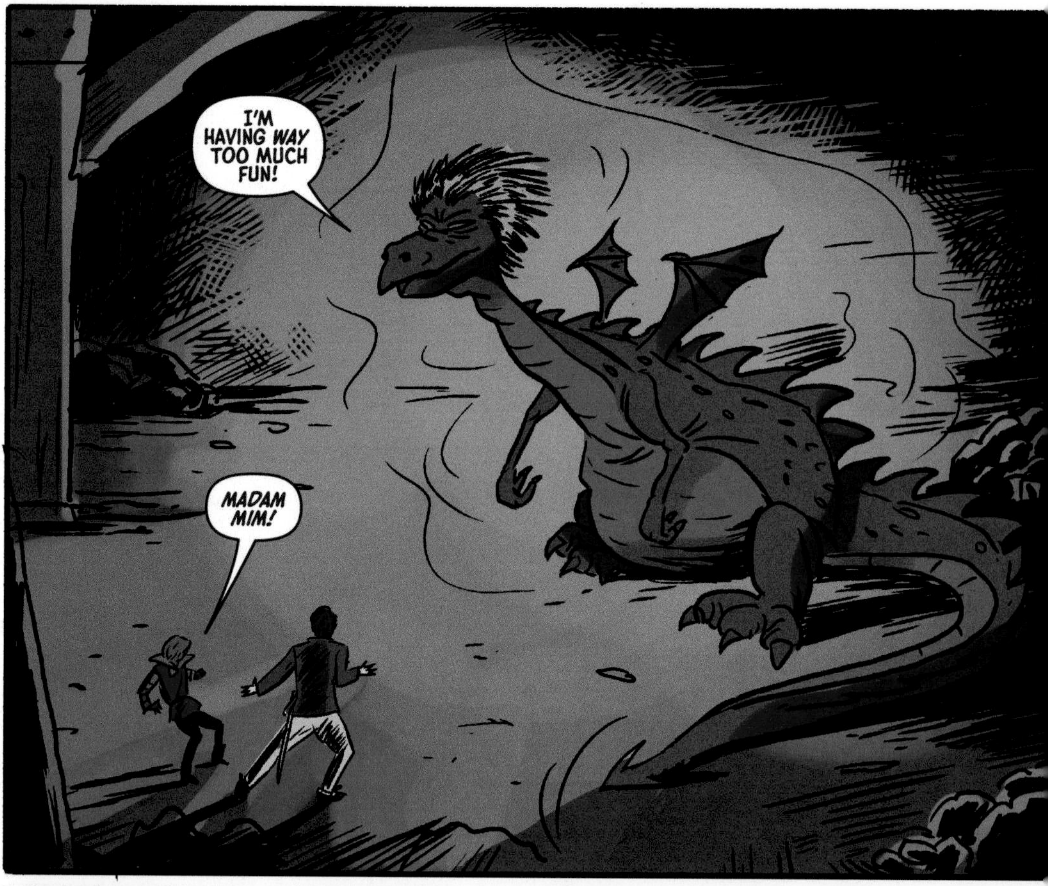
I'M HAVING *WAY* TOO MUCH FUN!
MADAM MIM!

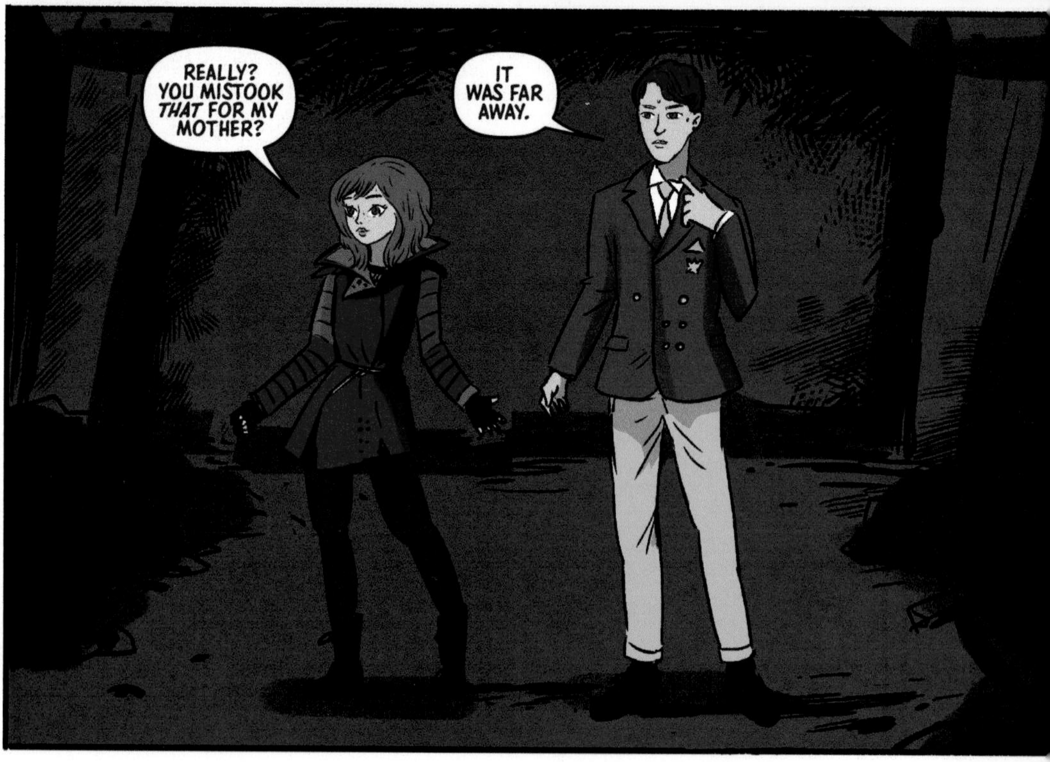
REALLY? YOU MISTOOK *THAT* FOR MY MOTHER?
IT WAS FAR AWAY.

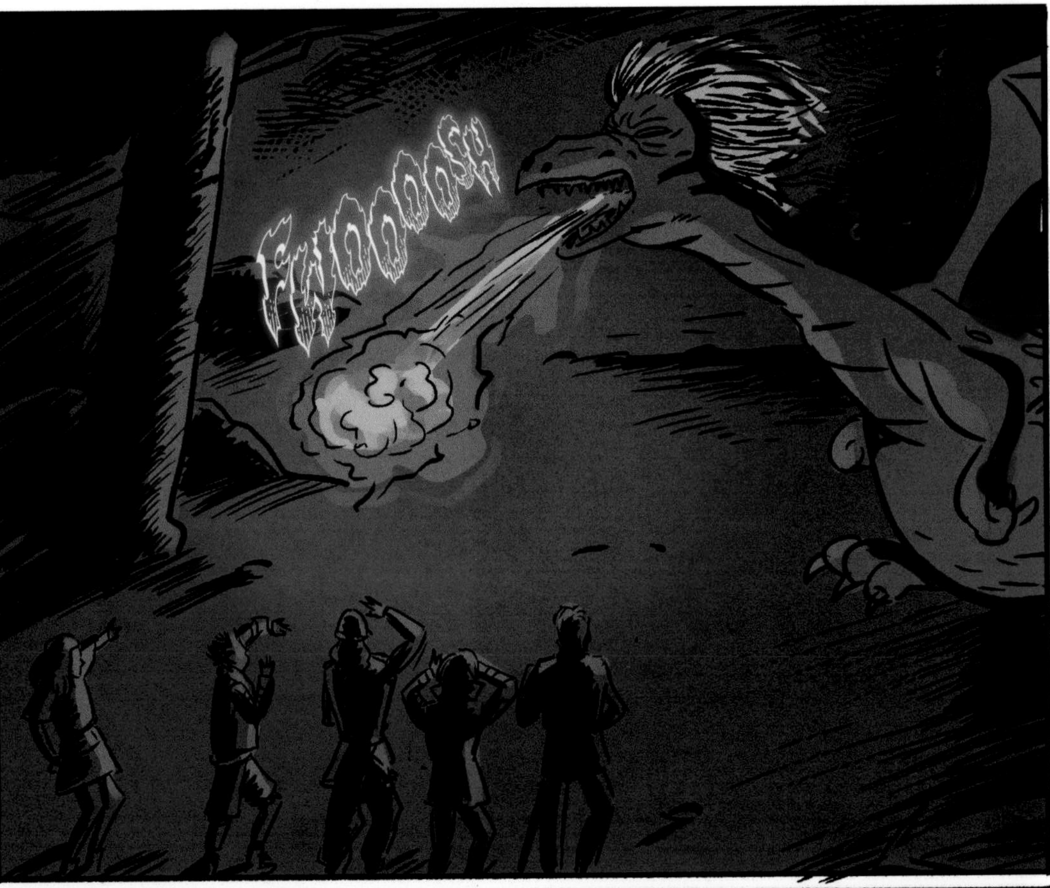
FWOOOOSH

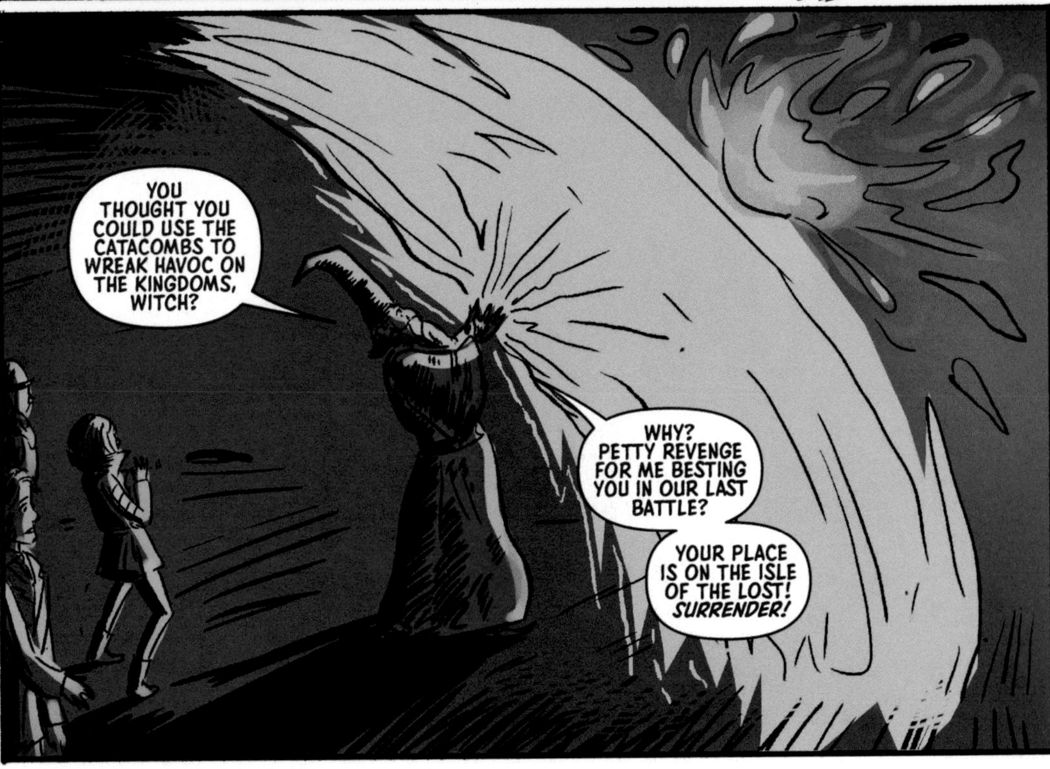
YOU THOUGHT YOU COULD USE THE CATACOMBS TO WREAK HAVOC ON THE KINGDOMS, WITCH?
WHY? PETTY REVENGE FOR ME BESTING YOU IN OUR LAST BATTLE?
YOUR PLACE IS ON THE ISLE OF THE LOST! *SURRENDER!*

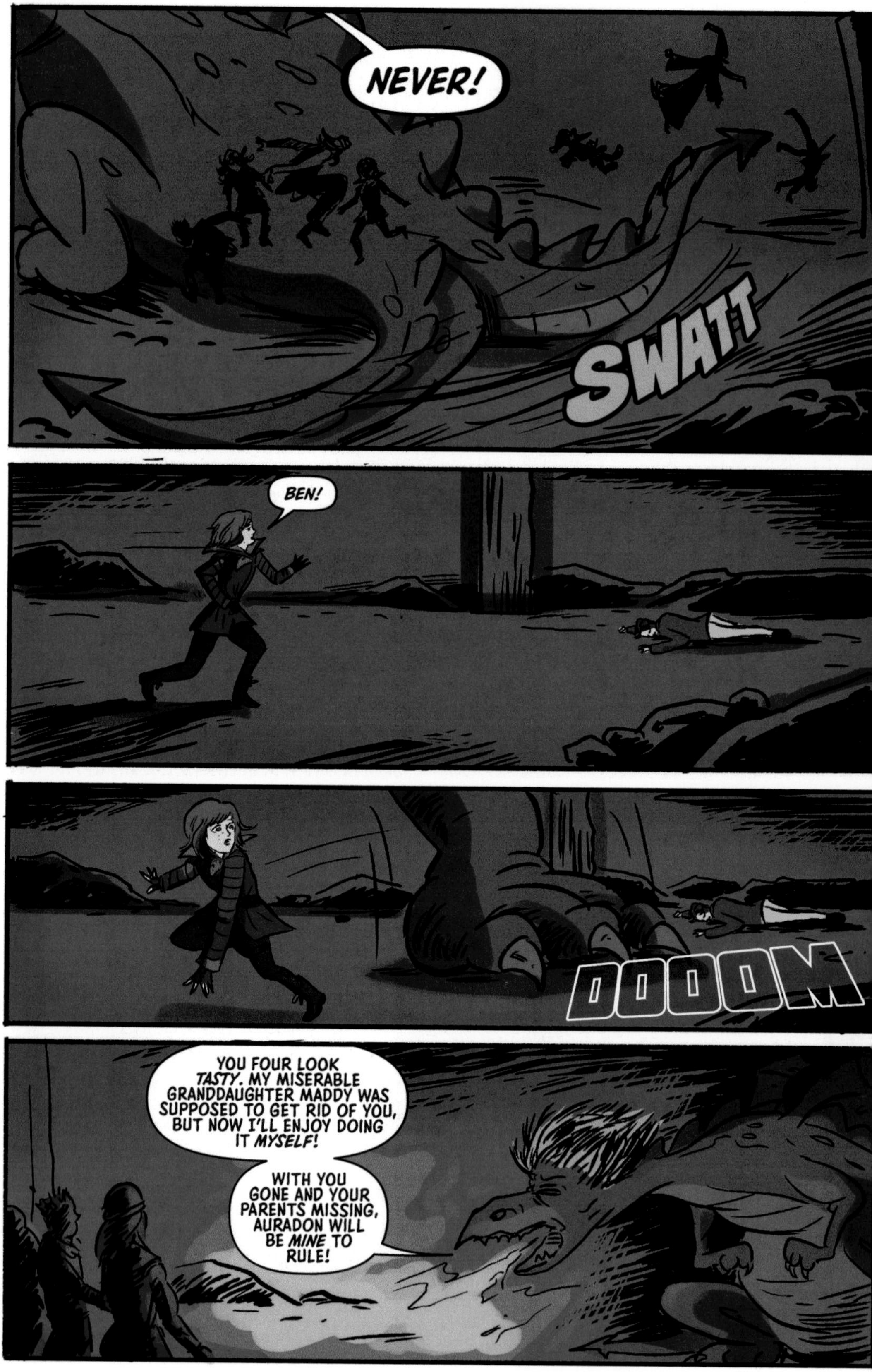
NEVER!
SWATT
BEN!
DOOOM
YOU FOUR LOOK TASTY. MY MISERABLE GRANDDAUGHTER MADDY WAS SUPPOSED TO GET RID OF YOU, BUT NOW I'LL ENJOY DOING IT MYSELF!
WITH YOU GONE AND YOUR PARENTS MISSING, AURADON WILL BE MINE TO RULE!

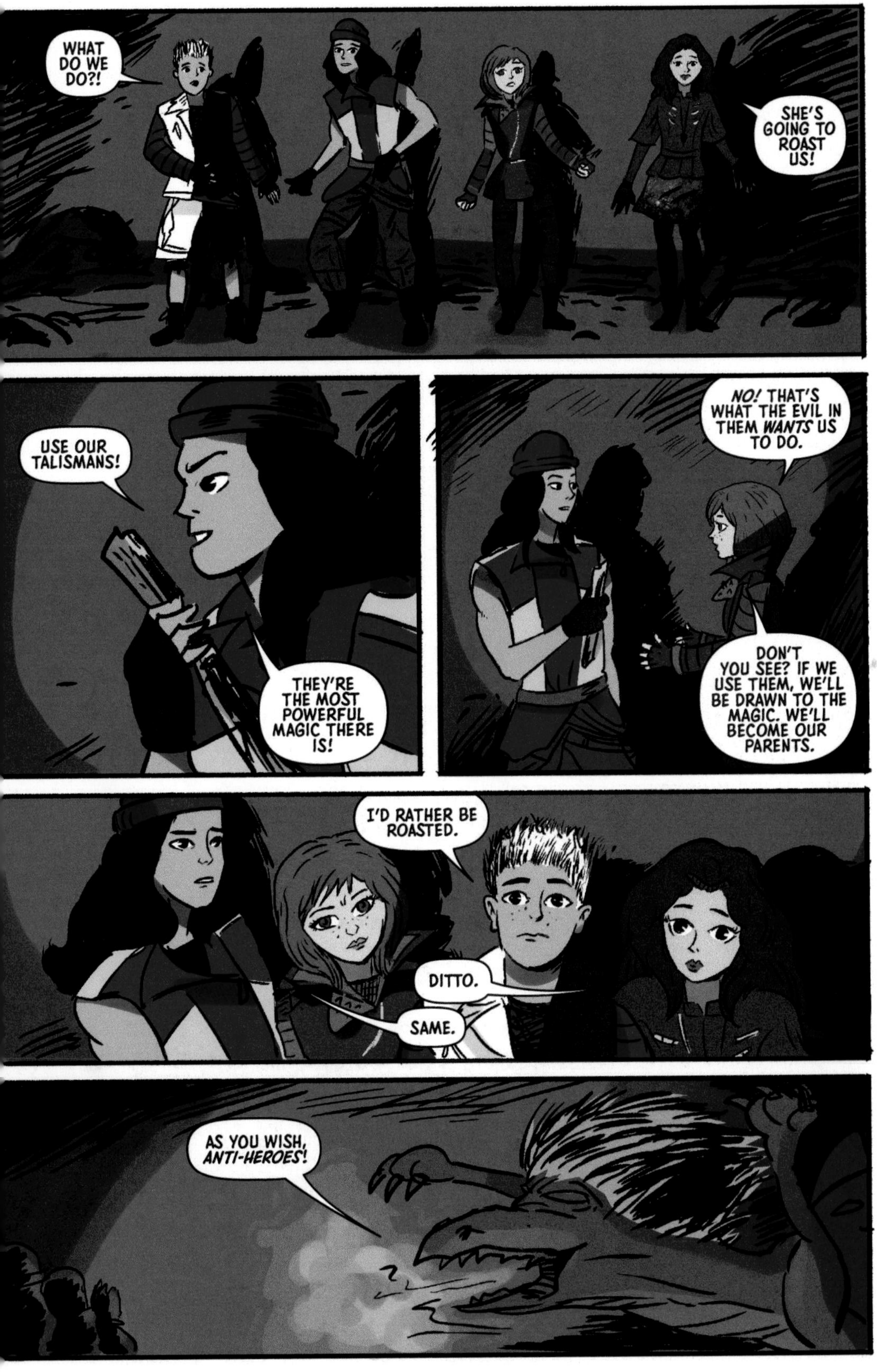
WHAT DO WE DO?!
SHE'S GOING TO ROAST US!
USE OUR TALISMANS!
THEY'RE THE MOST POWERFUL MAGIC THERE IS!
NO! THAT'S WHAT THE EVIL IN THEM WANTS US TO DO.
DON'T YOU SEE? IF WE USE THEM, WE'LL BE DRAWN TO THE MAGIC. WE'LL BECOME OUR PARENTS.
I'D RATHER BE ROASTED.
DITTO.
SAME.
AS YOU WISH, ANTI-HEROES!

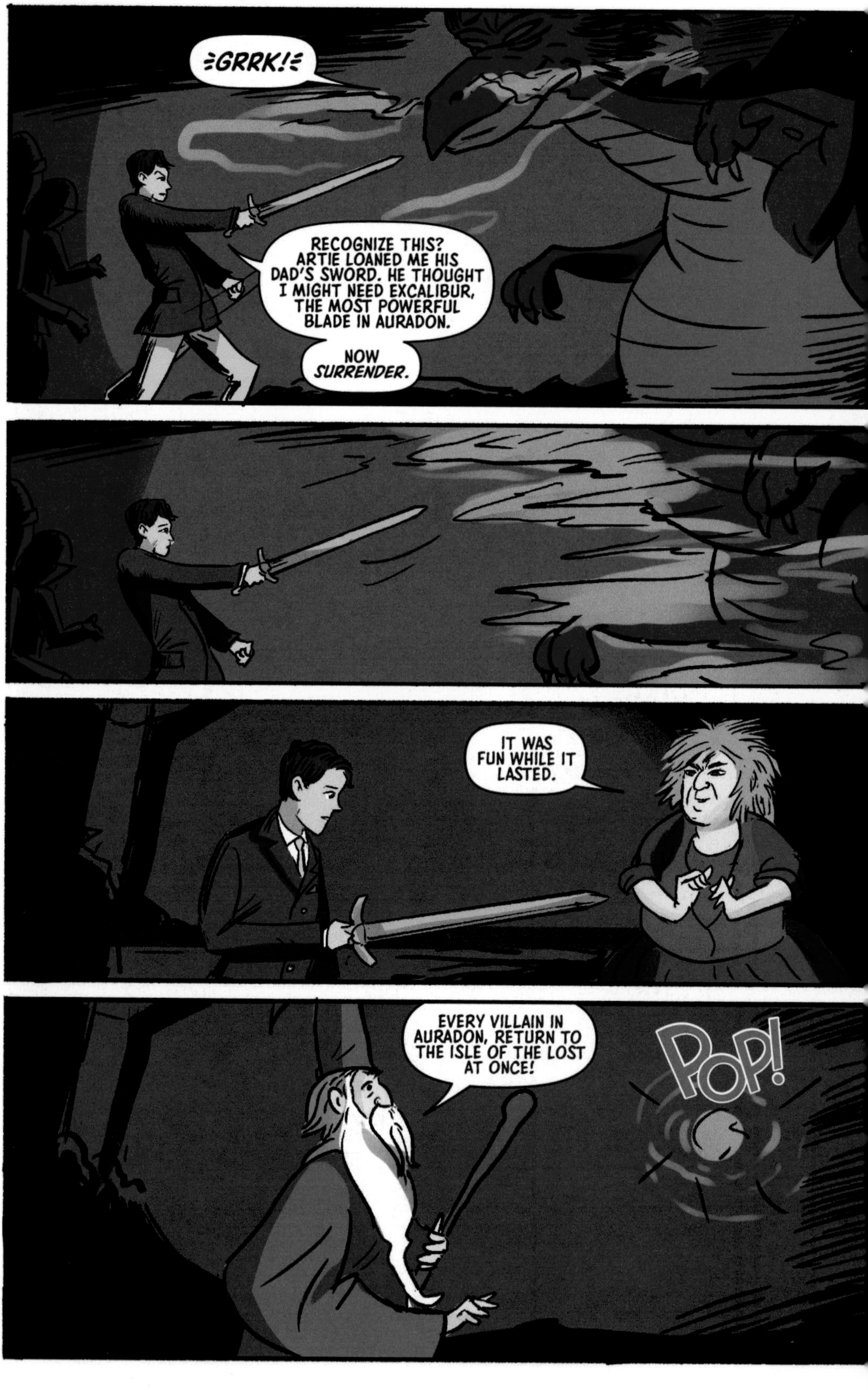
GRRK!
RECOGNIZE THIS? ARTIE LOANED ME HIS DAD'S SWORD. HE THOUGHT I MIGHT NEED EXCALIBUR, THE MOST POWERFUL BLADE IN AURADON.
NOW *SURRENDER.*
IT WAS FUN WHILE IT LASTED.
EVERY VILLAIN IN AURADON, RETURN TO THE ISLE OF THE LOST AT ONCE!
POP!

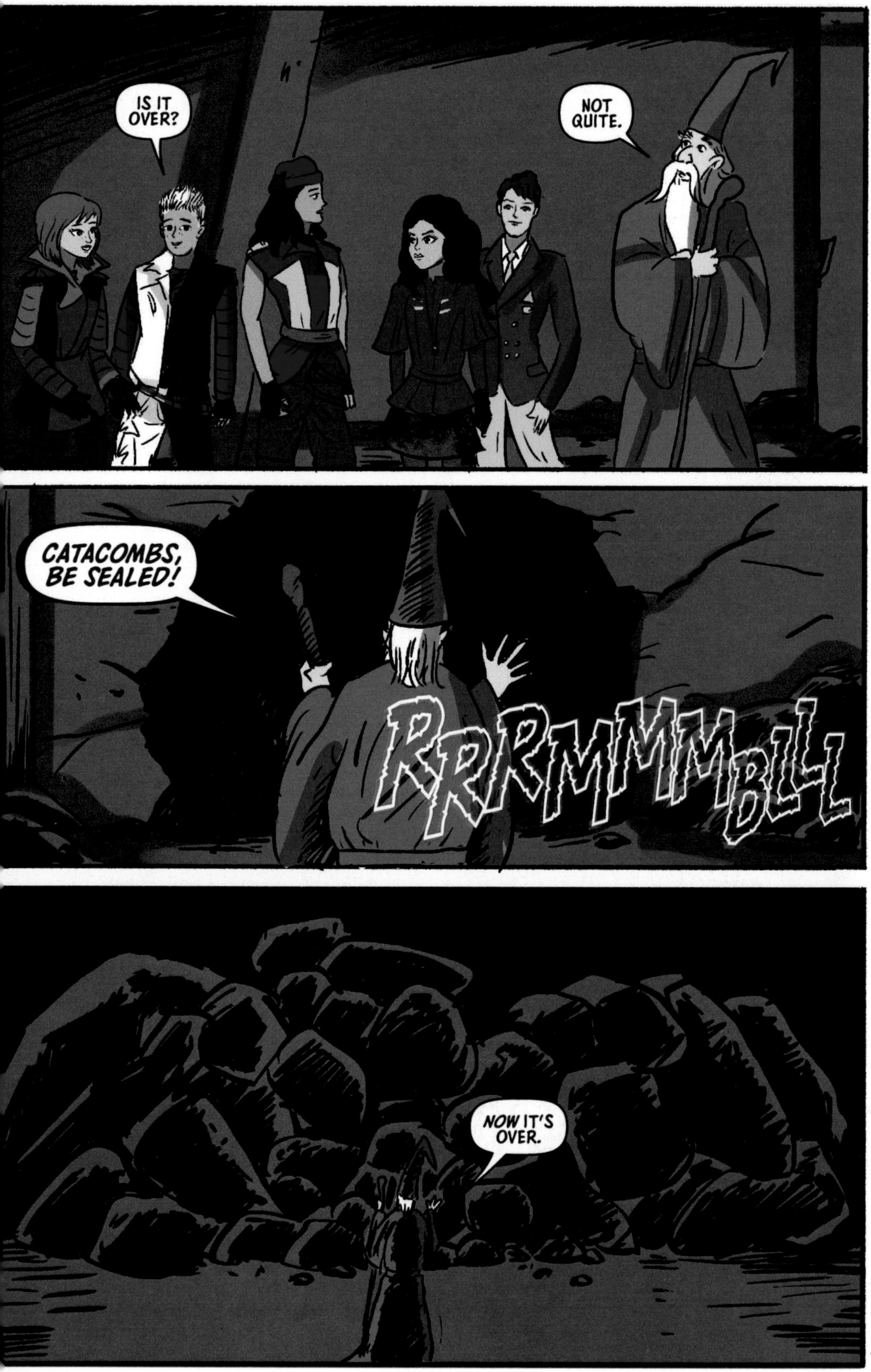
IS IT OVER?
NOT QUITE.
CATACOMBS, BE SEALED!
RRRMMMBLL
NOW IT'S OVER.

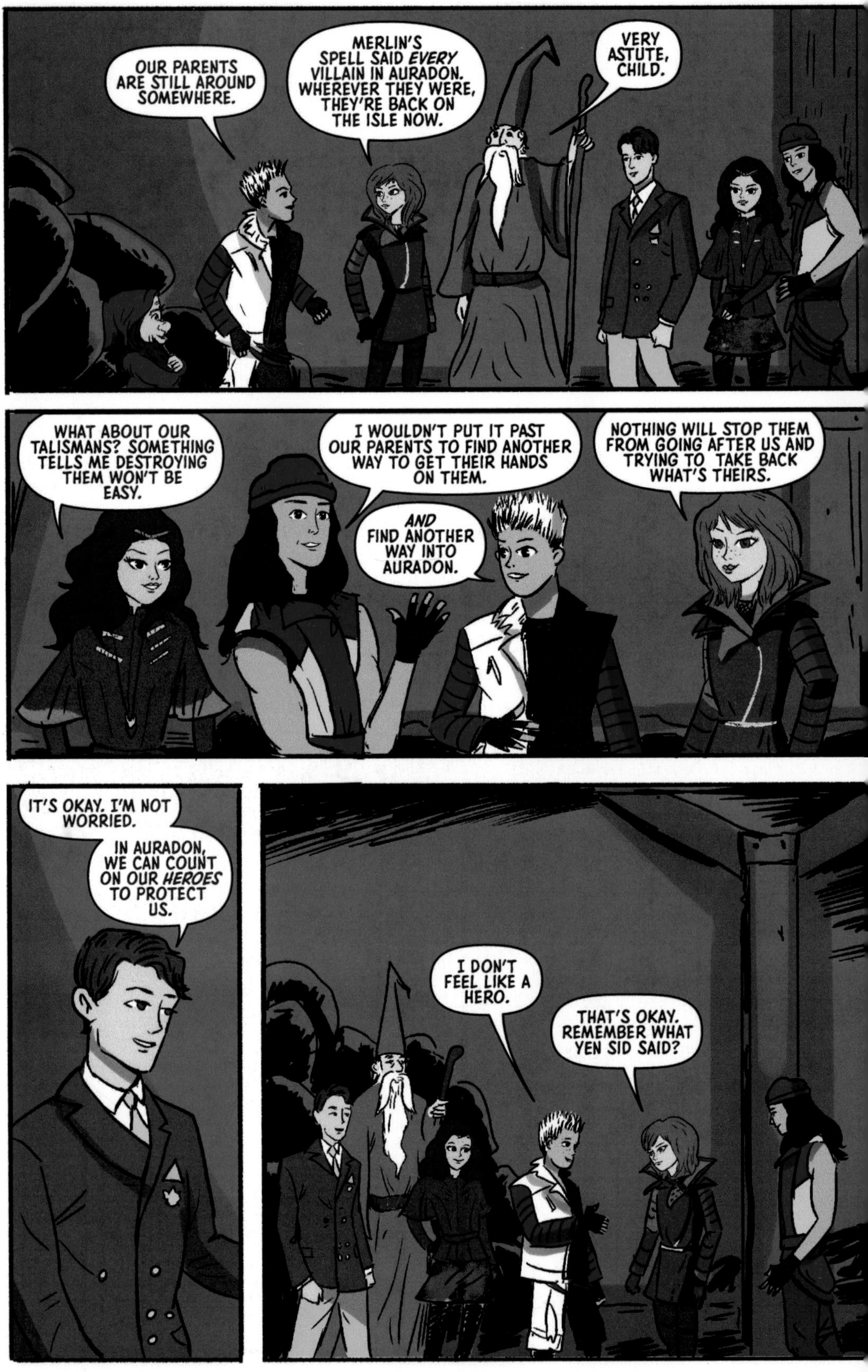
OUR PARENTS ARE STILL AROUND SOMEWHERE.
MERLIN'S SPELL SAID *EVERY* VILLAIN IN AURADON. WHEREVER THEY WERE, THEY'RE BACK ON THE ISLE NOW.
VERY ASTUTE, CHILD.
WHAT ABOUT OUR TALISMANS? SOMETHING TELLS ME DESTROYING THEM WON'T BE EASY.
I WOULDN'T PUT IT PAST OUR PARENTS TO FIND ANOTHER WAY TO GET THEIR HANDS ON THEM.
AND FIND ANOTHER WAY INTO AURADON.
NOTHING WILL STOP THEM FROM GOING AFTER US AND TRYING TO TAKE BACK WHAT'S THEIRS.
IT'S OKAY. I'M NOT WORRIED.
IN AURADON, WE CAN COUNT ON OUR *HEROES* TO PROTECT US.
I DON'T FEEL LIKE A HERO.
THAT'S OKAY. REMEMBER WHAT YEN SID SAID?

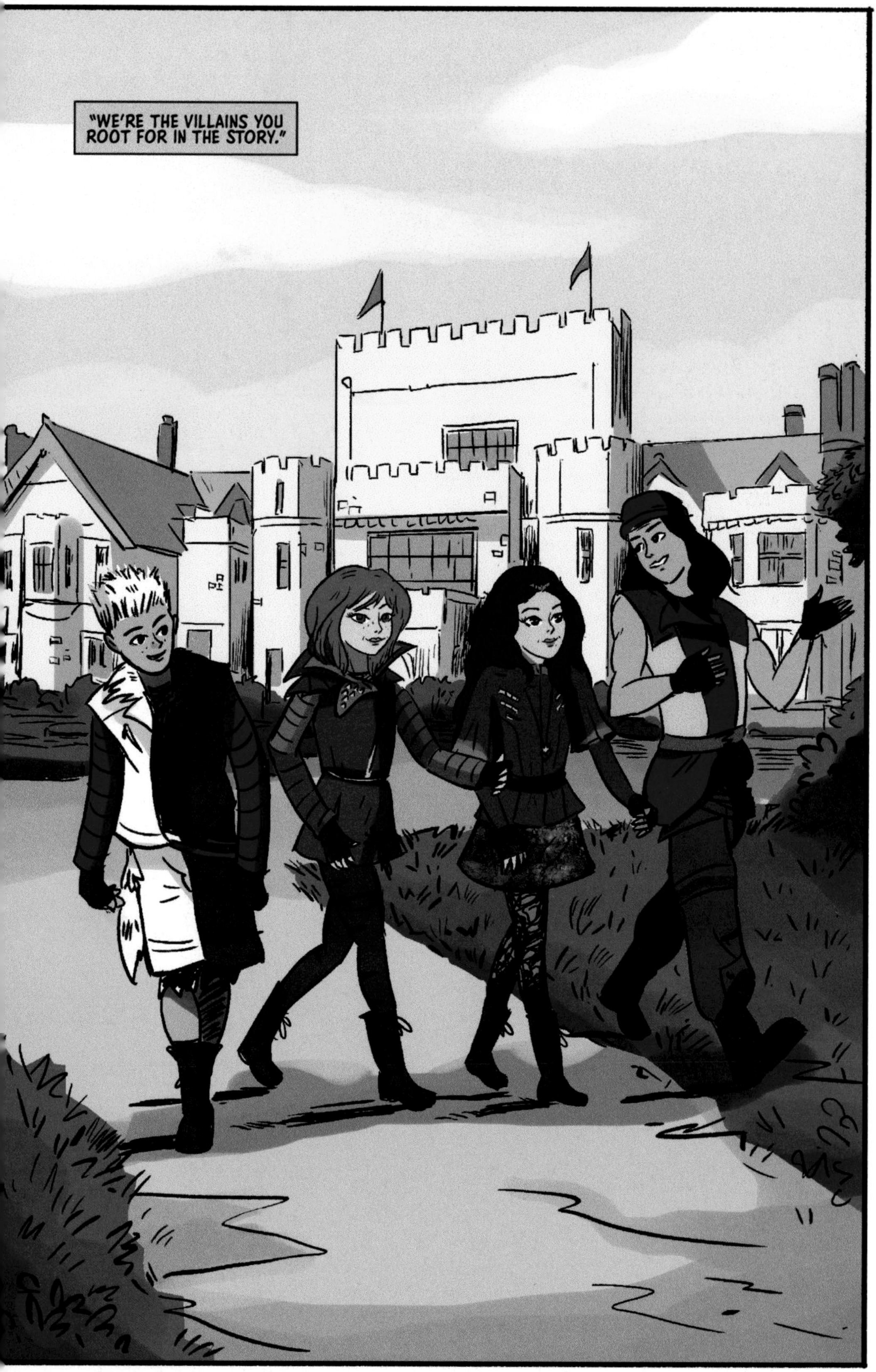
"WE'RE THE VILLAINS YOU ROOT FOR IN THE STORY."

Sometimes being good ISN'T SO BAD

BOOK ONE

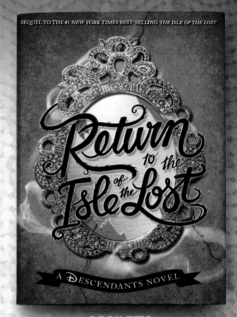

BOOK TWO

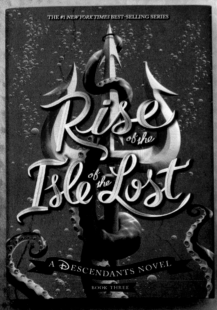

BOOK THREE

BOOK FOUR